THE GOOD LUCK CAFÉ

ANNIE RAINS

FOREVER

New York Boston

Copyright © 2023 by Annie Rains

Cover design by Daniela Medina

Cover illustration by Allan Davey

Cover image © Trevillion; Shutterstock

Cover copyright © 2024 by Hachette Book Group, Inc.

Forever

Hachette Book Group

1290 Avenue of the Americas, New York, NY 10104

read-forever.com

@readforeverpub

Originally published in trade paperback and ebook by Grand Central Publishing in March 2023

First Mass Market Edition: March 2024

Forever is an imprint of Grand Central Publishing. The Forever name and logo are trademarks of Hachette Book Group, Inc.

The publisher is not responsible for websites (or their content) that are not owned by the publisher.

The Hachette Speakers Bureau provides a wide range of authors for speaking events. To find out more, go to www.hachettespeakersbureau.com or email HachetteSpeakers@hbgusa.com.

Forever books may be purchased in bulk for business, educational, or promotional use. For information, please contact your local bookseller or the Hachette Book Group Special Markets Department at special.markets@hbgusa.com.

ISBN: 9781538710081 (trade paperback), 9781538710104 (ebook), 9781538710098 (mass market)

Printed in the United States of America

OPM

10 9 8 7 6 5 4 3 2 1

PRAISE FOR ANNIE RAINS

"Rains has a light, tasteful touch with hard truths."
—*Publishers Weekly*

"I am such a fan of the way Rains weaves a story and makes me feel hope and love. She is always a perfect choice for me when my beach bag needs to be filled."
—KTBookReviews.blogspot.com

"Every time I pick up an Annie Rains book, I know I am going to end my day smiling. There's something about the way that she writes that just speaks to something deep within, like she has peeked inside me and then written a story that I can relate to. It sounds dramatic, but I genuinely feel that she can do this for any reader out there."
—LadyWithAQuill.com

"Annie Rains delivers hope."
—ReallyIntoThis.com

"Annie Rains puts her heart in every word!"
—Brenda Novak, *New York Times* bestselling author

"Annie Rains is a gifted storyteller."
—RaeAnne Thayne, *New York Times* bestselling author

"Romance author Annie Rains was blessed with an empathetic voice that shines through each character she writes."
—NightOwlReviews.com

Sweetwater Springs

Christmas on Mistletoe Lane

A Wedding on Lavender Hill (short story)

Springtime at Hope Cottage

Kiss Me in Sweetwater Springs (short story)

Snowfall on Cedar Trail

Starting Over at Blueberry Creek

Sunshine on Silver Lake

Season of Joy

Reunited on Dragonfly Lane

Somerset Lake

The Summer Cottage

The Christmas Village

A Forever Home (short story)

The True Love Bookshop

Chapter One

The March sun beat against the top of Moira's head as she stepped in front of Sweetie's Bake Shop and pulled open the door. She breathed in the familiar aroma of coffee and pastries as she walked inside, and sighed happily. *Home sweet home-away-from-home.*

"Moira!" her mom called from behind the counter. Darla Green had bright red hair that she'd kept long since Moira was a little girl. The only hint that she and Moira were even related was the stamp of rust-colored freckles that both women had across the bridges of their noses and cheeks. "You're running behind, aren't you? I thought you might not be coming in this morning."

Moira headed in her mother's direction. "My shift starts in half an hour. I'm sorry to say I'm getting my coffee and bagel to go this morning."

Darla frowned as she started preparing Moira's breakfast. Moira didn't come in every morning, but two or three times a week she found herself here to see her mom and satisfy her cravings. Call her superstitious, but the fact that it sat catty-corner on Good Luck Avenue always made her feel like there was something lucky in dropping by. Maybe there weren't the leprechauns of her childhood imagination, but she was fortunate to have a place to come where she could visit with friends and family *and* get her daily dose of caffeine all in one.

Moira glanced around the room as she waited, spotting several locals in their regular spots, including Reva Dawson, who had her laptop front and center. Reva was undoubtedly working on her latest blog post. Moira did her best to avoid being fodder for Reva's town blog. Moira kept a quiet life out of the spotlight. As a 911 dispatcher, she worked behind the scenes of the goings-on in town. She knew every bit as much as Reva, probably more, but she didn't feel the need to gossip like the infamous town blogger did.

Beyond Reva, Moira spotted her best friend Tess sitting at a table on her own. Tess had her phone in front of her and was swiping a quick finger up the screen, a telltale sign that she was looking at TikTok or, in Tess's case, more likely BookTok. Tess owned the local bookstore a few doors down the street and ran the weekly book club that Moira attended.

"Here you go, sweetie." Darla slid a cup of coffee and a bagel wrapped in wax paper toward Moira.

"Thanks, Mom. Love you."

"Love you too." Darla flicked her gaze at Tess. "You going over to say hello?"

Moira nodded as she collected her breakfast items. "A very quick one. Being late for the dispatch is, in actuality, a life-and-death thing. Or it could be." Maybe, if Moira didn't live in Somerset Lake, where the biggest day-to-day emergency was a lack of parking on Hannigan Street.

Darla tsked as a smile spread through her rosy cheeks. "You always have been a dramatic one, haven't you?"

"I'm not being dramatic right now. A lot could go wrong if no one's there to answer the call for help." This wasn't exactly true. There was always one other dispatcher on shift. Since Somerset Lake was a small town, that was all that was needed. Moira was proud to be one of the few. She loved her job and knowing that she was quite possibly saving people's lives. Or, more often, kittens that were stuck in trees and couldn't figure out how to make their way down. But she liked saving them too.

Moira waved at Tess and walked over to where she was sitting. Tess looked up from her phone as Moira paused at the head of her table.

"Hey, you. I was hoping you'd come in today. Have a seat?" Tess asked. Today, her black hair was pulled back in a low ponytail with a few loose curls framing her face.

"I wish I could, but I have a shift in twenty-five minutes," Moira said. "I need to get home."

Tess visibly wilted. "Boo-hiss. I'm so jealous that you get to work from home."

Moira offered back an eye roll. "Oh, please. You own your own business. It might as well be home for you."

"True." Tess grinned. "Tomorrow then?"

Moira nodded. "Sure. I'll come in a little earlier so we can have breakfast. Sound good?"

"I'll look forward to it." Tess checked the time on her phone's screen and heaved a sigh. "I need to get to the bookstore anyway. Lara doesn't mind opening for me, but I don't want to take advantage of her. She's the best thing that's happened to me in a while. I don't want to run her off." Tess stood and pulled the strap of her purse onto her shoulder.

"Don't you mean River Harrison is the best thing

that's happened to you?" Moira teased. River was Tess's fiancé, and Moira was sure she'd never seen her friend so happy. The fact that her best friend had found love—for a second time—did Moira's heart good. Those who wanted a life partner should have one. Moira, on the other hand, wasn't interested in sharing her home, her bed, or her life with anyone. Maybe it was because she had grown up as an only child. It hadn't made her spoiled, but it had definitely molded her into a fiercely independent woman who didn't mind being alone.

"You're right. River is the best thing, and Lara is a close second." Tess laughed as she collected her trash to discard on her way out. Then she and Moira waved at Darla before pushing through the exit doors. "So tomorrow?"

"I'll be here. See you then." Moira started walking. The parking on Hannigan Street was scarce, which meant she'd parked the length of a football field away. Maybe that was a slight exaggeration, but she was glad she'd chosen sneakers when she'd left the house this morning.

Moira started hurrying toward her vehicle when her cell phone pinged from the front pocket of her purse. She fumbled with her coffee and bagel, shifting them to one hand so she could free up the other and dig inside her purse. When she pulled out her phone, there was a text waiting for her.

> ***Dad:*** Did you see your mom this morning?
> How was she?

Moira frowned at her dad's message. Her dad didn't usually check up on Darla. He'd retired last year though.

He seemed to be loving his newfound freedom, but Moira thought her mom seemed to be struggling with the fact that he was discovering new hobbies while she was working long hours—although it was doing what she loved.

Hugging her coffee to her side with the bagel resting on top, Moira used her opposite hand to tap out a return text with her thumb.

> ***Moira:*** I just left Sweetie's. Mom seemed fine to me.

Moira didn't have time to wait for her dad's reply. She picked up her pace, still holding on to her phone and breakfast. The aroma of the Asiago from the bagel wafted up to her nose, making her belly grumble. Then a gust of wind blew her hair into her eyes and mouth.

Ugh. She didn't have a free hand to swipe it away, so she blinked through the curtain of dark hair, spotting her car up ahead.

"In a hurry?" someone asked.

The unexpected voice startled her. She whirled to find its source, her subconscious already matching the deep voice to a name before she looked into the man's bright blue eyes. The sudden movement made her bagel tumble off the top of her coffee cup, where it was balanced. Moira tried to snatch it out of the air before it hit the pavement, which made her coffee slip from her grasp.

Gil Ryan attempted to catch the bagel and drink as well. He lunged toward Moira and stretched out his hand, bumping his forehead into hers.

"Ow!" She straightened and pressed a hand to her

forehead, her eyes open to see the rest of the ordeal pass in slow motion.

Gil caught the bagel—*success!*—but the coffee hit the pavement and exploded like a water balloon, dousing both of their shoes.

Not my new Converse sneakers! Coffee stains will be the death of them.

Gil straightened, holding the bagel with one hand and his forehead with the other, his gaze trained on her. "At least your breakfast was salvaged."

Moira hesitated before taking it, feeling awkward. She'd always felt this way with Gil, knowing he had a crush on her that she didn't reciprocate. "I wouldn't have dropped any of my breakfast in the first place if you hadn't startled me," she snapped. The awkwardness frequently made her come off as defensive and maybe a little cold. She knew this about herself. "*Of course* I'm in a hurry. That's why I was walking so fast. Reason would tell you not to call out to a person who looks like they're on a mission, unless you have something important to tell them."

It was like she couldn't control her mouth when Gil was around.

"I'm sorry. Why don't you let me buy you another coffee?"

Gil was pretty much a saint. Everyone thought so. She'd never known him to do anything wrong, unless he could be found guilty by association with his former roommate, whom Moira wished she'd never met. A person couldn't rewind time though. If they could, she'd dodge the handsome town mayor and have her coffee back this morning.

"I have to get home for work at nine. In fact, thanks

to you, I'm running late." She turned and started walking toward her car without a proper goodbye, which made her feel like a jerk. She immediately regretted the whole interaction with Gil, but if she turned around now, she'd be late to dispatch. So she kept walking.

Gil stepped inside Sweetie's Bakeshop and headed toward Darla behind the counter.

"Hey, Mayor Gil," she said with a broad smile. Unlike her daughter, Darla was always happy to see him.

"Morning, Darla. Can I get a hot coffee with a squirt of chocolate syrup?" he asked.

"Only you." She laughed, reaching for an empty cup off to her side. Then she prepared his drink as he pulled his wallet from his back pocket. "I had a little run-in with Moira before walking in."

Darla glanced over her shoulder as she poured from the pot on the back counter. "Oh? She was just in here."

"Yeah. We bumped into each other. I kind of spilled her coffee. Or she spilled it, but she firmly blamed me."

Darla chuckled. "Well, you know Moira," she said, as if that explained her daughter's attitude.

He did know Moira. She was as nice as her mother, to everyone except him. Somehow he'd found himself on her bad side, and that's where he stayed no matter how hard he tried to win her over. And he did try.

Gil was a people pleaser, and he knew it. It bothered him when a person didn't like him, especially someone whom he'd grown up with. And admittedly he'd had a crush on Moira Green since kindergarten when she'd sported long, black pigtail braids with green ribbons

tied at the bottoms. While the other girls declared pink
as their favorite color, Moira had always chosen green.
While those pink girls had played hopscotch and dolls,
Moira had dominated the swings and monkey bars.

Moira didn't do what was expected, especially back
when she and Gil were growing up. She was an outlier,
which some might call a negative. Not him though. Moira
had caught his eye when they were only kids. "You know
what, Darla?"

Darla slid his coffee across the counter toward him and
raised a questioning brow. "What's that, Mayor?"

"Can you make me whatever kind of coffee Moira had
this morning? She didn't have time to come back in and
get another. It'd be a shame for her to work her shift
without caffeine."

Darla's green eyes narrowed. "You're going to drop it
off at her house?"

Gil nodded, warming up to the idea. Maybe he'd
finally win Moira over this morning. She didn't have
to reciprocate his attraction, but getting off her bad
side would be nice. And he kind of was to blame for
causing her to dump her coffee. He'd called out to her,
seeing that she was obviously in a hurry. What was he
thinking?

"I don't know, Mayor Gil. My daughter doesn't like
unannounced visitors."

He could guess as much. Moira wasn't an introvert,
but she was a private person. "I won't stay. I won't even
go inside. I know she's working. I just want to bring
her a replacement coffee. She can't fault me for that,
can she?"

Darla looked skeptical. After a long pause, she grabbed
a cup and set about making another coffee for Moira.

A minute later, she slid it toward him. "That'll be four dollars and seventy-six cents."

Gil zipped his card through the reader, tapped in his PIN, and collected the two coffees. "Wish me luck."

Darla shook her head on a soft chuckle. "Good luck, Mayor Gil. I think you're going to need it."

Chapter Two

Gil was uncharacteristically nervous as he stood in front of Moira's front door. He was typically a laid-back kind of guy, which was good given his profession. Being the mayor wasn't easy. Yeah, Somerset Lake was a small town, and the folks here were agreeable for the most part. But one truth he'd discovered in life was that you couldn't make everyone happy all the time, and that fact kept Gil up more nights than not.

Gil shifted Moira's coffee to his left hand and rang the doorbell. Then, seeing the little note that read *Doorbell Broken*, he finally knocked. From inside Moira's home, he heard movement. She lived in a tiny one-story house in Wimberly Cove, a small neighborhood featuring one- and two-bedroom homes that catered to singles.

The door opened, and Moira crossed her arms over her chest. "What are you doing here?" she asked by way of greeting. She had on a headset, reminding Gil that she was on shift right now.

"Uh, hi." Gil held out Moira's drink, hoping she wouldn't knock it straight from his hand. "I know you're working dispatch. I just thought you could use that coffee I made you drop earlier. As the mayor, I want to make sure the ones keeping us safe are wide awake."

She looked at the cup, not budging to take it. "That's for me?"

"It is. Your mom made it just the way you ordered yours this morning. I may have driven a little bit over the speed limit to make sure I got it to you while it was still hot." He offered a smile, hoping he didn't look as nervous as he felt as he continued to extend the coffee to her. "Please, take it. I can't stand to waste anything. If you refuse this coffee, I'll be forced to drink it along with the one I have waiting for me in my truck. That'll leave me tightly wound for the day. I might have to call nine-one-one on myself."

Moira finally relaxed her guarded stance, extending a hand to take the coffee. Her gaze hesitantly met his. "Thank you. That was nice of you."

"You're welcome." He stood there a moment, finding it difficult to actually leave. They used to be friends— the kind that could laugh at everything and nothing at all. Then things changed between them. Gil never should have introduced Moira to his college roommate. He shouldn't have brought Felix Wilkes to Somerset Lake at all. Hindsight was twenty-twenty though. Foresight was twenty-seventy on a good day.

Finally, Gil backed away and stepped off her porch. "See you later, Moira." He turned and walked back in the direction of his truck in the driveway.

"Gil?"

He turned eagerly toward Moira's voice. "Yeah?"

Her expression was sheepish and hesitant. Even though she'd called out to him, she seemed to be at a loss for words. "How did my mom look to you? When you saw her this morning?"

Gil knitted his brows. "What do you mean?"

Moira shrugged. "I didn't notice anything different, but my dad seems to think she's not acting herself."

Gil thought back on his interaction with Darla twenty minutes earlier. "She seemed fine. The same old Darla. Did your dad mention how she's acting differently?"

Moira shook her head, her dark hair scraping along her shoulders. "No. I'm sure it's nothing. Thanks again for the coffee."

"Anytime."

She stepped back and closed the door, leaving Gil standing there, feeling a bit foolish and off-balance. Wasn't that how Moira always made him feel?

He continued toward his truck and got inside. Then he took a sip of his coffee before setting it in the cup holder and cranking his engine. *Onward.* He had things to do today, namely meeting with the town council about funding for a new parking lot on Hannigan Street. The next election for town mayor was this fall, and he wanted to promise his voters that he'd do whatever it took to ease the congestion on the main downtown stretch. But first he had to get the budget approved and find the perfect location, which was easier said than done.

The refrigerator was humming like one of those annoying flies that just wouldn't go away. Normally, Moira could block out background noise, but today she was on edge, probably from her run-in with Gil. He always left her feeling a bit discombobulated. Or he had since their early twenties and that night that should never be discussed. It wasn't Gil's fault that she'd gone on a date with his roommate, Felix. It was Gil's fault, however, that she'd gotten herself arrested the very next night. Gil had called law enforcement on her. That whole horrible weekend was one she'd rather just forget, and every time she saw Gil, she was reminded.

Moira blew out a breath and stared at her computer screen, blinking past the sting in her eyes, a hazard of too much screen time. Dispatch was dead. Not that Moira would ever wish an emergency on anyone, but no one had even called to report a deer munching on their greenery. Or a bird that had flown into their garage and was squawking angrily at anyone that entered. That was yesterday's call, and it was the most exciting thing that had happened on the dispatch all week.

Moira closed her eyes for a moment, becoming increasingly aware of the refrigerator's hum. She tried to block it out by following her stream of thoughts, which led her back to thinking about the mayor of Somerset Lake.

Great.

Her alert buzzed, announcing an incoming call on the dispatch. Adrenaline shot through her veins the way it always did.

"Nine-one-one, what's your emergency?" she answered.

"Yes, hi. There's been an accident on Hannigan Street. It's three cars," the caller said breathlessly. "There's a child in the middle car, and I can hear him crying loudly. Oh, poor thing. I hope he's okay."

Moira typed the details as fast as she could while simultaneously alerting the local sheriff's department and paramedics. "Crying is good. That means he's breathing easily. Have the other drivers or passengers gotten out of their vehicles yet?" Moira asked, typing quickly into the system.

"Just me," the caller said. "I'm in the third car. I'm fine. I'm just..." The person hesitated.

"Ma'am? Are you still there?" Moira asked.

"Yes. Yes, I am. I can hear sirens now. That was so fast."

The sheriff's department was right down from Hannigan Street. "Ma'am, are you hurt?"

"Well, um, my forehead seems to be bleeding. I just feel a little woozy, that's all. The child inside the other car is still upset. Should I go get them?"

"No, stay where you are, ma'am. You need to sit down. Do you see an ambulance yet?"

"Not yet," the woman said. "I don't know how it'll get through to us though. This road is so narrow, and there are cars parked all along the sides."

Lunchtime on Hannigan Street was like that, mostly because of Sweetie's and Choco-Lovers, which served up everything chocolate. Folks wanted to eat, and there was nowhere to park. "Are any of the vehicles smoking?" Moira asked, worried that one might catch fire. That had happened a few years back, and the driver had barely escaped.

"No, I don't think so." The caller's words slurred as they stopped and started. Moira thought maybe the woman had hit her head harder than she'd realized. "Oh, there's an ambulance. And a fire truck too. I see their lights down the street," she said.

"Good. Stay on the line with me until someone attends to you."

"Okay."

Moira waited with the caller for what seemed like forever. She was sure the other dispatcher on shift right now was probably talking to another of the accident victims or a nearby onlooker. Finally, one of the paramedics on the scene stepped over to check on Moira's caller.

When Moira finally disconnected, she felt jittery. She always ended her calls before she knew that everyone would be okay. She had no idea what had happened to the child or the caller or anyone else involved in the pileup. Sometimes Moira got the rest of the story through word of mouth or via Reva's town blog, but at other times, she was left to wonder if the person on the other line was okay.

Getting up, Moira stretched and went to pour herself a glass of water. She drank it while standing over the sink. Then she turned as the alarm on her dispatch went off a second time. *Again?* For a dead day, two back-to-back calls was unusual. Perhaps someone else was calling about the same accident.

Moira tapped a button on her wireless headset, connecting the call. "Nine-one-one, what's your emergency?"

"Hello? Are you there?" a man's voice asked.

"I'm here. Do you have an emergency, sir?" Moira asked.

"Yes. I…" He groaned painfully into the phone's receiver.

Moira waited, worry growing. "Sir, are you there?" she asked after a few seconds went by. "Are you okay?"

"Yes, my name is Doug Ryan. I live at 213 Lakeside Drive, but I'm at my brother's house right now."

Moira knew this caller, which wasn't so unusual. She knew most of the callers who dialed in. She usually tried not to let callers know she knew them though, in case it made them self-conscious or worried about privacy. In this case, she thought letting Doug know who she was would help establish trust. "Doug, this is Moira Green. What's going on? Are you all right?"

"Moira? Gil's friend?" Doug asked, sounding confused.

"I'm a dispatcher. Do you need me to send help?" she asked. Doug had Down syndrome. He had graduated from high school a couple of years ago and lived with his parents on the lake.

"Yes. My parents are running errands. And Gil's at a meeting. I'm at his house."

Moira knew Gil lived on the lake right next door to his parents. The house had belonged to Gil's grandmother when she was alive. It was about a five-minute drive from Moira's neighborhood.

"And what's going on with you?" she asked. So far, Doug was talking just fine, which meant he was breathing normally. She didn't know if he was badly injured though.

"I was feeling dizzy, and Goldie knocked me down."

Goldie was Gil's golden retriever. He'd had the dog for years, and she'd seen him walking it in a nearby park on several occasions. "Can you get up?" she asked.

"No, I hurt my foot when I fell. I'm still feeling dizzy too," he said, sounding increasingly distressed. His words were coming out slower, and he was slurring.

Moira started typing into her computer, sending details to local emergency crews. "When you fell, did you hear a snap or a pop in your ankle?"

"I don't remember. It happened so fast...Uh-oh. My foot is swelling and turning purple." Doug took several audible breaths.

"It's okay, Doug, I've notified authorities. Try to stay calm, okay?"

"O-okay."

Moira stared at her computer screen while she waited

impatiently for emergency personnel to acknowledge the call. *What is taking them so long?* "Are you doing all right?" she asked Doug after a minute.

"I think so. I'm feeling kind of hot though. I think I need my medicine."

Moira sat up straighter. She didn't know Doug's full medical history. "What medication are you on, Doug?" she asked, gaze trained on her computer screen. It had now been over five minutes. Usually someone had responded to her alert by now.

"I take it when I feel sick like this." Doug's words tumbled over each other.

"Doug, can you tell me exactly where in Gil's house that you are?" Moira asked, trying to keep Doug talking so she could better assess his condition. The last thing she wanted was for him to lose consciousness.

"Yes, I'm in the kitchen. On the floor."

She impatiently tapped her fingers against her desk. She usually got an alert when ambulances, fire trucks, or sheriff's cars were deployed to the scene. Then she stayed on the line with the caller until emergency crews arrived. No one was responding right now though. Were they all at the three-car pileup on Hannigan Street? Yes, this was a small town, but surely they could spare a couple of essential workers to help Doug.

"Moira? Are you still there?" Doug asked. "I don't feel so good."

"I'm here, Doug. I've alerted officials, and someone is coming to help you." She stared at her dispatch screen, heart racing in her chest. Finally, a message came on her screen.

Emergency personnel are currently working a MVA. Someone will respond to this call shortly.

MVA. Multiple vehicle accident. What did they mean they'd respond shortly? In all her years working dispatch, there'd never been a delay. She picked up her cell phone and attempted to call Gil, but the call went straight to voice mail. Next, she dialed the other dispatcher, Riley, who was also on shift. Instead of answering the call, Riley texted Moira back.

> ***Riley:*** I'm on the line with a MVA victim right now.
> ***Moira:*** I know. I got that call too. I need to step away from the dispatch. I need you to cover all incoming.
> ***Riley:*** What? Why?
> ***Moira:*** I'm responding to an emergency. I owe you.

Without waiting for Riley's objection—because there was no way she wasn't going to object—Moira stood. "Hold on. I'll be right there," she told Doug, who was still on the line. "Answer the phone when I call you, okay? I'm hanging up on the emergency line and calling you from my cell."

"Okay," Doug said.

"Make sure you answer," Moira stressed. She wasn't quite sure of his condition, and she didn't want to leave him alone in case he passed out.

"I will."

Moira reluctantly hung up. She pulled off her headset, hoping Riley would be able to handle any incoming calls on her own. Then, with a shaky finger, Moira dialed Doug from her cell phone.

He answered immediately. "Hello? Moira?"

"Hi, Doug. It's me." Moira grabbed her car keys from the counter as she ran out of her home. She got into her blue Hyundai and reversed out of the driveway, wishing she had a little flashing light to put in her windshield. When she was growing up, she'd fantasized about being a cop or paramedic. She'd always loved the idea of helping people. A lot of her friends had grown up saying they wanted to be like their parents, but Moira had never wanted to run a bakery or café. She'd worked at Sweetie's during high school, and while the money was nice to have, she'd dreaded working behind the counter. "I'm on my way, Doug. Just stay on the line with me, okay?" She drove faster than normal, heading in the direction of the lake. When she pulled into Gil's driveway, she asked, "Is the front door open?"

"No. I always lock it behind me when I come inside," he replied weakly.

Moira frowned as she parked. "Does Gil have a spare key that I can use to let myself in?"

"Yes," Doug said.

Moira exhaled as she hurried out of her car, crossing the lawn toward the front porch. "Great. Where is it?" she asked, taking the steps two at a time.

"It's on the kitchen counter."

Moira froze behind the front door. "What? Why is it there?"

"That's how I let myself in," he said.

"Well, is there any way you can come to the door, Doug?"

"I don't think so. My ankle really hurts, and I'm feeling shaky."

Moira didn't like the sound of that. Was Doug going into shock from the pain? If his ankle was broken, that was a real possibility. She looked around, trying to decide how to get inside the little yellow house. She could break a window, but that seemed extreme. Maybe she could pick the lock.

"Maybe you can fit through Goldie's doggie door?" Doug's voice was growing notably quieter.

"Doggie door? Where is that?"

"At the back door."

Moira jogged behind the house and let herself in the fence. Then she climbed the deck steps and looked at the doggie door in question. She would fit, but if anyone found out, she might never live this down.

"Please hurry." Doug moaned softly. "I need my medicine."

Without another thought, Moira dropped to her knees and started crawling. "Hold on! I'm on my way, Doug!" She stuck her hand inside the doggie door first, planting it on the cold tile floor inside, screaming as something wet and slimy slid across the back of her fingers. Moira quickly withdrew her arm, heart ballooning into her throat.

"That was Goldie. Please help me," Doug said.

Okay. I can do this. Moira stuck her arm through the doggie door again, and this time she followed with her head and her body, coming face-to-face with a large dog that ran its tongue over her cheek. Moira pulled the rest of her body through the door, glancing around for Doug.

"Over here!" he called.

"Good dog." Moira patted Goldie's head as she stood. Then she hurried over to the man lying on the floor near the kitchen counter. "Hi, Doug." Moira squatted next to him and inspected his foot, noting the pockets of dark purple swelling on both sides of his ankle. She gently palpated around the bone of his ankle.

"Ow!"

"Sorry. It doesn't appear to be broken. It does look like a bad sprain though. I'll get you an ice pack." Moira headed over to Gil's fridge, noting all the photos of Doug and him attached to the surface with magnets. Gil had always been like best friends with his brother. It was something she admired. Growing up, she'd had a lot of friends who refused to hang out with their younger siblings, but not Gil.

Locating an ice pack in the side door of the freezer, she carried it over to put on Doug's ankle, crouching beside him. "You mentioned needing a medication. What kind of medicine are you taking, Doug?"

"Orange juice," Doug said matter-of-factly.

"Orange juice?" Moira furrowed her brow. "That's the medicine you were talking about?"

He pointed at the fridge. "For my blood sugar."

"Oh. Okay." Moira stood and walked over to the fridge. She opened the door and pulled out a carton of juice, setting it on the counter. Then she checked the cabinets and located a glass. Once she'd filled the glass halfway, she handed it to Doug, watching as he drained the entire thing in one huge gulp.

"Thank you for coming to my rescue," he finally said. He didn't look as pale anymore. A faint smile lifted the corners of his lips.

"Just doing my job," Moira said. But going to a caller's home wasn't her job. Her job was to stay on the dispatch. Would she get in trouble for this? Or even fired?

The sound of the front door opening and closing got Moira's attention.

"Doug?" a man's voice called.

Moira immediately felt her face flush. She knew that

voice well. She'd just heard it this morning when she'd been unnecessarily rude.

"In the kitchen!" Doug's voice no longer sounded shaky or weak. The orange juice really had made an immediate difference.

Gil hurried into the kitchen, stopping short when he saw Moira crouching at Doug's side. "What happened?"

"I called nine-one-one," Doug told him.

Gil's eyes widened. "Why? Are you okay?"

"I got dizzy, and Goldie knocked me down. Moira came over and gave me an ice pack," Doug told him.

"He also asked for orange juice," Moira said.

Gil's gaze hung on Doug for a minute. He seemed to be analyzing whether Doug really was okay. "Juice is a good way to raise blood sugar levels quickly. Doug has type two diabetes. It's a recent diagnosis."

"Oh. I didn't realize." Moira straightened back to a standing position. "Well, he seems to be doing better now. I don't think his ankle is broken, but I do think it's sprained. He might need a doctor to check it."

"Of course. I'll see if Dr. Reynolds can work him in."

Moira nodded. "Now that you're here, I really do have to go. I'm not supposed to leave the dispatch. But no one was responding to Doug's call."

"Everyone is working the accident on Hannigan," Gil said.

"Yes, they are. Why didn't you answer Doug's calls?" she asked, not meaning for her tone to come out ac- cusatory.

Gil looked rattled for a moment. "I was in a meeting. I had to put my phone on silent mode. It was a media interview."

"It's okay, Gil," Doug said, looking offended by the

conversation. "I can take care of myself, you know. I'm an adult."

Moira turned to Doug. "Of course. Even adults need someone they can call when they're in trouble though. Are you feeling better?"

Doug's offense melted away, and he smiled. "It still hurts, but Gilly is here now."

Moira shared a glance with Gil. "Gilly, huh?"

"It's a childhood nickname that Doug won't let go." Gil laughed. "I guess it's better than how my friends call me Gilbert."

Moira had heard Jake and Miles tease Gil with his full name on several occasions. She'd always loved the name Gilbert though, ever since she'd read *Anne of Green Gables* one summer and had fallen in love vicariously through Anne's character.

"Thank you for coming over, Moira." Gil offered his hand to shake. "I'm sorry if this caused you any inconvenience."

"You're welcome." Moira stared at Gil's outstretched hand before slipping her palm against his, wondering at the way her heartbeat quickened. "I, um, really have to go," she said a second time, pulling her hand away.

"Of course." Gil nodded. "I'll stay with Doug until his blood sugar is back to normal and see about getting his ankle looked at by Dr. Reynolds."

"Sounds good." Moira hitched a thumb behind her. "I'll, um, see you later," she said. Then, with a small wave, she turned and left. She practically sped back to her own house. She ran inside and pulled her headset back on, exhaling when she noted that there were no missed calls on-screen. Then she relaxed into her chair and exhaled.

What had started as a dead day had become dramatic.

It was days like this she felt most fulfilled by her job. Some days she helped folks more than others. Some days she pretty much just sat at her desk and read books that she'd purchased from Tess's store.

Moira grabbed her cell phone and texted Riley.

> **Moira:** I'm back at the dispatch. I'm sorry for bolting on you like that.
> **Riley:** It's against regulation to go to a scene. What were you thinking?

Moira frowned at the text message. She hadn't really felt like she'd had a choice in the matter. Doug needed help, and that's all there was to it. Moira knew Riley was a stickler for rules though. She would never feel compelled to do what Moira had just done.

> **Moira:** I was thinking that someone needed help.
> **Riley:** Yes, but not from you. We're not trained as medics. If Sheriff Ronnie finds out, you'll be reprimanded.

Moira took that to mean that Riley didn't plan on telling the sheriff. At least she hoped that's what it meant.

> **Moira:** Thanks again for covering while I stepped out.

Moira's shift ended later that evening without another call. She removed her headset and walked into her kitchen to prepare a dinner for one. After the day she'd had, she didn't bother cooking. Instead, she would settle for a bowl of Cap'n Crunch cereal. It was quick and easy, and she was starving.

She pulled the box out of the cabinet and then went to retrieve a bowl, startling when someone knocked on her door. Who would be visiting her now? Her mom always went straight home to her father after leaving the bakeshop, and her friends all had boyfriends, fiancés, or husbands to go home to these days.

Moira stared at her front door for a moment, reviewing the list of possible visitors, none of whom seemed likely. When her unknown visitor knocked again, she sighed. She wasn't in the mood for social hour. She'd prefer a glass of wine and a hot bath. Even so, she walked over and peered through the peephole.

Moira's heart sputtered and stopped along with all the breath in her body. When she'd shaken Gil's hand earlier in the day, she'd felt something unexpected. Her heart had fluttered. Skipped. Quickened. He had always had a crush on her, but not vice versa. She'd never felt anything for Gil Ryan—until today.

He knocked again. Moira pressed a hand to her overreacting heart. She considered pretending she wasn't home, but her car was in the driveway. She closed her eyes and blew out a breath. This was silly. Whatever she'd felt earlier was a fluke. It was just Gil. She'd known him forever. The least she could do was answer the door—and politely ask him to leave.

Chapter Three

Gil didn't have to be an expert on body language to read Moira.

She wasn't smiling, but the good news was she wasn't frowning either. She just stared back at him expectantly, her arms folded over her chest, her hazel eyes darting around anywhere except to look directly at him.

If his heart weren't in his throat right now, he might say something witty and make her laugh. Instead, he forced a nervous smile and offered a small wave. "Me again. I, uh, just wanted to say thank you again for earlier today."

"You didn't have to come all the way down here. I just gave Doug an ice pack and a glass of juice, that's all." She nibbled at her bottom lip, drawing his attention there. There was something uniquely beautiful about Moira. A combination of interesting facial features—heart-shaped lips, a constellation of freckles over her nose and high cheekbones—that made it difficult for him to look away. "I was on shift for the dispatch, so I'd appreciate it if you didn't mention this to anyone. I'm not supposed to leave my post." Moira shook her head. "But no one was responding to Doug's call, and I was concerned."

"I won't say anything, but…"

Moira narrowed her eyes, concern wrinkling her forehead. "But what?"

"Well, Doug is fairly active on social media. He's already made several posts about how you saved his life." He chuckled to himself, but Moira wasn't laughing. On the contrary, she suddenly looked pale.

"He can't tell anyone. I could lose my job if Sheriff Ronnie found out."

"Don't worry. I have an in with the sheriff's department." Gil winked, trying and failing to calm her down.

"I don't need the town's mayor to put in a good word for me. I don't need you to come to my rescue like a knight in shining armor again either."

Again?

"I was just being nice."

"I know Sheriff Ronnie, too, you know. And I wouldn't have gone to your house if there were deputies available to respond."

"I know that. We need a new parking area on Hannigan Street. Or even Good Luck Avenue."

"I don't know where you'd put one. It's always been a problem," she said.

"It's a safety issue. I wouldn't be a good mayor if I didn't try to resolve it."

Moira almost smiled as she looked at him. The reason Gil hadn't gone on many second dates in his adult life was that there were never any sparks on his first dates. Every time he ran into Moira though, despite the fact that she clearly hated him, there were fireworks. At least where he was concerned.

If not for Moira, he would probably believe the whole spark thing was a myth and that finding *the one* came down to going on several dates with someone who shared common interests. Who knows? Maybe he would have settled down by now, like most of his friends.

Gil cleared his throat and blinked, watching Moira tuck a dark lock of hair behind her ear where several tiny earrings were stacked. "How's your dad these days?" he asked, hoping to defuse her tension. Granted, he was jumping from one stressful topic to another. A couple of years ago, Moira's father had a cancer scare, and for a time, it hadn't looked good. Now he was in remission.

"Dad is doing well—really well. He's loving retirement."

"I bet." Gil smiled back at her.

"To be honest, I think Mom is a little jealous even though she loves her work. Dad is sleeping in while she's still heading out early for the breakfast crowd."

"I'm sure it's an adjustment for both of them."

Moira nodded. "Doug seemed a little upset that I asked why you didn't answer your phone when he called today. I think he thought I was suggesting he needed supervision."

Gil let out a sigh. "Doug has accused my parents of being overprotective of him lately. Me, too, I guess. He's probably right. It's not because he has Down syndrome. Doug is also the youngest kid—my mom's baby and my younger brother."

"Nothing wrong with being independent," Moira said. "In fact, I admire that quality."

Gil watched her. "I've always considered you to be fairly independent yourself." He thought he saw offense settle on her features. "In a good way. You like to do things by yourself and in your own way." And at times, Gil had noted that she resented someone trying to step in and offer her a hand. Or maybe it was just him she resented.

"Is that why you hired Doug to be your campaign manager? To give him more independence?"

Gil shook his head quickly. "No way. Doug could have had any number of jobs about here. Your mom offered him one at Sweetie's as a matter of fact."

Moira's lips parted. "She didn't tell me that."

Gil lifted a shoulder. "Well, I snagged him first. He's a hard worker, and he understands what makes people smile. He's not afraid to tell me what I'm doing wrong either. And he believes in me more than anyone. He was the best guy for the job. Still is."

Something changed about the way Moira was looking at him. He wasn't sure what she was thinking, but whatever it was, he didn't think it was a bad thing. After a second, she looked away. "Well, thanks for stopping by. I need to get dinner started."

"Dinner for one?" he asked, immediately wanting to kick himself. He was so hopeless.

"Mm-hmm."

"Yeah. Me too. Well, one plus Goldie. Maybe Doug, too, if he doesn't like what my mom is cooking."

She nodded wordlessly, fidgeting with her hands in front of her. He thought she looked nervous and wondered if he was the reason.

"Well, have a good evening, Moira."

"You too," she said quietly, still looking at him in a way he'd never seen from her before. Her cheeks were flushed too.

Turning, he headed down her porch steps, hearing the door close behind him. Whatever had softened in Moira's eyes would return to disdain once she found out how the town council had voted today. It was nine against three, and mayor or not, he couldn't overrule the majority.

Gil got into his truck and drove home. When he unlocked and opened the door, he came face-to-face with Goldie, who seemed to be giving him the stink eye. He was getting home later than usual, but it couldn't be helped. *I'll make it up to you, girl.* Goldie was good-natured and upset for only a moment. Then she broke into happy tail wagging and charged forward to greet him, stopping short to sniff around his legs.

"You remember Moira, right?" he asked, feeling like he'd cheated on his dog somehow. "Don't worry, Goldie. You're the only girl I love." After a full minute of petting his dog, he headed into the kitchen for a glass of water, his thoughts retracing today's three run-ins with Moira. Even though she'd seemed to let her guard down around him on the last visit, he wouldn't be winning any votes from her this coming election. Not after she got the news about her mother's business being evicted from Hannigan Street.

His stomach clenched. He'd never been one for popularity contests, which is what running for office felt like. He wanted a second term though. He thought he'd done a lot of good for the town since he'd been elected to office, and there was still more he wanted to do. It was time to start making a concerted effort to secure votes for reelection this fall.

The doorbell rang, and Goldie took off in that direction. Gil set his glass of water down and walked over to open the door.

"Hi, Gilly." Doug was wearing his usual ball cap that read VOTE GIL RYAN FOR MAYOR in large block font.

"Hey, buddy." Gil looked down at Doug's foot. "How's the ankle feeling?"

"All better. Mom wrapped it and gave me some ibuprofen."

"Ah. I should have thought of that."

Doug shrugged. "You're not as smart as Mom is," he teased.

Gil shook his head and chuckled. "True enough. Do you think the water will be good for a boat ride tonight?"

"The lake is calm," Doug said with a nod.

"What do you say? Want to come out with me? An evening ride sounds like just what the doctor ordered."

Doug adjusted his hat. "Sure. We need to discuss how to make other people like you."

Gil grabbed his own ball cap from the hook by the door and put it on. "I suppose we can do that on the boat. You think there are folks out there who don't like me?"

"I made a list," Doug said without cracking a smile.

Gil matched Doug's slower pace, guessing his ankle was still achy from his earlier fall. They headed toward the dock where Gil kept his pontoon boat. He also had a sailboat stored in a building off to the side of his house. While his friend Jake loved his small planes, Gil was a boat guy. "A list of people who don't like me, huh? Is it long?"

Doug blew out a dramatic breath. "Let's just say we have our work cut out for us."

Gil hoped his brother was teasing him. If he had to guess who was at the top of that list, though—especially after tomorrow—it would be Moira Green.

Sheriff Ronnie never called. Moira hoped that meant her job wasn't on the line. She'd left her post for a good reason. Then again, an argument could be made that there was never a good reason to leave the dispatch when you were one of the few people responsible for responding to emergencies. Each eight-hour shift had two operators, with ten dispatch operators employed in total. That made for a small department that held a great responsibility for the town.

After changing into a pair of cotton pajama pants and a lightweight tank, Moira climbed into bed, begrudging the fact that Gil was still lingering in her thoughts. He was perhaps the nicest guy she knew, and all three times she'd seen him today, she'd treated him like the enemy. There was no excuse for being anything less than friendly, but she couldn't seem to help herself when he was around. Tomorrow, she'd apologize for acting rudely. Until then, she'd marinate in her guilt and try to get some much-needed sleep.

Moira burrowed under her covers and reached up to turn off her bedside lamp. Then she forced her eyes closed. It seemed like she'd just shut them when her phone's alarm clock started chirping on the table beside her. Moira squinted at the light splintering through her bedroom window. *Morning already?* She felt like she had a hangover as she sat up and draped her legs off the edge of her mattress, pulling a deep breath into her lungs. Then she yawned and stretched her arms overhead, feeling her muscles pull taut over her joints. Her shift didn't begin until nine a.m. Before that time, she wanted to get to Sweetie's, grab some coffee and a bite with Tess, and hopefully run into Gil.

When had she ever thought that?

Moira stood and walked into the adjoining bathroom to freshen up and get dressed. Working from home meant that she could wear whatever she wanted. Today that was jeans with a stylish rip in one knee and a soft lavender tee.

Moira combed her hair, brushed her teeth, and grabbed her keys on the way out of her house. Sweetie's was only a couple of miles away. Moira crossed the distance in the span of one song on the radio. She had to park all the way at the end of the street and walk to her destination, which was fine when the weather was nice. When it wasn't, she either got drenched or stayed home and settled for subpar coffee.

She pulled her keys from the ignition and got out, spotting Gil's truck nearby. Nerves bound her chest. The history between her and Gil was complicated. He wasn't like his former roommate. It hadn't been Gil who'd slipped a drug in Moira's drink when she was twenty-one with the intention of doing who knows what.

On the contrary, Gil had been the one to stop his friend from following through on his sordid plans. Because of Gil, Moira had been spared what might have been the most traumatic night of her life.

Moira's thoughts bounced around as she walked. The whole night was a big blur. All she really remembered was waking up at home and finding Gil in her kitchen. He'd explained that he'd driven her home. He told her that she was so intoxicated that he didn't feel right about leaving her alone, so he'd stayed and slept on the couch. Moira had gone through that day confused about why she'd been so drunk after having only half a beer. She hadn't wanted to believe Felix would have slipped something in her drink, but as the day went on and her brain tried to make sense of the night before, that was the only explanation.

A little bell tinkled above Moira's head as she entered Sweetie's Bakeshop. She waited for her mom's greeting, but it didn't come. Her mom wasn't even behind the counter.

"Oh, Moira. There's the hero of the hour!" someone said, gaining Moira's attention.

Moira turned toward Reva Dawson, her guard immediately rising. Friendly or not, Reva was the town's biggest gossip, and Moira didn't want to draw any attention to herself. "Hi, Reva. What exactly do you mean by hero?"

"You didn't read my blog post this morning, did you?" Reva tsked. "That's okay. As you know, I have eyes and ears all over town. I heard about what you did for Doug."

Moira felt the blood drain from her face. "Oh? What exactly did you hear?"

"That you saved the day. The local authorities were too caught up in that multiple vehicle accident, so hearsay is that you took it upon yourself to crawl through Mayor Gil's doggie door and help Doug in his moment of crisis yourself. Bravo, Moira."

Moira's lips parted. She couldn't decide which part of this realization horrified her the most. "You didn't put that on your blog, did you?" *Please say no.*

"Of course I did," Reva said, a proud gleam in her eye. "It's bullet point number one."

Reva's blog consisted of bullet points to offer the most recent gossip in an easy-to-read-and-pass-along format. "You beat out the three-car pileup news."

"Lucky me. But, Reva, can you please take what I did for Doug down? I wasn't supposed to leave the dispatch. I could get in trouble for that." Sheriff Ronnie was a reasonable guy, and Moira thought he liked her, but he was a stickler for rules. Staying on the dispatch during your shift was a biggie.

"Heavens no. Why would I take that down? You're a local hero around here, dear. The blog has already had nine hundred hits, and it isn't even eight a.m." The gossiper was practically glowing.

Moira was about to argue some more, when someone cleared his throat behind her. A sense of dread knotted her stomach before she even turned to face him. "Sheriff Ronnie. Good morning."

The sheriff wasn't smiling. Moira guessed he was one of the nine hundred visitors to Reva's blog. "Can you come by the department after your shift today?"

Moira swallowed past a tight throat. "Sure, Sheriff," she practically squeaked. "Will do."

Sheriff Ronnie looked past Moira to Reva. He didn't seem thrilled with her either. He tipped his head in greeting and then turned to leave.

Moira's heart was pounding, the sound reverberating in her ears. Reva gave her a sheepish look when Moira met her gaze again.

"Well, I best be going," she said. "Say what they will, but you're still a hero in my eyes," she added before walking away.

Moira watched the older woman leave the bakeshop. She felt a lot of things right now, but heroic wasn't one of them.

Chapter Four

Moira eyed the space behind the counter where her mom should be standing. It wasn't like Darla to leave the counter unattended for long. Moira walked to the front and eyed the little bell that read RING ME. Everyone knew that workers didn't enjoy being summoned by the bell on the counter, especially when it was a child doing the ringing.

Moira stood there a moment, and as she was about to tap the little bell, her mom appeared from the back room.

"Oh. Moira." Darla's smile was hesitant and forced. Her eyes looked red, which caught Moira off guard. Her mom was rarely ever upset.

"Mom, are you okay?"

"Oh, yes, of course." Darla waved a dismissive hand in Moira's direction. "It's just hot in the kitchen, you know that."

Moira did know that. She'd worked here during the summers and on weekends when she was growing up. She knew what her mom's hot face looked like though, and this wasn't it. She was about to press her mother on what was bothering her, when Darla turned and began preparing a coffee for her.

"Are you getting this to go?" Darla asked. "I'm assuming you're on shift today."

"I'm actually meeting Tess for coffee. At least that was the plan." Moira glanced behind her in case she'd somehow missed her friend sitting at one of the tables when she'd walked in.

"She hasn't come in yet," Darla said. "So…" She trailed off until Moira turned back to her. "I hear yesterday was an interesting day for you."

Moira groaned. She leaned over the counter, propping herself up on her elbows. "I wish Reva would stop broadcasting everyone's business."

Darla slid Moira's cup of coffee across the counter. Steam wafted up from the rim as Darla pressed a top over it. "You know that gossip is like an addiction. A person can't just kick the habit."

"An addiction is a disease, Mom. Gossip is a behavior." Moira grabbed the coffee and took a grateful sip. Sweetie's coffee was smooth on her tongue. "Mm. Best brew in Somerset Lake." She assessed her mother over the rim of her cup. There was something off in her green eyes. "Mom?"

Darla raised her brows in response. "Hmm?"

Moira was about to ask what was going on, when a voice interrupted behind her.

"Fancy meeting you here."

Moira turned toward her friend's voice. "Hey, Tess. There you are."

Tess broke into a tired yawn. "Sorry, I'm running a bit late. I overslept, and I'm in desperate need of coffee."

"I'm on it." Darla turned to prepare another cup.

"Late night?" Moira waggled her brows, making Tess roll her eyes.

"Mind out of the gutter, please. I stayed up reading our selection for book club, thank you very much."

"If you say so."

Tess sighed and looked at Moira. "Are we still having coffee together?"

Moira checked the time. "I can if you can."

"The bookstore doesn't open until nine, and Lara is with me today, so I'm in no rush."

Darla handed Tess her beverage and rung her up.

"I'll talk to you later, Mom." Moira made a mental note to do exactly that. There was something wrong—she could tell—and she needed to know what it was.

"Enjoy your coffees, girls," Darla called after them.

"I love that your mom still calls us girls," Tess said as they walked to a table along the wall. "It makes me feel young again."

"We're not exactly ancient." Moira plopped down in the chair across from her friend, pondering that statement. A restless night tossing and turning did make her feel a little ancient this morning. "Today is going to be miserable," she said with a sigh. "Did you happen to see Reva's blog?"

"I did!" Tess said enthusiastically. "You're a local hero."

Moira harrumphed. "Sheriff Ronnie might say otherwise. He wants to see me after my shift."

Tess didn't look concerned. "I wouldn't worry. You went above and beyond the call of duty."

"And abandoned the dispatch for fifteen minutes. Fifteen minutes can be life or death in some cases, Tess."

Her friend shook her head. "Not in Somerset Lake. Not usually, at least."

"Well, Reva's blog didn't do me any favors. All I did was get Doug an ice pack and pour him some juice," Moira said.

"You crawled through a doggie door to do so." Tess grinned over her coffee cup, her brown eyes twinkling.

Moira let her face drop in her palm for a moment. "Ugh. I wish she could have at least left that detail out."

"And Goldie licked your cheeks before you stood," Tess added.

Moira's mouth fell open in surprise. "Did she write that?"

Tess lifted a brow, one side of her mouth quirking in amusement. "So it's true?"

Moira pulled her cup of coffee to her. "The secret is out. I've gotten more dog kisses than romantic kisses so far this year."

"Despite your New Year's resolution of going on at least one date per month?"

Moira offered an exaggerated eye roll. "That wasn't my resolution. It was the book club's goal for me, and it was completely unnecessary. Not everyone needs a romantic interest in their life to feel complete." She'd been saying this to her friends and family for years whenever they'd asked why she was still single. She'd said it so often that she was starting to believe it.

"Well, we'd just like to see you go on a few dates. All of us at the book club are coupled up now. We need to live vicariously through you."

"How about I live vicariously through you and stay happily single?" Moira took another sip of her coffee. The bell above the entrance jingled as someone else walked into the shop. Moira immediately turned to see who it was, subconsciously looking for Gil.

It wasn't Gil.

When Moira faced forward again, Tess gave her a questioning look.

"Expecting someone?"

Moira shook her head. "No." She couldn't lie to Tess though. Tess always knew when she was holding something back. She was Moira's wisest and most perceptive friend. "Fine, I was hoping to see Gil Ryan this morning."

Tess's eyes rounded. "That's new."

"I was kind of rude to him yesterday." Moira shrugged. "I guess I want to relieve my guilty conscience."

Tess gave Moira an assessing look. In another life, Tess could have been a counselor instead of a bookstore owner. "Being rude to Gil has never bothered you before."

"I'm that awful to him?" Moira asked, dreading her friend's answer.

"So much so I'd worry about you if you weren't."

That didn't help alleviate Moira's guilt. "Maybe I'm warming up to him." She held up a hand. "Not romantically. I just…Everyone has always told me that I should date him."

"Because everyone with eyes can see that he has a thing for you."

"An unreciprocated thing," Moira said, although some little voice in her head argued that truth. She'd felt something yesterday. The smallest of somethings. "So subconsciously, I guess I've just avoided him."

"Like the plague," Tess said.

Moira sipped her coffee. "And, I guess, I've realized that's not fair to him. He's a nice guy."

Tess grinned behind her cup of coffee before taking a drink. "The nicest guy I know."

"Then why don't you date him?" Moira asked, already knowing the answer.

"Because I have River, and the mysterious, silent type is more my speed." Her smile grew at the mention of her fiancé. Tess had lost her first husband years ago, and everyone had thought she'd never fall in love again. Then River came along.

"Maybe the nice guy isn't my type either," Moira said.

"Gil is so much more than just a nice guy though. He's loyal, noble, sweet, and"—Tess pretended to fan herself—"pretty handsome, if you ask me."

Moira raised her brows, as she looked at her friend. "Uh-oh. I'm going to tell River."

"Not as handsome as him, of course." Tess laughed. "But Gil is cute. There's no arguing against that." She shrugged. "And how do you know the nice guy isn't your type? As far as I can tell, you don't have a type because you're never interested in anyone."

"My type is the kind who makes the world a better place. Who makes my world better."

"That's a pretty tall order," Tess said.

"Which is why I'm still single." Moira grabbed her cup of coffee and pushed back from the table. "I need to get home for my shift and do my small part in making my corner of the world better," she teased. "After abandoning my post yesterday, being late would not bode well for me."

Tess also stood. "And I need to get to the store. But first I'm going to grab another coffee to bring Lara."

"Best boss ever," Moira said.

"I don't know about that. If I see Gil, I'll tell him you're looking for him." Tess winked.

"Not necessary. I'll just apologize next time I bump into him," Moira said, equal parts hoping that was never and just a few minutes from now.

∞

Gil had seen Moira coming toward Sweetie's Bakeshop, and he'd ducked around the corner of the building. It was usually the other way around, where Moira avoided him at all costs. Not this morning though.

He couldn't face Moira after the conversation he'd just had with Darla. Darla was surprisingly calm about the news, but Gil suspected she was in shock. If things went as the town council had planned, her beloved business would be moving out of its longtime home at the center of town. She'd have to find a new building. Move. Unpack. There'd be time lost in the transition, which meant lost sales. It wasn't ideal, and Gil knew it.

Being the mayor sometimes meant that he had to do the dirty work though. And he did feel dirty about the council's decision to uproot Darla's business. Sweetie's Bakeshop had been housed at its central location on Hannigan Street for nearly three decades. It was like the massive oak tree near the lake that the town had once considered chopping down in order to build a public dock. A few townsfolk had surrounded the tree, including Moira, practically hugging the trunk and pleading for its reprieve. Gil had to agree with them. Things that lasted that long should be rewarded. In Gil's experience, the things that endured were the ones that made the most difference.

He got into his truck and cranked the engine, preparing to head to his next stop. Sheriff Ronnie had asked to see him this morning. As the town's mayor, he was sometimes called to the sheriff's department. Over the last four years, Gil had grown close to Ronnie. He guessed the good sheriff wanted to discuss the upcoming Spring into Somerset Festival happening next weekend. As far as Gil knew, everything was on track for the big day. There would be live music and food, and arts and crafts booths. Gil was planning to use the local gathering to announce his running for a second term as mayor. Like the giant oak tree on the lake, he wanted to endure and make his mark on this town.

Pulling onto Hannigan Street, he followed it to the corner of Good Luck Avenue. His phone rang while he drove. He tapped a button on his steering wheel to answer. "Hello?"

"Gilbert," the caller said.

Gil rolled his eyes as he came to a stop sign. "Hey, Jake." Jake Fletcher was a lifelong friend who lived on the other side of the lake from Gil. He and the other guys Gil had grown up with often liked to call him by his full name as a way of teasing him. "What's going on this morning?" Gil asked. A truck passed in front of him, and then the road was clear for him to continue driving forward.

"Oh, you know. Same old, same old. Mr. S is back to his morning shenanigans, sleeping in the buff on the lake." Jake helped his grandmother Vi and his wife, Trisha, run the Somerset Rental Cottages. "Between moving Mr. S back into his cottage every morning and making sure Vi is following doctor's orders, I'm staying pretty busy on this side of the lake." Jake's grandmother Vi had had a stroke a couple of years back. She was doing well these days, as far as Gil could tell, and was just as feisty as ever.

"Not to mention running a law practice and tending to a pregnant wife," Gil added. "How's Trisha doing, by the way?"

"She's great. She's sending me to Choco-Lovers every chance she gets, claiming the baby wants chocolate. At this rate, I'm considering naming the kid Godiva."

Gil laughed. "That's not a bad choice."

"Listen," Jake said, "I was just calling to touch base with you on what you asked me about."

Gil's foot lifted off the pedal just a touch as a car pulled in front of him a ways ahead. "Okay." Jake was a lawyer and Gil's go-to guy for all things legal. "And?"

"And I don't see that Darla has much of a leg to stand on if she wanted to fight the council's decision. The town owns her building. The lease is coming up and it's their right not to renew. They can legally evict Darla without any repercussion."

"Even if she's been the model tenant?" Gil asked.

"Even if. The one who holds the deed gets to call the shots. In this case, that's the town."

"I see." Gil didn't want to fight Darla, but his job was to look out for the town's best interests. He'd needed to make sure evicting Darla was completely legal, although, admittedly, some part of him had hoped Darla would have a leg to stand on if she wanted to fight the decision.

"I hope Darla can find a new location," Jake said. "Maybe call Della and see if she knows of a commercial real estate spot for her."

Della Rose was the best real estate agent in town. If there were another central location that was available though, then the new parking lot would have gone there. There was nothing. This was a small town with limited space. The only other commercial real estate available was on the outer reaches of Somerset Lake. Folks would have to go out of their way to grab coffee and breakfast from Darla. That meant they'd likely just go to the diner around the corner, even though the coffee wasn't nearly as good, in Gil's opinion.

"Keep this between us for now, okay?" Gil asked.

"Of course."

"Great. See you at the tavern on Thursday."

The guys got together every Thursday night without fail. They met at the tavern for wings and drinks while most of the guys' female counterparts met for book club. Gil wondered what really went on at the book club in Tess's bookstore. He somehow doubted those meetings were solely for members to talk about the books they read.

"I'll be there," Jake said.

They disconnected the call, and Gil drove the rest of the way to the sheriff's department in silence, which only allowed his thoughts to be amplified. The big, pressing question right now was whether Darla had told Moira the news about the bakery yet. If she had, Moira was somewhere hating him, which he regretted. He'd accepted that she'd never return his interest, but he still wished they could be friendly toward one another. He admired Moira— that was a huge part of his attraction to her. She had never been a person to stay quiet when there was an injustice. Like the time their eleventh-grade Language Arts teacher was let go after another student told blatant lies about her. Moira had marched down to Principal Russo's office in support of their teacher, leading a dozen or so other students. Or the time Moira had gathered with the community to save that oak tree near the lake. Moira was a force to be reckoned with, and he didn't want to be the one reckoning with her.

After a few minutes of driving, Gil turned in to the lot of the sheriff's department and parked out front. The air felt cool against his skin as he walked toward the one-story brick building. The department's administrative assistant looked up from the front counter as he stepped inside.

"Hey, Mayor Gil," Bonnie Weston said. "Are you here to see Sheriff Ronnie?"

"I am," Gil confirmed, looking around. He could hear a few deputies laughing in one of the offices down the hall.

Bonnie pointed down the hall opposite the one with the laughter. "His door is open. Good luck," she said, brows raised.

Gil narrowed his eyes on the woman who was about his mother's age. "Luck? Why would I need luck?"

Bonnie looked at him over her blue-rimmed glasses. "You don't know why you're here?"

Gil placed his hands on his hips, processing her question. "I guess I don't."

"Well, it's not my place to tell you." She pointed down the hall. "Go on. He gets a bit grumpy when someone makes him wait too long."

Gil had a sudden flutter of nerves in his belly. He and Ronnie were friends. There was no need to be nervous. Gil glanced down the hall and started walking, wondering just what he was walking into.

"Gilbert!" Ronnie said when Gil stood in front of his open door.

"Not you too." Gil gauged the sheriff's relaxed demeanor. *See? Nothing to worry about.*

"Come on in. Close the door, if you don't mind," the sheriff said.

Gil was back on alert. He stepped inside and closed the door behind him. "Should I also sit down?"

Ronnie's smile fell into a straight line. "That would probably be best."

Chapter Five

Gil took a seat across from Ronnie at his desk. "Let's have it. What's going on?"

The sheriff was laid-back and relaxed as much as he was serious and hard-edged, depending on the situation. Right now, it was the latter. "I was older than you in school," he started by saying.

Gil nodded. "By about three years, right?"

"About that much." Ronnie leaned back in his chair, crossing one boot over his opposite knee. "But even I remember when you and Denise Berger ran against each other for student government president."

Gil laughed out loud. "Of all the things I'd expected you wanting to discuss, I hadn't considered that you might bring that up this morning." He hadn't even thought about that fiasco in quite a while. The year he and Denise went head-to-head had been rough. Denise was voted most popular in school, but it wasn't because of her likability factor. Her popularity was due to her family's wealth and her parents' prominent roles in the community. Denise acted entitled in every area of her life, including student government. She was ruthless when she ran against Gil, digging for all the dirt she could find on him. When she hadn't been able to uncover any, she'd taken jabs at his character, making out his niceness to be a flaw. "She was a fierce opponent."

Ronnie pressed his fingertips together in front of him in a contemplative stance. "How would you like to repeat history?"

Gil gave his head a hard shake. "I wouldn't. That's one chapter in my life not worth rereading," he said, not following the sheriff's train of thought.

Ronnie frowned. "I suspected as much. That's why I wanted to be the one to tell you first," he finally said.

Gil wasn't sure what to think about this conversation so far. "Tell me what, Sheriff?"

"Denise has decided she's running for mayor this fall. She's going to be your opponent, and I'm afraid she hasn't changed much since high school."

The clock had been ticking extra slow today as Moira waited for her shift to end.

Sheriff Ronnie wanted to see her this afternoon, and she could only guess at the reason why. And she had been guessing all day and imagining the very worst. So much so that she was convinced Sheriff Ronnie was going to fire her for leaving her dispatch to help Doug yesterday.

To make matters worse, Moira had finally relented and gone to Reva's town blog to see what exactly the town gossip had said about her. Moira was the very first bullet point of the day.

Moira clicked on the open tab on her computer and reread the bullet point for the tenth time.

- Who knew that our very own Moira Green would become a local hero this week? When the sheriff's department failed to do their job, Moira took matters into her own hands, drove to the mayor's home, crawled through the doggie door, and gave medical attention to Doug Green just in the nick of time.

Moira groaned. As if leaving her dispatch while on shift wasn't bad enough, this blog post made it sound like the sheriff's department was deficient. Sheriff Ronnie had likely flipped his lid when he read this.

She eyed the clock over her kitchen sink. Five minutes until her shift was over. There had been only one call today, for someone who thought they'd seen a coyote on the outskirts of the woods. Moira had contacted the sheriff's department, who she assumed had contacted the new ranger for the area. The coyote in question was likely just a stray dog, but she hadn't heard one way or the other.

Three minutes until her shift was over.

The dispatch lit up.

A sudden spike of adrenaline shot through Moira as she answered. "Nine-one-one, what's your emergency?"

"Moira Green?"

Moira wrinkled her brow. "This is she. Who is this?"

"It's Mrs. Denny. Conner's mother. You remember Conner Denny, don't you, dear?"

Moira glanced at the clock. Two minutes until her shift was over. "Yes, I think so. He was a year behind me in school."

"I believe you're right. Well, I was just calling to let you know Conner is on the market again. I was telling my bingo friends, and they mentioned you were also still single. Is that true?"

"Um." Moira wasn't sure how to respond to this conversation. "Is this an emergency, Mrs. Denny?"

"Oh, well, a single man with a good job and manners is hard to find, dear. Trust me on that." Giddy laughter trailed her words.

"I'm not looking for a relationship, Mrs. Denny," Moira said, trying her best to be polite. This call wasn't really all that surprising. Over the last year, there'd been more and more attempts to set Moira up, as if people were trying to do her a favor. What was so wrong with a young woman remaining happily single though?

One minute until the hour.

"I'm sorry, Mrs. Denny. I'm sure Conner is very nice and that one day soon he'll meet the right person, which I'm sorry to say is not me."

"Oh. Are you sure? You haven't even given him a chance. He works at Hannigan's Hardware. Maybe just stop by one day and say hello. You never know when sparks will fly."

"Perhaps I will," Moira lied. She had no intention of stopping in the hardware store for anything anytime soon.

Five o'clock!

"I've got to go, Mrs. Denny. This is an emergency line only. Are you aware that it's a crime to call under false pretenses?"

"Oh!" Mrs. Denny gasped. "No, I didn't realize that. I am so sorry. I do apologize. Have a nice evening."

"You as well." Moira disconnected the call and exhaled. Then nerves wound their way around Moira's chest as she stood. Her legs suddenly felt wobbly. As frustrating as working dispatch could sometimes be, she loved her job, and she wanted to keep it. What if Sheriff Ronnie fired her this evening?

Before removing her headset, Moira made sure the evening dispatcher took over. Then she slipped on her shoes, grabbed her purse and car keys, and headed out the door. Once she was inside her tiny car, she cranked the engine and sent up a silent prayer that the good sheriff would go easy on her. She'd had a very good reason for leaving her dispatch. She was sure that the sheriff's department would have eventually made their way to Gil's home, but by then Doug could have had a serious issue with his blood sugar.

Moira's mind spun out various possibilities for Ronnie's request all the way to the sheriff's department. Her mind didn't stop spinning possibilities until she parked and walked inside.

"Hey, Moira," Bonnie Weston said, looking up from the front desk. "Sheriff Ronnie is waiting for you. It's been a busy day for him."

"Oh? He's had others stop by?" Moira asked, hoping maybe she was wrong about the reason she'd been called here. Maybe there was some other reason she hadn't thought of.

"A few," Bonnie confirmed. "His door is open. Good luck," she said in a lyrical tone.

What did she mean by that? Did she know something?

Moira nearly stumbled over her feet as she made her way down the hall. Then she lingered in Sheriff Ronnie's doorway until he looked up from the file he was reading. Sheriff Ronnie was a large man who took up most of the space behind his desk. He was intimidating until he smiled. Then he looked like a big teddy bear, if you asked Moira. He wasn't smiling right now.

He closed the file and pushed it off to the side. "Moira. You made it," he said. "Come on in and shut the door."

She swallowed past a tight throat. Then she began to talk immediately. "Sheriff, I am so sorry about yesterday. When Doug called for help, it sounded urgent, and in my opinion, it truly was. I knew the department was busy with the pileup, and I didn't want him to have to wait." Moira was talking so fast that she forgot to breathe, which consequently made her head feel dizzy. "It will never happen again, Sheriff. I promise."

Ronnie leaned back in his chair and pressed his fingertips together. "Are you going to give me a chance to speak or would you like to pass out from a lack of oxygen first?"

Moira blinked and inhaled deeply. "Sir?"

He gestured at the chair across from his desk. "Have a seat, Moira."

Her body felt weak and shaky as she walked closer. Maybe sitting was a good idea. She'd never been fired before. She'd never even gotten a warning from a superior. She plopped down in the seat and fidgeted with her hands as she forced her breaths to come in and out more evenly. It would be okay. She could always work at her mom's bakery. Since Darla had added the café seating last year, business had only increased. Moira didn't enjoy working in food service, but if she didn't have a choice, she'd do what she had to.

The sheriff reached across his desk and offered his hand.

Moira stared at it for a moment.

"I'd like to shake the hand of the woman who took action in an emergency and quite possibly saved someone's life."

Saving a life was a stretch. Doug hadn't been in that bad a shape, but hyper- or hypoglycemia could get dangerous. "You would?" Her mouth dropped.

Sheriff Ronnie looked at his hand, which was still extended, and back up at her.

"Oh, sorry." She shook his hand, wondering if her palms were sweaty. She couldn't remember the last time she'd been this nervous.

"It's not your job to risk your life for others," he said, drawing his hand back to his side. "Don't misunderstand. You shouldn't have left your dispatch to go to Doug's aid. There could have been another emergency that needed tending to."

"Yes, sir," Moira said, lowering her face. If Sheriff Ronnie wanted to chew her out, she would sit here and take it. She'd broken a rule after all. Not to say she wouldn't do it again. At the time, she'd felt like she had no choice. She'd used her judgment.

"And if there had been another emergency that had gone unattended, you would be facing serious consequences right now," the sheriff said, his eyes narrowed at her from across the desk.

"Yes, sir."

Ronnie waited a long second before continuing his lecture. "Fortunately, there wasn't another emergency, and if there was, Riley was on shift to respond." He cleared his throat, gaining her attention. "You didn't know what you were walking into by going to Doug's aid, Moira. My emergency responders are trained for all kinds of situations. You could have been hurt."

"Or licked to death by a large dog," she said, hoping to ease the tension.

Ronnie smiled, which she took as a good sign. "If you want to know the truth, I'm proud of you, Moira. The town seems to be impressed by your actions as well."

"Only because Reva put it in her blog." Moira shook

her head with a slight eye roll. "I wish she wouldn't have included me as a bullet point."

"Well, you deserve the recognition. Enjoy the spotlight for a moment," Ronnie said.

Moira released a breath. She'd really thought she might be walking out of this office unemployed, but it didn't appear that was the case. "I'd hardly call making a bullet point being in the spotlight, but I am breathing a bit easier. I thought you were going to fire me," she told him on a small laugh.

"No. I'm not firing you. In fact, the town wants to give you an award, Moira."

"Me?" She'd never been given anything more than a perfect attendance certificate in elementary school. "What kind of award?"

"A public service award. We're planning to formally give it to you next weekend at the Spring into Somerset Festival."

Moira blinked again, waiting for the sheriff to start laughing like this was some kind of joke. "You're serious?"

"Noontime next Saturday," he confirmed with a nod.

Moira's argument rested on her tongue. She didn't want to receive an award, but at this moment, she was just glad not to be getting a pink slip. "Thank you, sir."

"Thank *you*," he said with an easy smile. Why hadn't he shown her that smile this morning instead of making her sweat all day?

"Is that all?" Moira asked.

Sheriff Ronnie leaned back in his chair. "Yep. I already spoke to the mayor. He'll be presenting the award to you next weekend. It'll shine a nice light on the department as well. Maybe offset the shade that Reva tried to throw our way in her mention of us in the blog."

Moira's brain was still processing what he'd said. "Mayor Gil is going to be presenting me with the award?"

Sheriff Ronnie narrowed his gaze. "Doug is his brother, and he's usually the one who presents these kinds of awards. He said he'd be more than happy to do it. Unless there's a problem?" Ronnie's brow lifted subtly.

Moira shook her head, feeling even guiltier over the way she'd treated Gil yesterday. She still hadn't had a chance to apologize. She was also still confused over the little spark she'd felt at their last interaction. She didn't feel sparks. That wasn't like her at all. Hopefully those feelings would be gone when she saw him again. "No. No problem at all."

"You sure? Because the town council's decision isn't his fault. Your mom's bakery spot is the only solution to the parking issue."

Moira tilted her head, trying to piece together what exactly he meant by that. For the life of her, she had no idea. "I'm sorry?"

"As you know, parking is a nightmare on Hannigan Street, especially during the holidays and the festivals that occur every time you turn around. That three-car pileup never would have happened if there'd been ample parking on Hannigan Street. And you wouldn't have had to help Doug if the crews had been able to navigate that street efficiently. As much as I hate to see your mom's business get booted, a parking lot is necessary for the good of the town."

Moira was speechless. She really didn't know what to say. Sheriff Ronnie must be mistaken. She hadn't heard anything about Sweetie's Bakeshop being evicted. She stood and offered her hand to shake. "Thank you again, Sheriff."

Ronnie took her hand. "You're welcome. See you next weekend. Good job, Moira."

Moira walked out of the sheriff's office and past Bonnie at the front desk. She left the building in a blur and got inside her car. A few years ago, her mom had sold the building that Sweetie's Bakeshop was in. They'd needed money to pay for her dad's medical expenses. Darla had sold the building under the agreement that her business could remain, however. The town couldn't just kick her out, demolish the building, and put a parking lot in its place. Could it?

Moira cranked her car's engine and started driving. She needed to clear this up right now. It wasn't true. Whatever the sheriff had been talking about, it had to be a misunderstanding. When she arrived at Sweetie's Bakeshop and walked in, her mom's part-time help was behind the counter.

"Hey, Bailey. Is my mom here?" Moira looked past the nineteen-year-old into the back room.

"Nope. She left a while ago. It's just me," Bailey said.

Moira found that strange. Even when Bailey was here, Darla typically stuck around to cook or clean. "Was she feeling okay?"

"Oh, yeah. I think so, at least. She just said she had some errands to take care of."

"Thanks." Moira turned to leave and nearly bumped into none other than Gil himself. Anger flared hot over every square inch of her body.

"Moira. Hi." Gil had this intense way of looking at her. No one else had ever looked at her quite that way before. It used to annoy her to no end, but she'd felt differently the other day. Right now, however, the look was more than annoying. She was infuriated.

"How can you smile at me like that after what you decided to do to my mom's business?"

Gil frowned. "She told you?"

Moira tried not to cry. "It's true then? You're kicking her out of the building she's been in for nearly three decades? How can you do that?"

Gil held up a hand, his gaze darting around the room to see who was watching.

Moira didn't care who was overhearing this. Maybe the people of this town should know what their beloved mayor was planning. "This is wrong, Gil."

"Let's sit down, okay?" His voice was low in contrast to hers. "I'll explain."

Moira shook her head. "I need to find my mom." She stepped past him, feeling him turn and follow. "Stop following me, Gil," she warned.

She felt him step out of the bakery and stop on the sidewalk behind her. "Moira?" he called after her.

She stopped walking and turned to look at him, hoping he wasn't close enough to see the tears in her eyes. She waited for him to say whatever it was he thought would make this right.

He didn't say anything though. Instead he looked at her before dropping his head.

Disappointment settled over her. Some part of her had hoped he'd have something that could make this all better. Her mother had to be devastated right now.

Moira turned and kept walking to her car parked alongside the road. She got inside and released a breath as tears clouded her vision. She blinked them away as she pulled out her phone and texted her mom.

Moira: Where are you? I need to see you.

She waited for her mom to respond, but she didn't.

Moira: Mom? Are you okay?

No response.

Moira wiped at her eyes. When she was able to see clearly, she pulled onto the road and started driving. There were a handful of places her mom might be. She would check them all, one by one, until she found her. Then she'd make sure her mom knew that Moira wasn't going to let this happen. Over her dead body would Sweetie's Bakeshop be shut down.

Chapter Six

Gil crossed the lawn between his home and his parents' house and headed up the porch steps of his childhood home. Even though he lived just next door, he didn't walk over on a daily basis. He needed his mom's clear head and her glass-half-full perspective on life this evening though.

He rang the doorbell and watched the lake while he waited. There was a sailboat out there, which made him long to put his own boat out on the water. The wind wasn't ideal though for sailing. If anyone asked him, the pontoon was a better choice for evening boat rides.

The door opened, and his mom furrowed her brow. "I've told you a million times, this is your home. You don't have to ring the doorbell."

Gil tipped his head across the lawn. "My home is over there now. I *do* need to ring the doorbell."

His mother shook her head and tugged him toward her in a huge hug. One might have thought Gil had been away for a year the way she seemed to struggle to let go of the embrace. "You're staying for dinner?" she asked when she finally pulled away.

Gil had to roll his shoulders out after she'd squeezed the life out of him. "If you'll have me."

She nodded. "Of course. Your father is working late at the firm, so you can eat his portion." She winked and turned to lead Gil into the kitchen.

"He'll want some leftovers when he gets home," Gil warned.

"Well, that's what he gets for working long hours. I've been telling him it's time to cut back."

Gil chuckled as he took a seat at a stool along his mom's counter. "He loves being in a courtroom. He'll never do that." Gil hadn't loved practicing law though. He'd followed in his dad's footsteps and had gotten his law degree, which he'd used for only a couple of years to work at his dad's firm. He wasn't a lawyer at heart though. He was a public servant, a mayor, and he wanted to remain in office.

"You're here because of Denise Berger's decision to run against you?" his mom asked, stepping up to the stove to stir a large pot of food. Whatever she had cooking, it smelled delicious.

"How'd you know about that already?" Gil asked.

She looked at him over her shoulder. "I have my sources."

Gil's mom was good friends with Reva. She always had been. They took walks around the lake together and were part of a women's bunco group. Sometimes Gil wished he were a fly on the wall for those meetings. At other times, he thought the less gossip he heard, the better off he was.

"I never did like Denise," his mom said with a head shake.

"That's saying a lot since you like everyone."

Gil's mom looked at him. "Not her. She was awful to you when you were running for class president in high school. Don't you remember how badly she behaved?"

Gil choked on a laugh. "Of course I do. She made just as many signs about me as she did about herself." And the signs about Gil had been full of half-truths and embarrassing photos. One of her minions had snapped a peripheral picture of him scratching his nose, and the photo had labeled him a nose picker. It was mortifying and demeaning, but he'd done his best to be a good sport, tapping the side of his nose good-naturedly whenever anyone had tried to rib him.

"Principal Russo finally put an end to her defamation of me," Gil said, "but not before I was teased mercilessly." That's when Gil's friends had started calling him Gilbert, because all of Denise's posters against him had a slogan: GILBERT NOSE BEST, BUT DENISE IS THE (WO)MAN FOR THE JOB. It was childish, but they were technically still kids back then. "Hopefully, Denise has done a lot of maturing in the years since our high school election."

His mom put down her wooden spoon and turned toward him, crossing her arms over her chest. "You can't allow her to treat you that way this time. This is your career. You're a good mayor, and I won't have that woman making up stories about you. Want me to talk to her mom?"

Gil thought maybe his mother was joking at first, but her expression was serious. "Mom, I don't need you talking to Mrs. Berger about her daughter's political tactics. I'm just hoping that, since we're adults, Denise will behave as a grown-up in this election."

His mom scoffed. "You always were the optimist."

"I get it from you," he accused.

"And it's why you are a good mayor. There's too much negativity out there. I know Somerset Lake is just a small corner of the earth, but you make the world a better place."

Gil knew his mom was a little partial, but he appreciated the sentiment. "Thanks, Mom. If it eases your mind at all, Denise joined the town council a couple months ago and she's been more than civil to me. She didn't mention that she had her sights set on my position, however."

"Well, she does and I don't trust her."

Gil didn't either. "So, what are you cooking over there anyway? It's making me hungry."

"Vegetable stew."

Gil got up from his stool and walked to where his mom was standing. He glanced at the stovetop from over her shoulder, eying the array of potatoes, sliced carrots, and beans floating in a tomato base. "What can I do to help?"

His mom looked at him. "Beat Denise Berger."

"I'll do my best."

She nodded and then tipped her head toward the cabinet to his right. "Do you mind getting out three bowls?"

"Sure." Gil opened the cabinet where the dishes were held, and pulled down three soup bowls.

"There's something else I need your help with," his mom said as she reached for a ladle on the countertop. Her hesitation got Gil's attention.

"Oh? What is that?"

She pressed her lips together as if she didn't want to say what was on her mind. "I'm a bit concerned about Doug."

Gil laid the bowls on the counter for her to start serving the soup into. "Because of the whole nine-one-one incident?"

"Partly for that reason. He has it in his head that he's ready to move out on his own." She stopped stirring the pot and turned to face him, her expression strained.

Gil wasn't exactly surprised by this news. "Okay. I had moved out by the time I was twenty-one."

"Yes, but that was different. Doug isn't ready to move out," his mother said. "He may never be ready to leave this house."

Gil frowned. "A lot of people with Down syndrome live on their own. It depends on the individual, of course. Just like with anyone else, there's a wide spectrum of abilities. For the most part, Doug is as independent as I am."

His mother sighed. "This isn't a debate, Gil. I need you to back me up on this. I want you to talk to Doug and tell him that he can't move out. He has to stay here, where he belongs."

After looking everywhere for her mom, Moira finally circled back to her parents' house and found her mom's car in the driveway. She got out of her own vehicle and headed up the porch steps, when she heard her mom call to her from the back porch.

"Back here!"

Moira headed around to the back of the home, spotting her mom sitting in her deck furniture. Her mom's back-yard was beautiful. Since Moira's dad had retired, he'd taken to transforming the yard into a small slice of heaven on earth with his gardening. Everything was abloom for spring and rich in color.

"Dad has really outdone himself, hasn't he?" Moira asked, climbing the steps and taking a seat next to her mom.

Darla glanced over. "I love seeing him discover new things that he's passionate about. Has he told you he's going to take a beer-making class?"

Moira laughed. "Dad doesn't even drink, does he?"

"He likes a taste here and there." Darla shrugged and continued looking out on the backyard, her expression slowly wilting.

"Mom," Moira said, reaching to take her mom's hand, "I heard about the town's decision to move Sweetie's and make a parking lot in that location instead. It's despicable. I can't even fathom what the town council is thinking."

Darla released an audible breath. "They're thinking about what the town desperately needs. Downtown parking has been an issue for as long as I can remember."

"Sweetie's Bakeshop has been a staple for as long as I can remember," Moira said softly. "It's not right, and I won't sit around while your life's work is demolished."

Darla looked at her now. There was something so sad in her eyes. It broke Moira's heart. Her mother was always smiling. She was one of the happiest people Moira knew, even during the times when her life had seemed like it was crashing around her. Like when Moira's father had cancer. And like now.

"I don't want to see that happen either, but what can I do? I don't own the building anymore."

Moira really wished her mom had never sold it. It seemed like the right thing to do at the time though. "When you sold it, you were promised that you could stay. We can fight this in court."

"With what money?" Darla's red hair caught the sunlight as she shook her head.

"We know lawyers, Mom. Jake Fletcher is a lawyer.

Maybe he'd do it pro bono." Gil Ryan was a lawyer, too, although he wasn't practicing anymore. His dad still was, but there was no way Tony Ryan would take on a fight against the town and its mayor, who just happened to be his own son.

"I'm not going to ask for charity. Jake is busy. He and Trisha are expecting their first baby, and he's working and running the Somerset Rental Cottages. No." Darla lifted a stubborn chin. "Sometimes life gives you lemons, Mo."

"And you just have to make lemonade with them." Moira had been listening to her mom say that phrase all her life. It was usually when Moira had been going through some sort of drama at school or work. "Well, I'm making lemonade by fighting those lemons and turning this plan to demolish Sweetie's around."

"No," Darla said forcefully. "As much as it breaks my heart, I love this town. What's best for one shouldn't outweigh what's best for all. If a parking lot will make our downtown more accessible and safer, then that's what should happen. I can find a new location for Sweetie's."

"Where?" Moira asked. "It wouldn't be on Hannigan Street. People love your bakery and café, but they won't go out of their way to get there. They might at first, but then they'll stop because location is important for your business too. Then what, Mom?"

Darla fidgeted with her hands the same way that Moira did when she was nervous. Darla's hands were cracked and wrinkled, effects of years using them to make pastries, pies, and breads. It wasn't fair that she'd given so much of herself and would have to watch it disappear. "I went to the diner on Good Luck Avenue earlier this afternoon," she said quietly. "Angela is a good friend of mine. She always has been."

"Okay?" Moira wasn't sure what this had to do with anything.

"Her business has been struggling for a while now. Truth be told, I've always kind of thought she resented me a little bit for taking some of her business away when we opened the café part of Sweetie's."

Moira shook her head. "There's more than enough business for both of you."

"In theory." Darla nodded. "She's stopped serving breakfast to save on costs because the café has taken her morning crowd. I didn't tell her about the town's plans for Sweetie's, but I can't help but think she'd be happy to see me move somewhere else."

"Then she's not a good friend," Moira said.

Darla chuckled. "All's fair in friendship and business."

"You mean in love and war. And that's a complete lie." Moira blew out a breath. "What if we create a petition for people to sign in support of saving Sweetie's? You can have your customers sign it when they come in. I'll get people to sign it too. I'll go door to door if I have to. I'm sure Tess would put a petition out in Lakeside Books." Moira's excitement and determination gained momentum as she talked. She hadn't considered this idea yet, but it just might work.

Darla reached over and laid a hand over Moira's. "Sweetie, I appreciate the sentiment, I really do, but I want you to stop right there. As much as it breaks my heart, I'm not fighting this decision. And I don't want you to either."

∞

Later that night, Moira lay in bed staring up at the ceiling, mulling over her mom's words. She was disappointed that her mom wasn't willing to go up against the town council when she was obviously brokenhearted about the prospect of Sweetie's being uprooted from its current location. Darla would have to start over again, which seemed so unfair. While Moira's father was enjoying retirement, her mom would be back at square one, reestablishing her customer base and creating a homey environment that would never replace what Sweetie's currently had.

No. This can't happen. Moira had heard her mom's words tonight, but she didn't believe for a moment that Darla meant them. How could she? Maybe she was tired after all these years of taking care of Moira and then Moira's father when he got sick. Perhaps there was no fight left in Darla.

Well, Moira wasn't tired. In fact, she was energized, fueled by frustration and anger and a need to protect what belonged to her family.

Moira blinked back hot tears as she stared up at her ceiling. It was time for sleep, but she wasn't tired at all. On a sigh, she got up and walked into her kitchen to pour herself a glass of water. As she gulped it down, she began to construct a plan of action, eager for daylight so that she could fight hard enough for both her and her mom.

Chapter Seven

The following evening, Moira pulled her knees to her body as she sat on the leather couch in Lakeside Books.

Her friends had all arrived and were discussing how Trisha's belly was so much larger than last Thursday. They weren't wrong.

"This is the only time in my life that I won't be offended by how much you-all are commenting on my stomach," Trisha said, leaning forward awkwardly to get a piece of fudge off the coffee table.

"You're the most beautiful pregnant woman I've ever worked with," Lucy Hannigan said. Lucy was a midwife who owned and operated the Babymoon B&B in a prestigious neighborhood called The Village.

"You're partial because I'm your friend." Trisha rolled her eyes just slightly. "But thank you. I'm lucky to be under the care of the best midwife in town."

"The only one," Lucy said, "but thank you as well."

Moira sighed, pulling her book from her bag. "Is this a lovefest or a book club?" she asked, not meaning it to sound as grumpy as it came out.

The women all turned their attention to her. Tess, Lucy, Trisha, Della, and the newest member, Lara.

"Okay, something's up with you." Tess leaned back into her leather recliner and crossed her long legs. "What's going on?"

Moira hadn't gotten a chance to fill any of her friends in on the town council's decision. She was still in denial about it all, hoping it was just a bad dream. On a sigh, she said, "Mom sold the building that Sweetie's is housed in a couple years ago when my dad was sick."

"What?" Lucy's mouth dropped. "I had no idea."

Moira nodded. "She wanted to try some experimental therapies that insurance didn't cover. So instead of asking me for help, which she's too proud to do, she sold the building with the verbal agreement that she could still run her business here."

"Unwritten agreement?" Lucy asked, obviously thinking like her lawyer husband.

"I would have told her to at least get that in writing," Moira said. "But first I would have told her not to sell her building. The town has been champing at the bit for this piece of real estate for years."

"Why?" Trisha asked.

Moira shrugged. "Because they own most of the downtown area. And now Gil and the town council are proposing a new parking lot for Hannigan Street."

"Oh, thank goodness," Lucy said reflexively. "That is a welcome change."

Moira narrowed her eyes. "Where do you think they'll put the parking lot, Luce?"

Lucy seemed to consider the question. She finally shook her head and shrugged. "I have no idea. If there was a good spot, they would have done it years ago."

"Exactly. In order to put a parking lot here, they'll need to tear something down."

Lucy blinked, and then her mouth fell open. "You're not serious."

Moira reached for a piece of fudge. No amount of chocolate would make this news any better though. "I wish I weren't."

Tess reached out and rubbed Moira's arm. "I'm sorry. I know how much Sweetie's means to you. It means a lot to all of us."

Moira sucked in a breath. "Well, I'm not going to let this happen."

"What are you going to do?" Tess asked.

"I don't know yet. I was thinking about starting a petition. I'll get the whole town to sign it. Then the council has to listen, right?"

"I think the council would at least have to reconsider their decision," Tess agreed. "It's a good idea."

Moira broke a piece off her fudge square as she explained the idea she'd come up with last night. "Next weekend is the Spring into Somerset Festival. Everyone will be there."

"It'll be the perfect place to get your signatures," Lucy said excitedly. She was the eternal optimist of the group while Tess was the wise one. "I have a booth already set up to take reservations for the B and B. You can put your petition at my table. Or one of them. I'm sure other people would be willing to help you with this too."

"And you can keep a petition here," Tess added.

Moira looked around her circle of friends. "Mom already told me to drop any plans to fight this. She doesn't like others to make a fuss where she's concerned. That's why I'm doing this on my own and not telling her."

Tess made a face. "I don't like the sound of that. Keeping secrets from family is never a good idea."

Tess's late husband had kept a wealth of secrets from her. She and River Harrison, a private investigator in town, had done some undercover sleuthing last year to unravel the mystery of her late husband's death. The secret Moira was proposing was on a much smaller scale though. It would be harmless, really.

"My mom will get over it," Moira said. "This is for the best. For the town's best. Sweetie's Bakeshop can't be turned into a parking lot. It just can't."

"That's the spirit," Lucy said. "Now let's talk about this award you're receiving at the festival."

Moira rolled her eyes. "I was considering playing sick to get out of it. But now, with the petition idea, I can't really do that. I need to be there."

"Yes, you do." Lucy's green eyes lit up. "It's perfect, actually. You'll be onstage. You'll have everyone's attention. That's a perfect time to plead your case."

Gil bounced his leg under the table and glanced around the busy tavern. He was usually able to relax when he was at the weekly get-togethers with the guys. Tonight, however, he wished he were at home. All he wanted was to lie in bed and close his eyes.

"Earth to Gilbert," Jake said.

Gil blinked his friends into focus. Jake and Miles, a local deputy, shared a look. River cleared his throat and started chuckling quietly across the table.

"What? What are you guys laughing about?" Gil asked.

Even Roman was chuckling, and he was the newbie of the group, ruling out any kind of inside joke he might not get.

"Denise has already got you worried, huh?" Out of

their group of friends, Jake loved to tease Gil the most. It was just his easygoing way.

"What do you know about that?" Gil asked.

"She's already started her campaign against you, buddy. Have you seen her ads?"

"Ads?" Gil looked at his pals. "What ads?"

"She's running ads on Reva's blog," Jake said.

Gil scrunched his face. "Since when does Reva offer paid advertisement? Is that a thing?"

Miles shrugged. "Denise is calling herself the 'Family choice for mayor.'"

Gil pulled back, bracing his arms on the table in front of him. "Why? Because I'm single and without kids, that means I'm not the family choice?"

"That's the natural assumption." Jake tipped his drink back and took a long swallow.

"You were voted Most Eligible Bachelor last year," River added. "That's the antithesis of the family choice."

"Doesn't mean I'm living a bachelor's lifestyle." Gil reached for his soda. The carbonation popped on his tongue as he took a sip. "I thought Reva liked me," he said as he lowered his glass back to the table.

"She likes everyone," Jake said. "Don't take it personally. Just ask her to put in an ad for you too."

Gil frowned. For his last mayoral election, he hadn't needed to do any of that stuff. All he'd needed to do was get signatures petitioning for his run as mayor. He'd spoken at a few events, informing folks of his views and his goals for the town, and that was all. The previous mayor, Bryce Malsop, had been so unpopular that Gil was the shoo-in.

"She's going to play dirty." Miles reached for a chicken wing at the center of the table and placed it on the plate in front of him.

"We're not kids anymore," Gil said. "Can't we just let the best person win?"

The guys laughed at this.

"Oh, Gilbert, Gilbert." Jake patted Gil's back. "Buckle up. This fall's election is going to be a wild ride for you, friend."

Gil took another drink of his soda and listened as the conversation moved on to other topics. When he was about to leave for the night, someone walked into the tavern and headed straight to the bar. He thought his mind was playing tricks on him at first because Moira was supposed to be at book club with the women who regularly gathered at Lakeside Books.

Gil got up and started moving in her direction before he could talk himself out of it.

"Where are you going, buddy?" Miles asked before noticing who was sitting at the bar.

"I thought you were over her," Jake said, lifting his brows high on his forehead.

"I am." Gil turned his back to his friends and continued walking.

Moira straightened when she noticed him sit beside her.

"I've been looking for you," Gil said in a low voice meant only for her ears.

She averted her gaze. "Oh? What for?"

The bartender slid a drink in front of Moira. She took it between her hands but didn't move to take a sip. Instead, she just stared into its liquid depths.

Gil wondered what she was doing. There was something about her that looked lost tonight. She must be to find herself here at the bar instead of Lakeside Books. "Was book club canceled?"

"We ended early. Pregnancy makes Trisha tired." Moira shrugged and continued to stare at her beverage.

"Is something wrong with your drink?" he asked.

She finally met his gaze. The color of her hazel eyes was more green than brown tonight. Maybe it was the low lighting, but he also saw golden flecks in the irises. "I don't usually drink alone. And never at bars." Her chin lifted as she stared back at him.

Gil looked at the drink again. "So why did you just order that one?"

She shrugged, her gaze once again falling on the drink in front of her. "If there's ever been a week when I needed one of these, it's this one. No thanks to you."

"Moira..."

She shook her head and held her hand out to the side, halting his words. "I miss the days when a drink was easy. A way to kick back and leave your cares at the door."

Gil looked at his reflection in the mirrored backsplash on the wall. He wondered if something had happened to make Moira gun-shy with public drinks. "If you want to have that, I'll make sure you get home safely."

In the mirror, he saw her look at him through their reflections. "Just like you did that night?"

Gil knew exactly which night she was referring to. "You should know that you can trust me, Moira. Always."

"Trust you not to take advantage of me, yeah, of course. Trust you not to kick my mom when she's down? Nope." She pushed back from the bar and stood. "I forgot you'd be here tonight. This wasn't a good idea anyway." She gestured to the drink. "You can have it. It's on me."

"Moira..." he said.

She stopped walking but didn't look back at him.

"For what it's worth, I tried to find alternatives for Hannigan Street parking. I really did. There weren't any other options."

"My mom only sold her building because my dad got sick. She had no choice. But the town does have a choice in this matter. She never would have sold the building if she'd known it would be demolished one day." Moira finally looked at him, her eyes suspiciously shiny. "Do you know at one point she was planning to rename her shop the Good Luck Café?"

Gil shook his head. "No, I didn't know that. Because it's on the corner of Good Luck Avenue?" he asked.

"No, because once she opened, the business brought her nothing but good luck. It's where she met my dad. It's where she found out she was pregnant with me. She even got a hundred-dollar tip one time from a movie star who was passing through town. She kept her business as Sweetie's because that's what everyone in town already knew it as, and some things should never be messed with." Moira narrowed her eyes.

Gil cleared his throat. "I've already spoken to Della. I'll help Darla find a new spot to relocate. I'll even help her move. I'll do whatever I can to make this transition as smooth as possible."

Moira looked defeated. Gil wanted to wrap his arms around her and comfort her, even though he was technically the villain in this story.

"You've already done enough, don't you think?"

Gil's eyelids were hanging heavily, and the world was disappearing little by little as he lay in his bed later that night. Then someone knocked, and Goldie leaped off the bed, charging toward the front of the house.

Gil eyed the digital clock on his nightstand. It was only nine thirty p.m., early by sleep standards, but he was eager to put the day behind him. Who would be visiting this time of night? He sat up and slipped his feet into a pair of slippers. When he got to the front door, he peeked out the peephole. *Should've known.*

Gil opened the door and greeted his brother cheerily despite the fact he'd been pulled out of bed. "Hey, Doug. What are you doing here?"

Doug patted Goldie's head as she greeted him. "I want to go over the campaign." He walked past Gil into the house.

Gil closed the door behind his brother and turned. "It's a little late, isn't it?"

Doug pulled out a chair at the kitchen table. "Mom and Dad are still up."

"Did they say you could come over?"

Doug looked offended, not for the first time lately. "I'm twenty-one years old, Gilly."

"Right. Sorry." Gil massaged a hand over his face. Technically Doug had become an adult when he'd turned eighteen. It was only within the last couple of months, however, that he'd pointed out the way Gil and their parents were still treating him like a kid. "Would you like a cup of tea or something?" Gil asked, heading toward the kitchen.

"Hot cocoa?" Doug asked.

Gil gave him a strange look. "It's March, buddy. Hot cocoa is for winter."

"Who says?"

Gil chuckled softly. "You're right. You can drink

whatever you want whenever you want. I think I've got some mix left over in the cabinet."

"With marshmallows." His brother offered a wide smile that made his glasses slide down his nose. One thing about Doug was that he could be offended one minute but drop his hard feelings in a quick second. Doug didn't hold bitterness or grudges. He was as easygoing a guy as they came.

"Of course." Gil turned toward the cabinet and grabbed the cocoa mix. Then he turned the kettle on and leaned against the counter as he waited for the water to boil. It only took a minute before it was bubbling.

"Here you go." Gil walked the mug over to his brother, who'd taken a seat at the table. Gil sat down beside him with his own mug of decaf coffee.

"Gilly, you need to run an ad in Reva's blog," Doug said from over his cup of hot cocoa, its steam curling in the air and fogging his glasses.

"What do you know about running ads on Reva's blog?" Gil took a sip of his drink.

"I talk to Reva when I walk Goldie," Doug said. "She said she'd help me. She said Denise shouldn't be the only one promoting herself."

Gil sighed. "If you want to run an ad, that's fine by me. Just make sure I see it first. And not until after I officially announce my intention to run for reelection. I'll do that Saturday at the festival." Gil was guessing everyone already assumed he was running again, but he hadn't said as much. Hopefully, the announcement would rally his supporters in a big way.

Doug set his mug down. "I had pins made. To go on people's shirts. *Gil Ryan for Mayor.*"

Gil sipped his coffee. "That's great. Thank you."

"And I'll be wearing my hat and shirt." He gestured across his chest. "It says *Vote Gil Ryan for Mayor*."

Gil leaned over and laid a hand on his brother's shoulder. "Best brother ever."

Doug looked at him. "And campaign manager?"

"Of course. Love you, buddy."

"Love you, too, Gilly." Doug looked down and stared into his cocoa but didn't take another sip.

"Something else on your mind?" Gil asked.

"Yeah." Doug looked over at him. "I need you to talk to Mom for me."

"Oh?" Gil asked. "About what?"

Doug offered what seemed like a hesitant smile. "I want to find my own place to live."

Gil had hoped he wouldn't have to be brought into this matter. His mom had already asked him to start defense on this issue, which he didn't want to do. "Mom doesn't think that's a good idea."

The skin between Doug's eyes pinched. "She talked to you?"

"Yeah. The other day."

"So you're on her side?" Doug asked, pushing his mug of cocoa away.

"I didn't say that."

"I've always supported you, Gilly. Always. Now it's your turn to support me." Doug pressed his index finger into the center of his chest. "I want to live on my own."

"Okay, but why now?" Gil asked, feeling like he was straddling a fine line that separated his mom and Doug's stance.

Doug narrowed his eyes from behind his glasses. "Why not now?"

Chapter Eight

Moira's shift had been long and unremarkable. No one had called the dispatch today. Not a single person. At one point, Moira had even wondered if the dispatch was working. She'd checked all the cords and lines. She'd even gone as far as using her cell phone to call 911 herself to make sure she got through.

Now it was five o'clock, and she was clocking out. Throughout the day, Moira had been thinking about her idea to create a petition. It was a good idea, but would it work? Some part of her wondered if appealing to Gil one more time would make a difference. She wasn't exactly friendly with him, but maybe if she were, he'd work harder on her behalf. There had to be something he could do, right? What was the point of being mayor if he couldn't stop a travesty like this?

Moira stood from her desk and walked to the kitchen to pour herself a glass of water. After drinking it down, her mind was settled. It was still early. She could drive over to Gil's home and ask if they could talk. She'd be friendly and honest, and Gil would be exactly what he always was: a charming, good listener with a big heart.

Something fluttered around in Moira's chest. Ignoring it, she grabbed her keys and headed out the front door. The closer she got to Gil's house, the more intense the flutters became. She considered turning back and going home. The bakery was on the line though. Moira's second home. Sweetie's wouldn't be the same if it moved across town. People would likely choose to go to the diner on Good Luck Avenue instead. Sweetie's sales would go down. It was hard enough keeping a small business afloat on the main stretch downtown. Keeping one running in the middle of nowhere wouldn't work at all.

Moira's resolve thickened as she pulled into Gil's driveway and cut the engine. Everything would be okay. Gil was a nice guy. A good guy. And, like Tess had pointed out, he was handsome too.

She stepped out of her car and headed up the driveway. Her legs felt shaky as she climbed the porch steps. Then she took a breath before ringing his doorbell. When no one came, she rang it again. His truck was in the driveway, so he had to be here, right?

"Looking for Gilly?"

Moira turned to see Gil's brother standing off to the side of the house. "Hi, Doug. How are you feeling?"

"Much better. Thanks to you."

"Good. I'm glad. Do you know where Gil is?"

Doug smiled. "On his boat."

"Oh." Moira's heart took a dive. She guessed she wouldn't be talking to Gil tonight after all.

"He hasn't left yet. You can still catch him," Doug said.

Moira furrowed her brow. "He's still here? At the dock around back?"

Doug nodded. "I can't go out with him tonight. I'm working on the campaign," he explained. He pointed behind the house. "Better hurry if you want to catch him."

Moira headed quickly down the steps. "Thank you, Doug. I'll see you later, okay?"

"Okay, Moira," Doug called behind her.

Moira picked up her pace, hoping to catch Gil before he set off. She saw movement on the dock and started walking faster. Gil's dog barked when he saw her coming, and ran up to meet her.

"Goldie, heel!" Gil called before seeing where his dog was running. He straightened and watched Moira approach. "Hey. What are you doing here?" he asked when she was standing just a few feet away.

"I was hoping to talk to you." She crossed her arms over her chest. "I see that you're about to set out, but could you spare a few minutes?"

Gil hesitated. "The water is pretty calm right now. Why don't you join me?"

"On the boat?" She immediately shook her head. "What I have to say won't take long."

"Great. There'll be more time for us to enjoy the sunset. We have to hurry though."

Moira glanced between Gil and the boat floating off the dock. Some part of her wanted to say yes. Another part of her knew that wasn't the best idea. "I don't know."

"I dare you," Gil said with a grin.

Moira narrowed her eyes. That was something Gil used to say to her when they were younger—before he'd developed an obvious crush on her. "That's just wrong."

"I know how hard it is for you to pass on a dare."

He winked, and everything inside her turned inside out. "I haven't been dared in about a decade now."

"Then you're overdue." He tipped his head toward the dock. "I'm chasing a sunset tonight. Come with us." He gestured at Goldie.

"Your dog goes with you?"

"Always. She'd be disappointed if I left her behind." Gil watched Moira. "If you don't want to go, that's fine. I can call you when I get back."

She swallowed. "Okay."

He looked a little disappointed. "I have your number."

"No, I meant okay, I'll go with you." She took a step toward him. "I've never not accepted a dare, and I won't be starting tonight."

Gil wasn't sure what to do right now. Moira was on his boat, which was probably the last thing he would have guessed would be happening tonight. His gaze slid over to watch her sitting against the boat's rails as he motored away from the dock.

Moira's hair blew behind her with the gentle breeze off the lake. Gil liked to take the boat out this time of day because there was nothing more stunning than Somerset Lake at sunset. Except maybe watching Moira enjoying the view.

She turned and caught him staring. Her eyes dropped momentarily, and then, as if he'd dared her a second time, she looked up and boldly met his gaze. "Do you take your boat out every night?"

Gil shook his head. "Not every night. Several times a week though. I try to take the sailboat out on the weekends as much as I can. It's not as often as I'd like. I'd live on a boat if I had my way."

Moira's eyes seemed to light up. "A houseboat, huh? I don't know. You have a pretty amazing house."

"You'll have to come in through the front door next time," he teased, referring to when she'd crawled through his doggie door to help Doug. As soon as he made the suggestion, panic swept over him. "Not that I'm inviting you inside tonight." He cleared his throat. "I mean..."

"I understand what you meant. You're the last guy who'd ever invite me inside for anything more than a true nightcap."

Gil relaxed a bit. "Is that so? I guess that means you think highly of me?"

She narrowed her eyes. "Are you fishing for compliments, Mr. Mayor?"

"Well, this is a boat." He chuckled softly. "I'm glad you're out here on the water with me. The sunset will happen in about ten minutes. If you've never seen it from the water, you've never seen it."

"Hmm. Well, you're building it up pretty good. I hope it meets my expectations."

Gil was enjoying their friendly back-and-forth. "It's my promise that it will."

"And Mayor Gil Ryan always keeps his promises," Moira said, her tone shifting to something that sounded resentful.

He dropped his gaze for a moment. "I try to. I might have made a few too many promises during my last campaign. You step into something like the mayor's office and you think you can change the world. That's what I thought, at least. It's easier said than done. There's red tape to get through. Green tape, yellow tape, purple tape. If you make one person happy, you make another one livid." He ran a hand through his hair. "I know I've left a lot to be desired as a mayor."

"Don't get me wrong. I think you've done a lot for this town," Moira said. "You have made positive changes."

"Yeah, well, some people focus on the things that didn't happen."

"Like the parking lot," Moira said knowingly.

Gil kept the speed of the boat slow and easy, just like the lake's current. "When I made promises about solving Hannigan Street's parking issue, I just knew there was a need and that I would meet it. I didn't have a plan. Didn't have a single idea about how to make things happen. I certainly wasn't thinking that your mom's location would be the place."

"Gil, you can't move my mom's bakery. That isn't right. It isn't fair. There must be another way."

"This is what you wanted to discuss tonight, isn't it?"

Moira looked at him. "It's my family's business. I won't apologize for fighting for it."

"You don't need to. I'm the one who should be apologizing to you." He cut the motor and walked over to where he kept the anchor, tossing it into the water. Then he took the seat across from her, suspecting she needed her space. There was an invisible bubble around Moira that he always respected. "I love your mom and her bakery. I don't want to do anything to hurt your family."

She searched his gaze and then looked past him. Gil followed her gaze to the sinking sun, melting into the mountainscape beyond the lake with brilliant oranges and pinks. "I didn't even know Mom had sold the building until after it was a done deal. She never told me." Moira pressed her lips together and seemed to swallow. "There were treatments my dad needed when he first got diagnosed. She wanted him to have the best care, so she sold the building with the unwritten promise she could keep her business there."

"Nothing was supposed to change."

Moira wrung her hands together in her lap. Gil had never known her to be a nervous person. She was confident and went after the things she believed in. She was always the first to sign up to help a worthy cause in town. He'd always respected that about her. "Can we buy the building back? To keep the parking lot from happening?"

Gil grimaced. "Moira, it's not up to me, and honestly, I don't think the town council would agree. There's no place for a new parking lot except where Sweetie's is currently located. It's at the end of the shopping strip. A vacant spot in the middle of one would never do even if there was one available. It's what's best for the town."

"The town has been just fine all these years," Moira objected.

"Has it? You know what happened with the accident on Hannigan Street this week. It took twice the time it should have to get medical attention to those involved. A new parking lot would eliminate street-side parking and free up room for emergency crews," Gil said.

Moira leaned forward and grabbed Gil's hand. The unexpected touch took him by surprise. For a moment, he didn't breathe, didn't blink.

"What can I do? I'll do it. I'll do anything to save Sweetie's."

Gil wanted to make this right for Moira. He suspected she rarely ever asked for help, and he was probably the last person she would go to. This was important to her. "Moira, I'm still racking my brain for ways to make everyone happy." The sad truth though was that a politician couldn't make everyone happy all the time. There was always someone who was left sad, mad, or disappointed. "Putting a parking lot on the corner of Hannigan and Good Luck Avenue isn't written in stone."

She looked down at her feet for a moment, drawing Gil's attention there. She was wearing a pair of leather sandals, her toenails painted a soft blue. She wore a delicate-looking anklet with a tiny, heart-shaped charm that draped over her anklebone. "I appreciate that, Gil," she finally said. "If there's anything you can do to turn this decision around, I would be forever grateful." She looked up, and there was something vulnerable in her eyes.

He'd said it wasn't written in stone, but that was just him letting her down easy. Misleading her in any way was wrong, but he didn't want to witness the complete devastation on her face. He knew he had no earthly chance with Moira romantically, but he didn't want her to hate him anymore.

A soft breeze blew off the water, sending a lock of Moira's dark hair dancing over her cheek. Gil had to suppress his desire to swipe the hair away for her. He cleared his throat. "About that night...We never really talked about it," Gil said. His brain was already screaming at him to back away from the subject. Moira was in his boat. She was actually having a civil conversation with him right now. *Don't ruin it, Gil.* "I'm sorry."

Moira looked up at him with wide eyes. "What exactly are you apologizing for?" There was something fragile in her tone of voice, but he wasn't sure why.

He shrugged. "I ruined your date. You were having a good time with Felix, and I came over and insisted on taking you home." He realized later that he'd probably embarrassed her. That hadn't been his intention. "And I'm sorry for calling the police on you when you trashed my apartment the next night." He shook his head. "Granted, I didn't know it was you. If I had, I would never have called them. I probably deserved to have my place trashed. It was rude of me to interrupt your date."

Moira stared at him expectantly. It suddenly felt like she was waiting for him to apologize for something else. "Yes, you were roommates, but I didn't intend to ransack your stuff, Gil. I was targeting Felix. I just didn't know which stuff was his and which was yours," she finally said. "What I did, when I broke into your apartment, wasn't against you."

Gil felt like there was something he was missing. He would wonder if Felix had made unwanted advances on Moira if it weren't for the fact that Gil was the one who'd driven her home. Felix had never gotten a chance to even try for a good night kiss. "Why? What happened?"

Moira dropped her gaze to her feet and shook her head. "Nothing." She looked back up at him, her gaze searching his. "Thanks to you."

Gil let that sink in. For so long, he'd thought she was upset with him for ruining her date—so upset she'd broken into his apartment the next day and trashed it. And then she'd been upset with him for getting her arrested. "How much did you have to drink that night?" he thought to ask. She'd been so intoxicated when he'd walked up to their table that she could barely sit up in her chair.

"Less than one," Moira answered.

Gil shook his head. "That doesn't make any sense. How could one drink...?" His throat suddenly felt dry as he tried to swallow. "He—he drugged you?"

Moira looked down at her hands, fidgeting lightly in

her lap. "I can't prove it. The drugs were out of my system by the time I went to a doctor the next day. The police department wouldn't even make a report. It was my word against Felix's." She looked back up and met Gil's gaze. "I was mortified and embarrassed, but mostly just really angry about what he'd planned to do to me." Her eyes grew shiny, and she looked away.

"So you went to our apartment and trashed it." Gil nodded, understanding the situation now.

She nibbled on her lower lip. "Sorry. I know it was immature and foolish."

"It's understandable." Gil felt sick to his stomach. How could he not have seen this before? He guessed it was because he hadn't wanted to see it. He'd never known Felix to be anything other than a good guy. "Moira, I didn't know. If I had, I would have…" He shook his head, searching for the right words. How could he not have realized the situation? He'd never seen Moira drunk before, and on that night, she'd been barely able to put a sentence together. It was her first date with Felix. He had thought that maybe she'd been nervous, and she hadn't realized how much she'd had to drink to relax. "I'm so sorry, Moira."

She shook her head. "You don't need to apologize, Gil. You have nothing to be sorry for. I just kind of always assumed you knew."

"And that I approved of what Felix did? What he wanted to do?" Anger took root in the pit of Gil's stomach as he thought about it. Not at Moira, of course. "I haven't seen Felix in at least ten years, but I'd really like to meet him in a dark alley right now."

Moira looked at him. "Then we'd both get thrown in jail."

Gil held her gaze for a moment, wishing there was something he could do to right this wrong. Felix had drugged Moira and gotten away with it. "It'd be worth it."

Moira broke eye contact, turning her attention to their surroundings. "Anyway, thanks for taking me home that night."

Gil wanted to tell her that thanking him wasn't necessary, but instead he just nodded.

"And thank you for saying you'll help my mom keep her bakery on Hannigan Street."

Gil cleared his throat. He really needed to explain to Moira that there wasn't much he could do at this point. He thought she'd understood that. "I can't make any promises."

"I know. But I also know you'll do what's right." She turned to look at the sky again, and Gil heard her quick intake of breath. "Oh, wow."

He'd seen a million sunsets, so he watched her face instead. The awe in her eyes was worth a million sunsets on Somerset Lake. "Does it meet your expectations?" he asked.

"It surpasses them. I wish I could sit out here every night and see this."

"You can. My boat is always open to you."

She gave him a strange look.

"What?" he finally asked.

She shrugged and shook her head simultaneously. "It's just, you're so nice, even when I haven't been the nicest to you."

"Girls never like nice guys," he said with a soft groan.

Moira's grin was slow in coming. "I don't think you have anything to worry about, Mr. Mayor. You were named Most Eligible Bachelor last year, after all. If my memory serves me correctly, you had a lot of women interested in dating you."

Gil chuckled. "And yet I'm still single."

Her gaze lingered on his. There was a look he couldn't pinpoint in her eyes. "You just haven't found the right one yet."

He held his tongue. He thought maybe he *had* found her, but his ex-roommate had ruined his chances a long time ago. Whether Moira admitted to holding what Felix did against Gil or not, there was a wall there that he had given up on breaking through. He just hoped one day she was able to find a guy who treated her the way she deserved. "What about you? Why are you still single?" He wondered if one bad date with Felix had ruined her desire to go on more dates. He wouldn't blame her if that were the case. It would be hard to trust someone after such an experience.

She looked away, dropping her head for a moment before turning to look out onto the water. "People around here act like being single is a bad thing. It's not. I like my independence. I'm happy."

"I'm sure you are."

She looked at him again as if trying to gauge if he was being sincere or sarcastic.

"And, if and when you meet the right one, maybe you'll be even happier," Gil said quietly. "Who knows?"

"Maybe. But maybe love isn't out there for everyone."

"I don't know. I think it's out there for everyone who wants to find it." He cleared his throat. "At least I hope it is."

Chapter Nine

Coffee at Sweetie's Bakeshop was usually Gil's first stop when he went to Hannigan Street. Today he was procrastinating though because he hadn't seen Darla since breaking the news to her about the council's decision. He wouldn't blame her if she was furious with him. In her shoes, he probably would be.

He got out of his truck and headed toward Sweetie's. Hopefully Darla would have another employee with her today so he could pull her aside and talk to her again. He wanted to make sure she knew how sorry he was about the situation. He also wanted to offer to help her find the perfect spot to relocate.

Opening the door, Gil glanced around, subconsciously looking for Moira.

"Mayor Gil!" Darla said with her usual cheerfulness—no trace of resentment about what he'd told her the other day.

"Hey, Darla. How are you?"

"Great. Your usual?" she asked with a ready smile.

"Actually, I was hoping you had time for another chat. Do you have help here this morning?" he asked, glancing past Darla toward the back room.

Darla's smile wilted slightly. "I sure do. I'll get Bailey to work the counter for me. We can talk in the back room for privacy."

"That would be great. Thanks," Gil said.

Darla held up a finger. "But first, I'll make you a coffee. Knowing you, you haven't had a cup just yet."

"That would be correct." Darla was so considerate of others. That was one of many reasons why closing her bakery would be an unthinkable wrong. She didn't deserve this. He watched as she prepared a coffee just the way he'd always ordered it for the last decade. Then she called Bailey to handle the customers while she led Gil to a table in the back room.

"Please have a seat, Mayor." She pulled out her own chair.

Gil cupped his coffee between his hands, soaking in its warmth. "Darla, I want you to know that I did everything I could to turn this decision around. I never wanted to see this bakery of yours be relocated. This is its rightful spot. If there was any other way—"

Darla held up a hand. "Stop right there. It's okay, Gil. I'm not upset with you."

"You're not?"

Darla smiled calmly. "As mayor, your priority is the town. Not just one person. I know that." She leaned in toward him and lowered her voice. "Everything in life can be compared to a good card game. Regardless of who you're playing, you have to put down the best card for you. Not for your opponent. That's how you play the game."

He'd never compared his life or his job to a card game, but it made sense. "At what cost though?"

Darla shrugged and leaned back, folding her arms over her chest. "You can't see my hand, Mayor Gil. You use your best cards, and I'll use mine. It's not personal. I know that."

Since Gil had become mayor, everyone had bombarded him with demands and wishes. Everyone had their own agenda, and it seemed like no one was ever satisfied. But here Darla was, sitting across from him just as carefree as ever, still smiling in the face of possibly losing her business location. "I see where Moira gets her heroic qualities."

Darla chuckled. "My daughter is the spitting image of her father. Always has been."

"Maybe on the outside," Gil said, which was definitely true. Moira and Allen both had the same dark hair and hazel eyes. "But she has your heart."

Darla's gaze narrowed. "Gil, I know you've always liked my Moira."

He looked away. His crush had never been much of a secret. His demeanor unconsciously shifted when he was around Moira. He could actively work to be "normal" around her and fail miserably every time. "Moira is a great person."

"Yes, she is," Darla agreed. "But she's not without her flaws."

"None of us are."

"Mm. True enough. I don't know why she stays single. She says she has no interest in dating, but no one wants to be alone. Her friends are all finding love. I want the same for her."

Gil cleared his throat. He wasn't sure why Darla was telling him this. "Some people really are happier single."

"Are you?" Darla asked.

He cleared his throat again. He could use a bottle of water right now instead of a hot coffee. "I'm not unhappy. When the right person comes along though, I'll be ready."

Darla nodded. "Sometimes the right person just needs a little extra time to figure things out."

Was she insinuating that Moira was the right person for him? If so, she didn't have a good bead on her daughter. He was probably the last person Moira would ever want to begin a relationship with—even if he'd felt something different coming from Moira lately. Or maybe that was his imagination.

"I want you to know that turning Doug down for a job here had nothing to do with me being upset about the town's plans."

"A job here?" Gil asked.

Darla gave him a strange look. "He didn't tell you? Doug has come in a few times asking about a part-time job. I tried to hire him a couple years ago, and he turned me down. After he came here last month inquiring, I was planning to hire him. Then you gave me the news. I'd love to have Doug work for me but, safe to say, it's not the best time for me to be taking on new employees."

"I understand," Gil said, even though he didn't. Doug worked for him. Was Doug planning to quit, or was he going to take on two jobs? Granted, Gil didn't pay much more than minimum wage, and being a campaign manager for a small-town mayor wasn't exactly a full-time position.

"Maybe after I relocate," Darla said. "*If* I relocate."

"If?" Gil blinked back at Darla. "You have to. Somerset Lake needs you."

"Not as bad as they need a parking lot, apparently."

∞

At five o'clock, Moira signed off the dispatch and headed into her bedroom with intention. There was a town hall meeting tonight, and she planned to be there. Her mom should be attending as well. It was her bakery after all. Her livelihood.

Moira stepped into the bathroom and brushed her hair into place. She wasn't one to wear a lot of makeup, but she was addressing a room full of people tonight. She wanted to look and feel her best. She also wanted her mom to come with her. When Moira had called to ask Darla earlier in the week, Darla had made excuses. That's why Moira was heading over to her parents' house right now to make a convincing argument that her mother couldn't resist.

After a short drive, Moira pulled into the driveway of the home she'd grown up in. She'd spent half her childhood here in this ranch-style brick house and the other half in Sweetie's. They were both a part of her. Even though she'd grown up here, Moira rang the door-bell like any other guest. After high school and moving into her own place, she'd learned her lesson about not stepping inside unannounced. Her parents took advantage of their empty nest in ways Moira wished she never knew about.

"Oh, Moira. This is a nice surprise," Darla said as she opened the door wider. "I thought you had something else to do tonight."

Moira stepped into the living room and turned to face her mom. "I do. I'm going to the town hall meeting, and I still want you to come with me. That's why I'm here."

Darla frowned and started walking toward the kitchen, where Moira could smell Italian herbs in the air. "I already told you, I have no interest in going to tonight's meeting. I've never had any interest in politics, you know that. That was always you."

Moira had dabbled in student government in high school. She'd never been the student body president or anything, but she'd been treasurer and she'd loved being involved during that time in her life. Growing up, she'd also taken an interest in local events and causes like saving the old oak tree on the lake when the town had wanted to chop it down. Moira had joined all the protests organized by her school, and she'd been part of the journalism club as well.

"Mom, this is about more than just being involved in politics. This is your business. Your livelihood. You need to speak up while there's still time to change things. Bringing up this issue at tonight's meeting will mean more coming from you."

Darla kept her back to Moira and talked over her shoulder, tending to a pot on the stove. "Why? Nothing I say will change anyone's mind. If the town thinks a parking lot would better serve Hannigan Street, who am I to argue?"

"You're the business owner who's going to be put out of business, that's who!" Moira practically yelled.

Her mom finally turned to her. Her cheeks were a rosier shade of red, thanks to the heat from cooking. She sighed wearily as she wiped her hands on the apron tied at her waist. "Well, perhaps that's for the best. Then I can join your father in retirement."

Moira wanted to scream. Why was her mom just lying down and taking this? "Dad is ten years older than you, Mom. You'd be miserable if you retired, and you know it. What are you going to do, take up knitting?"

Her mom put her hands on her hips. "What's wrong

with knitting? Your grandmother loved knitting. Maybe I would too."

Moira threw her hands up in the air. "Fine, if you won't fight for Sweetie's, I will."

"Mo, do you really think that's a good idea?"

"Yes, I do. And you should too."

Her father walked into the room, skidding to a stop when he realized the tension in the room. He looked between Darla and Moira. "What's going on?"

Moira gestured toward her mother. "I want Mom to come to the town hall meeting with me tonight and fight for Sweetie's, and she'd rather spend the rest of her days knitting," she said with exasperation.

"Knitting?" Her father furrowed his brows. "You don't even like knitting," he said to Darla.

"My point exactly." Moira turned, talking to her mom over her shoulder as she walked out of the kitchen. "I'll see you tomorrow, Mom. I have somewhere important to be right now."

Chapter Ten

"What's wrong, Gilly?"

Gil looked up as Doug approached. Gil was sitting on his back deck watching the lake. This was one of his favorite views in all the world. At least the parts of the world he'd seen. The lake sparkled in different shades of blue depending on where the sun or moon sat in the sky. Tonight, the lake was a deep hue reflecting the moon's beams.

Gil looked over at his little brother and shook his head. "Nothing's wrong."

Doug put his hands on his waist. "I can tell."

Gil released a breath. "It's just not always easy being mayor. That's all."

"Still running?" Doug asked.

"Yeah, I'm still running." Gil watched Doug sit in the seat beside his.

"If you're still running, I'm still your manager," Doug said proudly.

Gil smiled gratefully. "Glad to hear it. I couldn't do this without you, you know."

"Yes, you could," Doug said, his smile faltering for a moment.

"Well, maybe, but I wouldn't want to." Gil cleared his throat. "Doug, Darla mentioned to me that you were applying for a job at Sweetie's."

Doug glanced over. "Yes."

"Why? You just said you wanted to stay on as my manager."

"I can do both, Gilly," Doug said without missing a beat. "I want to earn a living and move out."

Gil wasn't sure right now was the best time to get back into this conversation. "You sure you're ready for that? Living on your own isn't all it's cracked up to be."

Doug frowned. "Neither is living with Mom and Dad. Joey has his own place." Joey was one of Doug's friends from high school. He didn't have Down syndrome but he had been in a lot of the same classes Doug had attended.

"That's great for Joey." Gil chose his words carefully. "How would you work at Sweetie's? You don't have a driver's license."

"Not yet."

Gil nodded. "I see."

"No, you don't. You're just like Mom. You don't think I can drive or live alone."

Gil pressed his lips together. "What about the other day? When you had an insulin issue and fell down?"

"I called nine-one-one," Doug said, lifting his chin a notch. "The same thing I would have done if I lived on my own. The same thing you would have done for yourself."

Doug had a point. Gil scratched the side of his face where his five-o'clock shadow was filling in. "I'm your brother, not your mom. It doesn't matter if I think you're ready to live on your own."

Disappointment settled in the deep divot between Doug's brows. "It matters to me. I want you to believe in me the way I've always believed in you."

Gil held Doug's gaze. "I do. I just…" He trailed off because he didn't know his reasons for anything he was thinking about this issue. He just knew that his mom had asked him to discourage any talk of this kind from Doug. Surely she knew what was best. Right? "I'm not sure what to say right now, if you want to know the truth."

"Say you'll talk to Mom for me," Doug said. "Please. She'll listen to you."

Gil closed his eyes and nodded. This was a sticky situation that he didn't like being in the middle of. One of many sticky situations weighing on him tonight. He'd love nothing more than to take his boat out and unwind, but the town hall meeting was in an hour, and he guessed Moira was planning to speak. She would be expecting him to publicly support her.

"Gilly?" Doug said, reminding Gil he wasn't alone.

Gil opened his eyes and looked over. His brother peered back through his round glasses. "Yeah?"

"Can I come with you tonight?"

"To the town hall?" Usually Doug stayed home. He didn't like what he referred to as "boring" meetings.

Doug nodded. "Yes."

"I guess. If you want. It's not exactly fun though."

"I'm your campaign manager. I should be there. It doesn't have to be fun."

Once again, Gil thought Doug looked defensive. "You're right. A lot of things aren't fun, but we do them anyway. I just meant, you don't have to go, whereas I have no choice in the matter."

"I want to go," Doug said.

"Okay then."

"I've got to shower and change clothes," Doug told him, standing suddenly.

"Sure. Meet me back here in forty-five minutes?"

"Okay, Gilly." Doug walked down the steps, taking them slowly. Gil wasn't sure, but he thought Doug's ankle injury from the other day was still bothering him. Goldie ran over to Doug's side, matching his pace and following him next door.

Gil guessed he needed to get ready too. How did one dress when they were preparing to let down one of the people they admired most? He kind of felt like putting on his best funeral suit, because that's how he felt walking into tonight's meeting.

Standing, he walked into the house, opened the fridge, and reached for a cold bottled water. He twisted off the cap and drank half in one long gulp. Then he set the bottle on his kitchen island and continued walking toward his bedroom. Tonight wasn't going to be pretty. He just wanted to get it over with. Or skip it altogether, but as the mayor, he couldn't do that.

He changed into a short-sleeved shirt with a pair of jeans and brown leather boots. To give the jeans a more formal look, he pulled on a navy linen sports coat. He combed his hair, brushed his teeth, and then stepped back onto his deck to sit in his Adirondack chair and wait for Doug.

Goldie walked up to him and pressed her nose into his palm. He rubbed her head and scratched behind her ears, telling her, "At least I have one female in my life who'll love me after tonight."

∞

The town hall was a full house. *Great.* Gil had hoped for scarce attendance tonight. He was also hoping somehow Moira wouldn't actually show up. He should have known better though. Moira was strong-willed. Independent. If someone told her what to do, she dug her heels in harder to do the opposite.

He liked those qualities of Moira's. Once, in third grade, their teacher had told Moira to take off her coat because it wasn't cold in the building, and Moira had zipped her jacket up and told the teacher she didn't want to. Even though it was hot, she'd kept it on all day just to prove a point—she couldn't be forced. Being drugged by Felix must have hit Moira hard. Knowing what might have happened probably devastated her all those years ago.

Gil looked around the town hall from his seat onstage, spotting Moira in one of the middle rows. She waved when he looked in her direction. Gil waved back, stricken by mixed emotions. They'd made progress toward rebuilding their friendship the other night, and more than anything, he wanted to be friends with Moira. If he went against her tonight, that wouldn't happen.

Gil swallowed hard.

"Hey, Gil." Jake stepped onto the stage with him. Jake had joined the town council this past year. He followed Gil's gaze. "Could you be any more obvious, man? I thought you were over Moira."

"I am," Gil said. "I was just waving at her."

"Uh-huh. Sure." Jake chuckled. "Looks like there's a lot of interest in town talk tonight. I even see Reva here."

Gil glanced toward the blogger. "She's always here."

"Moira doesn't always attend though. I assume she's here about her mom's bakery?" Jake asked.

Gil nodded. "Yeah."

"And I assume you're going to back her up."

Gil turned to look at Jake, dread hanging heavy in his gut. "No."

Moira didn't often find herself nervous, but right now, she kept having to remind herself to breathe. Her palms felt slick as she rubbed them against the thighs of her black pants. She knew everyone in this room, and as far as she was aware, everyone here loved Sweetie's Bakeshop. They'd stand behind her. She'd be fine. All she had to do was speak what was in her heart. It didn't hurt that Gil was the town's mayor, and he was on her side. Wasn't that what he'd said last night? That he wasn't done looking for alternative locations for the parking lot?

Moira was barely listening as the first community member took their turn at the mic. The woman was saying something about a neighbor's free-range chickens going into her yard and taunting her fenced-in dogs.

"I don't let my shepherds run around free range in the neighborhood. Why does she get to keep her chickens loose?" Mary Edwards wanted to know.

The neighbor in question made loud comments from across the room.

Mary turned to her neighbor. "It's rude and inconsiderate."

"*You're* rude and inconsiderate!" the neighbor yelled back.

Then they started arguing in front of everyone. Moira's gaze slid over to Reva, who was tapping away on her laptop.

"Hey. Sorry I'm late." Tess slid into the seat that Moira had saved for her best friend. "What'd I miss?"

Moira was so relieved that Tess had made it that she wanted to throw her arms around Tess and hug her. Moira wasn't much of a hugger though. Instead, she fidgeted nervously with the strap of her purse. "Free-range chickens that poop all over Mary's lawn. I haven't gotten a chance to speak yet."

Tess reached for her hand. "You can do this."

Moira nodded. "Thanks for the vote of confidence."

"Of course." Tess glanced at the other seat beside Moira, where Darla was not sitting.

"Your mom didn't come?"

Moira shook her head. "Long story that I don't want to get into right now. I'll tell you over coffee tomorrow." Which they would have at Sweetie's like they normally did. If there was a parking lot in Sweetie's spot, where would they go?

"Thank you for those very valid concerns, Mary," Gil said, speaking into his microphone. He and several town council members were seated behind a long table on the stage upfront. "Who would like to talk next?"

Tess elbowed Moira. "Go for it."

Moira sucked in a breath, but it didn't seem to calm her nerves. Standing on shaky legs, she walked up to the microphone that was set up at the end of the aisle between rows of chairs. "I would like to talk," she said, pinning her gaze to Gil's. Her heart fluttered around nervously, and this time, it wasn't because of public speaking or the topic at hand. It was because of Gil. She swallowed past a tight throat.

"Go ahead, Miss Green," Gil said, addressing her more formally than he usually would. The other night on his boat, he'd promised to do whatever he could to support her. If he was on her side, she couldn't go wrong.

"Um, hi, everyone." Moira licked her lips, moistening them. Her throat was dry, too, and she wished she'd had the forethought to bring a bottled water. "I'm here because of the town council's proposal to demolish Sweetie's Bakeshop and put a parking lot for Hannigan Street there instead."

Several loud gasps filled the room. The decision wasn't public knowledge among the townspeople yet. That was one reason Moira wanted to be here tonight. She wanted to get ahead of the decision and reverse it. "Sweetie's Bakeshop is one of the staples of Hannigan Street. Small businesses are crucial to towns like ours, and while parking is an issue, I can't envision Hannigan Street or Somerset Lake without my mother's bakery. Not just because the business belongs to my family, but because that's where I grew up going after school. That's where I still go to meet up with people. Sweetie's Bakeshop is like a family member or friend in and of itself, and we stand up for our family and friends. We need to stand up for Sweetie's Bakeshop too. If we don't, what's next?" Moira looked at Gil, but he wasn't watching her. Instead, he had his head lowered, and he was staring at his clasped hands. *That's weird.*

Moira looked around the room. "Who else here loves Sweetie's Bakeshop?"

Applause broke out.

Moira returned to looking at the council. "So, that's why I'm here. To appeal to you to find another way to build a parking lot on Hannigan Street. I don't know how. I just know that's what we need to do."

Gil finally looked up, but he didn't meet her gaze. "Thank you, Miss Green. Your concerns are noted and will be discussed at the next town council meeting."

Moira blinked, waiting for him to say more. To verbally agree with her and give her his support the way he had last night. He wasn't even smiling right now. "That's it?"

Gil finally looked at her. "Unless you have something more to say."

She felt like the breath had been knocked out of her. "No. That's all I came to say." She stood there a second longer until Gil said, "Who else would like to talk tonight?" That was her cue to sit back down. Moira turned and headed back to her seat next to Tess.

"Good job, Moira," Tess leaned in and said.

Moira glanced over. "Why do I feel like it won't make a difference in the long run then?"

Tess reached over and squeezed Moira's hand. "At least you tried."

Moira nodded, too stunned to say anything more. She'd tried, but she wasn't done yet. This fight was far from over.

∞

When Moira got home that night, she retreated straight to her bedroom and stripped off her clothes, changing into a pair of pajama shorts and a tank top. Then she stepped out on her deck and looked out on the starry night. Something about the way Gil had been so distant tonight really bothered her. No one on the town council had said anything to make Moira believe they were going to look for alternate locations for the parking lot.

Moira glanced down at her cell phone. She wanted to text Gil and ask him what the deal was. She really had no right though. She'd been shying away from him for years. One night didn't erase how she'd treated him. Maybe this was payback. If it was, it wasn't okay. She didn't want her mom's bakery to suffer. Whether her mom said so or not, she didn't want to lose her business. It was her life.

Moira swallowed back tears and looked up at the sky again. She was long past wishing on stars, but what else could she do?

"Hey."

Moira startled at the unexpected voice. Her eyes searched the darkness, finding Gil standing there. She hadn't heard him drive up.

"You didn't answer your door, so I decided to walk around back." He shrugged. "I know my deck is where I usually am if I'm not inside."

Moira's heart was still pounding. "You scared me."

"I didn't mean to."

She relaxed a little bit. "I'm surprised you're here. After the way you ghosted me at tonight's meeting."

"About that…" Gil headed in her direction. He climbed the bottom step and stopped, leaning against the deck railing.

His attractiveness struck her more and more lately. "Yes?" she finally asked.

Gil held out his hands. "Moira, there's nothing I can do about your mom's bakery."

"That's not what you said last night."

He shrugged. "I shouldn't have led you to believe I could help. I wasn't thinking. I was too caught up in the moment."

"What moment?" she asked, inwardly denying there'd been any kind of moment between them. Had there been? Was it just her imagination? She looked down and realized she was wearing only a tank top and skimpy shorts. Heat flared through her chest.

Gil seemed to understand what she was thinking. He cleared his throat and looked away. "As the mayor, I have to do what's best for the town as a whole. The parking issue is a safety concern as much as an inconvenience."

"I refuse to believe there's no other way. As the mayor, it's also your responsibility to protect the livelihood of the people here."

Gil turned his attention to the starry sky where she'd been looking a few minutes ago. "I know. I would find another way if there was one."

"That's a cop-out, Gil. I thought we'd come to an understanding. I thought we were becoming friends."

He looked at her. "I hope we are. I don't want to fight with you, Moira. That's why I came by."

"Why exactly?" she asked.

"To shoot straight with you about your mom's bakery."

Moira lifted her chin. "Well, thank you for being straight this time. I guess I'll see you around."

"On Saturday at the festival," he reminded her. "I'm presenting you with an award."

"Are you going to take that back too?" she asked, knowing she sounded defensive, but she *was* defensive.

"No. You deserve it, Moira. If it's any consolation, I'm sorry."

Moira gave her head a shake. "It's not."

Chapter Eleven

On Thursday morning, Gil hesitated before stepping into Sweetie's Bakeshop. Some part of him felt like he had no right to be here after basically telling Moira last night that he wasn't going to fight to save her mom's business. What could he do though? Nothing. So why did he feel so guilty?

"Mayor Gil!" Darla greeted him as he stepped inside and headed toward the counter. "I'm so glad you came by this morning."

"Oh?"

"Breakfast is on me." Darla turned to start preparing his coffee. He always got his brew the same way, with a squirt of chocolate syrup. "Do you want a bagel with cream cheese too?"

"That'd be great, Darla. But I can pay."

"Well, of course you can. You're the mayor." She glanced back at him with a conspiratorial smile. Then her mouth slid down at the corners. "It's the least I can do for you after what Reva wrote."

Gil felt the corners of his own mouth falling. "What do you mean?"

Darla shook her head. "It doesn't matter. Everyone around here knows you have the town's best interest at heart. Even me." She reached for a lid for his drink, popped it on, and slid it across the counter to him. Then she grabbed a piece of parchment paper and some tongs to lift his bagel out of the case.

"What did Reva write?" Gil asked.

"Well, you can go to her blog to read it, but I wouldn't recommend it." She grimaced slightly.

"It's about me?" he asked.

"And the town council." Darla lowered her voice. "I tried to get Moira not to go last night, Gil. I really did." Darla placed his bagel on the counter and looked at him. "But she's so headstrong. She always has been."

Gil wasn't sure what to say right now. He needed to sit down with his breakfast and see what Reva had written. Sometimes the blogger was here with her laptop open this time of day, but not this morning. He was grateful for that. "Thank you for breakfast, Darla."

"You're welcome, Mayor." She offered an apologetic smile.

Turning, Gil looked for an empty table that offered the most privacy. He decided on one along the wall and sat down. Then he took out his cell phone while he sipped his coffee and pulled up a browser to search for Reva's blog. No sooner had the blog loaded on the screen than a customer walked into the shop. Gil looked up at the sound of the jingle, and his blood slowed. He came into the bakery on the regular, and Denise Berger was never here. What was she doing here this morning?

Gil ducked his head, hoping Denise wouldn't spot him. He didn't want to associate with the enemy if he could help it. He strained his ears to hear what Darla and Denise were saying. Their tones were cheerful, but he couldn't make out the words. Not that it was any of his business. His beef with Denise was from high school. Those days were long past, and there was no reason they couldn't be civil to one another now, even if she was planning to run against him as mayor.

He picked up his bagel and took a bite. Then he focused on Reva's blog for the day. There were four bullet points on his screen, each with a tidbit of gossip that would spread like wildfire through the town in the next few hours.

Gil took another bite of bagel and read.

- There's a sale at Choco-Lovers! In honor of it being Saint Patty's month, Jana has shamrock-colored fudge half price. Come and get it!
- Have you heard? Denise Berger is running against our very own Mayor Gil this year. Hearsay is an announcement is coming soon!
- Here's another interesting tidbit for you: Last night at the town hall meeting, Moira Green told everyone that the town council is gunning to demolish Sweetie's Bakeshop and make a new parking lot. We need more parking space, but we also need coffee. Am I right?
- Farewell to our friend Louise Herman. She's been staying in one of the Somerset Rental Cottages for two decades now. I never thought she'd leave, but grandkids are a big motivator, especially when they're in Florida. Ha!
- Don't forget: This weekend is the Spring into Somerset Festival. Hearsay is Mayor Gil is presenting an award to one of our own. You know I can't keep a secret. If I

knew who it was, I'd tell you. I sure hope it's not someone from the Green family though—they might just toss that award right back at him. And in my humble opinion, he might deserve it.

Gil frowned at his screen. The whole town was reading this blog. The last thing he needed, going into another mayoral campaign, was his potential voters thinking he was out to shut down the small businesses here.

"Mayor Gil," a woman's voice said, approaching him from behind. "Is that you?"

Dread coated Gil's stomach. He turned to face his old classmate. "Hey, Denise."

"How are you this morning?" She offered a sympathetic look. "Have you read Reva's blog yet?"

Gil sighed. "Unfortunately."

She clucked her tongue and shook her head. "Don't let her comments get to you. Everyone knows to take it all with a grain of salt."

"Yeah. Thanks, Denise."

Denise gestured toward the seat across from Gil. "Do you mind if I sit down?"

Gil did mind. He didn't want to sit across from his competition. Denise had been brutal to him in high school. He realized that was a long time ago, but some wounds didn't quite heal. "Have a seat, Denise."

She pulled out a chair, propped her elbows on the table in front of her, and narrowed her eyes. "I'm guessing you heard about my plans."

Gil sucked in a breath. "Yeah. I heard something about you running for mayor."

"I hope you don't take offense. I think you've served this town wonderfully."

"No offense taken," Gil said. "Let the best person win."

"Well, I haven't completed the process for registering. For all I know, I won't have the backing to make it to a real campaign. But that is my intention."

Gil reached for his cup of coffee, wishing he had something a little bit stronger than Hershey's syrup in his cup.

"I assume I'm the only one planning to run against you?" she asked.

Gil set his cup of coffee back on the table. "I haven't heard about anyone else."

"I wasn't sure if Bryce Malsop wanted to try to get his spot back. He was so upset when you beat him last time."

Gil chuckled. "I think our former mayor is enjoying his retirement these days."

Denise looked at him for a moment. "I was at the town council meeting last night. I was surprised to hear that you want to shut this bakery down."

"I don't want to," Gil said. "Being the town's mayor sometimes comes with tough choices though."

"I can't believe you, Mayor Gil," someone behind them said.

Gil turned to face Vi Fletcher. Vi was Jake's grandmother and the original owner of the Somerset Rental Cottages. "I told Jake how I feel this morning, and mayor or not, I intend to tell you the same." Vi was a tiny woman, but she was a mighty presence.

"Hello, Vi. Nice to see you."

Vi frowned. "I've always adored you, Gil, but I have to say, this is disappointing. You can't put Darla out of business."

Gil sighed softly. This was the crux of what he did.

"I'm the mayor, but I'm not the be-all, end-all. I don't make these decisions on my own."

"Well, as mayor, they all come back on you," Vi said, not sympathizing. "You need to fix this, Gil. I can't back a mayor who will allow the very roots of our town to be cut out."

Gil dared a glance at Denise and caught a glimmer of a smile on her lips. *Great. Just great.* He pushed back from the table and then stood, collecting his coffee and bagel. "It was nice to see you, ladies," he lied. "Have a wonderful rest of your day." He started walking toward the exit, slowing when he saw Moira approaching the door from the other side. His heart jolted. In Moira's eyes, he saw the same disappointment that he'd seen in Vi's. He felt cornered, physically and metaphorically.

Moira used to be so much better at avoiding Gil. These days they seemed to be a magnet for each other though. And ever since their boat ride the other night, she couldn't seem to get her emotions in check. She preferred it when she pretended to hate him and they didn't speak. Now she was just frustrated. And mad. And confused.

She stood on one side of the bakery's glass door and stared at him on the other side. Neither of them reached to open the door for a long moment. The tension in the air was thick enough to cut even though there was a door between them.

"What are you doing?" River asked, coming up behind her. "Do you need help opening the door?"

Moira broke eye contact with Gil and turned to River. "No, sorry. I just got lost in thought for a moment."

River seemed to notice Gil now. "Oh. Yeah, I've heard you two have chemistry."

"What?" Moira's mouth dropped open. "Tess told you that?" she asked.

River's brows furrowed. "No, all the guys at the tavern say it. They rib Gil on a weekly basis." River reached past her and opened the door. "Hey, Gilbert. How are you?"

Gil met Moira's eyes as he answered the question. "I've had better days. Hey, Moira."

She flitted her gaze toward him. "Mayor Gil," she said, sounding too polite and stiff to her own ears. "Excuse me. I have to get a coffee and then get to my shift." She hurried past, walking to the counter, where her mom was watching.

"I hope you were nice to Mayor Gil," Darla said.

Moira rolled her eyes. "I'm sure you were nice enough for both of us."

"I like him. And he likes you. You should be nicer."

"I am nice," Moira protested. "If you must know, we actually had a little truce the other night."

"Yeah?" Darla turned and prepared Moira's coffee.

Moira leaned against the counter and sighed. "That was when I thought he was going to help us though."

"Gil is just doing his job, Moira." Darla turned back to her and slid a coffee in her direction. "Tess isn't joining you today?"

"No, she got some new inventory in. She's unboxing and shelving this morning," Moira said, reaching for her drink. "I'll see her at book club tonight. Thanks, Mom. Love you."

"Love you too. Be nice to the mayor," she said again. "I told you how I feel about things."

"You did, and I don't understand it." She felt someone

step up behind her in line. "But you have customers, and I have a dispatch shift. Talk to you later, Mom."

Moira turned and walked out of the store. Or tried to.

"Moira Green?" Vi called from her table. She was seated across from Reva Dawson this morning.

Moira turned toward the women. "Good morning." She looked between them. "Do you need something?"

"We just wanted to tell you how proud we are of you, standing up for the small businesses here. I'm a small business owner myself," Vi said.

"And I am, too, in a way," Reva added.

"It was inspiring watching you go up against the council last night," Vi told her.

"You were fearless," Reva said. "I should have written that on my blog. I might have to edit it."

"No, that's okay." Moira wished Reva would just leave her out of the blog from now on.

"Have you ever thought of running for office?" Vi asked. "You would be great at it. You were so passionate up there."

"Well, I am passionate. Sweetie's is my mom's business."

"Even so, you were take-charge."

Moira looked between the women. "Thank you. That's nice of you to say."

"And we support you one hundred percent," Vi said.

"In keeping the bakery open?" Moira asked. She really needed to get that petition going. The more signatures, the better her chances.

"No. In running for office," Vi said matter-of-factly.

"A woman mayor. Imagine that," Reva said, as if it were a novel idea.

Moira hated to break it to Reva that women were occupying all kinds of offices these days. But she wasn't one of them. "Oh, no I'm not..." She trailed off. She'd never even considered running for a public office before. "I have a job. I work dispatch." And she was good at it.

"Well, being mayor in Somerset Lake doesn't have to be a full-time job, you know? You can still work at the dispatch. Change keeps us young," Vi told her.

"Well, she is young," Reva pointed out. "But change keeps things interesting for sure. You should consider it."

"It" meaning a run for office. No, Moira was all for keeping things fresh, but she was a dispatcher. She had no experience in politics. She couldn't just up and decide to run for mayor—against Gil.

After excusing herself and wishing the ladies a good day, Moira headed out of the bakery and toward her car. It was a long way to walk if there were no spots at the curb, like today. And when folks parked along the curb, it made driving down Hannigan Street a tight squeeze. Moira looked around for alternative locations for a parking lot— there was nothing—and thought about what the women had said, as she made the hike to her Hyundai.

Moira for Mayor? Vi and Reva had to be joking. Only, they'd seemed serious. She couldn't run against Gil though. Could she?

The idea continued to percolate as she sat through her shift. There were five calls to the dispatch, which made it a busy day. Only two were actual emergencies, however. The first emergency involved a minor fender bender. The other one was a caller reporting that Mr. S was sunbathing in the nude down on the lakeshore outside the Somerset

Rental Cottages again. Instead of calling the sheriff's department, Moira dialed Trisha.

"Hello?"

"Hey, Trisha. It's Moira calling from the dispatch."

Trisha groaned. "Not again."

"Afraid so," Moira confirmed.

Trisha audibly sighed. "I'll handle it."

"Thanks. See you at book club tonight?" Moira asked.

"Looking forward to it. Now, if you'll excuse me, I have a tenant to throw a towel over and send home."

Moira laughed. "I choose my job over yours."

Trisha laughed as well. "Right about now, I'd choose your job too. I have an entire cottage to clean up today. Louise Herman lived there for twenty-plus years, and I don't think spring cleaning was ever on her to-do list."

"That sounds like a lot of work for you while you're pregnant. Do you need help?" Moira asked. "I could come by after my shift one day."

"No, but thanks. Della has already offered. I have the best friends ever."

"Same here," Moira said. "Good luck."

"With the cleaning or Mr. S?" Trisha asked.

"Both."

They said goodbye, and then Moira stood from her desk and stretched her arms up in the air. She hadn't yet read Reva's blog, so she hesitantly decided to take a peek. Moira tapped a finger over her screen and pulled it up, glancing at the first bullet point. Jana was having a fudge sale. Moira would have to stop in this week and get some. She kept reading.

- Have you heard? Denise Berger is running against our very own Mayor Gil this year. Hearsay is an announcement is coming soon!

The news left Moira feeling a little disappointed. She could do better than Denise. Maybe Moira didn't have any political experience, but she had years of experience in public service. She knew the sheriff's and fire departments and the medical services, and she had connections with all the small businesses in Somerset Lake because of her mom's bakery. Denise Berger was a local accountant. She probably had connections, but Moira doubted she had a servant's heart, which was what a mayor needed. Gil had that. He wasn't looking out for Sweetie's though.

Moira refocused on the blog and read the last bullet point of the day.

- This weekend is the Spring into Somerset Festival. Hearsay is Mayor Gil is presenting an award to one of our own. You know I can't keep a secret. If I knew who it was, I'd tell you all. I sure hope it's not someone from the Green family though—they might just toss that award right back at him.

Moira cringed. She didn't plan to chuck the award at Gil. She was better than that. Even if he deserved it.

Chapter Twelve

Gil was wearing his smile like the worn jeans and loose T-shirt he had on tonight. The smile covered the fact that he wasn't listening to a word the guys at the table were saying right now. When they laughed, he laughed. When they groaned, he groaned. Otherwise, his thoughts were on the crummy day he'd just had.

Days like this made him reconsider running for another term as mayor. In the last twelve hours, he'd gotten a half dozen emails complaining about the issue with Sweetie's Bakeshop and another half dozen calls about it. Not to mention the folks he'd run into today who'd frowned at him while bringing up the town hall meeting last night. Yeah, those people made up a small percentage of folks in Somerset Lake, but it still weighed on him.

"What do you think, Gilbert?" Jake elbowed Gil, and everyone focused their attention on him.

"Oh, uh…" Gil scratched the new growth of hair on his chin. "I haven't really thought much about it," he said, wondering what they were discussing.

"You haven't?" Miles asked from the other side of Gil. "Why not?"

Gil cleared his throat. "Well, you know, I've had other things on my mind. What do you think?" he asked Miles, deflecting.

Miles narrowed his eyes. Then he looked past Gil at Jake, and both men broke into wide grins.

Gil looked between them. "What?"

"You have no idea what we're even discussing, do you?" Jake asked on a small chuckle.

"Yeah, of course I do. I'm sitting right here." Gil looked at the other guys. River was seated across from him along with Román.

"Gilbert Ryan, don't lie to us." Jake patted his back. "We were talking about Denise Berger running against you. There's no way you haven't given that any thought. What's on your mind tonight?"

Gil blew out a breath. "There are a few people in town who would probably rather see Denise as the mayor instead of me after last night's debacle of a meeting." Gil reached for his soda and took a sip. Most of the guys had beers, but Gil didn't usually drink alcohol in public. He didn't think it was good for his public image.

"What I can't understand is why you aren't fighting this decision to shut Sweetie's down," River said. "Yeah, we need more parking, but not at the cost of someone's livelihood."

Gil sighed. "It's not like it was my idea. I voted against it. But at the same time, it's the only solution, and this parking problem isn't something we can continue to ignore. Let's discuss something else, okay? I've been thinking about this issue nonstop, and I came here to forget my troubles."

"Fine, fine. Let's talk about this weekend. Who's going to the Spring into Somerset Festival?" Miles raised his own hand. "I have to work it, which Lucy isn't thrilled about. She's going with Moira, who as word has it is only going because she's getting an award from you." He looked at Gil.

So much for forgetting his troubles. They seemed to be following him around tonight. "Obviously, I'm going then," Gil said.

"Tess is dragging me with her." River looked regretful. He wasn't much for huge social gatherings.

"Della has already informed me that we're going as well," Roman said. He shrugged. "I don't mind. I love festivals."

Jake nudged an elbow against Gil's on the table. "Reva's blog suggested that Moira might throw the award back in your face. Need a few of us to go up onstage with you as bodyguards?"

Gil slid a look to his friend. "Ha ha, very funny. Moira won't be throwing anything at me."

"Well, she certainly won't be kissing you." Miles placed a hand on Gil's shoulder. "Sorry, buddy," he said in mock seriousness.

Gil expelled a heavy breath. "I thought being the mayor would win me some respect in this town."

"It has. But it doesn't win you anything among friends," Jake joked. "Friends don't let friends get too full of themselves."

Saturday's weather couldn't have been more perfect for the Spring into Somerset Festival. Moira glanced around as she approached the town green, where the festival was set up. She was supposed to be meeting Tess here, but Tess had texted ten minutes ago to say she was running late.

Moira didn't mind. She was on a mission today. Call her crazy, but the more she'd considered the idea, the more it sounded like something she could do. Something she wanted to do. Forget appealing to those in power in this town to ensure that Sweetie's stayed put. She'd never liked putting her trust or faith in someone else if she could help it. She preferred to do things herself. Which was why she'd made a very important decision.

Moira felt flutters of excitement in her stomach. Was she really going to do this?

"Hey, Moira." Lucy stepped up beside her.

"Hey." Moira pushed a clipboard into Lucy's hand.

Lucy furrowed a brow as she looked up. "What's this?"

"It's my petition," Moira told her matter-of-factly.

Lucy looked at the clipboard she'd been handed, reading the title. *"Petition to Run for Somerset Lake Mayor,"* she read. Then she looked up at Moira. "I still don't understand. I thought you were creating a petition to save your mom's bakery."

"Well, in a way, that's what that is. I'm going to save my mom's bakery by running for mayor," Moira said proudly.

Lucy looked stunned. "You are? You?"

"Mm-hmm. Me." Moira continued to smile. Ever since she'd made the decision, she'd felt this giddiness growing inside her. She couldn't remember the last time she'd felt this kind of excitement.

Tess stepped up to the two. "Hey, you two. What's going on?"

Moira handed her a clipboard as well. "I'm running

for mayor, that's what. And I need my friends to help me collect signatures to support my campaign."

"Running for mayor?" Tess repeated, her brows drawing together in a similar way to what Lucy's had done a moment earlier.

"Are you even qualified to run?" Lucy asked, still looking confused. "I didn't think someone could just decide to jump into politics."

"I've done my research," Moira said. "The only qualifications one needs to run for mayor are a high school diploma, proof that they live in the town where they're running, and a petition with signatures supporting the candidate."

"Okay. But why?" Tess asked.

Moira shrugged. "Because this is my town and Sweetie's Bakeshop is my home. I want a say in what happens here. And because I think I'd be good at the job."

"Are you kidding? You'd be amazing at it!" Lucy finally said. She gestured between her and Tess. "We'll be your campaign team. We can help. Right, Tess?"

Tess hesitated, but then a slow smile curled at the edges of her mouth. "Of course. I actually love the idea of my best friend running for mayor. All of us in the book club can help."

Moira's heart pounded. "Really?" Having the support of her friends meant so much to her.

"What about Gil?" Lucy asked.

"What about him?" Moira shot back.

"Come on. Don't pretend with us." Lucy hugged her clipboard against her chest. "We've always known the truth."

"Then please enlighten me." Moira wondered for a moment if Lucy was talking about the night Gil's roommate had drugged her. Or the following day when she'd trashed Felix's apartment and had gotten herself arrested. None of Moira's friends knew about that though. Neither did Moira's family. The whole situation was Moira's best kept secret, and that's how she wanted it to stay. "What truth do you think you know?" Moira asked nervously.

"That you're wildly attracted to the man," Lucy said with a waggle of her brows. "Just like he's madly attracted to you."

"Oh." Moira exhaled softly.

Tess narrowed her eyes. "Why? What did you think we knew?"

"N-nothing." Moira shook her head and quickly changed the subject. "Gil might not like the fact that I'm running against him, but I don't like the fact that he wants to demolish my mom's business."

"Hey, ya'll. What's the story?" Della stepped up beside them.

"I thought you were coming with Roman."

"I did. He's gone in search of a funnel cake," Della said. "I spotted you ladies, so I came over to say hello."

"I'm glad you did." Moira pushed a clipboard toward Della. "Can you help me get signatures?"

"What's this?" Della looked down at the board.

"She's running for mayor," Lucy said with a confident grin. "And all of us in the book club are going to be her winning campaign team." She turned to Moira. "You'll be onstage with Gil in thirty minutes. You're going to have everyone's admiration and attention. That's the perfect time to make your announcement." Lucy waved a hand in front of her. "Moira Green believes in small businesses and big changes."

Moira blinked, remembering how Reva had said that change keeps things interesting. "I love that as a slogan. Did you just come up with that off the top of your head?"

Lucy grinned. "See? We've got you covered. All you need to do is smile and inspire people. We've got your back."

Moira's excitement grew as she looked at the enthusiasm on her friends' faces. "Thank you. I can't believe I'm actually going to do this."

"I can't either," Tess said. "It's so unlike you, but also exactly like you. You don't like to draw attention to yourself, but you've always been one to shine the light on issues that need addressing." She reached for Moira's hand and gave it a squeeze. "No offense to our current mayor, but you're the perfect person for the job."

"Hey, ladies," a man's voice said, approaching the group from behind.

Moira turned and found Gil smiling back at her. "Hey, Gil," she said as guilt flooded through her. This decision she'd made would put her at odds with Gil.

"Ready for your moment in the spotlight?" he asked, completely oblivious to what was about to happen when he invited her onto that stage in a minute.

Moira swallowed and looked at her friends. "Ready as I'll ever be."

Gil gestured at the clipboards in her arms. "What's all this?"

Moira hugged the petition to her body. "N-nothing. It's not important."

Gil narrowed his eyes just slightly, but he didn't ask any more questions. "Well, I'm looking forward to giving you an award in a little bit. You deserve it."

Moira looked at Gil, feeling a surge of confidence—along with a thick layer of guilt and maybe a few flutters because her friends were right, she was attracted to Gil these days even if she'd never admit it. "I'll see you onstage."

Chapter Thirteen

There was a nice breeze blowing off the lake in Somerset today. The weather was perfect for a town festival. Everyone seemed to be in a good mood, and unlike yesterday, no one had asked Gil about tearing down Sweetie's for a parking lot yet. That was a good sign, especially considering Gil was officially announcing his decision to run for a second term as mayor today.

Gil stood off to the side of the stage, where a band was playing live bluegrass music for the occasion. This was as good a place as any to make his announcement. Almost everyone in Somerset Lake was out today. Gil sat and watched folks walking around, hitting up the vendors, and enjoying the music.

"Gil!" Doug's voice was easy to recognize in the crowd.

Gil turned toward his brother, who was walking with their mom and dad. They were all wearing VOTE GIL RYAN FOR MAYOR T-shirts, which was both embarrassing and appreciated. "Hey, guys. Fancy meeting you here."

"Well, we wouldn't miss the big announcement," his mom said. She wore a long dress and had her dark hair secured with barrettes on the sides today. She'd always taken Gil's events seriously and had dressed for the occasion.

Gil gave her a hug as she stepped closer.

"Also, Doug wouldn't let us stay home," his father said, hugging Gil as well. Gil's father appeared to be dressed for a game of golf, which was probably where he'd be today if not for this event. The courtroom and the golf course were his go-tos.

Gil's mom elbowed his dad. "Not that we would have missed being here, because our son has a big announcement to make."

Gil loved how proud his mom acted on his behalf. She supported Doug in his endeavors just as much, except for Doug's latest endeavor to move out.

"What's this about you shutting Sweetie's Bakeshop down to create a parking lot?" his father asked.

Gil sighed. "Not you, too, Dad. Sometimes sacrifices have to be made for the greater good. This is something the town needs. The only place for the lot is where Sweetie's currently is."

His father's frown told Gil everything he needed to know. If Gil weren't his father's son, even his father might not vote for him.

His mother placed a hand on his shoulder. "You always do the right thing. I'm sure that whatever decision you make will be a good one."

"Thanks, Mom." Gil gave his dad a pointed look.

"Just don't mention the parking lot up there." Doug pointed to the stage. "It's not good for your image."

Gil sighed. "Some folks are upset, yeah, but others realize that a parking lot is needed. There are a lot of people who will vote for me based on my commitment to fix this problem."

Doug frowned. "Gilly..."

"Fine." Gil held up his hands. "I'll do my best to avoid the topic."

"Well, we're going to have a seat out front," his mother said. "Break a leg."

Gil slid his gaze over to her. "This isn't theater, Mom."

"Anytime you're onstage, it's theater," she said wisely.

She wasn't wrong. There was always some element of acting that went on with public speaking. Gil glanced around and spotted Moira heading in his direction. For instance, he had to act like he wasn't still smitten by this woman when he absolutely was. Was it him, or did she get more beautiful every time he saw her? Today she was wearing a beautiful baby blue sundress that fell just above her ankles. She had on a long necklace and bangle bracelets that gave her a feminine vibe that she didn't always play up. He guessed she was dressed more formally to receive the award the town was giving her.

"Hey," he said as she drew closer.

"Hey." She stopped a couple of feet away from him. The clipboards she'd been carrying earlier were gone, leaving her hands empty. She nervously interweaved her fingers, drawing his attention to the light coating of lavender polish on her nails.

"You ready for the spotlight?"

"Not really." She blew out a breath and met his gaze. "I've never been much for public speaking."

"Could have fooled me the other night at the town hall meeting."

Moira winced, but her hazel eyes were smiling. "Sorry. I was a bit passionate. I am passionate," she corrected.

"Can't fault someone for that. My dad always told Doug and me to never apologize about fighting for something we believe in. There are so few things that inspire a person to break out of their comfort zone."

"Speaking at the town hall was definitely out of my comfort zone." Moira laughed.

"If I remember correctly, you were front and center a lot when we were growing up. Band. Journalism. Student treasurer."

"I can't believe you remember all my extracurricular activities," Moira said with a disbelieving voice.

Gil suddenly felt self-conscious. He threw one out that wasn't true just so he didn't look like he'd been keeping tabs on her since grade school. "Cheerleading."

Moira narrowed her eyes. "I was never in cheer."

"You weren't?" He scratched his chin. "Huh. I could have sworn you were."

The look Moira gave him told him she wasn't buying his act. Then she eyed the stage. "So you're going to give me the award and then what? Do I get to address the crowd?"

Gil rocked back and forth on his feet. "If you want to."

"I do," she said quickly.

He was surprised, considering how nervous she looked right now. She hadn't looked nearly this nervous at the town hall meeting, but there, there were fewer people and she hadn't been standing on a stage. "Okay. Wonderful. I'm sure everyone here will be happy about that. They all seemed to enjoy listening to you the other night."

Moira narrowed her eyes. "Did that upset you?"

Gil shook his head. "Why would I be mad at you for speaking up about something you believe in?"

"Because it isn't what you believe in," she said quietly.

Gil wished things were different, but she was right. They were on opposing sides right now. "I believe in you." He noticed how Moira's eyes narrowed just slightly. Had he said too much? He always seemed to wear his feelings on his sleeve where Moira was concerned.

"Gil! It's time." Doug stepped up to Gil and looked at Moira. "Hi, Moira," he said with a large smile.

"Hi, Doug. I like your shirt." She wrung her hands in front of her as she spoke. Gil hoped he hadn't made her even more nervous than she already was.

"Do you want a shirt? I can get you one too," Doug offered.

Moira grinned. "That's sweet, but, um, it's okay. I don't want you to go to any trouble for me."

"It's no trouble," Doug said. "I know how much Gil likes you. He'd love for you to wear his shirt."

Gil avoided Moira's sideward glance. He'd have to thank his brother for that later. "So, uh, I'll go onstage first and talk for a few minutes before inviting you up. Sound good?"

She nodded, looking flushed and beautiful. "Yep."

"Great. I'll see you soon," he said. Then he turned toward the stage and headed up the steps. He didn't typically mind public speaking, but he was a little gun-shy after all the hate mail he'd gotten this week. And since Denise Berger had put in a bid for mayor.

The crowd clapped as he took the stage. Was it less applause than usual? Were there folks who weren't smiling in the audience? Maybe even some who were frowning?

Where is this paranoia coming from?

He stopped behind the microphone and glanced out on dozens of familiar faces. "Hello, Somersetters!" he said, forcing more enthusiasm than he was feeling right now. "It's a beautiful day to celebrate spring at Somerset Lake. It's also a good day to make a very important announcement to you-all." Gil spotted his parents in the crowd. "I don't think this will come as a shock to any of you, but I thought at this happy occasion, I'd take the time to make my decision to run for another term as mayor official. The last four years have been amazing, and I am so fortunate to have such wonderful support from this town," Gil said, scanning the faces.

"We support you, but you don't support us!" a man's voice shouted from the crowd.

Gil's stomach dropped. He pretended not to have heard that comment and continued with what he had planned to say. "It has been an honor to represent Somerset Lake, and it would be an honor if the good people here were to vote me into office again this fall."

"What about Sweetie's Bakeshop?" a woman's voice called out.

Gil tried to locate the source of the voice, but there were too many faces. He took a breath and turned to see Moira waiting on the side of the stage. She offered a reassuring smile, which told him she had heard the comments. Then he gestured toward her. "I have some more great news for you-all. I'm sure you've all heard about our local hero, Moira Green, and how she went above and beyond the call of duty last week. In fact, I have something special to present to Ms. Green today." Gil held out his arm to Moira. "Moira, will you please join me up here onstage?"

Moira headed up the steps, her smile deepening as she approached him in the middle of the stage. She turned to the crowd and waved as the applause grew.

Were the cheers louder than what he'd just gotten? Was he losing ground with his supporters over this parking lot issue?

"No one owes Moira more gratitude than me because the person she helped is my brother Doug. As you-all may have heard, Doug called the emergency dispatch last week. He had fallen and twisted his ankle. He told me that he doesn't mind if I tell you that he's also recently discovered that he's diabetic. He was struggling on the day he called Moira, and as luck would have it, bad luck at least, several drivers and passengers in a three-car pileup on Hannigan Street were also having a difficult afternoon." Gil cleared his throat. "Long story short, all of the available emergency personnel were sent to the accident, and no one was immediately available to check on Doug, including me. So Moira went above and beyond her job description and drove over to where Doug was and helped him herself."

More claps resounded from the crowd.

"My family owes her a debt of gratitude, and that's one reason I was extremely pleased when Sheriff Ronnie told me that he wanted to present Moira with an award today. A hero is someone who helps another without any concern for themselves. They are sacrificial, honest, generous, and capable. All the qualities that I believe Moira Green portrays." Gil connected gazes with Moira, and his heartbeat quickened. She was definitely more beautiful every time he laid eyes on her.

"Then why are you tearing down her family's business?" someone called from the front row.

Moira's smile slipped at the corners.

So did Gil's. He could address the comment or pretend he didn't hear it—again. He didn't hide from things, but he also didn't want to tarnish Moira's time onstage. She deserved this award and the town's admiration. This was her moment.

Reaching for the plaque on the podium, he held it up for the crowd to see. Then he held it out for Moira. "Moira, it's my great honor to present you with our Hero Among Us award."

Moira stepped toward him, her fingers brushing against his as she took the plaque and held it against her midsection. "Thank you all. This is such an honor. Everyone who knows me knows how much I love my job as an emergency dispatcher. Being there for people when they need me the most is something I am passionate about. I love serving the people here in Somerset Lake."

Gil wasn't sure why she was anxious speaking in front of others. She was amazing up here, smiling and talking so naturally. He wouldn't even know she was nervous if she hadn't told him so.

"This is my hometown," she continued. "And I am so very proud of that. In my opinion, there is no other place in this state, maybe even the country, with people who are as friendly, smart, resourceful, and honest." Moira shook her head, deepening her smile.

Gil couldn't take his eyes off her. *Wow.* She really was amazing. It almost sounded like she was a politician at this moment instead of a Good Samaritan accepting an award. He found himself grinning as he listened to her go on about how much this town meant to her. It was inspiring really, and he felt the same way. That's why he had wanted to be mayor in the first place. It was why he showed up every day, even on the hard ones.

Moira hugged the award to her body and looked out on the crowd. "This is why I've made a decision that I would like to share with all of you today." Moira seemed to take a breath. "I am so excited to announce that I am planning to run for town mayor this fall."

Gil's mind stumbled over her words. There was no way he'd heard her correctly. Moira for mayor?

"I believe in Somerset Lake and all the people here. I believe in the small businesses that make our town unique. As mayor, I won't allow your livelihoods to fall to the wayside in order to save folks a couple extra steps with parking."

Gil felt like the breath had been knocked out of him. This was about more than saving steps. He'd just gotten through telling everyone here how paramedics and fire-fighters had struggled to get to an accident on Hannigan Street. That was why there was no one available to help Doug.

"I will fight for the things that matter," Moira continued. "I don't think I'm a hero just because I did my job or because I helped someone in need. I do think those qualities are something a good mayor should have though."

"Yeah!" someone called out. "Unlike Mayor Gil!"

Gil turned to locate the source of the voice, and this time he spotted the person in the crowd. It was Donavyn Wilber. That guy hadn't liked Gil since middle school when Gil had accidentally tripped him in the cafeteria, making him spill his tray of spaghetti. *It was an accident, Donavyn. Get over it already.*

"I think Mayor Gil has been amazing for this town," Moira said, casting him an apologetic glance, "but I also think I'm up for the challenge. Sometimes change is necessary, but not at the cost of what makes us special. Like Sweetie's Bakeshop."

"Yeah!" Someone clapped, and then someone else joined in. Then the entire crowd was clapping, and Gil just wanted to slink off the stage and disappear.

∞

Moira felt energized from the crowd's response to her announcement. Was she really going to do this? She'd never wanted to run for public office before. How hard could running for mayor of Somerset Lake be though?

She turned toward Gil once they were off the outdoor stage, and her heart dipped.

He looked deflated in a way she had rarely ever seen him. Gil typically carried himself with confidence. That was one of the things she secretly admired about him.

"I'm sorry," Moira said, at a loss for anything more to say.

"You just took me by surprise, that's all." He ran a hand through his dark blond hair. "I had no idea you were even considering running for office."

"Well, it's something new. I haven't even filled out the paperwork yet."

"So you just announced onstage to the whole town that you're running when you're not actually serious about it?" he asked, sounding tense and suddenly irritated.

"I am serious."

"Just because of what's happening with your mom's bakery?"

"Isn't that reason enough? If you aren't going to support small businesses here, I will."

Gil crossed his arms over his chest. "I *do* support business owners."

Moira shook her head, hackles rising. She didn't need to explain herself to Gil. "Not all of them."

They stared at each other for a beat. Gil was obviously upset, but she wouldn't apologize for this. Maybe she hadn't been keen on this idea when Vi had first suggested it, but now she was. This could be good for her, and for the town.

Gil simultaneously shook his head and blew out a breath. "I can't believe this. First Denise and now you. Good luck," he said, facing her, his tone incredulous. "May the best person win."

"Thanks. I think."

Gil headed off, leaving Moira standing there alone, but only for a second. Then Lucy, Tess, Della, and Trisha stormed her.

"You were amazing up there!" Lucy said, grinning from ear to ear.

"You're a natural for sure." Tess was more subdued with her enthusiasm, but she was beaming.

"This feels like a dream. Am I really running for mayor?" Moira asked, not quite believing any of this. "Am I really doing this?"

"You are," Trisha said on a laugh, one hand holding the mound of her belly. "I heard it with my own two ears and so did the rest of the town."

Moira still felt shaky but also exhilarated. Maybe there were more things she wanted to do. The world suddenly felt like her oyster. She looked among her friends, enjoying the moment. Then the guilt hit her. "I think Gil is mad at me."

"Serves him right," Lucy said. "Two of us are small-business owners. Not saying he's done a bad job, but knowing what's planned for Sweetie's scares me. We need a mayor who's going to look out for our businesses' best interests. You'd be great."

Moira just wished it didn't mean going up against Gil. He'd never been anything but nice to her until this parking lot thing. And he was still being nice.

"We can meet on Monday morning at Sweetie's and begin discussing your campaign," Tess said, taking the lead as always. Whenever there was anything that required planning, she always took charge.

Lucy lifted a hand. "I'll be there."

"I still have the dispatch to work," Moira said, "so I won't be able to stay long."

"We'll just have mini–planning sessions. It'll be fine." Lucy narrowed her eyes. "You're not in this alone. We're going to be the best campaign team you never knew you needed."

All the women took turns giving Moira a hug. Then Della returned to Roman, and Trisha left to locate Jake.

"I have to find River," Tess said. "He's not a fan of crowds. I promised not to leave him to suffer through this festival alone."

Lucy hugged Moira last. "You can do this. I'm inspired by you."

"Thanks." When the ladies were gone, Moira was left standing alone. She sat on the steps of the makeshift stage and took a couple of deep breaths.

"Hey, Moira."

She looked up to find Doug standing in front of her. "Oh, hey, Doug," she said, feeling another wave of guilt. She knew how much he loved having his brother as the town's mayor.

"Why are you running against Gil? He's a good mayor."

Moira forced a wobbly smile. "Yes, he is. But I think I could serve this town well too."

"He would never hurt you. But you're hurting him."

"It's complicated, Doug," Moira said.

Doug shook his head, his frown thickening. "No, it's not. It's simple. You're trying to steal my brother's job."

Moira took a steadying breath. "There'll be an election. The people here will vote and determine if Gil gets to stay."

Doug pointed a finger. "My brother fights for the people here. He fights for you. And it's my job to fight for him."

Moira offered Doug a small smile, hoping to lessen the tension. "Of course it is."

Doug folded his arms over his chest. "I thought you were my hero, but if you're running against Gil, you're the enemy." Turning, he walked away with his head held low.

Moira loved Doug. She didn't want to disappoint him. She didn't want to hurt Gil either. He was her hero once upon a time, and no one had ever given him an award for doing the right thing. He hadn't even known exactly what he'd done when he'd insisted on taking her home the night she'd gone out with Felix.

Darla stepped up in front of Moira and put her hands on her hips. "Just what do you think you're doing? Running against Gil for mayor? Where did that come from?"

Moira breathed a sigh as she faced her mom. "You know exactly where it came from. I told you, I'm not going to let you lose your business."

"Moira, what's happening is not Gil's fault."

"It kind of is. And running for mayor is something I want to do. I think I could do good for this town," Moira said honestly.

Darla hesitated. "You know I'll support you no matter what you do. This is a commitment though, Moira. If this is just about the bakery, what happens when it's demolished and there's nothing else to fight for?"

Moira narrowed her eyes. "It sounds like you've

already given up on the bakery. Why are you letting this go so easily, Mom?"

Darla took a seat on the step next to Moira. "Why does everything have to be a fight with you? It's always been that way."

"I fight for things I believe in. Like this. I don't understand why you don't."

Darla sighed and looked out on the festival. Practically everyone in town was here. There was food, crafts, music, and laughter—everything a person could want for their Saturday afternoon. "All I'm saying is, make sure you're running for the right reasons. The bakery is my responsibility, not yours. Taking on the role of mayor will be a difficult job, Moira."

Moira stood and looked down at her mom. "You still talk to me like I'm fifteen years old. In case you haven't realized, I'm an adult now. I know what I'm doing. And you say you'll support me no matter what, but I don't feel like that's true. You fought me when I decided to become a dispatcher. You question me constantly about why I'm still single. You don't support me fighting for your business, and I don't feel supported right now when I've possibly made one of the biggest decisions of my adult life."

"Moira…"

Moira shook her head, ending the conversation for now. "I'm going to walk around. I need to get signatures from people who are happy about my decision to run for mayor. I'll see you at the bakery on Monday morning," she said, turning her back to Darla. "I'll be meeting with my new campaign team, who support me one hundred percent."

∞

A couple of hours later, after walking around the festival and garnering dozens of congratulations and words of encouragement, Moira slipped away from the crowd and walked toward her car.

"Moira! Wait up!"

Moira turned to see Reva bustling toward her, a laptop messenger bag bumping against her hip. "Hey, Reva. Do you need something?"

"Yes. Oh, I am so excited about your announcement, dear. I mean, I love Mayor Gil, of course, but I love you too. I think most of the town feels that way. I would love to interview you for my blog so that the people in Somerset can get a feel for what you're passionate about. It'll be great promotion for you. What do you think?"

Moira couldn't believe she was actually going to agree to this because she'd always avoided being spotlighted on Reva's blog at all costs. "Yes, thank you, Reva. I'd love that."

"Perfect!" The blogger looked giddy about the idea. Then she waved. "I'll call you next week!"

Chapter Fourteen

The festival was mostly a success, at least for the town. For Gil, it was a bit of a dumpster fire. Not only did he have one competitor gunning for his job, but now he had two. And the second one, Moira, wasn't someone he ever wanted to fight with.

"Wanna go for a boat ride?" He petted Goldie's head.

She gave a bark as if she knew exactly what he was asking and her answer was an enthusiastic yes.

Gil stood from his Adirondack chair on the back deck and headed down the steps. He could always count on his dog and his boats.

"Hey."

Gil stopped walking but didn't turn. "Here to trade campaign strategies?"

"No." Behind him, Moira was as quiet as the night. He could almost hear her breathing.

Finally, Gil turned and faced her. She looked mesmerizing under the quarter moon and starry night sky.

"I just wanted to make sure you knew what happened today, onstage, wasn't personal."

Gil laughed dryly. "No? Trying to take my job isn't

personal?" He nodded and shoved his hands into his pockets. "Good to know."

Goldie ran over to greet Moira. She reached out to run her fingers along Goldie's back as she talked. "Is making plans to demolish my mom's bakery personal?"

Gil stared at her. "Point taken."

"Anyway, I was glad we were able to have a sort of truce the other night. I'm still upset with you, but I'm funneling that energy into my campaign. And I don't want this to affect our friendship."

Gil took a breath and nodded. "Your announcement surprised me, but I can handle a little friendly competition."

"Me too," Moira said. "And, in case you were wondering, I'm not going to shoot below the belt in this campaign."

Gil narrowed his eyes and grinned. "I'm glad to hear that. I don't play dirty either."

Now Moira narrowed her eyes. "Good to know."

"I meant it earlier. May the best person for the job win, whether it's you or me." He shrugged. "As long as it's not Denise."

Moira hugged her arms around herself. "My mom is not happy that I'm running against you."

Gil tore his gaze from Moira and looked at the lake. "I'm sure it just shocked her. As it did me." He tipped his head toward his boat. "I was about to go for a ride. Care to come along, seeing that we're friendly competition and nothing more or less?"

Moira seemed to consider his invitation. "No, that's okay. I should probably get home. It's going to be a busy week planning how I'm going to beat out the mayor of Somerset Lake."

Gil chuckled. "It won't be easy."

"Nothing worthwhile ever is."

He took a retreating step. "Last chance for a moonlit boat ride tonight."

"Tempting, but it was a long day. I'm tired." As if to make her point, she broke out into a yawn.

Gil wasn't the kind of guy who pushed. He liked to think he didn't keep company with that kind of guy either, but apparently he had at one time. Gil hadn't kept up with Felix Wilkes, because, roommate or not, he hadn't particularly liked the guy. He hadn't disliked him either though. "See you later, Moira."

"See you." She turned and headed back toward her car.

Gil waited to ensure she made it okay. Then he led Goldie onto his boat, thinking about Moira as he skimmed the water. If he weren't running for the mayor's office, he would vote for Moira. Experience or not, she would make a good town representative. Other than high school government, Gil hadn't had any political experience when he'd run for the position either. Just a dream and a desire for change. Back then he'd wanted to change the world, thinking it was easier than it actually was.

Had he made good changes since he'd been in office? He'd tried, but there was always more to do. Maybe he wasn't as passionate or as hungry as he was four years ago. He always told himself he'd step down if he was at risk of becoming like the former mayor, who'd become a grumpy fixture in the town. Gil wasn't anywhere near the likes of former mayor Bryce Malsop, but he could do better. Be better. He wasn't about to give up his position to Denise or Moira. They didn't have nearly the experience that he did. If either of them won, they'd have to do it fair and square.

∞

"You were conspiring with the enemy?" Lucy asked Moira on Monday morning.

Moira was sitting with her makeshift campaign team at a table in the bakery. "What are you talking about?"

"If you're going to run for mayor, you should know that all eyes will be on you at all times. You went to Gil's house on Saturday night after the festival," Lucy said, raising her brows high on her forehead.

Tess's mouth dropped open. "You what? What were you doing there?"

Moira shook her head. "I went to his house, yes, but I didn't go inside. I just stopped by to make sure he wasn't upset that I was running against him. My conscience started to get to me, especially after Doug disowned me as his real-life hero. And where did this piece of information come from anyway?" Moira asked.

"Denise has spies. You and Gil are the enemies in her eyes. She's going to be pulling out all the stops to find dirt on you," Lucy announced.

"Dirt?" Moira asked. "This is Somerset Lake. We don't run our elections with mudslinging."

"Well, apparently she does," Della said with a frown. "That woman can be pretty nasty. I helped her buy her current home. She hassled the previous owner of her house until the seller finally just gave her everything she wanted. I will never take Denise on as a client again."

Moira reached for her cup of coffee. "Well, I don't play that way. So now that we have enough signatures to put my name on the ballot in November, what else do I need to do?"

Tess tapped her finger on a list in front of her. "I did some online searches over the weekend. The process is fairly clear-cut. You just need to show up to the community events, shake hands, and push your platform as much as you can."

"My platform?" Moira asked.

"It starts with the slogan. I love what Lucy came up with the other day. 'Moira Green believes in small businesses and big changes,'" Tess said, adjusting her reading glasses on the bridge of her nose.

"I love it too," Trisha said with a nod of approval. "Your focus is on the small businesses here. If they thrive, everyone thrives."

The other women uttered their agreement.

"I like it as well," Moira said with a growing smile. "Reva wants to interview me for her blog. I told her yes."

"The one and only time you'll ever willingly make bullet points on her blog," Lucy said with a giggle. Then Lucy turned to Tess, who suddenly looked very serious. "We probably need to take her shopping."

Tess looked at Moira, her gaze lowering to Moira's T-shirt. "Shopping is a good idea."

"What? Why?" Moira objected, looking down at her current attire. To be fair, she'd just pulled on the first thing she'd found in her drawer before leaving the house this morning. "I happen to like the way I dress. It's comfortable."

"You're projecting an image. A brand. Right now, you are way too relaxed to be taken seriously," Della said. "You have to dress the part. I never wear T-shirts and jeans when I'm showing a house. A first, second, and third impression starts with how you look."

"Black pants and a simple blouse go a long way," Lucy

agreed. "It won't be drastic. Just enough to project that you can be mayor of this town. We need people to take you seriously."

Moira guessed they had a point. She'd never seen Gil looking anything less than polished. Denise on the other hand was just a little bit too polished. She wore fitted skirts and ruffled blouses 24/7, and her hair was practically a helmet of waves and hairspray. "Okay, you're right. I guess I do need to go shopping."

Lucy slid her gaze toward Tess. "Can we trade book club for a girls' night shopping trip this week?" She pressed her hands together in a prayer position.

"You're asking me?" Tess sipped her coffee. "I'm not the leader of our book club. It just happens to take place at my store. I'm game though."

"Me too," Trisha said.

Della frowned. "Unfortunately, I have to show a couple houses that night."

"On a Thursday?" Tess gave her a disapproving look.

"Just this one time. My client couldn't meet any other time. Send me pictures, okay?"

"Will do." Lucy stood. "But right now, I need to get some bagels from your mom and take them back to the bed and breakfast for my guests."

"Aww. How far along is the mother-to-be?" Moira asked. The Babymoon Bed &Breakfast catered to expectant parents.

"Eight and a half months." Lucy grimaced. "She could go into labor at any moment, really."

"Good thing they have a midwife running their inn." Tess stood as well. "Lara is out this week so it's just me at the bookstore. I need to head over and open shop."

"And I have a dispatch to get to." Moira collected her

purse and coffee and stood. "Hopefully it'll be a calm, emergency-free day."

"In which case, you need to start building a website." Tess pointed a finger in her direction. "'Moira Green believes in small businesses and big changes,'" she repeated.

"Yes, Campaign Manager," Moira quipped.

Tess turned back. "I don't run the book club, and I'm not the campaign manager here. It's a team effort on both counts."

Lucy put a hand on her friend's back. "You're a natural leader. Accept it."

"Maybe you should be the one running for mayor," Moira told Tess.

Tess put up a hand. "Not it. My plate is full with the bookshop and River." Her cheeks flushed at the mention of her fiancé's name.

"I'll bet it is," Della said on a chuckle.

"Look who's talking," Tess said with a smile as she headed toward the exit, glancing over her shoulder at Della.

Moira felt a little left out whenever the subject of romance came up among her friends. She was always the single one. Albeit happily single, but maybe not quite as contented as she once was. Now that all her friends were part of a couple, she was feeling more and more alone. She'd always said she didn't need a romantic interest in her life, and she still didn't. But maybe it would be nice to have one.

Where did that thought come from? First she was running for public office, and now she was reconsidering her stance on her love life or lack thereof.

Moira headed toward the bakery's exit and paused as

she saw Gil approach the door from the other side. They'd met this same way the other day, only from opposite sides. His gaze connected with hers, and her heart skipped.

He opened the door and gave her a warm smile. "We have to stop meeting like this," he teased.

Butterflies fluttered around in her chest. Moira ignored butterflies. They made her uncomfortable. She didn't necessarily enjoy the skipped heartbeats or flushed feeling of her skin either. "If this bakery becomes a parking lot, I guess we will stop meeting like this," she said.

Gil didn't seem to let the comment get to him. "Planning your campaign this morning?"

"Mm," she agreed. "Apparently, Denise has spies on us. Rumor has it we met up on Saturday night at your house."

Gil chuckled. "Well, it's true. We did."

"Do you have spies on her?" It was a serious question. He'd told Moira he didn't play dirty, but maybe keeping tabs on your competition was part of the game.

Gil shook his head. "I don't stoop to Denise's level. I focus on my plans and promises, not on the opposing teams' perceived flaws or misgivings."

"Good to know." Moira glanced past him toward the door. "Well, I have a shift to get to."

"And I have a coffee with my name on it." Gil stepped back to make way for Moira to leave. She was about to walk past him, but Sheriff Ronnie stepped up to the two first.

"Just the two folks I was wanting to talk to," he said with a huge grin on his face. Ronnie was a serious man. If he was smiling, something was up.

"Oh?" Gil asked. "You want to see both of us?"

The sheriff nodded. "I've already spoken to Denise,

and she says she'll be happy to help me out. Now all I need is for you two to agree."

"To what exactly?" Moira asked.

The sheriff rubbed his hands together. "As you know, this town responds well to fundraisers, and I'm doing a little spring cleaning in my jail. The cells need sprucing up. We need new cots and sheets, stuff like that. Those things are never in the budget though."

"I'm always happy to participate in a fundraiser," Gil said.

"Of course. Same here." Moira just didn't get invited to participate often because her job kept her tucked away inside her home. "Do you want us to sell something?"

"Kind of." The sheriff nodded. "I want to have a jail cell lock-in with all three of the mayoral candidates. We'll set bail for each of you, and the town will pitch in money to spring you out. If you don't make bail before sunset, you'll have to stay overnight in one of those cots that need replacing." He looked between them, a steady smile lining his lips. "Sounds like fun, right?"

Moira's belly flopped like a fish gasping for breath. She'd spent only one night in jail in her life, and she didn't fancy repeating it. The night she'd trashed Felix's apartment still haunted her, almost as much as the night before that.

"Yeah," Gil said enthusiastically. "That sounds like fun to me. I'm in."

Both men looked at Moira expectantly. What could she say? Denise and Gil had already agreed. If she refused, she'd look like a poor sport. She forced a smile that felt tight and unnatural. "Of course. Count me in as well."

"Great!" Ronnie said.

"When do you want us to do this?" Gil asked.

"Well, there's no time like the present. I was hoping for this weekend."

"That's pretty fast, don't you think?" Moira asked.

The sheriff shrugged. "All I need is for Reva to announce the lock-in on her blog. I got a connection at the *Daily Gazette* too. It'll be easy to spread the word, and I want to feed off your new announcement, Moira. People are excited about more folks throwing their hats into the ring for the mayoral race. This will be good for the jail and for you."

Moira shared a look with Gil.

"Okay, you two. Prepare to be arrested early Saturday morning," the sheriff said.

Anxiety twisted Moira's gut. "Wait. You're actually going to arrest us?"

"Oh, yeah. Handcuffs and everything. I might even put you in orange jumpsuits and parade you down Hannigan Street."

"Orange isn't really my color." Gil didn't seem rattled by this fundraiser at all. In fact, he almost looked excited about it.

Moira was rattled though. So much so that she was suddenly rethinking her bid for mayor. Was it too late to drop out?

Chapter Fifteen

Gil startled awake to the sound of his doorbell ringing. Goldie took off running out of the room ahead of him. Gil looked at the clock and blinked the blurry numbers into focus. *Six a.m.? Really?*

On a sigh that stretched into a sleepy yawn, he stood and stumbled toward the sound of the doorbell. He opened the door mid-complaint. "Doug, I told you not to—"

"Gilbert Ryan?" a gruff voice asked.

Gil blinked at Sheriff Ronnie flashing his badge. "Sheriff? What's going on?"

"Gilbert Ryan, you are under arrest." Ronnie smiled and lowered his tone. "Pretend arrest of course. Your jail time begins now."

Gil shook his head. Was this really happening? "I was sleeping, Sheriff."

"I figured as much. I wanted to milk this opportunity for all it was worth. Grab your cell phone. Posting some selfies from jail will help your cause when you beg for bail." He chuckled.

"Please tell me I get to put some decent clothes on too? Otherwise, there'll be no selfies happening."

Sheriff Ronnie's gaze dropped to Gil's Empire State Building boxer shorts. Gil had bought them two summers ago when he'd gone to the Big Apple to see friends. They were fun, but no one else was supposed to see them. "Hmm. Nice. I kind of pegged you as a guy who'd sport boxers with a puppy print."

"I have a pair of those too." Gil hiked a thumb behind him. "So, can I have a few minutes to change and maybe make a cup of coffee first?"

"Clothes, yes. But to get the full lockup experience, you'll be drinking jailhouse coffee. Best hurry up. Next stop is Moira's house."

Gil narrowed his gaze. "We're picking Moira up after this?"

"Mm-hmm. Miles is doing the honors of arresting Denise."

Gil looked past the sheriff to the cruiser outside. "You have your lights flashing? You'll wake up half the neighborhood."

"And they'll all know that their favorite mayor is being dragged down to the town jail."

Gil frowned. Everyone on his street would be talking for sure. His parents lived next door, and he hadn't thought to tell them he was participating in a jail lock-in this weekend. "Do I get one call once I'm at the station?"

Ronnie laughed. "I see you know your rights. We'll see about that one call. The phone lines might be a little busy."

Gil sighed. "I think you're enjoying this way too much, Sheriff."

"True. And I plan to take a lot of pictures to reflect fondly on this moment every time we bump heads on town issues in the future."

Gil opened his front door wider and gestured for Ronnie to step inside. Then he quickly walked back to his bedroom and changed. He texted his mom from his bedroom and told her about the fundraiser. Then he asked her to take care of Goldie for him. Thankfully, this was the first time his parents had ever gotten word that one of their children was being taken to jail, and it was for charity.

After changing into a pair of jeans and a T-shirt, and brushing his hair and teeth, he grabbed his cell phone and met Ronnie back in the living room. "All right, Sheriff. Let's go."

Sheriff Ronnie held up a pair of handcuffs and jingled them proudly.

Gil stopped in his tracks. "You're not serious."

"Oh, but I am. It's for charity, Mayor Gil."

Ten minutes later, the deputy cruiser pulled in to Wimberly Court. As it slowed at Moira's house, Gil had a sudden thought. This wouldn't be the first time she had been taken to jail. She'd been through this before. Would this be hard for her? Traumatic even?

Ronnie pulled the car into her driveway and put the engine in park. "You stay here. I'm giving her the same wake-up call that you just got."

Gil leaned forward in the back seat. "Uh, Sheriff, maybe you should let me do the honors."

Ronnie twisted his body around to look at Gil. "Why's that?"

Gil knew Ronnie was just having fun, but he was suddenly worried about Moira. She was a good sport, but this might be harder for her than Ronnie would understand. "Because, well, being woken by law enforcement was a bit of a rude awakening for me. I don't want you to startle Moira."

"And seeing you at her door would be less startling?" Ronnie asked, raising a wary brow. "I thought you two rubbed each other wrong."

"Yeah, well, we kind of made a truce the other night. And I'm not wearing a badge and jingling handcuffs. I'm also not her boss. You are."

Sheriff Ronnie seemed to consider this. "You're taking all the fun out of this, you know?" He pointed at Gil. "She doesn't get homemade coffee though. Jailhouse coffee."

"Got it. She only gets to change clothes and brush her teeth. Like me."

Ronnie frowned. "I'm timing you. No trying to escape," he warned.

Gil gave him a questioning look. "We volunteered for this. Why would we escape?"

Ronnie shrugged. Then he reached into the back seat and unlocked Gil's cuffs, setting him free. "Five minutes. Then I'm coming in."

Moira was having the best dream. She was on Gil's boat with him under a starry sky. She hadn't said no this time. She'd said yes, and she was so glad she did. The air was cool and crisp on her skin, and when she shivered, Gil took off the lightweight jacket he was wearing and wrapped it around her shoulders.

The unexpected touch of his fingers brushing over her skin made her belly flutter with anticipation of more. The dream was a blur, but there was a familiarity between her and Gil. They were comfortable around each other. The awkward tension that was always vibrating in the air between them was gone, and all that was left was this warmness along with something more. Something completely satisfying and addictive. She and Gil kept making eye contact and laughing, but she wasn't even sure what they were laughing about. They were just having fun.

Something knocked against the side of the boat, making a loud bang.

"What was that?" Moira asked in the dream.

Gil smiled and shrugged.

The knock came again until Moira stood and walked over to the sidewall of the boat to see where the sound was coming from.

"Do you hear that?" she called behind her.

Before Gil could respond, the boat rocked, and she went tumbling forward. Just in the nick of time, Gil reached out and grabbed her, pulling her against him before she fell overboard. For a moment, she stopped breathing. They were so close. Close enough to kiss, and some part of her had always wanted to kiss Gil.

The knock came again. Harder this time. Then the boat rocked, and both of them went tumbling forward into the cold ocean with a startling splash.

Moira sat up and gasped for air, blinking the view of her bedroom into focus. She ran a hand through her hair and realized someone was knocking on her front door. Her doorbell was broken. She needed to get that fixed. What time was it?

She eyed the bedside clock. *Six thirty a.m.?* Who in their right mind would be at her door this early on a Saturday morning? Grabbing a robe, she headed toward

the door and peered out the peephole. Gil's face came into
view, and all the heat and memories of the dream she'd
just been enjoying came rushing back to memory.

She was dreaming about him? And now he was on her
doorstep? Maybe she was still dreaming.

He knocked again.

Moira wished she'd taken the time to at least brush her
hair. She tightened her robe and finally opened the door
for him. "Hi. What are you doing here?" Her gaze caught
on the flashing lights in her driveway, where a sheriff's
car was parked. Her heart immediately took off racing.
"What's going on?"

"The lock-in that we agreed to," Gil explained. "Sheriff
Ronnie got it in his head that he'd arrest us first thing in
the morning. He's being a bit dramatic, if you ask me."

Moira took a breath. "Oh. I see."

Gil's brows lowered. "Why? Did you think you were
actually in trouble?"

"I just woke up." From a dream about Gil. "I'm not
thinking much at all." She looked at the cruiser again. "I
need to get dressed."

"That's fine, but no coffee," Gil said. "For some reason,
Sheriff Ronnie is pretty adamant about that part. Do you
want me to wait out here?"

She hesitated. "You can come in. I'll just be a few
minutes." She let Gil inside and gestured at the couch.
"I'll be right back."

She walked back to her bedroom, regretting that she
had to give up her Saturday to be woken this early and
hauled down to the town's jail. She pulled on a pair of
jeans and a T-shirt, her mind returning to that dream about
Gil. Why was she dreaming about him? They'd agreed to
play nice in this mayoral election, but that didn't mean

she should be fantasizing about kissing him. He was still planning to shut down her mom's bakery, and she was still planning to knock him out of office. Mayor Moira Green had a nice ring to it.

Moira brushed her hair and teeth and returned to the living room, where Gil had his eyes closed. He looked like he'd fallen right back to sleep. "All right. Let's get this over with."

He jerked awake and smiled back at her, making her insides warm. Then he stood and faced her. "You don't look like a criminal."

He was teasing, but his words hit her wrong. She had been a criminal once. She'd acted without thinking, and she'd been hauled to jail. She didn't want to relive that memory, but she kind of was right now. "Yeah, well, looks can be deceiving. You don't look like someone who'd vote to tear down a woman's livelihood for the sake of a few votes, and yet..." She trailed off as she walked past him toward the front door. Blame her rudeness on the fact that she hadn't had her morning caffeine yet.

Turning back, she looked at Gil. "Fair warning. It's probably best not to make conversation with me until after I've had a cup of coffee."

Gil smiled. "I completely understand."

And maybe he really did understand. He was one of the few people who knew she'd spent a night in jail.

"I was about to come looking for you two," Sheriff Ronnie said when they reached the car. "I told Gil you had five minutes, and it's been six."

Moira slid into the back seat beside Gil, keeping several inches of distance between them. "You never said anything about coming to our homes while we were still asleep."

"Or about handcuffs," Gil added, glad that the sheriff hadn't put those back on Gil's wrists upon entering the car. He was glad Moira didn't have to wear them either.

Ronnie offered a deep, rolling laugh. "I wish I was a fly on the wall to see how Denise is reacting right about now. Miles and I flipped a coin on who got to arrest her." He flicked his gaze in the rearview mirror and looked at Gil and Moira. "Arresting the town's mayor and our very own small-town hero is pretty fun too."

The ride to the sheriff's department was mainly filled with Sheriff Ronnie talking in between sips of his thermos of coffee. *Must be nice.*

Gil tapped Moira's hand on the seat between them. "You okay?" he half mouthed, half whispered.

She nodded. "I was kind of expecting to drive myself to this lock-in this morning."

"Me too. I'm hoping my friends and family pull through and bail me out pretty quickly."

They pulled into the sheriff's parking lot, and Ronnie parked the cruiser. "Let's go, you two. I'll get you some jailhouse coffee after I book you."

"Book us?" Gil said. "You can't be serious?"

"Mug shots and everything." Ronnie chuckled. "It's for charity, Mayor."

Two hours after Moira had entered the jail cell with Gil, Denise walked in with a full face of makeup and her hair washed and styled.

"Well, good morning, you two," she said, sipping from her cup of coffee from Sweetie's Bakery.

"How'd you get a coffee from Sweetie's?" Gil asked.

Denise smirked. "I insisted. And whenever I insist, I always get what I want."

Apparently, she'd insisted on showering and putting her look fully together first too.

Denise sat down on one of the chairs in the cell, making a show of trying to get comfortable. "Oh, this is just awful," she said with a distasteful expression. "This is one of the worst experiences of my life."

"You've only been here two minutes." Moira had given up on getting comfortable. She sat on the cot with her back against the cement block wall.

Denise shot her a look. "Deputy Bruno had his lights on when he came to get me. All of my neighbors saw me get into the front seat of his cruiser."

"Front seat?" Gil asked with a look of disbelief. "We had to take the back. And we didn't get showers or breakfast from Sweeties."

"Well, Mayor Gil, as I told you, I know how to get what I want," Denise said, casting him a pointed look. "That's why I'll make a great mayor for this town."

Moira glanced over at Gil, who seemed to stiffen. He was good at keeping his cool, but she thought she saw the muscles along his jaw slightly clenching.

"And I don't expect to be here too long before making my bail." Denise sipped her coffee. "What a horrible, horrible experience," she said again, shaking her head. Her hairspray helmet didn't move. "Being treated just like a criminal. Never in my life."

Moira massaged her forehead. She kind of hoped Denise did make bail sooner than later because she couldn't imagine staying trapped in a cell with this woman for an entire day. Or perhaps Moira's crowd would pull through and bail her out, leaving Gil to suffer Denise's company alone.

"Okay, my favorite inmates." Sheriff Ronnie stepped up to the other side of the bars. "We've got some media attention. Reva is here, and WTI-News is on their way over." He rubbed his hands together, looking practically giddy for the usually solemn-faced sheriff. "Make sure you look real sad and pitiful so that folks want to donate to your bail."

"That shouldn't be too hard," Denise whined.

"There's something we can agree on." Moira shared a glance with Gil, who was grinning. He almost seemed to be enjoying himself in this situation. Knowing him, he probably was.

"Hey, ya'll!" Reva walked into the room with her camera already raised to her face. "I just need a few pics for my blog. Smile pretty! I'm appealing to those who will be donating to your cause."

"How about all three of you stand right behind the bars and cling to them?" Sheriff Ronnie asked.

No one moved to strike his suggested pose. Reva took a dozen or more pictures, and then they all posed and smiled for WTI-News.

At noon, Sheriff Ronnie came back to see them, jingling a key in the air. "All right, one of you has already made bail." He looked between them, his gaze finally sticking on Denise. "It looks like your husband pulled through."

Denise huffed. "Well, he waited long enough," she said ungratefully. She stood and headed out of the jail cell without a backward glance.

Gil looked at Moira. "Looks like it's just you and me now."

Her heart skipped a beat as she looked at him and remembered the kiss they'd almost shared in her dream this morning. Being locked in a jail cell with Gil wasn't the most romantic of settings, and she really didn't want to be attracted to him, but here she was feeling flushed and all out of sorts. "It's kind of cheating if you post your own bail, isn't it?"

"Oh, it is, but I'm not a bit surprised. If Denise can cheat her way into the mayor's office, she will."

Moira looked down at her intertwined hands. "This is the strangest fundraiser I've ever been involved with." She looked up. "Is this the norm for a mayor's life?"

"No. Being a mayor is pretty boring most days. My brother wakes me up, we have breakfast, and then I handle paperwork and have meetings with people. I'm guessing your typical day is a whole lot more exciting than mine."

Moira laughed. "You're kidding, right? I'm a nine-one-one dispatcher for the town that has the least number of emergencies in the state."

Gil grinned. "I'm proud of that fact. Not that I can take credit."

"You take some. You're a good mayor, Gil. I know that and so does this town."

His gaze lingered. "We'll see come election. I have some steep competition this time. I'm talking more about you than Denise."

"Me?" Moira was surprised he'd consider her real competition. Some part of her felt like an imposter for even throwing her hat in the ring. Another part of her, however, really thought she could do this. She had ideas and thoughts, and she believed she could make a difference if she wanted to.

"Why not you? You never really know what you're capable of until you try. I don't want to give up my job, but I'm proud of you. That probably sounds strange, but I am."

Moira couldn't help grinning. "You're right. It does sound strange. But thank you."

He met her gaze and held it, and it felt like she was in that moment in her dream, on the boat, when he was looking deep into her eyes, seconds away from kissing her. "You're welcome, Moira."

Chapter Sixteen

Gil's stomach growled loudly. "Sorry about that."

Moira glanced up. She was sitting across the room from him, keeping her distance. Emotionally, she was hot and cold where he was concerned. She was frustrated and upset with him about wanting to displace Sweetie's. But at the same time, it was hard not to like Gil. "Do you think they'll feed us in this place?"

"I would say yes, but Sheriff Ronnie is enjoying our jail time way too much. Surely they feed the inmates though."

"It would be a crime not to," Moira agreed.

Sheriff Ronnie had been stopping by the cell on the half hour, updating them on their bail moneys. Gil was in the lead, halfway to making bail, which he felt a little guilty about. He didn't want Moira to have to spend the night in here alone.

"Hey, you two!" a cheerful voice said from outside the bars.

Gil looked up at Darla, who had two huge bags from Sweetie's in hand. "Please tell me one of those is for me," he teased.

"Of course it is." Darla winked. "I'm not going to leave my favorite daughter and favorite mayor in jail to starve." Her smile slid away. "Not saying my next vote is going to you, Mayor Gil." She looked at Moira nervously.

"It's okay, Mom. I get it." She gestured to Gil. "He's trying to put you out of business though. Why are you feeding him?"

Darla shook her head, her eyes rolling with amusement. "Don't mind her, Gil. She's protective. Always has been."

"Understandable," Gil said.

"I'm also right. And you have always been too forgiving and nice," Moira said.

Darla gave her daughter a wary look. "Mayor Gil is just doing his job. I know that. And, you know, maybe it's time for me to retire like your father."

Moira stood and walked over to where her mom was standing. "That's just silly talk. You still love what you do. You don't want to retire, Mom."

Gil watched the two interact. He'd always been fascinated by a mother-daughter relationship. It was so different from the way he and his own mother interacted. Moira wasn't afraid to speak her mind. He supposed that was one thing that would make her a good mayor. He always wanted to satisfy everyone involved, whereas Moira picked a stance and stood by it.

Darla handed a bag through the bars in Gil's direction. "Here you are, Mayor. I made your favorite."

He got up and walked over to her now. "Thank you, Darla. You're too kind."

"Yes, she is," Moira said pointedly.

Darla bounced a pointer finger between them. "You

two play nice, okay? You're alone and having a meal together." She shrugged. "If you ask me, that's kind of like a date."

Moira looked at Gil.

He couldn't help but chuckle. "It's the closest I've been to a date in a while," he agreed to Darla.

"No." Moira shook her head. "Don't even say that. Next thing you know, that'll be a headline on Reva's blog."

Darla laughed too. "Well, I think a first date in a jail cell is romantic."

"This is not a date." Moira took her bagged lunch over to the corner of her cot. "Thank you, Mom. Did you donate to my bail?"

Darla nodded. "Of course I did. Never thought I'd need to bail you out. You've always been so straitlaced."

Moira shared a look with Gil, confirming that not even Darla knew about Moira's night in jail. He doubted anyone knew about her date with Felix either, except maybe Tess, who was the closest of Moira's friends.

"I donated to yours, too, Mayor," Darla said, looking suddenly guilty.

Moira's mouth dropped open. "He's going to demolish your business and build a parking lot in its place."

Gil swallowed. Moira made him sound like a real-life criminal. "The building. Your mom's business can relocate. I'll personally help her find the perfect place to do so."

Moira shook her head. "You're right. We shouldn't talk about this topic."

"Especially not on your jail cell date," Darla said, making Moira roll her eyes. "Well, I've got to get back to Sweetie's. Good luck, you two!"

"Thanks, Darla. I appreciate it." Once Darla had gone,

Gil opened his bag and peered inside. "Mm. I love her grilled ham-and-cheese croissants."

"Enjoy it while you can. If you win the election, you'll never get another," Moira said.

Gil watched Moira open her own bag for a moment. "That three-car pileup the other day? It took emergency vehicles twenty minutes to get there because the road was clogged with cars and trucks that were parallel parked all the way down. Traffic stopped, and no one could get by. There was a five-year-old child in the back seat screaming because his mother was unconscious in the front. Things turned out okay, but it could have gone very differently. There was no one to respond to Doug. What if you hadn't acted? We need a parking lot, Moira."

Her shoulders seemed to round. "Isn't there another way though? Without tearing down what my mom has worked so hard to create?"

Gil wished he had a different answer to give her. "I've looked for one. If you know another solution, please tell me. I would do anything to make this right."

She lifted her chin subtly, looking equal parts stubborn and beautiful. "Well, when I'm mayor, I'll find a way."

At four thirty that afternoon, Ronnie stopped by to give another update on bail. "Looks like you're fleeing the coop," he said.

Both Moira and Gil looked up.

"Which one of us?" Gil asked.

Ronnie let the suspense hang in the air for several seconds before tipping his head at Gil. "You, Mayor Gil. You're free to go."

Some part of Gil wished it were Moira who was leaving. He couldn't just leave her here all by herself.

"Go on," Moira said, as if reading his mind. "I'll be fine." She forced a fleeting, fragile-looking smile in his direction. "Congratulations on making bail."

"Thanks." He hesitated for a long moment, not moving.

Sheriff Ronnie opened the jail cell door. "Better hurry before I change my mind," he threatened with a deep laugh.

Gil looked at Moira again.

"Go," she said a little more forcefully. "You made bail. You heard the sheriff. Escape while you can."

Gil reluctantly stood. "Okay. Well, it was nice spending the day in here with you."

She gave a stiff nod. "I'd say we should do this again, but I'd be lying."

"Right. Because you barely tolerate being in the same room with me."

"No, because this is jail. Being stuck with you wasn't so bad," Moira said. "Way better than being stuck with Denise."

That wouldn't normally feel like a compliment, but coming from her, it did. "Okay then. See you later, Moira."

"See you," she said in a quiet voice.

He left the jail and walked out, talking to Ronnie on the way. "How much more money does she need to raise to make bail?"

The sheriff grimaced. "About five hundred more dollars. She might be staying the night."

Gil lowered his voice. "Keep her here another hour or so and then let her go. I'll cover the remaining bail."

"You will?" Ronnie asked, thick brows lifting high on his forehead.

"Just don't tell her it was me, okay? Moira is stubborn. She won't accept it from me."

"Why are you springing her?" the sheriff asked.

Gil cleared his throat, looking for an answer that wouldn't make his real reasons obvious. "It's for charity, right?"

Sheriff Ronnie patted his back. "Exactly. I'll drive you home, Mayor."

Moira was lying on a cot, just about to drift off, when she was startled awake. That seemed to be a theme for the day.

"Your turn!" Sheriff Ronnie said.

"Hmm?"

"You've made bail. Lucky you, you don't have to sleep here tonight."

Moira sat up, her body stiff from the uncomfortable cot she'd spent most of the day on. "I did? Who posted?"

"Oh, you've had several supporters stop by and donate today. Your mom, your dad. Tess, Trisha, Lucy. All the usual suspects."

Moira knew they'd all been by earlier in the day though, and she hadn't been anywhere close to covering her bail after they'd donated. "Who else?"

Sheriff Ronnie avoided her gaze. "Why are you interrogating me? Do you want to stay overnight? Because I can arrange for that to happen, you know."

"No." Moira shook her head quickly and stood, her joints popping and protesting their lack of movement today. "I want to go home and shower."

"Good idea. Thank you for participating. The money raised today will really help spruce this place up."

"You're welcome."

"And it wasn't so bad, was it?" Sheriff Ronnie asked.

Moira narrowed her gaze. "It wasn't so great either. In addition to new cots, you need to invest in better coffee."

Ronnie laughed and patted her back as she walked alongside him. "Come on. I'll drive you home."

As soon as Moira arrived at her house, she sat on the edge of her bed and texted Gil.

> *Moira:* I know it was you who posted the rest of my bail.
> *Gil:* Are you out then?
> *Moira:* Home sweet home.
> *Gil:* Good to hear. Maybe we can do that again sometime.

He was joking, right? She tapped her thumb along her screen as she replied.

> *Moira:* Not a jail cell. Never again.
> *Gil:* What about my boat then? Monday night?
> *Moira:* For what?
> *Gil:* Well, I was thinking we might review the upcoming community events calendar. I know I'll be attending all the events. You should be at as many as possible too. To make this campaign fair.
> *Moira:* Helping the enemy?
> *Gil:* You're not my enemy.
> *Moira:* Is Denise going to be there as well?

Moira knew good and well Denise wouldn't be.

Gil: Denise can figure out the social events
          calendar herself. What do you say?

Moira nibbled at her lower lip. She knew that Gil always
had a thing for her. She also suspected his invitation was
more about his crush than the mayoral campaign. Would
spending a little time together under false pretenses really
be such a bad thing though? When she wasn't fuming
about the prospect of losing Sweetie's, she enjoyed Gil's
company.

Moira: Okay. I have to work dispatch Monday.
            Six o'clock?
Gil: Sounds good. See you then. To discuss
            the social events calendar.
Moira: Right. See you then.

Chapter Seventeen

On Monday morning, Moira stepped out of Sweetie's and headed to her car. She drove home and turned on the dispatch at nine a.m. As usual, there were no calls until about midday, when someone called to report a loose dog.

"Is it behaving aggressively?" Moira asked.

"Oh, no. It's a sweet little darling. I'm feeding her some baked chicken from last night's dinner."

Moira sighed. "So the stray is friendly?"

"Yes, of course it is."

Which didn't make for an emergency. Even so, Moira contacted animal control, which would likely see the dog and know exactly whom it belonged to. Somerset was a small town after all. The rest of the day, Moira worked on her website as Tess had suggested, creating one on a free platform.

She didn't exactly have a professional photograph of herself, so she put up one that her mom had taken of her accepting her Hero Among Us award the weekend before last. The award was a notch in her belt along with years of public service. By the time she'd completed her home page, Moira was impressed with herself. On paper, she actually did seem like a great candidate. This was getting real. She was doing this.

The dispatch lit up with another call.

Moira connected the line. "Nine-one-one, what's your emergency?"

"Yes, hi." The caller's voice was quiet, hesitating between breaths. "Um, I'd like to report a possible crime. I mean, maybe."

"Okay. What's going on?" Moira asked, sensing that the caller was nervous.

"Well, um, I had a date with a guy last night. Um, I'm not really sure what happened."

All the hairs on Moira's arms stood up. "Tell me what you are sure of."

"I just know I woke up this morning in my own bed. I feel like I'm hungover, but I didn't drink last night. I mean, I don't remember drinking. I don't remember much, actually."

Moira's stomach clenched painfully. "Are you safe right now? Is your date still there with you?"

"No, he's gone. I don't remember him leaving though. I don't even remember him taking me home. I didn't meet him here. I met him at a restaurant in Magnolia Falls." The woman sniffled, and Moira wondered if she was crying.

"What's your name?" Moira asked.

The caller hesitated. "You know what, this is a mistake. This isn't an emergency. I'm sorry, I shouldn't have called."

"No, wait. Please don't hang up. You need to file a report," Moira urged. "Let me send an officer to your address."

"No, that's okay. I don't even know if anything happened. I'm probably just being paranoid."

"But what if you aren't? You should go to the emergency room. They can do an evaluation and test you for any drugs in your system. Don't let this go, okay? You might regret it if you do."

"Or I'll be embarrassed and regret bringing this up to anyone at all," the caller said. "I mean, he was a nice guy."

Moira took a shallow breath. This was all hitting way too close for comfort. "A nice guy who took you to dinner and drove you home, leaving you feeling drunk and unclear of what happened."

"I've got to go. Sorry to bother you."

"Wait!" The line went dead. Moira had an address for the phone number, but the woman had changed her mind about asking for help. Moira couldn't send anyone to her house when she wasn't in immediate danger. She also couldn't make the woman get checked out by a medical professional.

Moira's insides twisted and tied themselves in knots. She felt helpless and devastated on the woman's behalf because the reality was that it was likely that her date had drugged her, and he'd likely gotten a lot further than Felix had with Moira.

Moira's eyes burned. She swallowed hard, willing the woman to call back but knowing she wouldn't. Moira stared at the phone number on the screen. The caller ID read AR RANCH. Perhaps the caller's last name was Ranch? On impulse and against her better judgment, she grabbed her cell phone and tapped the number into her contacts. She wasn't sure what she planned to do with that number, but keeping it felt like she was doing something versus the alternative of just forgetting the call had even happened.

Moira didn't budge from her spot behind her desk until her shift ended at five p.m. Then she got up and walked to the kitchen, preparing herself a glass of water. Her hands were shaking, and her heart was beating fast as memories of the night with Felix played in her mind.

It had been a good night, the parts she could remember at least. She was really enjoying getting to know Felix. He was funny, and she kept laughing because everything he said was so witty. Felix was also attractive. He and Moira had shared a lot of the same interests, and she was already considering a second date with him. That's how well they'd hit it off.

They'd had dinner and she'd had one beer—that's all. After she had taken just a sip, Felix had pointed out that Moira had something on her cheek. He'd leaned in and tried to swipe it off, but said he couldn't get it. That's when Moira had excused herself to go to the ladies' room. She didn't want to have a smudge on her cheek through an entire date. When she'd gotten to the restroom, though, she'd inspected her face closely and hadn't found anything. No smudge, no speck of dirt, nothing. She'd figured that Felix had taken care of it or the smudge he'd thought he'd seen was really just a shadow. Then she'd returned to the table where Felix was sitting, and they'd continued laughing about anything and everything.

That was all she remembered until she'd woken to Gil in her home. Whether he'd known what was happening or not, some part of Gil had questioned Felix's intentions that night. He'd listened to his gut and had stepped in. Where was her gut when she'd been enjoying herself with Felix during their date?

It'd taken her a while to figure out that Felix had slipped something into her drink when she'd gone to the bathroom. It was the only explanation. She'd gone to the Magnolia Falls police, who'd told her there was nothing they could do without clear evidence that a crime had been committed. She'd left the station completely devastated. That's when she'd taken matters into her own hands, which was rash and thoughtless, and why she always made her decisions carefully these days.

Even though Gil was her hero, her guard had been up around him ever since. He'd gotten her arrested after all. He was the one who'd brought Felix to town in the first place. She'd assumed he'd known, on some level, what kind of person Felix truly was.

Moira looked at the clock on her wall. She was supposed to meet Gil at his place for a boat ride tonight. After the 911 call she'd just answered, she didn't feel up to it now. She was worried about the woman caller. Moira had her phone number. She could call. She had her address. She could drive over there and try to convince the woman to change her mind. That would definitely break the rules and possibly get her fired though. Speaking up was a decision that a woman had to make for herself. Moira had made that decision on her own—not that it had helped in her case. It was her choice. And tonight, her choice was to stay home instead of meeting Gil on his dock.

Moira wasn't answering her phone.

Gil stared at his screen, willing her to return his five missed calls. She was supposed to meet him here on the dock thirty minutes ago. He looked at Goldie, who appeared desperate to go for a ride. "Not tonight, girl," he said, petting her head. "I need to go check on a friend."

Something had happened since he'd last seen Moira. But what?

He grabbed his keys as he headed out to his truck and then drove the short distance to her place. The windows were mostly dark, but there was one prick of light coming from the living room window. Maybe she'd forgotten about meeting him. They'd made the plan on Saturday evening after the jail lock-in. It was possible she was so exhausted after that whole day that she'd forgotten the plans they'd made.

He got out of the truck, headed up the walkway, and knocked on the door. When she didn't immediately answer, he began to shift back and forth on his feet. Maybe she was hurt. Did he need to call someone? He knocked again. This time he heard a shuffle of movement inside. A moment later, Moira opened the door and looked at him.

She pressed her lips together. "I'm sorry. I should have called," she said in a quiet voice. She swiped a lock of dark hair away from her eyes. "I thought you'd just go on the boat ride without me."

"No way. I needed to make sure you were okay." He narrowed his eyes, scanning over her. "Are you?" he asked. She didn't look okay. Her gaze was downcast, and her skin was pale. It was barely seven o'clock, and she was wearing sweatpants and had her hair pulled back in a messy ponytail. She didn't look like she was preparing to go out tonight at all.

She seemed to hesitate, and he instinctively knew she was trying to decide whether to be honest or shrug away whatever was going on. "Not really," she finally said.

Gil exhaled softly. "I'm a good listener, you know."

She shook her head. "I'm not sure I want to talk about this. I thought I wanted to be alone, but now that you're here…"

"Want me to come in?" he asked, hoping she'd agree. Not so much for himself, but because she looked like she needed the company. There was something vulnerable and lonely in her gaze.

She stared at him a long moment, rolling her lower lip between her teeth as she seemed to think on her answer. "I'm making dinner. Are you hungry?"

"Starving, actually."

She opened the door wider and gestured him in. When she'd invited him inside on Saturday morning before the lock-in, Gil had been half-asleep. He hadn't taken the time to look around her house. It was a small yet cozy space with modern furniture and homey items like soft throw blankets and shelves of books. There were framed pictures on Moira's mantel that Gil longed to walk over to and look at. His focus needed to stay on Moira though.

He turned to her. "Need help with dinner?"

She shrugged. "I wasn't prepared to make anything extraordinary. I hope you don't mind. It's just chicken noodle soup from a can." She cringed.

Gil chuckled softly. "That sounds good to me."

"Great. I'll grab the bowls, and we can sit at the kitchen counter. My dining room table has become my makeshift campaign center right now." She laughed quietly, but Gil didn't hear any trace of humor in the sound. She was obviously upset about something, but he didn't think it had anything to do with him for once.

"Hmm. Maybe I should sneak a glance over there and see what my rival is up to," he teased.

"Maybe you shouldn't," she warned, giving him a half smile.

A couple of minutes later, she served the bowls of soup and sat down beside him under the low lighting of the kitchen.

"Okay, I'll talk about it," she finally said after another minute of quiet. She hadn't even had a spoonful of her dinner yet. "I had a caller earlier in the day." Moira stared down into her bowl, stirring around absently. "The caller went on a date last night. She met the guy in Magnolia Falls. She doesn't remember getting home, and she felt hungover when she awoke this morning." Moira's voice cracked. Finally, she spooned some soup into her mouth.

"Wow," Gil said. "Did you send her to a medical facility to get checked out?"

"I tried, but she started second-guessing herself. She shied away from my advice and disconnected the call."

Gil waited for Moira to say more. When she didn't, he figured that was the end of the story. "I bet it's tough not knowing what happens with some of the people on the other line, huh?"

She looked at him. "The thing is, I kind of know what happens with this caller. Or I can guess. She'll question what went on in the space she can't remember. It's hard not knowing what happened to your own body. Not being able to fill in the blanks. I'm guessing she didn't have a Gil Ryan to come to her rescue." She offered another small smile in his direction.

"Hopefully, she decided to take your advice once she disconnected the call. You might have gotten through to her."

"Maybe." Moira visibly swallowed. "Some days the dispatch is so boring that I literally finish an entire book and start another. Other days, it rips my heart out a little piece at a time."

Gil reached for her hand and squeezed, leaving his palm covering hers. Her eyes subtly widened. They were green and brown, the most perfect hazel he'd ever seen. He searched them, drinking in the feeling of staring deeply into this woman's eyes. She'd avoided him for so long that this hadn't happened in nearly a decade. He'd missed the color of her eyes. Missed being up close enough to study the freckles dusting the bridge of her nose and cheeks. Did she even realize how beautiful she was?

"You're staring at me," she whispered.

He was scared to blink for fear she'd look away. "You're staring back at me."

She searched his eyes. "I always wondered. Why were you there that night?"

"Hmm?"

"I was on a date with Felix at the restaurant. You must have been there if you noticed that I was intoxicated. Why were you there?"

Gil finally blinked and looked away. He reached for his glass of water and took a sip, wondering how honest he wanted to be. "I was jealous. Felix asked you out, and you said yes. I was kicking myself for being too chicken to ask you out when I'd been wanting to for months. But Felix just marched in and seemed to sweep you off your feet. I guess I was there to make myself even more miserable than I already was."

Moira's expression revealed nothing if she was surprised. "Why didn't you ask me out?"

"Because I thought you'd say no." Gil glanced over, and his gaze unwittingly dropped to her mouth. What would it be like to kiss Moira? When his gaze returned to her eyes, she was looking at his lips as well. Was she thinking about kissing him too?

"What are we doing, Gil?" she finally asked in a small voice.

"Having dinner. That's all. Unless you want more." He was being bolder than he'd been with her before. He could feel her letting him in closer than she ever had though.

"It's a bad idea."

"Not from where I'm sitting," he said quietly, leaning in almost against his will. Was she leaning too?

Her eyes fluttered up to meet his as her lips came closer. There was something vulnerable there in her gaze. He also thought he saw a quiet longing. As he wondered, she closed the distance, and her lips touched his. He felt like his heart might burst right through his chest while his mind fed it instructions: *Don't move too fast. Don't move too slow. Don't do anything to ruin this moment.*

A kiss was just a kiss, but *this* was not just a kiss. Not with Gil. Moira knew he'd liked her for ages. Kissing him was leading him on, wasn't it? The moment felt too good to end it though. His lips were warm against hers. His hand was gentle as it hugged her waist, anchoring her to the stool and to this moment.

A soft moan tumbled out of her. She pulled back and stared at him.

"Wow," he finally said.

"Yeah, wow." There really wasn't anything more to say. "I'm still running against you."

He let out a surprised laugh. "I wouldn't expect anything different."

"So what do we do about what just happened? Forget it?" Moira asked.

"Not possible." He shook his head and straightened on his stool. "I can't forget that kiss, and I don't want to. Is there a law that says two people who are attracted to one another can't date and also run against each other for the same office?"

"Date?" she asked. Equal parts of her were thrilled that he would suggest the D-word and appalled at the same time.

"What would you call what we're doing right now?"

"Chicken soup between friends."

Gil tilted his head, one side of his very kissable mouth quirking at one corner. "Not once you add in kissing. Kissing over a romantic dinner is a date in my opinion."

Moira's heart beat fast in her chest. "Canned soup is romantic?"

"It is when it's with you."

She paused as she tried to decide what to do. One wrong move could ruin everything. She liked being able to spend time in the same room with Gil now without feeling the need to flee. She liked being able to face him, look him in the eye, and not have invisible twelve-inch-thick walls go up. She liked the idea of dating, even though for years she'd been protesting that she didn't need to date to be happy.

Dating wouldn't make her happy, it was true. Dating had never been all that enjoyable for her. It was awkward, and whenever she had sparks, her date didn't, and vice versa. But dating Gil might be different. He was nice, sweet, handsome. He was smart, and his heart was bigger than the charming lake that sat in the middle of this town of theirs. He was a keeper kind of guy, but she didn't think she was a keeper kind of girl. Therefore, kissing Gil would be leading him on.

Moira turned back toward her bowl, picked up her spoon, and dipped it into the quickly cooling soup.

From her peripheral vision, she saw Gil do the same. "So, this Friday then?" he asked as their soup began to dwindle in their bowls.

She turned to him again. "We're both running for mayor. Everyone will be talking if they see us together on a date."

Gil turned to her as well. "Here's the thing. People are going to be talking about us whether we go on a date or not. They'll just have to work harder to find something to say. I've found that giving the public something to talk about controls the narrative."

She looked for an excuse to say no as hard as she did a reason to say yes. Everything inside her was at war right now. "Okay," she finally said.

"Okay?" He looked surprised, as if he was certain she was going to shoot him down. Then a smile lifted at the corners of his mouth. "Okay." He nodded. "I'll pick you up at six thirty?"

"Sounds good. One condition," she said. "We can't discuss the campaign."

"Agreed. Or the bakery," he added.

Moira hesitantly nodded. "That narrows things down, doesn't it?"

"We'll figure it out." He offered his hand for her to shake.

Moira's heart fluttered as her skin slipped against his. Then Gil leaned in and kissed her cheek, holding her gaze as he pulled away. For a moment, she had a hard time taking in a full breath.

"Thank you for dinner. It was delicious," he said.

"You're welcome."

"See you Friday night, Moira." He stood from his stool and pushed it in under the counter.

"See you then." She watched him walk out her front door and close it behind him. Then she touched her fingers to her cheek. Had that really just happened?

Chapter Eighteen

True You was the one and only women's clothing boutique in Somerset Lake. Fortunately, it had a wide variety of stylish things to meet most women's needs.

Tess held up a cream-colored pantsuit. "What about this?"

Moira tilted her head. "It's a little formal, isn't it?"

"You're running for mayor," Tess stressed. "You're going to be doing interviews and participating in community events. You can't wear jeans and a T-shirt all the time."

Moira still hadn't told her friends about tomorrow's date with Gil. They were going to freak out. In a good way, she suspected, but still it would catch them off guard. "I just think I need something nicer than jeans and a T-shirt, but more casual than a pantsuit for *some* occasions."

"What occasions?" Lucy could always home in on something off in a conversation. "A pantsuit would work for anything. I think it's a good choice."

"Okay, I'll try it out. But what if I wanted to go, I don't know, like on a date?" Moira asked, trying to sound hypothetical.

"A date?" Trisha asked, sitting in a chair along the wall. Every time Moira saw her, Trisha's belly had grown. The baby wasn't due until this fall. At this rate, it was going to be a long, hot summer for Trisha.

Moira looked around at all her friends' faces, which seemed to be beaming.

"With whom?" Trisha asked. "You met a guy?"

Moira was starting to wish they'd just stuck with book club tonight instead of a shopping trip where all the focus was on her. "I didn't say that."

"You said *date*. The Moira I know doesn't prepare for hypothetical dates," Tess said.

Moira shrugged. "Okay, maybe I'm going on a date tomorrow night at six thirty." Her cheeks burned as she avoided her friends' gazes. "And if that were the case, what would I wear to a nice dinner with a nice guy?"

"Nice guy?" Tess asked as her brows drew impossibly higher on her forehead.

Moira swallowed, and looked at her friend.

Tess and Lucy shared a knowing look as both of their mouths curled into huge grins.

"Whoa. What's that look?" Moira asked, looking between them.

"You're going on a date with Gil?" Lucy practically shouted.

"What?" Trisha said, jaw dropping.

Moira wanted to hide in the racks of clothing nearby. "Who said anything about Gil?"

Lucy pointed a finger at her. "You did. You said *nice guy*. We all know that Gil is the poster boy for nice guys."

"So?" Tess prodded. "Are we right?"

Moira shook her head as her gaze bounced among

her friends. She couldn't lie to them even if she tried. Knowing this group of women, they'd be camped out on her doorstep at six thirty tomorrow just to find out who her mystery date was. "It's just dinner, okay?"

Lucy squealed and cupped a hand to her mouth.

"I am so happy for you, Moira," Tess said. "And you're right. A pantsuit will not do for this monumental occasion. We've been waiting for you to go on a date with Gil for years. This needs to be special."

"It's just dinner," Moira said again, her voice growing weaker.

Lucy pointed at a chair against the wall. "Sit there. We will find all the clothes and bring them to you," she ordered.

Moira plopped down in the cushy chair and watched as her friends went on a mission to make her over. Truth be told, she needed a makeover. She was stuck in a nondating rut, wearing the same holey jeans and fitted T-shirts much too often. She wasn't sure why tomorrow's date with Gil was special, but she had to agree with her friends. It did feel monumental in a way. Like she'd finally dropped this huge resistance and a tsunami was heading in her direction to slam over her routine and transform it into something new. Something that excited her in the same way that running for mayor did.

As she waited, she pulled out her cell phone and stared at it blankly. She'd been thinking off and on all day about the caller on her dispatch. She'd even gone so far as to pull up the number that she'd saved in her phone and let her finger hover over it. What would she say though? Whatever the woman had decided was none of Moira's business. She could even get disciplined or worse if she reached out to the woman.

"Here." Trisha held up a pair of dusty-rose-colored capri pants and a black sleeveless blouse.

Moira dropped her phone back into her bag and looked up.

"It's feminine but also simple and no fuss. It's very you. My best friend in Sweetwater Springs owns a boutique there. I learned everything I know about fashion from her. This outfit suits you."

Lucy stepped up to Trisha with a dress in her hand. She lowered it when she saw what Trisha was holding. "Yeah. That's it. That's perfect for Moira's date."

Moira studied the selection for a moment more. "I love it, actually." Her gaze lifted. "Okay, what shoes do I wear?"

By the time Moira left True You with her friends, she had four pairs of capri pants, five blouses, a pantsuit, and three different pairs of sandals.

"My debit card needs a rest for the next six months," she said in Tess's car on the way home.

"You rarely buy yourself anything." Trisha narrowed her gaze at Moira in the back seat. "There's no reason to feel guilty."

"Plus, these are work clothes," Lucy said. "If you're going to be mayor, you need to dress the part."

"Am I going to be mayor though? Can I really beat Gil?"

Trisha nudged Moira with her elbow. "Just because you're dating him doesn't mean we're going to go easy on this election. We believe in you. Yes, you can be mayor if that's truly what you want."

Moira nodded. "At first it was just about my mom's

bakery. I wanted to fight. Now I want more than that. I want to change things. I want to do things."

Lucy spun around from the front seat and winked at her. "Well, in that cream suit, you're going to convince anybody of anything you want."

Tess dropped off Trisha first, and then Lucy. Moira was grateful when Tess pulled into her driveway.

"Thanks for the ride and the shopping trip. It was great," Moira said, unbuckling her seat belt. She had moved to the front seat after Trisha and Lucy had been dropped off.

"Of course. You okay?" Tess asked, glancing over and peering at her. "I know you have a lot on your plate right now."

Tess really had no idea how true that statement was. "I'm fine. Thanks again." Moira pushed her car door open and stepped out. She retrieved her bags from the back seat and then waved at Tess on her way to her front door.

The biggest thing she had on her mind wasn't the campaign or even her date. It was the caller, and her will-power was wearing thinner every time her mind retraced the interaction. She closed her front door behind her and dropped her bags on the couch. Then she pulled out her cell phone, took a breath, and gave in to her need to dial the caller's number. Just to see if the woman was all right.

Moira's heart pounded as she listened to the dial tone. She was beginning to think no one would pick up. Then a woman's voice answered.

"Animal Rescue Ranch. This is Beth."

Moira froze. She wasn't actually planning to talk to this person. At least she didn't think she was. She'd just wanted to hear the woman's voice and make a judgment on her well-being based on the tone. She hadn't expected to get a name or a place of business.

Animal Rescue Ranch?

"Hello?" the woman, Beth, said.

"Um, yes. Hi." Moira had no idea what she was doing right now.

"Are you, um, looking for a pet?" Beth asked.

Moira's palms were sweating. "No. I mean, maybe."

"Do you have a reason for calling?"

Moira chewed her lower lip. Not a reason that she could give this woman. Not without putting her job in jeopardy. "Maybe a dog. My grandmother used to have a King Charles something."

"Cavalier King Charles spaniel," Beth supplied, her voice level and confident. "I love that breed."

"Oh," Moira said, feeling a flutter of excitement, even though she wasn't really in the market for a dog anyway. This call was completely about checking up on the woman who'd called in distress the other day.

"We don't get many Cavaliers in. I can put you on a list and call you if we get one though."

Moira didn't think that was a good idea, just in case Beth realized Moira worked at the dispatch and made the connection to why she was calling. Which she should not be doing. "I, uh, I'll call back another time," Moira said quickly. "Take care of yourself."

"Oh. Okay," Beth said. "Um, you too."

Moira disconnected the call and blew out a breath, shaking from head to toe. Beth had sounded okay. She was breathing at least. Maybe knowing that much would take Moira's mind off the situation. At least she hoped so.

∞

For the last forty-eight hours, some part of Gil had been waiting for Moira to cancel their date. He felt like he was walking a tightrope and couldn't allow his hopes to get up too high. He had liked this woman for what seemed like forever. And she'd been shying away from him for that same amount of time.

He pulled into her driveway, cut the engine, and checked his cell phone one last time to see if she'd canceled. She hadn't. This was really happening. He grabbed the bouquet of flowers he'd purchased at Somerset Florist, feeling only a little bit silly for buying them. He somehow suspected Moira hadn't been given flowers too often in her life. In Gil's opinion, every woman deserved flowers. He picked his mom up a bouquet several times a year just because.

The bouquet he'd gotten Moira was an arrangement of wildflowers, which he thought suited her best. They were simple, yet beautiful, and they represented a mountainous countryside in nature. Gil headed up the porch steps and rang the doorbell, still halfway expecting Moira to shoot him down once she answered. Instead, when she opened the door, she was dressed in a pair of soft-looking cropped pants and a sleeveless black top that shimmered in the dwindling sunlight. Her hair was down in loose curls that bounced near her shoulders as she smiled back at him.

Gil grinned foolishly as he looked at her, relieved that she wasn't backing out of their plans. He was also suddenly nervous that he'd screw this night up in a hot second and she'd slam the door on him.

"Are those for me?" She gestured toward the bouquet of flowers he was nervously crushing with his hands.

He held them out to her. "Oh, yeah, as a matter of fact, they are. I hope you don't mind."

"That you brought me flowers? Why would I mind?" She didn't wait for him to answer. Instead, she gestured him inside. "I'll just put these in water. Thank you. It's been a long time since anyone has given me flowers."

"Oh?" Gil asked. "Anyone I know?"

Moira glanced over her shoulder. "Benny Myer."

Gil stopped walking and watched as she reached for a vase in her cabinet. "Benny Myer? You two dated?"

Moira held up a finger. "One date. We only went out once."

"That good, huh?"

Moira seemed to be in a good mood tonight. She looked relaxed, and she was laughing easily. That boded well for their evening. She arranged the flowers in the vase, taking her time to spread them around evenly. Then she admired them for a long moment. "They're beautiful." She looked at up him. "Thank you."

"You already thanked me. Are you going to tell me this Benny story over dinner tonight?"

Moira walked around the counter and headed back in his direction. "Benny talked about the resale value of my car for half of dinner and offered to take me to his used car lot in Magnolia Falls to do a trade-in afterward."

Gil opened the front door for her. They stepped out onto the porch, and Moira turned back to lock up behind them. "If memory serves me, you've been driving that same car for a long time now."

She nodded. "I turned down Benny's offer and politely declined another date."

They walked to Gil's truck.

"I'm going to open your door for you because, in my mind, this is what a date does."

Moira gave him a strange look.

He held up his hands. "I just don't want you to think

I'm being old-fashioned or a brute somehow. I know that you are perfectly capable of opening your own door."

"I'm not looking for a reason to end this date, Gil," she said as he opened the door. She stepped past him and got inside. "I'm glad this date is happening. I'm excited about it, actually."

He looked at her. "Yeah? Me too." After closing the door, he took his time walking around to the driver's side, breathing deeply and willing his heart to slow down. He'd known Moira for his entire life. They were friends until they weren't quite friends. Now they were friends again, even though they were also rivals. It was complicated, but also simple. This was Moira, and more than anything, he wanted to spend the evening with her.

He got in his truck, reversed out of the driveway, and headed down the road.

"Where are we going?" she finally asked.

Gil glanced over. "I guess it would be nice if I told you, huh?"

"I wasn't sure if it was supposed to be a surprise."

He shook his head. "Not at all. I'm taking you to my place."

When Moira didn't immediately respond, he glanced over. Her face was suddenly pale, and her lips parted.

"That came out wrong. Let me rephrase. I've cooked you dinner and prepared us a table outside by the lake. It's waterfront dining without the nosy onlookers." He dared another glance at Moira, who seemed to have relaxed again. "I figured I could come off cheap or romantic. One or the other."

"Romantic," she said decidedly.

∞

Moira wasn't sure if she'd ever had a more romantic evening. The moon was full, the stars were out, and the air was crisp against her skin. Gil had tried to light a candle at the center of the table, but the wind kept blowing it out. They had wine. Moira had shied away from having alcohol on dates since Felix. She trusted Gil though. The lake also added to the ambiance of the evening.

"I had no idea you could cook like this." Moira scooped another bite of her eggplant Parmesan.

Gil shrugged. "I live alone. I cook all my own meals by necessity."

She tilted her head. "You live next door to your parents. I kind of imagined that you went to their house every evening for dinner."

Gil laughed. "No. I value my independence. Doug values his independence as well. When he wants to get away from Mom and Dad, all he has to do is cross the lawn and come here. Which he often does."

"You are a great brother," Moira said with a growing smile.

Gil reached for his wineglass and took a sip. "So is Doug. He's the one who first suggested I become mayor, you know. He was reading a sign that said *Bryce Malsop for Mayor*, and he replaced the name with mine. *Gilly for Mayor*. That's what he calls me. He was joking, of course, but it resonated so deeply that I just knew. It was like a lightbulb went off in my head, and I thought, *Yeah, that's what I want to do with my life*."

Moira looked down at her plate, feeling a tiny pang of guilt. She was going after a title that belonged to Gil. He was passionate about what he did, and he was good at it. She moved her fork around her plate, chewing on her thoughts momentarily.

"What's on your mind?" Gil asked, picking up his own fork.

She looked up. "I know it's not your fault that my mom's bakery is on the chopping block. I also know that you have a lot of pull in this town. You could change the council's mind. You could find an alternate location. You could do more than you are."

Gil rolled some noodles around his fork as he listened.

"Sorry. I know this isn't date-worthy conversation."

"If it's weighing on your mind, it is." His lips set in a small frown. "Moira, you should talk to your mom about this."

"My mom? Why?"

He shrugged. "I don't know. She mentioned retiring when we were in the jail. I believe everything happens for a reason. If the new parking lot does go in the place of Sweetie's, maybe it's a good thing for your mom too. Maybe retiring right now isn't so far-fetched."

Moira stiffened. "Nonsense. She's only fifty-five, Gil. And no one wants to see their life's work demolished."

"Is that why you're running for mayor? Because of the bakery and the parking lot?"

Moira hesitated. "Maybe that was my reason at first. Now it's about something more though. I don't know." She searched for the right words to describe this raw excitement accumulating inside her. "I feel like a lightbulb kind of went off in my head too. I want to make a difference. I want to be a vehicle for change."

"But you do make a difference. You save lives," Gil said gently.

Moira shook her head. "No. I take calls for the people who do the lifesaving."

"Doug thinks differently."

"Well, I left my post, risked getting fired, and crawled

through a doggie door to give him an ice pack and a glass of juice. That's not exactly heroic behavior."

"It is in my opinion." Gil smiled sweetly at her. "And the rest of the town agrees. That's why you were given the Hero Among Us award."

Moira reached for her glass of wine and took a sip. "We said no discussion about the campaign tonight, and that's one of the first topics I brought up. Sorry." She mimed zipping her lips. "I'm done discussing it. I promise."

They stared at each other for a moment.

"Maybe that leaves nothing else to discuss," Moira finally mused.

Gil shook his head. "There's plenty to talk about." He cleared his throat. "Speaking of Doug, he's been talking about moving out of my parents' house and into his own place."

Moira found this topic interesting. "Wow. Good for him."

Gil watched her. "You think so?"

"Yeah. Why wouldn't I?"

Gil shrugged. "It's just, my mom wants me to talk him out of this idea. She doesn't like it. But Doug wants me to talk her into it. I feel a little torn, I guess."

"Doug is fully capable of living alone, right?" Moira hesitated before expanding on that. "I mean, I know he has Down syndrome, and you said he was recently diagnosed with diabetes. That's a lot. Would it be safe for him?"

Gil leaned back in his chair. "My brother takes care of himself. When he was injured the other day, he called emergency services. That's exactly what I would have done in the situation. I just don't know why he would want to move out of Mom and Dad's. It's a pretty nice setup if you ask me."

Moira tilted her head and smiled. "Oh, come on. Why did you move out of your parents' home?"

"Because it was time. I wanted to be my own person."

"Exactly," Moira said. "I think it's great. I'm sure Della can help Doug find the perfect spot."

Gil nodded slowly. "So I should go against my mom on her request to talk Doug out of this?"

"Moms are hardwired differently than big brothers. Moms are overprotective by nature." Moira shook her head. "I'm an only child so maybe I don't know what I'm talking about, but big brothers are there to lead the way. They do everything first and then help the younger sibling follow suit."

The way Gil was watching her made her look away. "I'm glad I talked to you about this. You're a good listener," he said.

Moira reached for a slice of French bread from the center of the table. "I guess that's why I work dispatch." There were some people she couldn't help, however. Like Beth.

After dinner, Gil pushed his plate aside and tipped his head toward the lake. "Want to take a moonlit stroll?"

Moira grinned at him. "Flowers and a moonlight stroll? Wow. You really know how to make a woman feel special."

"I hope so." Gil pushed back from the table and offered his hand. She placed her hand inside his, noting the way her insides lit up like a strand of fairy lights at midnight.

While they walked side by side, Moira was very aware of how close they were standing. Once upon a time, she'd done everything in her power not to be in the same room with Gil. She'd convinced herself she hated him. Yet here she was tonight walking beside him.

"You're shivering. Are you cold?" Gil asked.

"Oh." She laughed quietly. "I didn't even realize. The breeze off the lake is kind of chilly, isn't it?"

"Sometimes." He stopped walking and turned to face her, stepping close and blocking the wind. "Is that better?"

"Mm." She looked up into his eyes, heart racing toward her throat. They'd kissed the other night, so it felt inevitable that, on their first date, they'd kiss again.

Gil placed his hands on her arms and ran them over her skin to warm her. "I wish I'd brought a lightweight jacket for you."

"It's okay. I'm feeling pretty warm right now."

His eyes seemed to sparkle. "Good." The way he was looking at her told her he was thinking about the other night too.

"I'm glad you planned something private for us this evening. We don't have to worry about Reva taking photographs of us kissing for her blog." Moira's cheeks burned as soon as the thought came out of her mouth.

"So, we will be kissing?" Gil asked with a growing smile.

"I was thinking we might," she said, suddenly feeling dizzy with anticipation and nerves.

Gil leaned closer to her. Her heart dropped into her belly. Then, unable to wait for him to reach her, she crossed the distance and brushed her lips to his. Her body immediately melted into the kiss, and all her senses awakened. Every smell, sound, touch. His hands were still anchored on her arms, tugging her gently into the kiss and grounding her. His mouth was warm and relaxed, just like the kiss itself. Moira wasn't sure she'd ever had a kiss quite so perfect, and she didn't want it to end.

By the time Moira had gotten home, she and Gil had kissed twice more. The second time was at her front door before she'd let herself inside and bid him good night. He hadn't suggested coming in or even looked beyond her door and into her home. He was ever the gentleman, even though her thoughts may have run slightly amok.

She wanted to take things slowly where Gil was concerned. The upcoming fall election was a huge hurdle that would eventually come between them. Right? Or maybe it wouldn't. They were both adults. Perhaps they could let the cards fall where they may and still be friends, or more, at the end of all this.

Or maybe she was getting too far ahead of herself and should just go to bed. She changed into a pair of pajamas and slipped under her covers. Then she reached for the switch on her bedside lamp and twisted it, and the room fell dark aside from the sliver of starlight cast through her blinds.

She and Gil had enjoyed being under those very romantic stars. Staring up at the ceiling, her mind replayed the hours before.

For a long time after Felix had drugged her, she'd retraced every detail of their date, looking for the warning signs that she should have caught. There were none. Not that she could see at least. That whole experience had made her distrustful of every instinct she had. She was in a better place now. She trusted herself to find the people worthy of her time and attention and not to allow some-one into her life who was going to hurt her. Gil wasn't going to hurt her. Not intentionally at least.

Moira rolled onto her side, her mind firmly rooted in thoughts of Gil. Somewhere along the way, she drifted off into a dreamless slumber only to be startled at two a.m. by a loud bang on her door.

Moira sat up in bed, suddenly wide awake. The noise had been loud, and it had definitely been at her door. Was someone trying to break in? Right about now, Moira wished she had a good guard dog, or at least a dog with a ferocious bark to deter any intruder.

Climbing out of bed, she grabbed a metal baseball bat that she kept in her closet, and flipped on all the lights as she walked into the front room, clutching it as a weapon. She wasn't just involved in student government in high school, she'd also played softball and had a good swing, if she did say so. She shakily stepped up to her front door and looked out the peephole, eying her empty porch, her driveway, and the road. No one was there.

She lowered her bat but didn't budge for a long time, as if whoever had banged on her door would come out of hiding. Finally, she stepped away from the door and headed into the kitchen to make a pot of coffee. There was no way she was going back to sleep tonight. Her heart rate was elevated, and her mind was whirring with possibilities, a result of too many true-crime books and TV shows. Instead, she was going to stand guard, just in case, and pay the price tomorrow when she would undoubtedly have a hard time keeping her eyes open.

Chapter Nineteen

Gil awoke to a sound at his front door. He groaned, and rolled to free his face from where it was smooshed into his pillow. One guess who was visiting at this hour.

He read the digital clock on his nightstand to see what time it actually was: 6:04 a.m. Aside from another arrest from Sheriff Ronnie—which he was not up for—the only person who would be ringing his doorbell right now was Doug. He considered ignoring the bell, but the last time he'd done that, Doug had gotten his hideaway key, let himself in, and walked straight back to Gil's bedroom anyway. Sometimes Gil wondered why he'd moved next door to his family.

Gil sat up and yawned, patting Goldie's head as she rushed over to greet him. Goldie must know who was at the door, too, because she wasn't barking or acting like there was a burglar the way she typically did. "I wish you could go let him in for me," Gil told Goldie as he stood and shuffled toward the front door, his eyes only open enough to make sure he didn't trip over the furniture.

He opened the door and squinted at the bright sunlight that burst through along with Doug.

"We have a problem." Doug walked past Gil.

Gil closed the door and turned to face his brother. "Is this about Moira?"

Doug sat on a stool at Gil's kitchen island and propped up his upper body on his elbows. If he thought Gil was going to get straight to making sausage for him, he was mistaken. Instead, Gil headed over to the coffee brewer. Coffee came first. Always.

"Want a cup of joe?" Gil asked Doug.

Doug's face scrunched. "Do you have orange juice?"

"You know I do." Gil pointed at the fridge. "Help yourself."

Doug got up and poured himself a glass of juice.

Within a few minutes, the coffee maker sputtered the last drop of coffee into the pot, and Gil inhaled the thick scent of java goodness. He grabbed a mug and poured himself a serving. Then he shuffled over to the stool next to Doug's.

"You mentioned a problem?" Gil asked.

Doug nodded. "Denise Berger."

Gil lowered his coffee mug to the counter and gave Doug his full attention. "Oh? What happened?"

Doug placed his cell phone on the counter in front of Gil. "Watch."

Gil picked up the phone, which had a paused news video pulled up. He clicked the play icon and turned up the volume so he could drink his coffee as he watched.

Denise was on the screen, dressed to the nines in a flashy houndstooth suit and talking to a reporter from WTI-News. "How can the town of Somerset Lake even consider reelecting a mayor who doesn't care about our small businesses? Small businesses are the heart of this town." The fake laugh that tumbled out of her mouth set

Gil's back teeth clenching. He tried not to keep enemies, but Denise rubbed him all wrong. "Gil Ryan is not the guy for the job if he can't support the things that matter to its citizens."

Gil watched as Denise made her case against him. Then the reporter asked about the other mayoral candidate.

"Is Moira Green still in the running? Was she ever even in it, or is that all talk?" Denise fake laughed a second time. "That woman has no political experience. All she has is a vendetta against what's happening to her mom's bakery. And who can blame her? She doesn't need to be mayor to fight for her family's business though." Denise pressed a hand to her chest. "*I* can do that. I have the experience, the team, and the passion to implement change in Somerset Lake."

The news anchor smiled and looked at the camera. "You heard it here at WTI-News. Denise Berger for mayor in Somerset Lake."

Gil slid Doug's phone back toward him. He sipped his coffee some more before talking. "How do you find this stuff so fast? Do you search my name in the news every morning?"

"Of course."

Gil should have guessed as much. "It's just talk. Negative press is expected when you're running for any position in the government." Gil didn't mind Denise's criticism of him, but he was bothered that Moira was on the receiving end too.

"You should do an interview with her," Doug said.

"With who? With WTI-News?"

Doug nodded. "I can set it up."

Gil massaged a hand over his face. "No thanks. I don't need to defend myself against Denise on a news station.

I might end up saying a few things about her on live TV that I'll regret."

Doug looked disappointed as he drank his orange juice. "What about Moira?"

Gil glanced over. "What about her?"

"Is it true that she doesn't count?"

That wasn't exactly what Denise had said, but Gil understood why Doug had interpreted her words that way. "No, it's not true." Gil shook his head. "If you ask me, she counts more than Denise." Gil stood and looked at Doug. "It's early, buddy. And it's Saturday. I'm going back to bed. Make yourself at home but don't wake me up."

Doug still looked upset.

"I'll make sausage for lunch, okay? We'll talk about possibly scheduling an interview."

This made Doug smile. "*I'll* make us sausage at lunch," he said. "Night."

Gil headed toward his bedroom. He wished it were still night. He wished it were still last night with Moira. He climbed back under his covers, thinking of that kiss. No, Denise was definitely wrong when she implied that Moira didn't count. She counted.

Moira yawned and blinked sleepily into the depths of her coffee.

"Must have been some date last night." Lucy waggled her eyebrows across from Moira as they sat at a table in Sweetie's Bakeshop.

Tess laughed wryly. "Didn't get much sleep, huh?"

Moira shook her head. "The date is not the reason I'm

tired. Someone threw a rock at my door at two a.m. and woke me up."

"What?" Tess sat more upright in her seat. "Who?"

Moira shrugged. "I have no idea. I was terrified for like thirty minutes, thinking someone was trying to break in. Finally, I got up the nerve to peek out the peephole, but I didn't see anyone. Then I glanced out the window onto the street. No cars. I didn't dare open the door until this morning. I found a rock on my doorstep."

"Who would throw a rock at your door?" Tess asked.

Lucy frowned. "Actually, Miles told me that's happened to several people here in town over the last couple of weeks. They think it's just a bunch of kids. A harmless prank."

"Well, that harmless prank cost me the rest of the night in sleep." Moira yawned again.

Tess narrowed her eyes. "You let that keep you up all night?"

Moira shrugged, realizing suddenly that maybe that wasn't a normal reaction. "It wouldn't keep you up?" she asked.

Tess shrugged. "I mean, not really. Once I knew there was no threat, I would have gone back to sleep."

"Well, I have a ferocious guard dog," Lucy said, speaking of the elderly French bulldog that she'd inherited from her mom. "And my fiancé is a deputy sheriff. I wouldn't lose much sleep either."

"Maybe the dispatch is making you a little skittish," Tess suggested.

"Yeah, all the scary stuff that happens in Somerset Lake," Lucy said sarcastically.

Moira smiled it off. Maybe she was a little skittish and untrusting of people without reason. "Well, I hadn't heard about this prank. Don't kids have better things to do than toss rocks at a sleeping person's door?"

"Apparently not. Not in Somerset Lake at least." Tess sipped from her coffee. "We're a small town. It's hard for the teens to get their kicks. Don't you remember when that kid was stealing Christmas decorations last year?"

Lucy raised a hand. "I remember very well because he stole mine."

Tess tilted her head as she looked at Moira. "I'm sorry you lost sleep over something so silly. Now stop stalling and tell us about your date."

Moira reflexively grinned. "It was... nice." She lowered her head, feeling a rush of heat scorch her cheeks.

"You have been avoiding this guy for ages. We have had your back in helping you dodge him because you've seemed to have an unnatural repulsion for him. And now you're blushing about him." Lucy popped a piece of bagel into her mouth and chewed while continuing to talk. "You don't get away with just saying it was nice. Details please."

Moira sighed. "Fine. Well, he cooked me dinner, and we ate outside by the lake. Then we took a walk along the lake."

"That is very romantic," Tess said. "Did you two...?"

Moira cleared her throat. "Yes."

"Wait, what?" Lucy looked between them, eyes rounding comically. "What are you saying yes to? What did you two do?"

Moira's mouth dropped, and she shook her head, realizing what Lucy was thinking. "No! We just kissed. That's it. I didn't even go inside his home."

Lucy squealed. "You kissed Gil?"

Moira's eyes darted around the room to see who was

overhearing. "Shh. There are people here. I don't want this to end up on Reva's blog."

Tess snickered. "So you're kissing the competitor? I can't say I'm disappointed. I'm actually really happy for you."

"Me too," Lucy said. "Gil is a great guy. You two would make a cute couple."

"Let's not get ahead of ourselves. It was just one date," Moira said.

"Will there be another?" Tess asked.

Moira shrugged. "Maybe. I don't know. He didn't ask for another date."

"But he kissed you good night?" Tess clarified.

Moira nodded as a giddy smile rested on her lips. "Yes."

Tess looked pleased as she leaned back in her seat and crossed her legs. "Then trust me. He'll be calling."

Chapter Twenty

The members of Somerset's town council were seated around a table with paper plates of cookies and plastic cups of soda. Sugar and caffeine were always the highlight of these meetings. Gil used to love attending as a town council member. He had loved discussing community topics and feeling like he made a difference where he lived. Being a member of the town council had evolved into his holding the mayor's office. It was a steady progression. Denise had only just joined the council. She'd barely attended three meetings. And yet, she was running against him. It didn't quite make sense in Gil's mind.

"Hey, Gil." Peter Blake stepped over and shook Gil's hand. Peter was a veterinarian in town. He and Gil had gone to school together, but they'd never really hung out. Peter was the academic type back then, and Gil was the type who got called down every five minutes for talking out of turn.

"Hey, Peter. How are you?"

Peter shrugged slightly. "Concerned, if you want the truth."

Gil narrowed his eyes. "Oh? What about?"

"You. There has been a bit of negative press. I don't want to see it harm your reelection chances."

Gil sighed. "You're talking about Denise Berger's interview with WTI-News? Folks who know Denise know to take whatever she says with a grain of salt."

"And those who don't know her, don't know that," Peter said matter-of-factly. "Then there's Moira Green. After receiving that Hero Among Us award, she's a rising favorite around here."

Gil wasn't aware of that, but instead of feeling threatened, this information made him happy. He didn't want to lose his job to her, but he loved seeing Moira in the spotlight. "Moira Green is a wonderful woman with a love for the town. I'm proud to have her as a campaign rival."

Peter stared at Gil as if he was trying to figure out a puzzle.

Missy Hendricks stepped up to the conversation. "You really do need to get out there and fight back, Mayor Gil. Sometimes playing dirty is a necessary evil."

Gil lifted his brows. "I'm not planning to stoop to Denise Berger's level. If I win another term, I'll do it honestly."

Gil's mind was still on Peter and Missy's advice as the town council meeting got started. Topics of interest for tonight's meeting were the dog park that Beth Chimes had been bringing up since Gil had taken on the mayor position, the upcoming summer festival (because once one festival was over, the next was always being planned), and the ongoing saga of needing a new parking lot for Hannigan Street.

"Several town residents are upset over the suggestion to shut down the bakery," one council person pointed out.

"Someone is always going to be upset over any decision we make. We do the best we can," Missy retorted.

"That is very true," Gil agreed. He'd been feeling that sentiment a lot lately. "I'm still looking for a good solution for where to move the bakery. It's a staple here in the community, and I think we can calm the concerns of those who are worried about it if we find a location that is still very central to our town."

"Good luck finding one," Chuck Morris said. Chuck was the group's pessimist. "This is a small town with limited options. No one wants to see more construction take place at the expense of nature."

Gil nodded as he listened. "I've asked Della Rose to keep an ear to the ground of any current businesses that might be considering closing their doors. That would alleviate any need for new construction." Which he knew Darla couldn't afford. Although maybe her financial situation had changed since she'd been forced to sell the building.

By the time the meeting was over, Gil felt exhausted. He got into his truck to drive home, but found himself driving somewhere else. He hadn't even made the conscious decision before he pulled into Moira's driveway and cut his engine. He wasn't even sure why he was here, but he got out of his truck and walked toward her front door anyway. He knocked and waited for her to answer.

After several long minutes, Moira opened the door and wrinkled her brow just slightly. "What are you doing here?"

"I'm not sure." He shook his head. "I guess I just wanted to talk to someone. Can I come in?"

Moira's eyes widened subtly.

He held up his hand. "I'm sorry." He took a step

backward. "It's late, and I should have called." He turned to leave.

"Wait," she called after him. Then she opened her door wider, revealing that she was already wearing her pajamas. Yeah, this was completely inappropriate to be here. "Come in. It's okay." She offered a small smile. "I'll make some tea, and we can talk."

Gil looked at her. "Are you sure?"

"Of course." She gestured him inside. "Better move out of the doorway before you get hit by a rock though."

"Huh?"

Moira laughed. "Some kids around here are throwing rocks at people's doors for fun. My door was hit last night." She pointed at a dent on her door.

"This is news to me." He stepped inside. "I'll talk to Sheriff Ronnie about it."

Moira closed the door behind him and led him into the kitchen. "Have a seat. I'll turn on the kettle."

Gil sat down on the stool at her kitchen island and clasped his hands in front of him as he watched Moira work. "I'm sorry for inconveniencing you."

"You aren't." She glanced over her shoulder. "I'm glad you're here, actually."

"Oh? Why is that?"

Moira faced him and leaned her body against the counter. "Because I need to talk to you."

Moira sat across from Gil with her warm mug of tea cupped between her hands.

"What's up?" Gil asked, sipping his tea. "You said you wanted to talk to me?"

She nibbled her lower lip. She was thinking that she'd be having this conversation tomorrow after tossing and turning and planning out what exactly to say first. "I don't know what I'm thinking lately. I think my decision to run for mayor was a misplaced way to help my mom save her bakery." Moira looked at Gil. He didn't look surprised by anything she was saying so far. Instead, he looked steady and calm. "At least, that's what it was at first. Then people started coming up to me, and I sincerely thought I could make changes for good in this town."

"Thought?" Gil asked.

Moira shrugged. "Maybe it was foolish of me to think an amateur like me could run the town. I'm considering dropping out of the mayor's race." There. She said it.

Gil lifted his mug of tea and sipped. "I don't think you should end your campaign."

Her mouth dropped open. "I thought this would make you happy."

He released a breath. "I want to keep my place as mayor, yes, but I want it to be because that's what the town wants. And if you drop your bid, that just leaves me and Denise." He ran a hand through his hair, looking frustrated and way too handsome for his own good. "Denise winning the mayor's spot would be a nightmare for this town. Her priorities align with herself, not what's best for Somerset Lake."

"There's no way the town would elect Denise. Gil, you're great at what you do," Moira said.

"That's why you decided to run against me?" he asked, one eyebrow lifting.

She looked down into the dark depths of her tea for a moment. "Maybe I don't agree with you on all your decisions. We can agree to disagree though."

He sighed. "I can't believe I'm persuading my rival to stay in the running, but just don't drop out until you've given this more thought, okay?"

Moira looked at him for a long moment. "Okay. We're both on the same page about Denise."

Gil nodded.

Moira sipped her tea some more. "I have another confession."

"Oh?"

"Part of me also thought that dropping out of the mayoral race would be good because there'd be no reason for us not to date. Last night was pretty amazing."

Gil grinned. "I already told you that I don't see a good reason for us to stay apart. We're two adults. We can handle whatever comes our way, right?"

"I'd like to think so." She tugged her lower lip between her teeth. "So what do we do now?"

"I can leave if you want me to. Or stay awhile. We could just talk or, I don't know, play cards."

"Cards?" Moira laughed softly. "I do have a stack for Uno."

Gil looked intrigued. "Wow, that's a blast from the past. I haven't played that in a while. It used to be mine and Doug's favorite."

Moira stood and walked over to what she referred to as her junk drawer. She grabbed the deck and held it up. "If we're going to play, we should have stakes involved."

Gil's eyes narrowed over his mug of tea. "How about, if I win, you go on another date with me this week?" he suggested.

Moira sat back down in front of him. "And if I win?"

Gil lifted a shoulder. "If you win, you still go on another date with me."

She tilted her head to one side. "Are you asking me out again, Mayor?"

He looked at her steadily. Calmly. "I am."

Moira cut the deck and started dealing the cards, making Gil wait for his answer. Then she fanned her cards in front of her face and looked at him. "Let the best person win."

∞

On Monday morning, Moira pushed through the bakery's front doors and breathed in the nostalgic aroma of her childhood. Darla smiled and waved from behind the counter where she'd always been during Moira's lifetime. The idea that this place might cease to exist was hard to swallow.

Moira stepped up to the counter. "Hi, Mom. Can I get my usual?"

"Of course." Darla turned to start preparing it, talking over her shoulder. "Dispatch today?"

"Yep. Nine to five. What about you?"

"I'm here until six." Darla slid a cup of coffee in front of Moira. "Then I'm meeting your dad for a walk along the lake. He's gotten romantic in his golden years. He likes to watch the sunset." She dipped to get a croissant out of the glass case for Moira's breakfast.

"I didn't know Dad was mushy." Moira thought of Gil. Sharing a sunset with him was the most romantic moment of her adult life. Then again, so was a night of playing Uno at her kitchen counter. Moira didn't have a lot of dating experiences to go off though.

Darla slid the croissant across the counter. Then she rang Moira up. Moira had stopped accepting freebies here a long time ago. She was an adult, and this was her mom's business.

"Are you doing okay?" her mom asked as Moira slid her debit card into the reader.

"I'm not planning a protest outside your business, if that's what you're asking." Moira smiled softly. "I'm okay. You?"

Darla looked tired. Her rosy cheeks weren't quite as pink as usual. "I'm good. And the campaign?"

Moira picked up her coffee and croissant. "It's going well."

"I'm glad. Your heart will always steer you in the right direction."

Right now, Moira's heart was steering her toward Gil. Moira turned toward the bell on the bakery door and waved at Tess as she headed inside.

"I'll bring her coffee and bagel out," Darla said.

"Thanks, Mom." Moira gestured for Tess to meet her at a table near the wall. "Mom is bringing your coffee and bagel out."

Tess pulled out a chair and sat down. "Perfect. I don't know what I'll do when this place is no longer here." She looked at Moira. "Unless of course you get that changed. Being mayor will give you some pull, I imagine."

Moira brought her cup of coffee to her mouth. "We'll see." She sipped quietly for a few minutes, looking around the bakery again. The walls were covered with old photographs of Darla and a bunch of musicians that Moira had only ever known through these pictures. Darla's first dream had been to be a singer. Then she'd gotten pregnant with Moira, and her dream had shifted to owning this place.

"Here you go." Darla set a coffee and cream cheese bagel in front of Tess. "Enjoy. I'll just put it on your tab."

Tess reached for her drink. "Thanks, Darla."

They waited to continue talking until Darla returned to the counter.

"I like the wardrobe, by the way. This new version of Moira Green is impressive." Tess picked up her bagel and took a bite.

"What do you mean?"

"Public speaking, standing up for what you believe in, dating. The Moira I know and love hides away in her living room most of the time. And hides from the swoony town mayor." Tess beamed back at Moira. "And now you're dating him and also trying to steal his job."

Moira face-palmed. "We have an agreement. Whatever happens, happens. It's not personal."

"Hmm," Tess hummed, chewing and swallowing her bite of bagel. "Seems very personal to me."

They enjoyed their breakfast together, and then Moira got up to leave. As she was making the trek to her car parked farther down the street, her cell phone rang. She dug it out of her purse and checked the caller ID, not recognizing the number. "Hello?"

"Hi, is this Moira Green, candidate for Somerset Lake town mayor?"

"Yes, it is." Moira reached her car and slid behind the steering wheel. Her dispatch shift started in twelve minutes. She needed to go home and get settled. "Who is this?" she asked, putting the call on speakerphone so that she could have both hands for driving.

"This is Jessica Marcus with WTI-News. I'm calling to see if you're available for a live interview for the news this evening."

Moira cranked her car and pulled onto the road. "News?"

"That's right. I don't know a mayoral candidate who would turn down free publicity. We're the most watched TV news station in the area."

Moira swallowed past the sudden flutters in her chest. Tess said she was proud of her, but public speaking still made Moira nervous. If she was going to do this though, she needed to get used to it. She'd been second-guessing herself with Gil last night, but she really did want to continue on this path. It scared her, yeah, but it also invigorated her. "Sure, I would love to interview with you. I have to work until five."

"We can set it up at six. Does that work for you?"

Moira's palms were suddenly slick against the steering wheel. "Y-yes. That works well."

"How about I interview you in front of Sweetie's? I know that's part of your running platform. We can meet, say, around five forty-five?"

Darla probably wouldn't be thrilled about this meeting place. She didn't want to draw attention to the town's plans. Moira did though. "That would be great. I'll see you tonight." Moira disconnected the call and grinned to herself as she drove home. Tess was right. She was doing things that the old Moira would never do. Moira liked this new version of herself as well.

Chapter Twenty-One

"I can't believe the most pressing thing on my list right now is looking for a few kids tossing rocks at folks' doors," Ronnie said with a drawn-out sigh.

Gil sat across from the sheriff at his desk. "Well, that beats the alternative, I guess. At least you're not looking for a serial killer or something."

"In Somerset Lake?" Ronnie looked amused. "You've been watching too many cop shows."

"More like reading too many true-crime books while I try to fall asleep at night...So you don't have any leads on the rock-throwing case yet?" Gil asked.

"All I know is that the perps are just a couple of kids being bored. This is the one time I advocate letting bored kids play video games versus driving around and looking for trouble. I have a few deputies patrolling the neighborhoods at night. That's all I can do. That and hope someone witnesses the rock throwing in action and calls in a description or a license plate number. Or catches one of the perps on one of those Ring cameras. Those things have solved quite a few crimes since they've come out." Ronnie ran his fingers over his overgrown beard.

"Small towns have perks and drawbacks. When kids throw rocks at doors for fun, that's a drawback."

Ronnie gave a low chuckle. "We have to make our own fun around here, that's always been the case. I remember the old days of catching fish in the lake with our bare hands as sport."

"And skinny-dipping too," Gil said. "Not that I ever joined in that recreation."

"I'm pleading the Fifth." The sheriff leaned forward. "I'm not sure I ever properly thanked you for agreeing to the lock-in here at the jail. We raised a lot of money to cover some much-needed sprucing up in the cells. Spring cleaning isn't just for our homes."

"You're welcome. I'm always glad to help."

"And you got a day with Moira out of the deal. I hear you two have gotten close these days."

Gil didn't agree or disagree. He wasn't ready to spread his and Moira's relationship around town just yet. It was new, and he didn't want to invite anyone else's opinions or negativity in.

"Well, if you two get married, maybe you'll have your wedding at the jail. For sentimentality's sake."

Gil scoffed. "A jailhouse wedding? No wonder you're still single, Sheriff." He stood and reached out to shake Ronnie's hand.

Ronnie shook it as he laughed. "I'm still single because it suits me. Thanks for dropping by, buddy."

Gil turned to leave.

"Hey, Gil?"

"Yeah?" Gil turned back.

"I just want you to know that you've got my vote. You're the best mayor this town has seen. I believe in you."

Gil swallowed thickly. "Thanks. That means a lot, coming from you."

"I also want you to know that I told Moira the same thing."

Gil narrowed his eyes. "You only get one vote, Sheriff."

Ronnie leaned back in his chair. "That's too bad because both of you would make an excellent choice, in my opinion."

"There's three of us running," Gil pointed out.

Ronnie shook his head. "Denise is a hard no for me."

"Well, I appreciate your support," Gil said. "Even if you're cheating on me with Moira."

Deep breaths.

The deeper Moira tried to breathe in, the less calm she felt. Who said this was a good technique for remaining calm?

Tess stepped up beside Moira and wrapped an arm around her. "You look amazing. That cream suit really looks good on you. Deep breaths," she coached.

Moira side-eyed her. "It's not working."

"You'll be fantastic. Just answer the questions honestly, and it'll be over in ten minutes or less. These things are hard to mess up."

Moira nodded. "You interviewed with this woman when you took over the bookshop from your aunt, right?"

"I did. She's a bit ambitious with her questions. Just try to remain calm, hold your smile, and don't answer anything too quickly. You're allowed to think about your responses. And if you don't want to answer a question, just say *no comment*."

Moira watched her friend. "Wow. You make a great campaign manager, you know that?"

"Don't flatter me too much or your other campaign managers will be jealous."

Moira laughed. "Thanks for being here. I feel a little better."

Tess leaned in and whispered only for Moira's ears. "But I bet you wish Gil was here."

Moira took a shuddery breath. "The reporter would really have a field day with that, wouldn't she? Two mayoral candidates dating."

Tess shrugged. "You don't choose who you fall for."

Moira glanced over. "We've had two dates."

"You never fooled me. You fell for Gil way before the first date."

Moira was about to argue that point when the reporter stepped up. "Hi, Moira. I'm Jessica Marcus." She offered her hand to shake. "I'm so excited you agreed to talk to me on camera this evening."

Moira's heart somersaulted in her chest. Was it too late to turn around and run in the opposite direction? "Me too," she said.

"Okay. Well, let's get set up and introduce you a little better to potential voters, shall we?"

Moira smiled through the start and middle of her interview. It was going pretty well as far as she could tell. She kept surprising herself at how capable she was. In grade school, she had nearly peed her pants during one oral report she had to do in Mrs. Givens's classroom.

"I have a little something I want to read to you, if that's okay," Jessica said then.

Moira glanced at a piece of paper that Jessica pulled from her pocket. "Um, sure." She just hoped this wasn't some kind of sneak attack.

"This is an email that our station received yesterday, and it's the reason I contacted you for an interview. This letter touched us at the station so much, and we just knew we had to read it to you on the air. Is that okay?"

Moira nodded. "Sure. I guess."

Jessica pulled a pair of reading glasses out and began to read.

Dear WIT-News,

I hope you will interview Moira Green, the candidate for Somerset Lake mayor. Ms. Green has inspired me, and I think she'd inspire many of your viewers. First, Ms. Green is an ordinary woman who goes out of her way to help others. She recently won a Hero Among Us award. Then, when her mom's bakery was threatened, she stood up for what she believed in, fought the decision, and decided to step out of her comfort zone and do something in her community to make a change. Most of us go through life doing what's easy, what's familiar, what doesn't stir the pot. Moira Green is an example of someone who is brave, generous, and kind. She's the type of mayor I want in Somerset Lake. I would love to see her as a guest on your news station.

Sincerely,
One Inspired Somersetter

Jessica looked up at Moira expectantly.

Moira was speechless for a moment. "Wow. I'm not sure what to say. I am just an ordinary woman. That part's true."

"We're all just ordinary until we do something extraordinary," Jessica said. "I think that's what you've done."

Moira was still reeling from her interview when she arrived home. The rock from the other night was still there on her porch along with the dent on her door. Not even that could mar her mood right now. She felt exhilarated, and the person she wanted to talk to most right now, to celebrate this moment with, was Gil.

She let herself inside her home, locked the door, and headed into the kitchen. Calling Gil would be wrong, right? She couldn't brag about doing such a great job when the job she'd done was competing with his. This was so complicated. After months of not dating at all, and years of only subpar dates, she was dating a guy who really didn't make sense for her on paper.

No. She couldn't call Gil. That would be rude.

Her phone rang. She reached to pick it up, and her insides turned to mush at the sight of Gil's name.

"Hello?"

"Hey. You were awesome," he said without missing a beat. His voice was scratchy and deep. She could almost hear him smiling.

"You watched?"

"Of course I watched. Me and Doug had a watch party, complete with popcorn."

"Ack. Doug was probably rooting for me to trip over my words."

"Just a little bit and only out of loyalty to me," Gil said.

"I was rooting for you to do amazing, and that's exactly what you did. I'm so proud of you."

Moira swallowed past a tight throat. She was proud of herself too. "I wish you were here."

"Oh? Why is that? What would you do?" he asked, his voice dropping deeper.

"Kiss you, I guess. You're the first person I wanted to talk to after the interview."

"I'm honored," Gil said quietly. "And, the truth is, I couldn't wait to talk to you either."

Moira heard a noise in the background of Gil's phone. It sounded like a door slamming. "Where are you?"

"Your driveway. Can I come in?"

"You're in my driveway right now?" she asked, hurrying toward her door.

"Mm-hmm. And I have champagne to celebrate an interview well done."

Moira went up on her tiptoes to peek out the peephole, and her head felt dizzy. He was here!

"If you don't want me to come inside, I'll just hand the bottle over and leave. I promise."

Moira opened the door, and her heart lifted into her throat. "Hi."

"Hi." He held out the bottle of pink champagne. "I've been saving this for a special occasion."

"And you're willing to waste it on me?" She took the bottle and held it against her midsection.

"Nothing is ever wasted on you, Moira." He stood there a moment. "Should I leave?"

She shook her head, opening the door wider and gesturing him inside. "No. You should stay."

∞

Moira lifted her head, looked at Gil, and gasped. The sound must have startled him because his body jolted on the couch where he was sitting with her.

He looked around sleepily. "What's going on?"

"I think we dozed off." She laughed quietly.

Gil seemed to blink heavily. "Sorry about that." He lifted his arms over his head and stretched, breaking into a loud yawn. Then he lowered his arm around her and tugged her against him for a moment. "I better go."

"Yeah." But some part of her wished he could stay. Not to sleep together—they weren't ready for that just yet— but just to keep her company. It was nice having him here, and she trusted him so much more than she'd ever trusted anyone. "I've never let a date come inside my home."

Gil looked at her. "Never?"

She was probably disclosing too much. Not letting a guy inside her home meant not bringing a guy into her bedroom. She cleared her throat. "Not since college, at least."

"That's a long time," he said.

"A very long time." They weren't talking about inviting someone in for a nightcap.

"I take responsibility for that," Gil said. "Because of Felix."

Moira shook her head. "You didn't know what kind of person he was. And I'm not telling you this to make you feel guilty. I'm telling you this to make you feel special. I let you in, and I'm not in a hurry for you to leave. That's a pretty big deal for me."

Gil reached for her hand and squeezed it. "I'm in no hurry to leave either, but if I don't go now, I'll end up falling asleep again. That might make it hard to keep this relationship of ours under wraps."

Moira didn't let go of his hand just yet. "It's going to get harder to do that anyway. When I see you, all I want to do is kiss you."

Gil leaned in and brushed his lips over hers, lingering for a long moment. "I feel the exact same way."

Chapter Twenty-Two

It took steel willpower to pull away from Moira. "I better go," Gil finally said. "It's after midnight, and I'm willing to bet my dog and possibly my brother are waiting up for me."

Moira's dark hair was messy from where he'd run his fingers through it. "Careful out there," she warned. "There are flying rocks."

Gil stood from the couch. "I should have brought my hard hat. Hopefully, the deputies who are patrolling the neighborhoods will catch the culprits soon before someone gets seriously hurt."

Moira followed him to the door. "Good night, Gil."

He turned and looked at her. "I want to kiss you right now," he confessed.

"Oh?" She tilted her head, letting her hair fall across her cheek. "What's stopping you?"

Gil looked at his feet for a moment. "I guess I'm still getting used to the fact that you can even tolerate being in the same room with me, much less kiss me."

She stepped out onto the porch and tipped her head back to look up at him. "I can tolerate it, and I even kind of like it."

Gil's heart squeezed. He liked it too—a lot. He also

liked seeing Moira this happy. He dipped his head and touched his mouth to hers in a brief kiss that lit him up like a sky full of fireworks. "Good night, Moira. Sweet dreams."

"Night."

He headed back to his truck and got inside, missing the feel of Moira in his arms. Some part of him had loved this woman most of his adult life. Now he had his chance with her, and he didn't want to begin this relationship in secret. He wanted to take Moira out to the nicest restaurant in town. He wanted to date her openly among everyone.

When he got home, Goldie had her nose pressed against his window, watching him as he walked up the driveway. He unlocked the door and took a moment to pet her. She spent extra time sniffing his clothes. "Yeah, Goldie, I was cheating on you with another woman. Her name is Moira. Looks like you might have to start sharing me," he told his dog.

Goldie tilted her head as if she was trying to make out what he was saying. There were a few statements Goldie knew for sure.

"Wanna go out?" he asked.

Goldie darted toward the back door. Gil let her out and waited on the back deck as she did her business. Then he called her back. "Bedtime."

Goldie was the only female who'd been in his bedroom for years. His dating life had been lackluster despite his being named Most Eligible Bachelor in Somerset Lake last year. Even if he wanted to, it was tough bringing anyone home because his parents lived next door and his brother was always dropping by unannounced. He missed having someone in his life. A romantic someone whom he could share dreams of the future with.

Gil changed into a pair of sweatpants for sleep and plopped down on his bed. Goldie jumped into the space right beside him. "What do you think, Goldie? Do you mind sharing me if the right woman were to come along?"

Goldie tilted her head, looking confused.

Gil wasn't confused though. There was no *if*. The right woman *had* come along. He'd found her, and all he needed to do was figure out how to keep her.

The next morning Gil yawned as he looked at his brother, standing on his porch.

"What is this?" Doug asked.

"Hello to you as well."

Doug was holding up a phone for Gil to see.

Gil blinked the screen into view. No matter how many times he asked Doug to hold off on coming over so early, Doug never listened. "Reva's blog? Doug, it's way too early for that."

Doug walked into the house and headed toward the kitchen.

How would this work if Gil ever did have a woman sleep over? No woman would want to be woken at daybreak.

"You made a bullet point," Doug said.

"Oh, good. Free publicity."

Doug slid his phone across the counter to where Gil was now standing. "Read it."

Gil frowned. "You're bossy, you know that?" He picked up the phone and read.

- Mayor Gil is rumored to have purchased a bouquet of flowers this week. My sources say they weren't for his mother, so who is the woman of the hour? Is our Most Eligible Bachelor about to be off the market? Who is the mystery woman?

Gil massaged a hand over his face. "Leave me alone," he growled under his breath.

"Me?" Doug asked.

Gil lowered his hand and shook his head. "Not you, Doug. Reva and all the spies who will now be trying to figure out who I'm dating. I'm supposed to be the mayor of this town. How can I be taken seriously if I'm being voted Most Eligible Bachelor and hounded about my dating life?" He turned to start the coffee maker. This news called for two cups today. "It's not easy being mayor, Doug."

"Nothing worthwhile is easy," Doug said, echoing what their mom always told them when they were growing up. Things had been easier for Gil than for Doug. When Doug was growing up, it had seemed like acquiring every new skill was a challenge. Doug never gave up though. He wasn't a quitter. Gil had learned everything he knew about perseverance from his brother.

"I vote Doug Ryan for mayor this year," Gil said, glancing at his brother over his shoulder.

"You're the mayor, and you're staying mayor," Doug announced.

Gil turned back to his coffeepot, which wasn't brewing nearly fast enough for his liking. "Well, I have two competitors. My future role in this town is up to the voters."

"We will convince them you're the best choice," Doug said.

Gil had always had a good self-image. It was just here lately, when some folks were more vocal about their dissatisfaction over some of his choices, that he was struggling.

"Why don't you want people to know you're buying Moira flowers?" Doug asked.

Gil sighed. He hadn't exactly told Doug he was seeing Moira romantically, but Doug had likely seen her over the other night when Gil had prepared a candlelit dinner by the lake. "Because Moira is running for mayor too. I don't know how it would look to folks if they knew we were dating." Gil shrugged. "I don't want people to be talking more about who she's dating than what her ideas and values are."

"What about you?" Doug asked.

Gil faced his brother. "I'm already mayor. I have experience. And I'm a guy. Sad to say, but sometimes people aren't as forgiving to women about stuff like this. I just want the focus on Moira to be her platform and what she's passionate about."

Doug looked disappointed. "Moira is my real-life hero, but so are you, Gilly."

"Well, you're my hero," Gil told Doug. "You always have been."

Moira took a bite of her bagel and then halfway choked on it as Darla read Reva's latest bullet point on her blog.

"Gil is buying someone flowers? Who is he buying flowers for?" Darla asked.

Moira beat a hand to her chest, making the bite of bagel go down her suddenly very dry throat.

Darla eyed Moira. "Did you read Reva's blog this morning, sweetheart?"

Moira ducked her head under her mom's watchful gaze. "No, I don't read that stuff if I can help it." Which was only partly true. A lot of days, Moira glossed over it just to ensure her name wasn't there. "Gil could have been buying flowers for anyone. A sick friend. His mom. Reva is reaching for news with that one."

Darla placed her phone down on the table in front of her. "You were great on WTI-News last night, by the way. I can't believe how poised and well-spoken you are. You are going to make an excellent mayor, sweetie. Nothing against Gil. I love him. But you're my daughter. I have to root for you."

Moira sipped her coffee. "You don't *have* to root for me, but thank you for your vote," she said. "The other night I was having a few second thoughts about running. Gil was actually the one who talked me out of dropping out."

Darla narrowed her eyes. "Oh? And when did you talk to Gil?"

Moira popped a piece of bagel into her mouth. "After the interview."

When Darla didn't immediately say anything, Moira looked up. "Why are you looking at me like that?"

The corners of Darla's mouth twitched in a barely there smile. "You saw Gil after your six o'clock interview? That must have been at least seven o'clock. Where did you see him?"

Moira glanced around the bakery, making sure no one was eavesdropping. Then she shrugged as if it were no big deal. "He came to my house, just to congratulate me on the news segment."

"Mm-hmm. He could have called to tell you what a great job you'd done."

"I guess he could have. He was probably just in the area," Moira said, wishing she hadn't disclosed that little nugget of information for her mom to run with. Her mom didn't get a chance to run with anything though, because Gil walked over to their table.

"Morning, ladies," he said in that deep Gil voice.

Goose bumps rose over Moira's skin, and she felt her own cheeks flush. Darla would be the one to notice. She felt her mom's eyes trained on her. In her mind's eye, Moira could practically see the giddy expression on her mom's face.

"Morning, Mayor Gil. How are you?" Darla asked, her voice a little more cheerful than usual.

"Doing well, thanks. Morning, Moira. How are you?" he asked, forcing her to look at him.

When she did, her heart melted a little. She was falling hard and fast for this man. She wasn't sure she'd be able to keep her feelings a secret for long, especially around her mom. Her friends already knew. It was just a matter of time before everyone had figured out who was on the receiving end of Gil's flowers. "I'm good. Mom was just telling me I have her vote."

Gil grinned. "I should hope so, seeing that you're family."

"If I could vote twice, Mayor Gil, I would." Darla cast him an apologetic glance.

"You sound like Sheriff Ronnie. He said the same thing. If I have to run against someone though, your daughter is a good choice. I'd vote for her, too, if it didn't mean booting myself out of a job." His gaze snagged on Moira's, and she couldn't look away. "Congrats again on a great news interview last night."

"Thank you," she said.

"Yeah, I hear you went by her home personally to tell her just how well she did," Darla said, brows lifting.

Gil glanced at Moira, a nervous smile twitching at the corners of his lips.

She cast him an apologetic look. She had never been all that great at keeping secrets. Except for the one about Felix. That was something she never wanted to talk about with anyone. Partly because she wished she had handled the aftermath better instead of landing herself in jail.

"I did drop by Moira's. Just briefly." He shifted back and forth on his feet. "Well, I guess I should probably go get my caffeine fix."

"Bailey's working the counter this morning," Darla told him. "Pretty soon Moira and her friends will all have to find a new place to grab coffees. Maybe you can take Moira around and help her find a just-right spot."

Yeah, Darla was onto Moira and Gil's relationship. And now that Reva had put the word out that Gil was purchasing flowers at Somerset Florist, it was only a matter of time before everyone would know.

"I'd love to do that," he said, gaze lingering on Moira.

She suppressed the need to argue that Sweetie's wasn't going anywhere. Nothing was set in stone.

"See you later," Gil told the two.

"Yes, I'm sure you will," Darla teased, giving Moira a hard stare. "He bought those flowers for you, didn't he?" she asked, once Gil had walked toward the front counter.

Moira looked down at her bagel, picking a piece off. She rolled it into a doughy ball between her fingers. "I'm pleading the Fifth."

"I knew it! I am so excited for you two. Wait. How can you be dating your rival?"

"He's not my rival, Mom." Moira looked around the bakery and made sure no one was close enough to even read lips. In this town, information was gold. "We're not looking at the campaign that way. We both just happen to want the same thing, and only one of us can have it." Moira glanced at the time on her phone. "Keep this on the down-low, okay? Don't tell Aunt Lois. Don't even tell Dad."

Darla pretended to zip her lips. "My lips are sealed."

"Good. Thank you." Moira stood and collected her half-full cup of coffee. Once upon a time, she would have thought of it as half-empty. Things were looking up though. Her perspective was brighter under the glow of new dreams and a romantic interest. "I have to get to the dispatch."

Darla reached for her hand and squeezed. "I am so thrilled for you, sweetheart."

"Thank you, Mom. It's new so it might not amount to much." Moira shrugged, telling her mom the same thing she'd been trying to tell herself. *This might be short-lived. Don't get my hopes up. Prepare my heart to be broken.*

"Or," Darla said, trailing off for a beat, "it might amount to a new son-in-law for me one of these days."

"Mom!" Moira said in a hushed whisper. "We're barely dating. Don't marry me off just yet."

Two days later, Moira headed over to Lakeside Books at six p.m., holding a box of cookies from Choco-Lovers. Moira set the box on the coffee table in the back of the store and curled up in her favorite leather recliner there. "Jana sends her love."

"Anyone else sending their love?" Lucy asked in a singsong voice.

The newest member of the book club, Lara, looked between the two women. "What's that about? Did I miss something?"

All the women were tuned in to the conversation now.

"Does this have anything to do with Reva's bullet point this week, saying that Gil was buying flowers for some lucky lady?" Trisha asked, one hand rubbing her belly.

Moira ducked her head. "Why on earth would you think that has anything to do with me?" she asked, trying and failing to dodge their suspicion.

All the women stared at her.

"Who wants to take a field trip to Moira's home and see if there is a vase of flowers on her dining room table?" Lucy asked, raising her hand first.

Moira shook her head. "Okay, yes. Gil bought the flowers for me, but it's not a big deal, you guys."

Della's mouth dropped open. "A date and flowers? Fancy."

"Flowers are a pretty big deal in my book," Trisha agreed. "The only guys to ever bring me flowers were the ones who were seriously working hard to impress me."

Moira held up the book they were supposed to be discussing. "Can we please talk about the book for *book club*?"

Tess folded her legs under her body. "Fine." She placed her book on her lap. "But what are you going to do if he wins another term as mayor? When the votes come in, it could get complicated between you two."

"Maybe, but I can be an adult about it."

"Mm-hmm. And what if *you* win?" Tess asked.

"Then he'll be an adult," Moira said as if the answer was obvious.

"Gil would be out of a job doing what he loves. Are you sure he'll be okay with that?" Della asked.

"The election is still months away. We have a lot of time. We might not even be together come election time."

Tess hummed thoughtfully. "I think you know that's not the case. I think that's why you've been avoiding Gil all these years. You haven't been ready to explore this thing between you two. And now you are."

Moira kind of knew Tess was right. Some part of her had always known that exploring the attraction between her and Gil would lead to so much more than she was ready for. At least what she was ready for before now. "All I know is running for mayor is something that excites me more than I've been in a long time. Gil excites me too. Maybe I shouldn't hope that I can have both, but I do."

Tess stuck her hand over Moira's. "You're my best friend. And if you want both, I say go for it."

"I wholeheartedly agree," Lucy said. "You've waited a long time for love."

"Love?" Moira pulled back, jaw dropping. "It's a little soon for that, don't you think?"

"Well, it's not a crush. You're way past crush. And we all know Gil has been in love with you since kindergarten," Lucy said matter-of-factly.

Moira looked at Tess, who didn't seem to disagree. Moira's insides churned. She was ready to explore this thing between her and Gil, but she wasn't quite sure she was ready for the big L-word.

Seeming to read her face, Tess held up the book again. "Okay, time to talk about this book. For real this time, ladies."

Chapter Twenty-Three

Gil wasn't naive. He knew what he was walking into tonight at the tavern. The guys were going to hound him about whom he'd purchased flowers for. His friends were pretty ruthless when it came to teasing each other.

He could lie, but that wasn't his way. It also wasn't his style to kiss and tell.

"So, Gilbert," Miles began, drawing out his syllables in a playful fashion.

All the men's heads swiveled in Gil's direction.

Uh-oh. Here it comes.

"Who is she?" Miles wanted to know.

Gil played dumb for a minute, focusing his gaze on the carbonated bubbles of his soda. "Who is who?" he asked casually.

"The mystery woman you bought flowers for," Jake said, following Miles's lead.

Gil cleared his throat. "She is a wonderful woman who I don't want to discuss right now."

Jake elbowed him from where he sat on Gil's left side. "I think this is great news, buddy."

Gil inhaled deeply and shook his head simultaneously.

"This new relationship of mine is in the beginning stages. We're trying to keep things private."

The guys stared at him. Gil thought they were probably trying to decide whether to pursue the topic some more or drop it.

"You and Moira looked pretty cozy at the lock-in the other weekend," Miles said.

"Uh-oh." Roman grinned. He and River were sitting across the table from Gil. "Don't let your new mystery girl hear that."

Gil reached for his soda and took a sip, tempering his reaction. "Speaking of fundraisers, I was considering doing another barbecue picnic at my house. Just like I did for my first campaign."

"Sounds good," River said.

"You and Tess will come then?" Gil clarified.

"I'm not sure about Tess. She's loyal to Moira so..." River trailed off.

"Gil, buddy, you might need to step up your campaign game this election. You have two people going up against you. It's not a sure deal this time around," Jake said. When Gil had run against former mayor Bryce Malsop, things had been different. The people of Somerset Lake were fairly unanimous in their desire for change.

Gil nodded. "Yeah, I get that. I'm not sure where to start though. I won't make promises that I don't intend to keep. I'm not that kind of politician."

"I'm sure Denise doesn't mind promising her voters the world on a platter," Jake said.

Gil sighed. "Hopefully my voters trust me to be honest with them. The moment I stop doing that is the moment I don't deserve the mayor's office."

Jake patted his back. "Well, I am one hundred percent behind you."

All the guys agreed.

Gil looked around the table. "Thanks, guys. I really appreciate it."

"Our counterparts, however, are voting for Moira. Sorry, buddy." Miles offered an apologetic look.

Gil chuckled. He wasn't at all offended. "As long as they're not voting for Denise."

"What will you do if you don't win?" Jake asked. "Return to practicing law?"

Gil shook his head. "No, I don't think so. Not in the traditional sense at least. I just want to help people. If I don't win this election, I'll have to find another way."

Miles lifted his drink. "A toast. To a mayor who cares."

Jake lifted his glass, followed by River and Roman. "To Mayor Gilbert."

Gil massaged his forehead in mock frustration. It wasn't that he minded his full name—much. He didn't mind being teased by his friends either. He lifted his glass as well. "To good friends."

Later that night, Gil felt like the weight of the world— or at least his small section of it—was on his shoulders as he walked through his home with Goldie trailing him. The question of what he'd do if he didn't win was weighing on his mind as he changed clothes and climbed into bed with Goldie at his side. He reached for his laptop to review a few documents for work, when his doorbell rang.

Gil groaned when Goldie took off running toward the front of the house. Who would visit at this time of night? The only person he could think of was Doug.

Gil got up and went to go answer, turning over reasons in his head to send Doug away. "Doug, I'm not up to visiting tonight—" He opened the door and stumbled over his words. They all got stuck in his throat.

"Um, hi," Moira said. "I know it's late."

"Not at all. Do you want to come in?"

"Unless you're busy."

"I'm not." Gil motioned her inside.

Moira stepped past the threshold and turned to face him.

"What's up?" They hadn't talked about meeting tonight. She had book club, and he had his Thursday night at the tavern.

"I don't know. I just..."

The look on her face made Gil's heart drop. She was hesitating to say something. She almost looked apologetic. "What is it?"

Moira took a breath. "My friends know. My mom knows too."

"You told them?" Gil was confused. "I thought we agreed to keep this under wraps."

"We did. I didn't have to tell them though. They just figured it out. I mean, you weren't exactly normal when you chatted with me and my mom earlier this week. It was kind of obvious."

Gil ran a hand through his hair. "Well, the guys didn't figure it out, but I'm sure they all know now, considering that your friends are all coupled up with mine."

Moira grimaced. "I'm sorry."

"Don't be." Gil stepped toward her, bracing her elbows with his hands. "We're dating. It's not a crime. Yeah, it might be better for us if we kept this thing between us private for a little longer, but"—he shrugged—"now that it's inevitable, we should probably control our own narrative."

"What do you mean?" Moira asked.

"I mean, instead of hiding and being found out, we should own this and go public."

The corner of Moira's mouth quirked. "I like the sound of that. How do you suggest we come out as a couple?"

"By having a date that's not at your place or mine. A real, out-in-the-open date."

Moira's smile grew. "I think I know the perfect place. There's an animal adoption fair for the local animal shelter going on at Hannigan Square tomorrow."

Gil grinned. "I know. I always attend those fairs. That's where I got my Goldie, you know."

"No, I didn't know that," Moira said excitedly.

"I'm kind of surprised you'd suggest that for a date though. I didn't realize you liked animals."

"Of course I do."

Gil loved the idea. "I'll woo you with my ability to make balloon animals for the kids."

Moira looked impressed. "You're a twister?"

"It's one of my many talents." He stepped closer to her, unable to resist. "If you're lucky, I might even make you a balloon animal."

"Sounds perfect."

Gil tugged her closer. "It will be. Nothing warms your heart like seeing a dog's or cat's large, hopeless eyes light up."

"Then count me in. It's a date."

∞

Moira angled herself right and left in front of her full-length mirror. An animal adoption fair wasn't exactly the kind of event you dressed up for. A date with the current mayor, however, was. She'd compromised by wearing a pair of white denim capris and a cardigan sweater over a soft, fitted tee. Even this was a far cry from the holey jeans and T-shirts she wore while working dispatch.

"Moira Green for mayor," she said to her reflection in the mirror. At one point, she hadn't believed that statement for a second, but the more she said it, the more she did.

That wasn't what this evening was about though. Tonight was about letting the community know that she and Gil were in a budding relationship. No more hiding. Tonight was also about laying eyes on her caller Beth. Moira now knew Beth worked for Animal Rescue Ranch—AR Ranch. Hopefully, she'd be working the event, and Moira could get some peace of mind that Beth was okay.

The doorbell rang, and nervous flutters stormed Moira's chest.

She hurried to the door and opened it to find Gil dressed in a pair of dark-rinse jeans and a collared shirt.

"You look..." His gaze dropped, making those butterfly flutters even more intense.

"You don't have to lie," she said before he could finish his sentence. "It's an animal adoption fair though. I didn't think a sundress would really be all that appropriate."

"It doesn't matter what you wear. You look amazing in anything." His gaze returned to hers.

"Aww." Moira's gaze dropped now. "What? No flowers this time?"

Gil looked taken aback. "I didn't want to become too predictable. I've heard predictability is a death sentence for a new relationship."

Moira laughed. "I'm just teasing. I don't need flowers anyway. I'm content to just hold your hand."

Gil reached out his hand for her to take.

When she placed her palm against his, he lifted her hand to his lips and planted a kiss below her knuckles, making her insides warm.

"Ready to give this town something to talk about?" he asked.

"I think they've already been talking about us," she said. "Seeing that we're running against each other."

"Maybe so, but we're about to give them something much juicier to discuss." He winked and tipped his head toward his truck in the driveway.

Moira stepped outside her door, pulled it shut behind her, and locked it. Then she followed Gil to the passenger side of his truck and allowed him to open the door for her. "Don't let me bring any critters home with me tonight," she said once Gil was settled in the driver's seat beside her.

"No? Why not?"

Moira shrugged. "I like to think things through. I don't make rash decisions if I can help it, and adopting a cute little dog or cat would fall into the rash-decision category."

Gil reversed out of her driveway. "I didn't think Goldie through when I brought her home, and she is one of my better decisions. Sometimes you just have to follow your heart."

Moira watched out the window as they passed the homes on her street. "Not this girl. Not tonight."

"Okay. I'll do my best to keep you from falling in love, but no promises."

Moira's gaze darted across the seat, meeting his.

Gil cleared his throat. "Falling in love with an animal, that is. If you want to fall for something or someone else, that's completely up to you."

Fifteen minutes later, they pulled up to Hannigan Square.

"It's so hard to find parking," Gil commented off-handedly. Then he glanced over. "Sorry. Not to bring up a sore subject."

"No, I agree with you," she said. "It is hard. It doesn't mean that my mom's bakery needs to be demolished to fix the problem though."

Gil circled the square and finally slowed. "Bingo. There's one I can squeeze into. It'll have us walking a ways though."

"I'm perfectly capable."

Gil parallel parked into a spot on the curb about a block from the square and then looked over. "Ready to go public?"

"Not really." Moira reached for his hand for a moment. "To tell you the truth, I'm a little nervous."

"Me too. But this will be fun. I promise."

Moira nodded. "Okay. Let's do this."

Gil pushed his truck door open. "Stay there. I'm doing this right tonight."

Moira waited as he ran around and opened her door for her. Then she stepped out and took his outstretched hand in hers.

Once again, Gil lifted her hand to his mouth and kissed it.

"Oh, my heavens!" someone said from behind them.

Moira froze and slid her gaze toward Gil. They'd

barely gotten started with this date, and they were already outed as a couple in a huge way.

"Are my eyes deceiving me?" Reva Dawson asked. Of course Reva would be the first one to see them together. Reva had a nose for news.

Moira turned toward the infamous town blogger, noting how Gil's hand tightened on hers. He wasn't letting go and neither was she. They were in this together.

"Your eyes are not deceiving you, Ms. Dawson," Gil said, trying to maintain a pleasant tone.

Reva hurried up to them, her gaze firmly set on their clasped hands. "You two are dating?" She looked up with a broad smile. "Oh, this is good."

Gil had no doubt this would be the first bullet point on her blog tomorrow. He could only imagine what she planned on saying.

"How long has this been going on?" she asked. "Is Moira the one you were purchasing flowers for the other day?"

Gil cleared his throat. "Good evening to you as well, Reva. Are you on your way to the animal adoption fair?"

She frowned slightly at his obvious change of subject. "Well, yes. I thought I'd see who was adopting a new pet. That would be good news for my blog tomorrow. My readers love a good dog story." Her smile returned in dramatic fashion. "They love a good love story too."

Gil squeezed Moira's hand, trying to reassure her that everything would be fine. He was nervous, too, though. It'd been a while since he'd dated anyone seriously, and he hadn't since he was mayor. This was a big deal for him. More than he'd realized when he'd suggested it last night. It was necessary though. He didn't want to live in secret, and he wanted this thing with Moira to work. A foundation of hiding didn't seem like the right thing to do anymore.

"Enjoy the animal fair," Gil told Reva. "Maybe you'll find a lovable canine or feline to bring home with you."

Reva chuckled. "I have four at home already. I think I have my hands full. They keep me in good company when I'm writing my blog though. They'll keep me company tonight, matter of fact." She winked and hurried past Gil and Moira.

Moira looked at Gil, and he couldn't quite read her expression.

"Hmm. By the look on your face, you're completely freaked and ready to bolt," he said, testing the waters.

"It's too late for that. Reva has seen us." She offered a nervous smile. "And I wouldn't turn around and run anyway. I want to do this. Like you said, we can't have all our dates at your place or mine, and I want more dates."

Gil leaned in and brushed his lips over hers. "I want more dates too. As long as they're with you."

Moira laughed softly. "You don't want to keep playing the field, Mr. Most Eligible Bachelor of Somerset Lake?"

"I never played the field to begin with."

They started walking again. The animal adoption fair could be seen up ahead now. There was a big banner that read FUREVER HOME sandwiched by huge red hearts with paw prints inside.

"I have to admit, when I attend these things, it's so hard for me not to bring home at least three or four dogs with me."

"You don't think Goldie should have a friend?"

"I know golden retrievers are traditionally happy-go-lucky, but she's the jealous type," Gil said. "It's going to be hard enough for her to adjust to sharing me with you."

Moira looked a bit more relaxed as they approached the crowd and entered a large gated area where the dogs were contained on leashes with their handlers. "It takes a lot of volunteers to work this place, huh?"

"Oh, yeah. All for a good cause."

Moira glanced around. "Since you come to these events a lot, I'm assuming you know the volunteers."

Gil nodded. "Yeah. All of them."

Moira looked at him hopefully. "Will you introduce me?"

He tilted his head. "You thinking about becoming a volunteer?"

Moira smiled and lifted a noncommittal shoulder. "You never know."

"First running for mayor and now volunteering with rescue animals. You are one surprise after another these days, aren't you?" Gil teased. "Come on. I'll introduce you to the organizer, Beth Chimes."

"Beth?" Moira asked, brows lifting.

"You know her?" Gil asked.

Moira shook her head quickly. "Not yet, but I'd love to meet her."

"Your wish is my command." Gil led Moira toward a table where three women were sitting. Folks had tried to set him up with Beth last year. She was young, single, and attractive, but there were no sparks between them.

"Hey, Beth," he said.

Beth looked up from a notebook set before her on the

table. "Mayor Gil." A broad smile formed on her face. "I'm so glad you could make it."

Gil gestured to Moira, who looked shell-shocked again. "This is my friend Moira Green."

"Um, hi. Nice to meet you," Moira said.

He got the feeling that Beth made Moira nervous somehow, which he found odd.

"You're running for mayor." Beth's gaze moved to Gil, and her smile faded. "Against you."

"That's true." Gil nodded.

"I was so sorry to hear about the town's plans to demolish your mother's business," Beth told Moira. "I speak to your mom all the time when I stop in the bakery."

"Right. I've seen you there," Moira said.

"Well, now we've officially met. We can speak to each other next time." She looked at Gil apologetically. "I mean, maybe there'll be a next time before Sweetie's closes."

Gil wanted to move on from the topic of Sweetie's and the Hannigan Street parking lot. "What can we do to help today?"

"Just being here is enough." Beth stood from her seat. "Having both of you here is sure to reel people in. If you could just walk around and love on the animals. That'll encourage others to do the same. Maybe snap a few pics and post on social media if you can. To draw more attention to the event. I would love it if every animal here found a good home today." Beth looked at Moira. "That never happens, of course, but one can hope, right?" She stuck her hand out for Moira to shake. "Nice to meet you, Moira."

Moira shook Beth's hand. "You too. Really. You seem happy."

Beth smiled awkwardly. "Oh, well, meeting new people and matching them with their ideal pet makes me happy, I guess. See you around."

Moira glanced at Gil as they walked away.

He still couldn't read Moira, and maybe that was part of her appeal. She was a good mystery, which he'd never been able to resist.

"Beth seems nice," Moira said.

"She is. She's really passionate about giving these animals good homes."

"Was she acting the same way she normally does, when you see her?"

Gil cast Moira a questioning look. "Why do I get the feeling there's a motive behind your wanting to meet Beth? Maybe Beth is your motive for wanting to be here today too?"

Moira fidgeted with her hands. "My main motive today is spending time with you."

Gil wasn't quite believing that in full, but he returned the sentiment. "Mine as well." He pointed at the dogs they were approaching. "Ready to pet on some lonely dogs?"

"Ready. You said Goldie was the jealous type. If you go home smelling like all these guys, you'll be in so much trouble with your dog."

Gil chuckled. "Yes, I will. But, if I'm with you, it'll be worth it."

Chapter Twenty-Four

Moira had stopped noticing the double takes and looks of surprise as she and Gil walked hand in hand, and she was now just focused on enjoying herself. And she was. This was the best date she'd ever had. "Who'd have thought an animal adoption fair could be so much fun?" She looked up at Gil from where she was kneeling in front of an adorable brown and white Cavalier spaniel mix.

Gil squatted beside her and petted the little pup's head as well. "I would have."

Moira's gaze hung on him for an extended moment. Then the puppy tugged on her sweater, regaining her attention. "You are pretty demanding, huh?" she asked the puppy, who licked her palm in response.

"I think she likes you. I can't blame her, really."

Moira side-eyed him. "Such a charmer."

He leaned in to kiss her, and she was very aware that this was their first public kiss. They'd been holding hands, so it was obvious they were here together, but a kiss confirmed their relationship for anyone who doubted.

Gil paused just a millimeter from her mouth. "You okay with this?"

"Mm-hmm," she said, her heartbeat quickening.

Gil leaned in again, and then the puppy jumped up between them and ran its tongue over both of their faces.

"Eww!" Moira laughed. "Either the puppy got us or you're one sloppy kisser, Mr. Mayor."

Gil used his shirtsleeve to wipe his face as well. "Wow. Goldie really is going to have a fit when I get home this evening." He patted the puppy's head again. "You sure you're not in the market for a puppy?"

Moira shook her head quickly. "I've always loved this breed. My grandmother used to have a Cavalier. I don't make rash decisions though, remember? Bringing Molly home with me would be impulsive."

"Moira and Molly has a ring to it. Just saying."

Moira straightened back to a standing position, and Gil did as well. She looked down at Molly. "Don't worry, girl. You'll find your forever home." Moira turned to Gil. "Just not with me."

Gil reached for her hand again. "Now, where were we before Molly so rudely interrupted us? Ah, yes. We were just about to kiss."

Moira grinned, heart leaping back into her throat.

"Hey, you two!"

Both Moira and Gil separated short of a kiss when they heard Denise Berger's voice.

"Well, this is interesting, isn't it?" Denise looked practically giddy. "My two rivals in the race for mayor are a little more than rivals with one another."

"Hello, Denise," Gil said politely.

Moira had to give it to him. He had grace in difficult situations. She guessed that made him a good mayor. She forced a smile and tried to do the same. "Are you here looking for a new pet?"

Denise offered up a fake laugh, pulling her hand to her chest. "Oh, no. Not me. I'm not a dog person."

Gil held on to his smile. "Maybe you should be."

"Excuse me?" Denise asked, smile slipping at the corners.

Gil shrugged. "This town loves dogs. A mayor without a dog just wouldn't seem right here. Plus, dogs make us better human beings. It's a fact."

"I'm a perfectly fine human being as it is." She looked at Moira. "Are you getting a new pet?"

"No. I'm just here with Gil."

"Well, that's fairly obvious." Denise's smile showed off lipstick-smudged front teeth. It served her right for having such a snooty attitude. "I wonder what voters will think of this new relationship of yours."

"I suspect my voters will be happy for me," Gil said. "I'm sure Moira's will as well. Dogs aren't the only things that make us better human beings. Sometimes people make each other better too."

Moira's heart skipped. Did he mean that? Was he talking about her?

"I see. Well, it's good to see you both," Denise said. "I'm going to continue forward."

"Shaking hands and kissing babies," Gil said, surprising Moira. She'd never known him to be remotely rude. She wasn't even sure if this qualified.

"Well, that's the nature of politics, right?" Denise winked. Then she looked at them both, her gaze hanging on Moira a little too long. It made Moira uncomfortable. She didn't really have anything against Denise other than the fact that she didn't think Denise should serve the town as mayor.

"That was a bit weird," she said once Denise was out of earshot.

"If she becomes mayor this fall, I'm moving," Gil said.

Moira playfully punched his shoulder. "No, you're not. You have lived here all your life."

"Except for college." As soon as Gil said it, his smile dropped. He cleared his throat, looking suddenly tense.

"It's okay," Moira said in a quiet voice. "Nothing really happened, thanks to you. I can't blame you for having a bad roommate."

"Understatement," Gil said. "I never would have forgiven myself if anything had happened that night, you know."

Moira nodded, believing him. "I know. You're a good person, and I think you're right. I'm a better person with you around."

An hour later, both Moira and Gil had actually shaken hands and kissed several babies.

"I didn't think I liked puppies," Moira said. "I always thought if I ever got a dog, I'd want an older one. But puppies are so much fun."

"Now that Goldie is all grown up, I miss the puppy stage," Gil said.

"Well, there are plenty here to go around."

Gil shook his head. "What about Molly? You've had an hour to consider her. It wouldn't be a rash decision to bring her home now."

Moira turned to him. Some part of her wanted to bring Gil home tonight. That would be rash though. And it would be crossing a line they couldn't uncross. She wasn't ready for that just yet. She liked taking things slow between them. "I don't have any pet supplies."

"They sell them here, you know."

Moira tilted her head to one side. "Why are you trying so hard to get me to bring a puppy home, Mayor Gil?"

He chuckled. "I meant what I told Denise earlier. Dogs make us better humans. Not that I think you need to improve in any way. I think you're pretty perfect as is."

Moira felt her whole body warm. "You might be the first man to ever think so."

He reached out and slid an unruly strand of her hair behind her ear. "Doubtful. You're a little intimidating, that's all."

"Me?" She laughed at the idea.

"Yeah. You're hard to read, in a good way. A man likes to know he's not going to fail. They look for all the signs that women send them to ensure them they're going to achieve success. You don't really send those signals out. It's a risk pursuing you."

"Hmm. I find your assessment of me very interesting. If I had known that's what was keeping the men away all these years, it might have saved me a little self-esteem."

"Trust me. You're beautiful, smart, sweet, funny. You're everything that any guy with half a brain is looking for."

"Including you?" she asked, wishing she could take the question back as soon as it left her mouth.

"Including me."

Moira cleared her throat. "Okay."

Gil gave her a strange look. "Okay, what?"

"I want to take Molly home with me. I want to adopt her. You've convinced me."

Gil looked pleased. He reached for Moira's hand, giving it a soft squeeze. "Let's go get her then."

∞

Gil's heart sank for Moira as soon as they approached the spot where Molly had previously been. The little Cavalier was no longer there on its leash. Instead there was a cardboard heart that read I'VE BEEN ADOPTED!

Moira seemed to visibly wilt as she stood there staring at the cardboard sign.

Gil cleared his throat. "Want to find another pup who'll steal your heart?"

She shook her head quietly and then looked up at him. There was a shiny quality to her eyes that took him off guard. And now he felt awful for even suggesting she adopt a pet here today. She was disappointed.

"I'm sorry," he said.

"Not your fault. I'm happy for little Molly," Moira said, putting on an unbelievable smile. "Whoever adopted her probably knows a lot more about raising a pup than I do. I don't know much. And I have my hands full with a day job and running for mayor."

"Not to mention dating me," Gil said, hoping to cheer her up.

Her eyes seemed to warm as she looked up at him. "You are quite the handful."

"So I'm told. Hey, do you want to go somewhere else? We've made our appearance here. How about we head out?"

"But you haven't made those balloon animals you told me about yet," she teased.

"Another time." Gil reached for Moira's hand. "If we're outing ourselves as a couple tonight, we should venture out and show everyone."

Moira laughed. "We can spread our own news before Reva has a chance to."

"That's the spirit. I have an idea of where to go," he said.

"Where?"

He shook his head. "It's a surprise. Do you trust me?"

"After you made me fall in love with a puppy, decide to adopt it against my better judgment, and broke my heart?" she asked.

Gil made a face. "Is that a no?"

"It's a yes. I trust you despite all that." She squeezed his hand. "Lead the way."

Twenty minutes later, Gil thought Moira looked a lot more relaxed. "Chocolate for the win, right?" he asked.

Moira grinned at him across the table. "Choco-Lovers always cheers me up."

"Good to know." He leaned forward and reached a hand toward her face.

Moira's smile dropped quickly.

"You have a little..."

"Oh. I have chocolate on my cheek?" she asked, trying to brush it off herself. "Did I get it?"

Gil shook his head. "You smeared it. Here." He brushed his finger over her cheek, trying to get it off for her. Her skin was soft and touchable, and he loved the fact that he could touch her now. "There." He lowered his hand.

Moira looked at him strangely for a long moment. Then she reached for her drink and pulled it closer to her but didn't take a sip. Her vibe was suddenly guarded.

"You okay?" he asked.

"Yeah." She nodded. Then she quickly shook her head, looking increasingly flustered. "That's how he was able to get me to leave the table and drug my drink. He pretended like there was something on my cheek. Felix." She visibly swallowed.

Gil's mouth dropped. "Moira, I'm sorry. I didn't know."

"Of course you didn't. And I know you would never put anything in my drink. It just...I don't know. The moment just hit me weird, that's all."

"Well," Gil said, "just so you know, I'm not pretending. You actually do have chocolate on your cheek. You're a mess, to tell the truth," he teased.

This made Moira smile. Then she blew out a breath. "My secret is out. Do you want to break up with me now?" she asked.

"If you're trying to get rid of me, you'll have to try harder than that."

"I'm not. I've decided that I like having you around." She took a sip of her drink.

"You do?"

"Mm-hmm." Picking up one of her chocolate puffs from the plate at the center of the table, she held it out to him. "I'm even willing to share my treats with you."

"Wow. That's serious." Gil leaned forward again to take a bite of the chocolate puff she held out. Just as he was about to taste it, Moira brushed it over his cheek.

"Oops." Her giggle turned into a full-on laugh.

"Accident, huh?" Gil asked. "And to think I tried to help you get the chocolate off your face. A future mayor should always be presentable."

"So should a current mayor," she teased.

As she was laughing, Gil lifted one of his chocolate truffles and swiped it over her chin. "There. We're both unpresentable now."

"No, you did not," Moira said on a small laugh, raising her chocolate puff again.

They stopped laughing when the shop's owner, Jana, walked over. She stood at the head of their table and looked between them. "No food fights, you two. If I didn't know better, I'd think you were a couple of teenagers in here."

Gil looked at Moira. "What can I say? Moira makes me feel like a teenager again."

"Aww." Jana shook her head. "That's sweet. You have a keeper, Moira. You also have a lot of chocolate on your face right now."

Moira reached for a napkin. "Sorry, Jana. We got a little carried away."

"No problem. I'm just happy to see you two enjoying yourselves. It appears the town's Most Eligible Bachelor is off the market. I wonder who Reva will pin the title on next."

Gil shrugged. "My condolences to whoever it is. You're right though. I'm definitely off the market."

Moira handed him a napkin and laughed. "And also covered in chocolate."

Gil wiped his cheek and then lowered the napkin. "Okay, so tell me the truth."

Moira paused mid-bite into a truffle. "Hmm?"

"You were acting very strangely around Beth Chimes. What was that about?"

Moira lowered her truffle. For a moment, she shrugged and looked like she might give him some excuse that wasn't exactly true. "She called me on the dispatch the other day. She's the caller who didn't remember what happened on her date the night before."

Gil stiffened. "Are you sure about that?"

Moira looked guilty. "I kept her number and called it back a couple days later. She answered as an organizer

of Animal Rescue Ranch. She said her name was Beth."
Moira looked down at her hands. "I just wanted to check
on her. I wanted to look her in the eyes and see for myself
that she was okay."

"And? Do you feel better?"

Moira nodded. "A little, I guess. Maybe someone came
along and helped her before things got too bad, the way
you did for me."

"I hope so," Gil said quietly. "I guess we'll never know."

Moira frowned. "That's the hardest part of what I do.
Sometimes there's no closure. Sometimes I can't help a
person the way I want to."

Gil reached for her hand and squeezed. "But sometimes you can."

"And that keeps me going, call after call." Moira
smiled, but it wasn't quite reaching her eyes. "This has
been a great date. Sorry for having a little bit of an
ulterior motive."

Gil chuckled. "I don't mind. Thanks for telling me
though. I'm glad you feel comfortable talking to me
about it."

Moira picked up another truffle. "You can't tell anyone.
Keeping the number of a caller in my phone is about the
equivalent of leaving the dispatch to go to a caller's house.
Ronnie definitely wouldn't be giving me any awards this
time. I'd most likely be looking for a new job."

"Well, you're already gunning for my job. I guess
you'd just have to up the ante."

She narrowed her eyes. "That assumes that I'm not
already going in full ante for the mayor's position."

Gil shook his head. "I'm not assuming anything. I
want you to go after this with everything you have, if this
is truly what you want."

Moira gave him a strange look. "I wouldn't run if it wasn't."

Gil hesitated. This date was going well to this point. He didn't want to mess it up. "I wanted to be a mayor for years before I actually decided to run, you know. There were baby steps I took that led me to taking the office. You said you didn't make rash decisions." He licked his bottom lip, tasting the chocolate there. "I think that's a good thing in some cases, like running for public office."

"What are you trying to say?" she asked.

"You should just know what you're getting into."

"I do." Moira averted her gaze.

Gil could feel an invisible wall going up. "Great. How about this? No more talking about jobs or politics or running against each other for the rest of this date. Let's just focus on us."

Moira turned her attention back to him, a small smile growing at the corners of her lips. "I think that's a great suggestion. Deal."

Chapter Twenty-Five

After breakfast with Tess and Lucy, Moira headed up to the counter to tell her mom goodbye and get a refill on her coffee.

"Can I see you in the back?" Darla asked. She looked serious this morning, like there was something weighing on her mind.

"Sure." Moira headed around the counter and followed Darla into the back room. It was the weekend, so Darla had Bailey working the counter. "Is something wrong, Mom?"

Darla sat down at the little table that she had set up and waited for Moira to do the same. Once Moira was seated, Darla took a breath and narrowed her gaze on Moira. "I need to be honest with you, and I need you to hear me."

"I'm listening." Moira's heart was thudding in her chest. Her mom was usually so cheerful and laid-back. She didn't often get so serious or look so troubled. Whatever her mom was about to say was important.

"Moira, I opened this bakery nearly thirty years ago. You were just a little baby at the time. It was hard, and I am so proud of this place."

"As you should be, Mom," Moira said.

"Some part of me always thought you'd take over one day, but it's not your path, and I would never force my dream on you. You have a life, and I am so amazed by who you've become. Who you're still becoming. You save lives, Moira."

Moira shifted uncomfortably in the small metal chair. "Not exactly, but thank you for understanding, Mom." Moira had never wanted to work at her mom's business. She didn't even enjoy baking.

"Moira, I've broached this with you a couple of times, but I don't think you've heard me. I know this bakery is like a second home to you. You said your first word in this building. You learned to crawl and then walk here. And don't think I'm not keen on the fact that this place is where you had your first kiss when you were fourteen."

Moira's mouth fell open.

"Peter Blake," Darla said with the faintest hint of a smile. "I had a talk with that boy at this very table the next day."

Moira gasped. "You didn't."

Darla laughed quietly. "I did. What I'm trying to say is, this bakery is special. It harbors memories that I hold dear."

Moira reached for her mom's hand. "Mom, I'm not giving up on saving this place. That's why I'm running for mayor."

Darla's smile dropped. "I was worried that was the case."

Moira shook her head. "What do you mean by that?"

"Moira, this bakery can't be your why for running for town mayor. Helping me can't be your *why*. Moira, the truth is, I don't want to save this bakery."

"What?" Moira sat up straighter. "Of course you do. Like you just said, this place is special. It's home."

"I'm ready to retire, Moira. I don't wake up eager to get to this place anymore. I watch the clock when I'm here because I want to be home where your father is. He almost died a few years ago. We have a second chance, and I don't want to waste it working behind a counter. I want to do the things we always said we would." She forced a smile.

Moira's dad was enjoying his retirement so much. Moira knew that. "You could hire more staff and work less hours."

"I could, and I've considered that option. But part of me feels like, when the doors are open, I need to be here interacting with the customers. I honestly think Sweetie's Bakeshop will go downhill if I delegate what I've always done to staff who aren't as invested in this place. I don't really want to see that happen. Sometimes it's best to go out on top."

"Mom, you don't really believe that."

Darla gave her a pointed, serious look. She didn't blink, didn't shift or fidget. "I do, and I want you to hear this. *Really* hear it, Moira. The parking lot is necessary, and it should be here. I'm ready to move on to something new, like your father. If your why for running for mayor is this bakery, then it's misplaced."

Gil walked outside onto his back deck and sat in one of the wooden Adirondack chairs. Goldie quickly joined him, pushing her head beneath his hand to force him to pet her. Gil absently obliged while his mind retraced his evening with Moira the other night.

"Hey, Gilly."

Gil blinked the blurry image of the lake back into view and turned toward Doug, who was heading across the lawn. He was wearing a VOTE GIL RYAN FOR MAYOR T-shirt in a dark gray color this time. "Hey, buddy. How are you?"

"You made Reva's blog again."

Gil chuckled. "I know. I'm dating the competition. That's big news."

Doug slowly climbed the deck steps. Goldie ran over to greet him, walking faithfully beside him until he sat in the chair next to Gil's. In another life, she would have made a good service dog.

Doug held up one finger. "You made one bullet point."

"All publicity is good publicity," Gil said. He didn't really believe that statement though. A time or two he'd gotten publicity that rattled him and upset his supporters, like this thing with Sweetie's Bakeshop.

"Hey, Gilly?"

"Hmm?" Gil looked over, squinting at the sun's rays.

"I don't want to hurt Mom's feelings, but this isn't a phase. I want my own place."

Gil remembered what Moira had said. If Doug could take care of himself, why shouldn't he have his own place? "Okay."

"I spoke to Della Rose already," Doug said, petting Goldie's head.

"Wow. What did she say?"

Doug couldn't seem to hide his smile. "Louise Herman moved out of one of the Somerset Rental Cottages. It's open, and Della thinks it would be a good place for me. It's more money than I was planning to spend though." He narrowed his eyes at Gil from behind his glasses. "Della told me to ask you for a raise."

Gil chuckled. "Did she now?"

"Yes, and I think I deserve one," Doug said earnestly. "I also spoke to Jake."

Gil was surprised at this. "Oh?"

"Jake said that Louise was the dog walker for the Somerset Rental Cottages. I can do that and be your campaign manager too. And live on my own."

"You've given this a lot of thought," Gil said.

"When you want something, you go for it, no matter what. I want this." Doug took a visible breath. "So?"

Gil hesitated. "So?"

"I want a raise. I want you to talk to Mom for me. And I want you to help me move."

Gil grinned. "Is that all? Would you like to run for mayor too? Seems like everyone else in town wants that."

Doug shook his head. "No, you're the mayor, and you're a good one. Almost as good at that as you are at being my brother."

Who could argue with Doug after he'd said that? "Okay. To all of it. I'll back you up and talk to Mom."

"Really?" Doug's eyes lit up behind his glasses. "Thank you, Gilly."

"Don't thank me yet. Mom might disown me after our talk."

"You'd still have me," Doug said, making Gil's heart squeeze. What had he ever done to deserve such a loyal and loving brother? He'd do anything within his power to help Doug. Doug would feel part of a community in the close-knit environment at the Somerset Rental Cottages. Why hadn't Gil chosen one of those cottages as his first place to live after college?

"If I move into my own place, you won't have to worry about me waking you up all the time," Doug finally said.

"Truth is, I'll probably miss that."

Doug looked at him a moment. "I can drive the golf cart around the lake and still wake you up then."

Gil laughed out loud. "No, thanks. I won't miss it that much, Doug."

Chapter Twenty-Six

Moira rolled onto her side and looked at the clock. She couldn't sleep. Now that she knew her mom didn't want her to fight for the bakeshop, Moira lay here wondering what she was even fighting for. Her why was gone. Or the why she thought she had, at least. Instead of counting sheep, she'd been staring at the shadows in her bedroom, listing the reasons she had for still wanting to be mayor. And why she didn't.

There was only one reason that fell in the "didn't" category. She didn't want to hurt Gil. They'd already discussed that to death though, and he had assured her that, whatever happened, it wouldn't affect their relationship. He was a man of his word. She believed that wholeheartedly.

So that left her with at least a dozen reasons to still run for mayor, which surprised her. This had stopped being about saving Sweetie's Bakeshop a while ago. She'd discovered a side of herself that she'd long suppressed, and it felt good to be taking a stand for her community.

Moira flopped around onto her other side. She wasn't losing sleep over fears or negative thoughts. She was energized. Excited. About the campaign and also about her new relationship with Gil. Everything was changing in mostly good ways.

On a sigh, because she really did need to get her sleep, she stood and walked into the kitchen for a glass of water. She drank it while watching outside her back window. The moon was full tonight. She stared at it in wonder for a moment. Even the moon and the stars looked different somehow.

Am I falling for him?

Moira stood there with that question. Maybe she was. The air was sweeter. Gil painted her world a brighter shade of all her favorite colors. Wasn't that how others described falling in love?

Moira set her empty glass down and turned back toward her bedroom, doubting she'd get any quality sleep tonight with this new revelation.

"I can't believe this place will be a parking lot soon." Moira popped a piece of her bagel into her mouth as she sat across from Tess the following week.

"So you've given up on saving Sweetie's?"

Moira shrugged. "I don't really have a choice. My mom wants to retire in the fall. It's her decision, not mine."

"Hmm." Tess looked around the bakeshop thoughtfully. "There are a lot of memories wrapped up in these walls."

Moira looked around as well. "Hannigan Street definitely won't be the same. But at least everyone will stop complaining about not having anywhere to park."

Tess laughed quietly. "True, I guess. I'm even nostalgic

about that. I mean, what will we all moan and groan about if not parking?"

Moira tore another piece of her bagel off but didn't eat it just yet. Instead she sat there thoughtfully for a moment.

"What's wrong?" Tess asked. "I can tell when something is on your mind. What is it?"

Moira blinked her friend into focus. "It's just... I like Gil."

Tess looked at her strangely. "I know you do. That's a good thing, right?"

Moira nodded. "I mean, I *really* like Gil."

Tess's gaze narrowed. "I know that too. You remind me of the way I felt when I was falling for River."

"So you think I'm falling for Gil?" Moira asked.

Tess angled her head. "Are you really looking to me for answers? I think you can answer this question yourself."

Moira tore another piece off her bagel, leaving it beside the first. She wasn't hungry in the slightest. She just needed something to do with her hands. "You know, I almost adopted a puppy the other night. A puppy."

Tess grinned. "Yeah, so?"

"So"—Moira shook her head and gestured at herself—"who is this person, and what did she do with the real Moira Green?"

"You *are* the real Moira Green. And it's nice to see you opening yourself up to new things. Like a puppy. Why didn't you adopt it?"

"Because someone else took her home before me." Moira picked another piece of bagel off. "Is this what happened with you and River? Did you start contemplating getting a dog all of a sudden?"

Tess chuckled. "Actually, yes. But River's dog is enough canine for me. I'm considering getting a cat for the bookshop though."

"Oh, fun." Moira finally popped the piece of bread into her mouth and chewed. "Maybe you can turn the bookshop into part cat café."

Tess pulled back and held up her hands. "That sounds like way too much work. I sell books, not coffee, tea, and pastries."

"Right. My mom is actually working on a new hangout for Sweetie's customers. Turns out the diner down the street lost a lot of its morning customers to the bakery, so it quit serving breakfast during the week."

"Things always work out the way they're supposed to." Tess pushed back from the table. "I've got to go open the store. Lara has a dentist appointment this morning. Talk to you later?"

Moira nodded. "I have to get home for dispatch."

"Maybe you'll save another life, Miss Small-Town Hero," Tess teased.

"Maybe so." But she would most likely sit at her desk and doodle Gil's name like she'd done the last several shifts.

On Thursday night, Moira stood in front of the mirror debating the third outfit she'd tried on for tonight. For the first time since she'd had the flu three years ago, Moira was skipping book club. There was a town council meeting scheduled and, even though she wasn't officially on the council, as someone running for mayor she had been invited to attend.

The doorbell rang and Moira hurried to answer it. Gil

had offered to pick her up and ride together. Now that the cat was out of the bag about their relationship, this was awkward. But also wonderful.

She opened the door and beamed at him. "Hi."

"Hi," he said, his gaze dropping to what she was wearing. She'd chosen a pair of black pants and a sapphire blue blouse that was equal parts dressy and casual. "You look like mayor material."

Moira tilted her head. "So do you," she said, noting his dark gray pants and yellow polo shirt. She stepped out onto the porch and locked the door behind her, gaze snagging on the dent in her door. She doubted she'd ever get rid of that. Turning back to Gil, she asked, "Does Denise Berger go to these meetings?"

"She has in the past. It's not usually her scene though. If she's not in charge, she doesn't want to be there. That's my guess, at least."

Moira nodded as they walked. "To be honest, I'm a little nervous. Some part of me feels like I don't belong at one of these meetings."

Gil opened her truck door for her. "That's called impostor syndrome. I've been mayor for three years now, and I still have it sometimes." He closed the door behind her.

Impostor syndrome. Moira had heard of that before. Was that what she was feeling? She pulled her seat belt across her and turned to Gil as he got behind the wheel. "You don't have to be my boyfriend when we're at the meeting, you know?"

This made Gil smile. "So I'm your boyfriend when we're not at the meeting?" he asked, cranking the truck's engine.

"No." She shook her head. "No, I didn't say that." She rolled her lips together. "Are you . . . saying that?"

Gil chuckled and reversed the truck out of the driveway. "It feels like we're in high school again. The whole *are we, aren't we* thing. Do you remember that?"

Moira laughed quietly. "I wasn't much for dating in high school, so I don't really recall anything like that. Not for me, at least. I remember friends agonizing over stuff like that though."

"Grade school dating was easier. You just asked a girl to be your girlfriend, and she said yes or no."

Moira held her tongue for a moment, tuning in to the faint sound of music streaming through Gil's radio. It was some kind of soft rock.

He slid his gaze over. "So?"

"So?" she repeated.

"Are we?"

Moira considered the question. "Tell me, what does being your girlfriend entail exactly?"

Gil pulled up to a stop sign and looked both ways. Then he looked at her for a long moment. "Hmm. Let's see. It entails allowing me to call you, visit you, bring you flowers whenever I choose, and try to make you laugh as often as I can. Also accepting compliments from me, having me check on you, and bring you soup when you're sick."

Moira laughed a little louder now. "Gee. What's in it for me?" she asked sarcastically.

Gil looked over with a serious expression. Then he continued driving. "Just my heart. That's all."

Doug was right. Town council meetings were typically pretty boring. Gil guessed that could be said about most meetings for anything. They had an agenda, and the same things were on it every time they met. That meant that they pretty much held the same conversations about the same items every time and kicked the topics they couldn't agree on down the road to the next meeting.

That wasn't true for the important stuff, of course. That stuff got handled right away. It was the menial stuff, like putting up an extra sign on the town green reminding folks to pick up after their pets. Or getting more volunteers for the school's career day this spring.

"Well, if that's all," Gil said, bringing the meeting to a close the way he normally did.

"Actually..." Moira raised a hand. She'd been mostly quiet during tonight's meeting. "I wanted to bring up a topic for the town to consider."

"Okay." Gil offered an encouraging smile. "Go ahead."

"Well, this has to do with the rock throwers." Moira looked around the long rectangular table where they were all seated. "I'm concerned that the culprits are a bunch of teenagers looking for a little fun. Frankly, if that's the case, I can't really blame them. There's not a whole lot around here for the younger crowd to do."

"There's the lake," another member, Bob Reynolds, said.

"Well, yes, but the kids would be waterlogged if they spent all their free time at Somerset Lake," Moira shot back with equal parts directness and politeness.

"The youth center," Denise Berger said. She'd shown up after all, and she'd done her best to control the narrative for every topic so far.

"Younger kids like the youth center, sure, but the older ones usually stop going. I mean, they're so bored that they're throwing rocks at doors. It sounds harmless, but someone could really get hurt. I think it would cut down on teens getting themselves into trouble if they had a place to go. We adults have our places, right? Sweetie's is mine." Moira looked down for a moment. Gil knew she was regretting that soon her place would be leveled and paved into a parking lot. Looking back up, she forced a smile. "So I wanted to suggest that we start considering creating a hangout for the teens."

"What kind of place are you suggesting?" Denise asked, practically looking down her nose at Moira.

Moira shrugged. "I don't know. A skate park, maybe."

"For skateboarders?" Sheriff Ronnie asked.

"Mm-hmm. There's one in Magnolia Falls. The kids skate for hours on end. There's also picnic tables for them to just sit and talk." She shrugged and glanced over at Gil.

He offered another supportive smile. "I like that suggestion a lot."

"You're just saying that because you two are dating," Denise shot across the table.

Gil cleared his throat. "And maybe you don't like the idea because it wasn't yours."

The room went quiet, the tension thick and palpable.

Gil cleared his throat again. He didn't usually let his tongue slip like that. "We'll put the suggestion on the list and discuss it some more at the next meeting," he finally said.

"This is what's wrong with you as a mayor," Denise said. "This is why I should take your place."

A few people in the room took audible breaths.

"Why exactly is that?" Gil asked, tempering his response.

"Because you sit on things for too long. You're a thinker whereas I take action. Moira's idea is a bad one.

If I were mayor, I'd strike it down and keep moving. If I were already in office, the parking lot would be built by now, and we'd all be discussing something else to improve the town." She lifted her chin and looked Gil directly in the eyes.

He was wondering how to handle the conversation when one of the town council members spoke up in his favor. "I don't agree, Mrs. Berger. A thoughtful mayor is a good thing. Only a fool takes action too quickly."

Denise's lips parted as she glanced over at the man. "A fool?"

"That's what he said," another town council member said.

Several members nodded.

"Mayor Gil has done a wonderful job for this town. The parking lot is coming at its own pace, and we're all doing our best here, which means we're not judging one another."

"Speaking of rock throwers, people who live in glass houses," one member said, wagging a finger at Denise, "shouldn't throw them."

Denise's cheeks flushed. "What is that supposed to mean?"

"It means you're not perfect, and you're surely not the perfect candidate for mayor," Vi Fletcher said, direct as always.

Gil had always liked Vi. She spoke her mind, even when hers wasn't a popular opinion.

"If you continue your run," Vi told Denise, "you'll lose. That's pretty clear. And after last year's fall talent show, we all know how much you can't stand to lose."

Gil had forgotten about that. Denise had objected loudly last fall when her musical act had gotten only fourth place.

She'd told everyone who would listen that the voting was rigged and she was robbed of the winning title.

"Lose?" Denise echoed as if that was an absurd idea. She looked around the room, where her peers either nodded to agree with Vi or lowered their gaze.

Gil didn't contribute to the conversation. He just sat back and watched everyone in the council fight his fight for him. It was a humbling show of support that left him speechless and proud of the job he'd done over the last few years.

Once the town council meeting was over, Gil walked Moira outside.

"I wasn't kidding. I like your idea," he said.

"Because I'm your girlfriend?" She turned to face him.

"Aha. So you *are* my girlfriend."

She stepped closer, tipping her face up to his, her hazel eyes catching the starlight.

He wanted to kiss her so badly right now. But there were still town council members lingering by their cars and holding side conversations, some of which were probably focused on Moira and him.

"Okay," she finally said.

Gil lifted a questioning brow. "Okay?"

"I'll be your girlfriend."

Gil opened his eyes the next morning and blinked his bedroom into view. Goldie was nuzzled up to his side, undisturbed until he made his first move. Gil glanced over at his bedside clock and blinked again. Nine a.m.? When was the last time he'd slept this late?

He sat up in bed, and Goldie huffed. Doug had usually knocked on Gil's door by now. Gil had stopped setting an alarm clock a long time ago because he didn't need one.

Yawning, he stood and shuffled to the bathroom. After that, he walked down the hall and opened the back door for Goldie to go out. Gil glanced across the lawn at his parents' home, hoping to see Doug heading in this direction. Maybe Doug had just slept in, too, and his absence wasn't because he was upset with Gil. Doug was nowhere to be seen, however.

On a sigh, Gil refocused on Goldie, who was now sniffing random patches of grass.

"Come on, Gold. I need coffee."

Goldie darted back toward the house, racing inside ahead of him. Gil went through the motions of drinking his coffee and taking a quick shower. Then he headed across the lawn to see Doug.

He stood at his parents' front door and knocked. A moment later, his mom came to the door. Her smile dropped when she saw him.

"Uh-oh," Gil said. "What did I do?"

"You know exactly what you did." She stepped back and gestured him inside. "Want a cup of coffee?"

"I just had a cup, but I wouldn't turn down a second one," he said, following his mom into the kitchen.

Apparently, his mom wasn't feeling humorous today. She pointed at the half-full pot. "Help yourself. I just made it and was about to enjoy my first cup."

Gil grabbed a mug from the cabinet. He reached for the pot of coffee and poured himself a healthy serving, guessing he was going to need the caffeine to get through the lecture he felt coming.

He turned and leaned against the counter as he sipped his coffee. "Go ahead." He gave her a *gimme* gesture.

"You're helping Doug find a place to live? On his own? You know how I feel about that. I thought we were on the same page."

Gil shrugged. "You're the parent, and I'm just the big brother. But Doug is an adult, and as his brother, it's my job to help him in any way I can. Isn't that what you always taught me?"

His mom frowned. She sucked in a deep breath as her eyes began to water. "You think I'm being over-protective?"

"If you are, it's allowed. You're our mother. A great mother at that."

"I'm trying to be. I thought a great mother would keep Doug here though, in case he needs us."

Gil set his coffee mug down on the counter and crossed the room toward his mom. "If he needs us, he'll call. And we'll call him to check on him. He'll have neighbors and two jobs."

"Two?" his mom asked, looking up.

"Doug is going to be the official dog walker for the Somerset Rental Cottages, and he's going to be great at it. He's going to be fine, Mom. Really."

Her shoulders rounded. "Maybe I won't be fine though. I'll have an empty nest."

"I'll be right next door." He wrapped his arm around her shoulders. "You okay?"

She sniffled. "I was planning to yell at you, but I couldn't because I know you're right."

Gil chuckled. "You want to tour Doug's new home

with us? I mean, it's not official yet, but I think the place is a good fit for him."

She leaned into his hug. "Yeah. I wouldn't miss it. Maybe he'll let me spruce the place up."

Gil pulled back and gave her a questioning look. "You didn't offer to spruce up my first place."

"Well, I guess the secret is out. Doug is my favorite."

Gil's mouth fell open. "I knew it!"

"No, you didn't." She punched him softly. "You're both my favorite. Do you want me to come next door and spruce up your house for you? Or do you have another woman in your life who can give the place a lady's touch?" She raised her brows.

Gil let go of the hug and returned to drinking his coffee. "No comment," he said, slipping back into mayor mode.

"Well, if you do, you should invite her over for dinner with the family. That would be nice. I would like to get to know Moira better."

Gil sipped his coffee, smiling behind the rim. "Maybe I will invite her sometime."

Chapter Twenty-Seven

Moira didn't make rash decisions, but she had followed an impulse this morning and ended up at the animal shelter where she'd heard that Beth Chimes volunteered when she wasn't running her private ranch. Apparently, the animal shelter worked closely with the ranch to ensure all the animals had a fair shot of finding their forever families.

Moira wanted to check on Beth one more time. She'd also kind of wanted to make sure that Molly had truly gotten adopted and wasn't on the market for a new home after all. Moira hadn't been able to stop thinking about the little puppy.

The woman at the front desk had sent her straight back when she'd told her that she wanted to volunteer with Beth.

Beth looked up with surprise as Moira entered the room. "Hi, Moira. What are you doing here?"

Moira shrugged. "You told me I was welcome to come help out anytime. I woke up today and just thought I'd come see if you needed anything."

Beth tilted her head. "We're always shorthanded. I

was going to bathe all the dogs today and take them on walks." She gestured at the kennels in the room. There were about fifteen or so, full of dogs and cats rustling around and checking out the room's newest visitor.

Moira's gaze ping-ponged from one to the next, but she didn't see Molly. That was probably for the best. She didn't know anything about caring for a dog. But she guessed she'd learn today. She made a show of rolling up her sleeves as she turned back to Beth. "I'm here to help."

"These dogs can't vote, you know. Most candidates would be volunteering where there are people who can sway the numbers."

Moira supposed that was true. "Someone once told me that dogs make you a better human. I guess I figure a better human makes you a better mayor." She shrugged. "Also, if I'm being honest, I was just looking for Molly."

Beth offered a sympathizing look. "I'm sorry. She's not here. She and her new owner are very happy with one another. You still want to spend your Saturday help-ing out?"

Moira nodded. "Absolutely."

Beth narrowed her eyes. "You work at the emergency dispatch, right?"

An *uh-oh* bubbled up in Moira's chest. "That's right. I'm one of several dispatchers." She felt Beth's eyes boring into her.

"You called me the other day, looking for a Cavalier. When I asked if I could put you on a list, you said no. Is that because you didn't want me to know who you were? Because you were checking on me?"

Moira didn't answer immediately. Instead she stood there, staring back at Beth at a loss for words.

Beth's gaze dropped momentarily. "You were checking on me because I called the dispatch the other day."

"I'm sorry," Moira finally said. She shook her head. "I didn't mean to invade your privacy. I just, well, I was worried about you after the call. I needed to see for myself that you were okay."

"You saw me at the adoption fair. But you're here now, seeing me again." Beth furrowed her brows. "Why?"

Moira swallowed. "I don't know. I guess some part of me felt a connection with you and your story."

Beth gave her a searching look. Then she offered a small smile. "Just so you know, I took your advice and went to a clinic. And then I filed a police report. I'm not sure I would have done those things without your encouragement. So, thank you. I'm okay—kind of. I'm getting there at least."

Moira didn't know the full story, but she guessed she didn't need to. All that mattered was that Beth was taking care of herself. "I'm glad to hear that." Moira glanced over her shoulder. "Do you want me to leave?"

Beth shook her head. "No way. I need your help with these animals. If you meant what you said about wanting to pitch in, I'll take you up on it."

"I meant it," Moira said, genuinely happy to be there.

Beth looked down for a moment. "And thank you for caring."

"Probably too much, if you ask my boss."

"There's no such thing as too much," Beth said.

Two hours later, Moira was covered in dog hair and slobber, but she felt fantastic.

"Their love is unconditional. That's why I do this," Beth said as she ran a brush down the fur of a small beagle mix. "You never have to wonder if they're going to turn their backs on you or leave one day. It's good therapy."

Moira could probably use that kind of therapy in her own life. "So you work with animals during the day and then volunteer with them in your free time?"

Beth looked up from her brushing. "Do what you love, right? What made you decide to be a nine-one-one operator?"

"I wanted to help people, but I'm too much of a chicken to be a cop. I never liked school enough to be a doctor or a nurse. I'm the first line of contact in an emergency. It feels good to help." Moira reached out for the cocker spaniel and ran her hand along his silky-smooth back. "Not that there are a lot of emergencies in Somerset Lake. The dispatch isn't too active."

"You can do a lot of good as mayor," Beth said. "Maybe you can spread the word about these lonely dogs."

"I will. Mayor or not, I'll definitely spread the word. Everyone should bring one of these adorable little guys home."

"You're sure you don't see any lovable pups here that you want to bring home with you?" Beth asked hopefully.

Moira shook her head. "I'm not ready for that just yet. But I'll be back another time to volunteer."

Beth looked pleased. "Good. We'll take all the help we can get around here."

By the time Moira left, she felt energized and exhausted at the same time. She needed to get home and take a nice, long bath and maybe have a glass of wine. She and Gil hadn't made plans for tonight. He'd mentioned wanting to spend some time with his brother, which Moira admired about him. Doug was lucky to have Gil, and vice versa. Moira wished she had a sibling some days. Some part of her—maybe a bigger part than she'd realized—also wanted a dog.

Moira got into her car and pulled out her phone to check any messages she might have missed while she was inside with Beth. There were three. One from Tess.

> *Tess:* Anything I can do for you?

Moira assumed she was talking about the campaign. She tapped out a quick reply.

> *Moira:* Not right now. But thank you!

The second text was from Lucy.

> *Lucy:* The nerve! Are you okay? Do you need me to come over and bring ice cream?

Moira furrowed her brow and reread that text before tapping out a response.

> *Moira:* Why do I need ice cream therapy?

Moira didn't wait for a response. She was ready to get home. She put her car into drive and pulled onto the road, hearing more text messages ping from her phone in the passenger seat. What was going on? Perhaps she should take Lucy up on the ice cream. That sounded nice, but not nearly as enticing as inviting Gil over. She'd prefer not to be covered in dog hair when she saw him—so a shower was in order—but she also couldn't wait to see him and tell him all about her day with Beth and the dogs. And to kiss him. Dog kisses were great, but Gil kisses were preferable.

Gil glanced around the Somerset cottage that was available to rent, scrutinizing it for safety. It was a one-bedroom cottage with a bathroom, kitchen, and living area.

"Fully furnished," his mom said, looking pleased. "That's good. You won't have to buy furniture."

Doug had been quiet since stepping inside the tiny quarters.

Gil stepped up to him. "You okay? Having second thoughts?"

"No." Doug smiled now. "I'm just shocked that this is happening. I'm going to move out and be on my own."

"We're just around the corner," Gil reminded him. "A golf cart ride away." Almost everyone here had golf carts and used them regularly to navigate around the lake.

Doug nodded. "I know. This is great. This place is perfect."

Someone knocked on the door, and they all turned to see Trisha Fletcher standing on the porch. Trisha not only was the rental manager but also lived with Jake a couple of cottages down.

Gil gestured her in. "Hey, Trisha. Please don't tell us this place has already been rented, because Doug just told us it's perfect."

Trisha clapped excitedly. "Oh, yay. I'm so glad to hear that. I think you'll love living here, Doug. I know I do. Petey always loved to walk the dogs with Louise. He's

hoping you won't mind if he goes along with you sometimes." Petey was Trisha's young son from a previous
marriage.

"I won't mind," Doug said. "I like Petey."

"Good. Anything I can help you with? Want me to
give you a tour?"

His mom laughed. "Well, the place is fairly small. You
can give us the tour without moving a foot."

"Which is perfect for a single guy moving out for the
first time," Gil said, catching his mom's eye. She was
still having a hard time letting go, but he knew she was
doing her best.

Gil's cell phone pinged with a text message. He
ignored it and continued looking around the cottage.
Whoever was calling could wait. This time with Doug
was important. As soon as the phone stopped buzzing, a
message pinged. Then another.

"Aren't you going to check it?" Doug asked, looking
concerned.

His cell phone alerted him of a third message. "Fine.
Let me see who it is." Gil pulled his phone from his
pocket and tapped on a message from Jake.

> *Jake:* There's an article you need to see.
>   Sooner than later.
> *Gil:*   I'll pass. I don't care what anyone says
>   about me in the media.
> *Jake:* It's not about you. It's about Moira.

Gil stared at the text, wondering if Jake thought he
should see it because it was bad for Gil because it shone
a positive light on Moira. Or bad because it shone a
negative light on Moira.

Another text came through. This one from Miles.

Miles: Why are politics so ruthless?

"Gil? You okay?" Doug asked.

Gil shook his head. "I'm not sure. I need to go though. Mom, can you finish touring the place with Doug?"

"Of course I can." She wrapped her arm around Doug's shoulders. "And I promise I won't try to talk him out of this."

"Thanks," Gil said, stepping out of the cottage and onto the porch. He dialed Jake's number as he hurried down the steps.

"I thought you'd be calling me," Jake said as soon as he answered. "Have you seen it yet?"

"No. Where is it?"

"The *Daily Gazette*."

The *Daily Gazette* was one of the bigger newspapers that served the western side of the state. Gil got into his truck. Before cranking the engine, he typed "the *Daily Gazette*" into a browser on his phone. "How bad is it?" he asked Jake, who was now on the speakerphone.

"For you, not bad at all. For Moira? Not great."

Gil sighed. The article loaded onto the front page of the digital newspaper with the headline MAYORAL CANDIDATE WITH A PAST MIGHT NOT BE GOOD FOR SOMERSET'S FUTURE. Gil really didn't want to read any further, but his eyes lowered just enough to see Felix's name. "Thanks for alerting me to this, buddy. I need to go," he said, turning the key and cranking the engine.

"I assume you're heading to Moira's house."

"As fast as I can," he said before disconnecting the call. Then he texted Moira.

Gil: I'm on my way. Be there in 10.

He waited a minute to see if she'd respond. When she didn't, he put the truck in drive. Gil had been on the receiving end of bad press a few times in his career, for something stupid he'd said or done in his past. The past had a way of rearing its ugly head. Something told him this would devastate Moira though. She was a private person, just dipping her toe into the public spotlight. This was too much. How had this information been leaked?

Gil pulled up to a stop sign and glanced at his cell phone in his center console. She hadn't responded to him. Maybe she hadn't seen the article yet. That would be the best-case scenario. He didn't want her to be alone when she saw it. If he could be by her side to support her and assure her that this would pass, maybe it wouldn't sting as much.

He looked both ways. Seeing that the road was clear, he kept driving, pressing the gas pedal a little heavier than he probably should and going a few miles over the speed limit to get to Moira.

When he pulled into her driveway, her car was parked, and she was still sitting in the driver's seat. Her forehead was lowered to the steering wheel and her body shook softly.

Oh no.

He was too late. Gil's gut tied itself into knots. She'd already seen what was written about her, and by the looks of it, she was devastated.

∞

Moira couldn't move. She wasn't even sure she was breathing right now. Or maybe she was breathing too much. Her head was spinning, and the world seemed to be falling away from underneath her.

She heard the vehicle pull in behind her, but she didn't lift her head to see who it was. Maybe it was Lucy with the ice cream therapy she'd offered. Or Tess. Or Gil. She wasn't sure whom she was hoping for. Maybe she just wanted to be alone or disappear, never to be seen again.

Her mom had sent the article to her while she was driving. She'd read it once she'd pulled into the driveway, and now she was having what could only be described as a small panic attack. The article had told only half the story.

The lock-in fundraiser at the sheriff's department was not the first time Ms. Green was thrown in jail. Reports have come in revealing that, when Ms. Green was twenty-one, she was arrested for destruction of property. At the time of her arrest, the targeted apartment was being leased to Gil Ryan, who is now Somerset Lake's mayor, and his former roommate, Felix Wilkes.

A knock on her window made Moira finally look up.

It was Gil. Tears immediately filled her eyes. *Yeah.* He was the one she was hoping for. She suddenly needed to melt into his arms. He opened her car door and stepped toward her, embracing her in a hug. "Hey, I'm sorry," he whispered in her hair. "I know you didn't want any of that information to become public knowledge."

"You read the article?" she asked, burying herself in his chest.

"Yeah."

"It's not fair. It paints him as the victim and me as the aggressor. When he's the one who…" She was struggling to manage her breaths. It felt like the cap had come off her bottled-up emotions, and her messy feelings were bursting out of her.

"I know." Gil's hand smoothed the hair on the back of her head. "Want to go inside? I'll make you a cup of tea. Or coffee. I can do whatever you need to make this better."

Moira sniffled. She pulled away and looked up at him. "Everyone is going to read this article, Gil. Everyone will know what I did. How can I run for mayor now? How can I ever show my face in town again?" More tears welled in her eyes until one slipped down her cheek. She quickly swiped it away with the back of her hand. "I could even lose my job over this."

"Lose your job? Don't you think you're overreacting just a little bit?" Gil asked.

Moira shook her head. "Gil, I never told Sheriff Ronnie about my criminal history. When Ronnie hired me, he asked me point-blank if I had ever had any run-ins with the law, and I said no."

Gil's face seemed to blanch. "I see."

"I was never charged with a crime. The charges were dropped because of you. I'm guessing Felix never filed charges because he didn't want me to tell anyone about what he'd done to make me lash out like that. Not that he would have admitted to anything or that I had any proof."

"You were young," Gil said calmly. "Once you tell people why you did what you did, they'll understand."

"Tell?" Moira shook her head and pulled away. "No, I'm not telling."

Gil furrowed his brow. "Why not? You have nothing to be ashamed of. Nothing even happened."

Moira's mouth fell open, and her eyes narrowed. "Really? Nothing happened?" She took another step backward. "Maybe my clothes stayed on, but I *was* violated. Maybe it could have been a lot worse, but it still affected me."

"Of course. I know. I didn't mean to minimize what he did to you. Drugging you with the plan to hurt you..." He seemed to swallow. "I don't know how that would feel."

"I'll tell you how it would feel. Horrible. I trusted him. I trusted myself to make decisions with him. And he broke that trust in me. I wanted revenge. That's why I did what I did."

"I know that now."

More tears streamed down Moira's cheeks. She hated crying in front of other people, especially Gil. "But I can't tell anyone what happened. I don't want to be a victim, and maybe no one would even believe me. Then I'd be pegged a liar." That's how she'd felt when she'd reported the next day what Felix had done. The officers taking her report had been nice, but they'd told her there was no evidence. It was a he-said, she-said case, which made her feel like she was making it all up. Felix was a stand-up guy. A college athlete. Mr. Popular. No one would believe he was capable of drugging a woman to take advantage of her. Not even Gil had considered that scenario.

Gil braced her shoulders between his hands, looking her square in the eyes. "I'll back up your story. I drove you home, remember? I saw how intoxicated you were. And I know you. You wouldn't lie about something like that."

Moira was shaking. This was all too much. "I need to

go inside."

"Good idea. We'll figure this out, Moira. And it's not as bad as you think. People will be talking about something else next week. They'll probably be talking about me."

Moira climbed her porch steps and then turned to look at him. "People won't forget this, Gil. I broke into a home and destroyed property. Those are felonies."

"You were never charged. No one can prove it."

Moira placed a hand on her chest. "Like I said, I'm not a liar. I won't lie about this."

"Breathe, okay. This is politics. Even if it's just small-town politics. Everyone has something they don't want the world to know. No one is without skeletons in their closet. If you're going to be in office, you have to get used to airing your dirty laundry."

She blinked wearily. "Maybe I'm not cut out for being in office then."

Gil narrowed his gaze. "Because of this? Moira, Felix has done enough, don't you think? If you let this story allow you to pull out of the mayor's race, you'll just be allowing him to hurt you again. To win. Come on, Moira. You're stronger than that."

She pulled back, inexplicably hurt by that statement. It made her feel guilty and angry that she wasn't stronger. At least she didn't feel strong at the moment. "Am I? Because right now I just want to quit everything."

"You don't mean that."

"Maybe the last month and a half was just one big mistake."

Gil gave her a searching look. "Which part?"

Maybe Moira was being overdramatic right now. Maybe she was leading with her emotions, but it felt like her world was collapsing around her, and all she wanted to do was retreat into her house, where she was safe. "All of it. And maybe you shouldn't come inside with me after all." She sniffled. "I think I just want to be by myself."

"Trust me, when you feel like you want to be alone, you really need to be with the people who love you. Like me."

Now Moira was the one giving Gil a searching gaze. Did he mean what he just said? Did he love her?

Wow, she really wasn't in a place for this discussion right now. "Gil, I just—I just need space, okay? I'm sorry." She stepped inside her home, needing air and maybe Lucy's ice cream therapy. She didn't look up at him as she closed the door, shutting him out.

Chapter Twenty-Eight

Gil stood there on the other side of Moira's door, unable to move for a moment as his thoughts and emotions went to war. He wanted to knock on Moira's door and try again. Leaving her right now when she was so upset didn't seem like a good idea.

There was another part of him that wanted to retreat to his own home and lick his wounds. He'd just told Moira he loved her, pretty much, and she hadn't responded. Or she had responded but not in the way he'd hoped. He got that his timing was off, but the L-word always deserved a response, right?

He turned and ran a hand through his hair. He'd always believed in honoring a person's wishes, so he would leave. But he wouldn't leave Moira alone. He pulled his cell phone from his pocket as he walked, and dialed Tess's number.

"Hey, Tess," he said when she answered. "I'm leaving Moira's house now."

"How is she?"

"Not great. Would you mind checking up on her?"

"Sure. But why aren't you staying with her?"

Gil opened his truck door and got inside. "She doesn't want me here."

"Did you two get into a fight?" Tess asked.

"Not exactly." No, instead he'd professed his love for her. That was the opposite of a fight. "Maybe having a good friend by her side right now would be better."

"Okay. I'll head over right now."

"Thanks, Tess. Let me know if there's anything I can do."

"Gil?" Tess hesitated. "Moira hasn't let a lot of guys in on a romantic level. The fact that she let you in is a big deal. Just be patient with her, okay?"

Gil looked up at Moira's home before backing out of the driveway. "I will. You can't stay where you're not wanted though. And right now, she doesn't want me here."

"I'll update you in a little bit," Tess promised.

"Thanks." Gil drove home, where Doug was still sitting on his couch along with Goldie.

"Hey, Gilly. Want to hear about the tour of my new home?"

Gil shook his head. "I do, but can we maybe talk about it tomorrow? I'm kind of beat, buddy. I think I'm just going back to my room."

Doug stood. "You're upset." He walked over to him and gave him a big hug.

Gil didn't think he wanted it, but mid-hug, he realized he needed it. He pulled back and looked at Doug. "What am I going to do when you're not right next door to cheer me up when I need it?"

"You'll just drive to my place. You'll always be welcome."

Gil smiled even though he didn't feel like it right now. "Ditto, buddy."

∞

Gil resisted calling or texting Moira until that night when
he was about to fall asleep and couldn't take it any longer.
He reached for his phone on his nightstand and pulled up
the thread of messages between them.

>   *Gil:*   Are you okay?

He waited for several long minutes for her to respond.
Finally, he decided she wasn't going to answer him. Maybe
she was already asleep, which might be a good thing for
her. Then his phone pinged with an incoming message.

>   *Moira:* I'm okay.
>   *Gil:*   I'm glad to hear it. Can we meet up for
>   breakfast for tomorrow?
>   *Moira:* I'm going to lay low for a few days.
>   *Gil:*   I'll come to your place then?
>   *Moira:* Maybe another time. Sorry.

Gil sent some follow-up texts, but Moira was no
longer responding to him. He pulled up Tess's contact and
called. If anyone knew what was going on with Moira,
it was her.

"Hey, Tess," he said when she answered.

"Sorry, Gil. I was supposed to update you. I just
got home."

"It's okay. How is she?"

"She's upset. I didn't even know about what she did to
that guy. She never told me. That is so unlike Moira."

Gil cleared his throat. "Well, Felix had it coming."

"What do you mean?" Tess asked.

Gil hesitated. "Because of what he did."

"I'm still not following," Tess said.

Gil froze. "Moira didn't tell you what happened?"

"Apparently not."

If she didn't tell her best friend, she wasn't going to defend herself to the public either. "Is she just hoping this will all go away by laying low?" Gil asked.

"Moira is good at laying low. Too good for her own good. I don't care that she terrorized some guy in the past. I'm shocked because that's not the Moira I know, but it sounds like there's more to the story."

"Yeah," Gil said. "It's not my story to tell though. Thanks for the update, Tess."

"Of course. Gil?"

"Yeah?" he asked.

"I'm not just Moira's friend, I'm yours too. I haven't really known you to get serious with a lot of people either. Speaking from experience, you don't get sparks often. When you do, they're worth fighting for."

"Thanks," Gil said for lack of anything better to say. "Bye, Tess."

"Bye."

He disconnected the call and set his phone back on his nightstand. Then he lay back in his bed and closed his eyes. Tess was right. Moira was worth fighting for, but how could he fight for her when she was emotionally MIA? And did she want him to fight for her? He was in love with her, but did she feel the same way?

Moira's phone rang. She stared at it for a long moment. The last three calls had been from the media. There'd also been one from an old friend she hadn't spoken to in six years. Everyone wanted to know about Moira's criminal past.

Moira finally reached for her cell phone and eyed the caller ID. Her stomach dropped. It was worse than the media. She loved her mom, but Darla wasn't calling for pleasantries. She'd want to know why she'd never heard a word of any of the things the article was accusing Moira of, and if Moira was guilty, why had she done them.

If Moira didn't answer, her mom would just drive over here. On a breath, Moira connected the FaceTime call and held the phone in front of her face. "Hi, Mom."

"Are you okay?" Darla asked immediately.

Moira was sick of being asked that question. She didn't want to lie anymore. "Not really."

"Is it true?"

"Yes," Moira said, suddenly feeling a wave of nausea. She'd always had a fear of disappointing her parents.

"I'm guessing it wasn't Gil's apartment you were wrecking. This roommate of his must have done something pretty awful to warrant you behaving so badly. I know you. You wouldn't harm anyone unless they hurt you first."

Moira swallowed. "He tried..." Her mouth was dry, and her heart was beating way too fast. "He tried, but he didn't," she managed to say.

Her mom exhaled loudly on the other line. "I see. Well, regardless of what did or didn't happen, I'm so proud of you, Moira."

"Proud? But I committed crimes. I broke into someone's home and destroyed their belongings."

"Yes, you did. And you also stood up for yourself.

Maybe not in the right way, but a woman in pain lashes out. I'm not here to judge you. I just want to make sure you're okay."

Moira swallowed past a tight throat. "Mom, I want to drop out of the mayoral race. I can't do it. I can't." Tears rushed to her eyes as she explained what she'd been thinking about for the last twenty-four hours. "Maybe that makes me weak or cowardly, I don't know, but having my life under this microscope for others to pick apart isn't for me. At least not right now."

"I'll support you no matter what you decide," Darla said. "As I'm sure your friends will too. And Gil."

"Mom...I just want everything to go back to the way it was. Life was easier before I started chasing things I'm not even sure I want. I had a job I loved. I met up with my friends at Sweetie's. I had book club. It was all so simple. Now everything is complicated. I just want to reverse time and have my normal life back."

"You can't. Sweetie's is still closing, and Gil is still part of your life. I won't call you weak or cowardly for dropping out of the mayor's race, but don't let fear allow you to push Gil away. Relationships are hard, and they can be messy, but sometimes the things that complicate our lives are the things that make life worth living."

"Speaking of relationships, I'm glad you'll be spending more time with Dad."

Darla sighed. "Well, I'm sure he'll drive me nuts, but it'll be a good change. Until a couple of months ago, I couldn't really imagine retiring from the bakery because the town depends on it so much. With your father being home more often, I was starting to want to slow down and enjoy my life a little more too. Sometimes things work out in the most unexpected ways."

"Yes, they do. Sweetie's turning into a parking lot was not on my radar." Moira laughed.

"Neither was Gil, I'm guessing," Darla said gently. "Just think about what I said. Don't throw the baby out with the bathwater."

Moira gave her mom a strange look. "I've never liked or understood that saying."

"You've made a lot of changes in a short time. In this case, it just means that not all of those changes should be scrapped. Some things stay the same and some things change—for the better."

When Moira was done with her mom's call, she sat on the edge of her bed and waited for the next call from the media. She knew which changes needed to take a back seat in her life. She wasn't ready to be mayor. Not yet, at least. She didn't believe in making rash decisions, and yet, that's exactly what she'd done when she'd launched her campaign against Gil. He'd told her he'd taken steps toward running for that office for years before actually becoming mayor. Maybe she could run now, but it didn't mean that she should.

Within five minutes of her waiting, her phone rang.

Moira held the phone to her ear. "This is Moira Green," she said.

"Ms. Green, can you comment on the accusations that you were caught breaking and entering and destroying a Mr. Felix Wilkes's property?"

"No comment," Moira said, breathing through her emotions. They were bittersweet, but she also felt a peace about the decision she'd already made.

"Reports say that Mayor Gil Ryan dropped his charges and that Mr. Wilkes did not press charges against you. Do you know why?"

Moira closed her eyes. Where were these reports coming from? "No comment."

"Do you have a comment on anything that has transpired over the last few days?" the reported asked.

"Yes. I would like to announce that I'm dropping out of the mayoral race for Somerset Lake. I wish the remaining candidates good luck. Thank you," she said quickly before disconnecting the call and placing her phone down on the table beside her, hands shaking.

Maybe this was the right decision for her life right now, but she was still sad. Lying back in bed, Moira rolled to her side and closed her eyes, hoping that sleep would silence her thoughts, and that when she woke up, life would be back to normal.

Normal was not the case when Moira woke up the next morning. Or the next. By Thursday night, at the end of Moira's shift, her new normal was living as a recluse. She'd managed to stay home for the last several days, but the big question of whether she would attend book club tonight still hung in the air. She loved her Thursday night get-togethers, but she was still in isolation mode. Despite Moira's dropping out of the campaign, this story wasn't fading fast enough. Everyone had questions that she didn't feel like answering.

The clock ticked to five p.m., and Moira stood from her desk. Her shift was over and uneventful, for the most part. She headed back to her bedroom to change clothes for book club even though she still hadn't decided yet if she was attending. The probability of running into anyone other than her friends was low. She could drive over and duck inside the closed bookshop before she came face-to-face with Reva.

Then again, what if her friends wanted to talk about

the things Moira had done? They hadn't really pressed her on the recent news, but she hadn't given any of them ample opportunity either.

"Maybe I won't go." She plopped down on her bed and blew out a breath. As soon as she did, someone knocked on her door. She didn't move until they knocked again. On a sigh, she stood and dragged herself to the front door. After peering through the peephole, she opened the door. "What are you doing here?"

Tess offered a knowing smile. "Making sure you come to book club tonight."

"Shouldn't you be at the bookshop?"

"Lara is closing for me. I had a sneaking feeling you might try to skip tonight, and then we'd be left without our goodies from Choco-Lovers."

Moira rolled her eyes playfully. "So you were worried about the lack of sweets at tonight's meeting?"

"No, I was worried about you. Go on, finish getting ready. I'll wait." Tess pushed past Moira and walked into her living room and sat on the sofa without another word.

Moira turned and looked at her friend. "You're a little bit bossy. Did you know that?"

Tess crossed her legs and leaned back. "River says the same thing." She made a shooing motion with her hands. "Go. I'll be here waiting."

Moira didn't budge. "I was thinking about staying home tonight."

Tess nodded. "I guessed as much. That's why I came."

An hour later, Moira was glad she'd gone to book club. Her friends always made her feel better.

"So tell us what happened," Lucy said, folding her legs beneath her.

"Lucy," Tess warned, narrowing her brown eyes at their friend. "We said we weren't going to press Moira. If she doesn't want to talk about it, she doesn't have to."

Moira blew out a shaky breath. "I really don't want to discuss it." She hesitated for a moment. "But sometimes the things you don't want to talk about are the exact things you should be talking about." She swallowed hard.

"If you're not ready..." Tess said, trailing off. "We're your friends no matter what."

"None of us are able to judge you," Trisha agreed. "I mean, my ex-husband robbed people right beneath my nose. I missed things I should have seen."

Tess raised a hand. "We've all made mistakes. It's part of being human."

Moira nodded and took a deep breath. She knew that everyone had things in their past they weren't proud of. It had always been hard for her to discuss *her* things though. "Way back in the day, I went on a date with Gil's college roommate."

"Felix." Tess nodded. "I remember meeting him once when he came to town with Gil. He was cute."

Moira rolled her eyes. She'd thought Felix was cute, too, before she'd realized he was such a despicable human being. "I feel so foolish. I didn't even like him that much." She shook her head, wishing for the millionth time that she could have a do-over.

"Hindsight is twenty-twenty," Lucy said.

Moira looked at her friends. "I can't prove this, but Felix slipped something into my drink when I went to the bathroom. I only had a couple swallows of my drink before I excused myself. Once I returned and drank a little bit more, I was completely intoxicated. I don't even remember what happened after that."

Tess pressed a hand to her chest. "Oh, Moira."

Moira held up a hand, needing to finish her story before she lost her nerve. "I do know that nothing happened, but only because Gil showed up and drove me home. Felix argued with him and wanted to drive me himself, but Gil insisted. When I woke up the next morning, Gil was in my kitchen making breakfast."

"You could have been assaulted," Lucy said. "If not for Gil."

Moira nodded. "I slowly started putting the pieces together and came to that same conclusion. I went to the police, but there wasn't enough evidence to make a case. It was my word against Felix's." She bounced her foot on the floor beneath her chair, trying to release her pent-up energy. "So I decided to take matters into my own hands and make him regret what he tried to do to me." Moira rolled her lips together, feeling a rush of anger and guilt all at once.

"What happened?" Lara asked.

"I called Felix and told him what a great time I had the night before. I asked him to meet me at a park so we could hang out again that night. Instead of meeting him though, I broke into his apartment. The one he shared with Gil. And I just ransacked it. I broke things. I smashed things. I was so angry, not just for me but for all the women out there who've been through something similar or worse. I felt this sadness deep inside me, knowing that guys like him hurt people and get away with it all the time." Moira sniffled. "It's not fair. They should pay. *He* should pay. That's what I was thinking."

Tess put a hand on Moira's shoulder. "It's understandable that you would be upset. Just hearing what happened makes me beyond angry on your behalf."

Moira glanced around at her circle of friends. There was no judgment in their eyes. On a breath, she continued. "Anyway, Gil showed up and called the cops before he realized it was me. The police came and arrested me, and I spent the night in jail. Not my finest moment."

"What are you talking about?" Lucy asked. "I am prouder of you than I ever have been. You are amazing."

"Because I got arrested?" Moira asked in disbelief.

"You were betrayed and hurt, and while violence is never the answer," Tess said, "I agree with Lucy. I'm proud of you too. Not for taking matters into your own hands but for being such a strong, beautiful person, inside and out. Don't let this news stop you from living your life and chasing your dreams. If you want to be mayor, go for it. If you want to be with Gil, be with him. The past is just that. The past."

Moira shook her head. "The story that everyone else got paints me as the bad guy."

"You don't owe anyone an explanation," Lucy said. "The charges were dropped, right?"

"Gil was the one who called the cops. Once he realized it was me, he dropped the charges. Felix threatened to file, but I think he thought better of it."

"So Gil knows all of this?" Tess asked.

Moira nodded. "He does now. Back then, he thought I was ransacking his apartment because I was upset with him," Moira said. "I felt so awkward around him for so long. I didn't want to face him. I felt foolish and embarrassed. I just wanted to forget that whole weekend."

"Like you said, you were young." Della stepped over to the couch where Moira was sitting, and sat on the edge of the coffee table, facing her. She leaned forward and wrapped her arms around Moira. "I'd tell you to forgive yourself, but there's nothing to forgive. You were just being human, lashing out at the things in this world that don't make sense. We've all been there." She pulled back and looked at Moira. "Maybe we all haven't trashed someone's apartment, but we've all wanted to. Trust me." She smiled at Moira. "The truth is out now. You can stop letting it haunt you. It's time for you to get back up on that horse and ride it."

"What horse exactly are you talking about?" Lucy asked, making everyone laugh.

"It's a figure of speech," Della said with a slight eye roll. "We're here for you, Moira. That's the point."

"I know, and I love you ladies. All of you." Moira fought back her tears. These were happy tears. She was so lucky to have friends like these in her life.

"Where is this Felix guy now?" Lucy asked, sitting back down.

Moira shook her head. "I have no idea."

Tess pulled her laptop to her thighs. "Felix Wilkes, right? Wasn't that his name?"

"You're searching for him online?" Moira wasn't sure how she felt about that. What if he was out living his best life? What if he was the mayor of some other town?

"Bingo!" A few minutes later, Tess looked up and met Moira's gaze. "He's in jail, serving an eight-year sentence."

Moira's heart dropped into her belly. "Did he…was he…?" If he hurt another woman, some part of her would feel guilty—even though she never could have pressed charges against him anyway. Nothing had actually happened. Not that she could prove, at least.

"No." Tess shook her head, calming Moira's worries. "Apparently, Felix had a prescription drug habit, and he also got into selling. He wasn't a good guy."

"Understatement of the year," Lucy said, folding her arms over her chest.

Moira sniffled. Some part of her felt relieved that Felix was serving time. That meant he couldn't hurt anyone. He couldn't hurt her either, unless she let him.

Chapter Twenty-Nine

The tavern was crowded tonight, filled with laughter and music. So much so that Gil could barely hear the guys at the table. Probably for the best. He wasn't in the mood for socializing. He just wanted to stay home with Goldie or maybe take his boat out on the lake. It was Doug who had pushed him to come here tonight. Sometimes Doug tagged along. He liked Gil's friends, and Gil's friends liked Doug. Actually, Gil's friends had stopped being just Gil's friends a long time ago. They were Doug's too.

"Why so quiet tonight, Gilbert?" Jake asked.

Gil didn't even have it in him to roll his eyes at being called Gilbert. "I'm just listening to you-all."

"He's sad that Moira isn't talking to him," Doug explained.

Gil glanced over at his brother. "Thanks for sharing that."

"You're welcome," Doug said with a smile. He reached for his Coke and drank it.

"Did you two get in a fight or something?" Miles asked. "Is she upset about ending her campaign for mayor? And that you're still running?"

Gil shook his head. "It's not like I won. She dropped out. There's a difference." He ran a hand through his hair, debating whether to get into this with his friends tonight. "She's ignoring my calls. She doesn't want to see me. The last time I saw her, I basically told her I loved her." He offered up a quiet, humorless chuckle. "In hindsight, I guess that might have been a mistake."

River cringed across the table. "Your timing might have been off by a little bit. Wasn't she still reeling from the news article?"

Gil took a sip of his Coke. "I stupidly thought it would put good news on top of the bad. I was trying to make her feel better, but it just made things awkward between us. Mine and Moira's timing has always been off."

"So you don't really love her?" Jake asked. "You were just trying to make her feel better?"

Gil looked at his friend, wondering how honest to be. He swallowed past a tight throat, his chest aching due to Moira's absence in his life. "Just breathing right now hurts because I know I can't see her tonight. Or tomorrow. I can't taste my food. I can't enjoy a sunset. Nothing feels good right now. Not without her."

"Wow," Jake said. "I knew you liked her and all, but I didn't know you liked her that much. That sounds like love to me."

"Me too," Miles agreed.

"Why can't you see her tonight or tomorrow?" Roman asked. Roman wasn't from Somerset Lake, so he didn't know that Gil had been pining for Moira for most of his adult life.

"Because Moira says she wants space and time. I have to give that to her. Don't I?"

Jake shrugged. "There's a fine line between respecting

a woman's wishes and making sure she knows you're going to stand by her no matter what. That you won't just disappear on her."

Miles nodded. "She needs to know you'll fight for her *while* respecting her wishes."

"How do you do that?" Gil asked, raising his glass of Coke to his mouth. Even his soda tasted flat with his current mood. "It seems contradictory."

"No one said love was easy." Jake patted Gil's back. "You did say you loved her though, right?"

Gil massaged a hand over his face. "I thought love was supposed to make a person feel amazing. Not like they are coming down with the flu."

"It does both. Just one question. Did Moira say she loved you too?" Miles asked.

Gil sighed, the ache in his chest deepening. He'd thought Moira's feelings for him were growing, but now he wondered if it was just him. "No, she didn't say it back."

"Ouch," Doug said, making all the guys laugh. "Well, I love you, Gilly."

"I love you, too, Gilbert," Jake teased, clapping another hand to Gil's back.

Gil laughed quietly, despite his broken heart. "You guys have a funny way of showing it."

When Gil got home later that night, he sat on his bed debating whether to text Moira. He'd waited awhile, trying to give her space, but something the guys had said tonight resonated with him. He needed to make sure she knew he was still there for her when she was ready. He'd thought it went without saying, but he needed to make sure.

He picked up his phone and pulled up Moira's contact. Then he tapped out a text.

> *Gil:* Maybe not tonight or tomorrow, but when you're ready for a sunset boat ride, let me know.

Some foolish part of him waited for her to respond and tell him that tomorrow sounded great. She didn't. She didn't reply at all. Gil set his phone down, lay back on his pillow, and closed his eyes.

He awoke with a start a few hours later when something hit his front door with a loud bang. Gil sat up and waited for his eyes to adjust to the dark, his ears tuning to the silence and waiting for something more. Goldie took off running toward the door, barking, and making that effort impossible for Gil. He followed her, checking the time on his cell phone as he walked. It was one a.m.

Gil looked out the peephole and noted a carful of teens. That's when he realized what the noise had been. A rock. It was finally his turn to have his front door rocked on. He chuckled to himself as he watched out the peephole. The kids weren't taking off per their MO. Gil waited, realizing they couldn't take off because they were having car trouble.

Gil really didn't want to call the police, but these kids had to be stopped one way or another. They could hurt someone. Reluctantly, he dialed 911. Moira didn't work the nightshift anymore, so he got a male dispatcher. "Yes, hello. There is a carful of teenagers outside my home. They threw a rock at my door, and they appear to be having car issues. If you send someone now, you'll catch your rock throwers."

Goldie looked up at Gil as if to say, *Aren't you going out there?*

Gil petted her head. "No way, girl. I'm going to let the authorities handle this."

Within minutes, two sheriff's cars pulled up, one on each side of the teens' car. Gil watched as the deputies talked to the kids. Then they took the kids, four altogether, and put them in the back seats of the sheriff's vehicles.

Gil felt bad about ratting them out, but this behavior had to stop. Maybe Moira was right, and the town needed more resources catering to the teenage population. Kids need after-school programs and places to socialize. He wanted to text Moira and tell her about this turn of events, but she'd find out tomorrow. Gil was sure that the dispatchers talked to one another, and catching the rock throwers was big news. It might even make a bullet point on Reva's blog.

Gil watched the deputies' cars drive away, leaving the teens' car parked in front of Gil's home. Once they were gone, he stepped outside and looked at his front door, where there was a huge dent in the painted metal surface. A dent that would unlikely come out. It wasn't the end of the world, but he'd have to live with it or take the door off its hinges and replace it. He walked back inside and locked up behind himself.

"I'll check on the kids in the morning," Gil told Goldie. "Tonight, we need to get our beauty sleep. Bed," he said.

Goldie knew that word. She took off running ahead of him and leaped onto the mattress in his room. Gil lay down beside her, but he was wide awake, and his brain was firmly on Moira's suggestion about a skate park.

Sitting up against his headboard, he pulled his laptop

to rest on his thighs. Then he began researching similar-type places to suggest to the town and possible locations. He wasn't sure where the money would come from, and it wouldn't happen overnight, but Moira was right. It would be a nice addition for the town's underserved population. Some might say, it would be a necessary addition.

The next morning, Moira parked and got out of her car. It was true. Going anywhere on Hannigan Street involved a long walk. She could use the walk this morning though. Part of her was still considering turning back and going home. Another part of her kept reminding herself that she was supposed to be a small-town hero. And the person who needed a hero the most right now was herself.

Jessica Marcus from WTI-News turned when she saw Moira approaching. Moira had asked her for a meeting, proposing a small outdoor dining area that sat to the left of Sweetie's Bakeshop. "Moira, I was glad you called. Are you ready to film?"

"Ready as I'll ever be, I suppose."

"Great." Jessica gestured to her cameraman, and Moira saw a green light come on in his equipment. The reporter turned toward Moira and smiled. "Moira, you recently dropped out of the race to become mayor. Any chance you'll reconsider?"

Moira shook her head on a small laugh. "No. Not this year, at least."

"Well, I'm sure when you're ready, your voters will still be out there waiting to cast their ballot on your behalf."

"We'll see about that." Moira laughed awkwardly, looking between Jessica and the camera.

"You left this race because of your past. Is that correct?" Jessica asked.

Moira took a breath, wanting to bolt, but this was why she'd asked Jessica to meet her here today. "You could say that. I was hiding from this part of my past for a long time. I guess I was embarrassed about my actions. I didn't want people to judge me."

"And now?" Jessica asked.

"Now I want to confront my past. Yes, I did those things that were reported."

Jessica's mouth fell open. "That is not what I was expecting you to say. I suspect you had a good reason."

It was almost worth telling the truth just to surprise a professional reporter like Jessica who'd likely heard almost everything. Moira rolled her lips together. "It's my word against his, of course. That's so often the case. All I know is I went on a date with this man, had one drink, and could barely walk out of that bar. He was going to drive me home. Luckily, a friend of mine was there, Mayor Gil. He stepped up and took me home instead. Mayor Gil actually insisted on doing so. I can't prove what happened that night, but I know in my gut, and in my heart, what could have happened." Moira took a breath. She'd been talking fast, trying to get her story out. She hadn't spoken Felix's name, and that was on purpose. The last thing she needed was a defamation lawsuit. "I wanted revenge. I was angry. I was hurt. That's no excuse for taking the law into my own hands though. I know that. Being young is also no excuse."

Moira took a breath. She had a figurative spotlight on her right now, and she needed to use it to help others. That was why she'd called Jessica in the first place. "I'd like to take this moment to encourage others who may find themselves in a similar situation as I was to report any potential crimes, even if you think there's nothing that can or will be done, report it. Tell someone. Tell law enforcement, tell your friends, a family member. If you don't have a good support system, find a counselor and talk to them. Holding the truth in doesn't help anyone, least of all yourself."

"Wow," Jessica finally said. "You are such an inspiring woman, whether you run for public office or not. Thank goodness for Mayor Gil insisting on taking you home. Are you still friends today?"

How did reporters seem to know exactly which questions to home in on? "We are, yes."

"Good. Well, in my opinion, when you're ready to run for mayor again, this town would be lucky to have you."

Moira went straight home after her interview with Jessica. It wouldn't air until tonight, but Moira was already feeling exposed. Jessica was right. Thank goodness for Gil. He was a lifesaver. Her very own small-town hero. And she'd been treating him like the opposite, avoiding him again the way she used to before their truce.

It was just hard being around him and not being with him, and she wasn't sure she was ready to jump back into their budding relationship. She didn't feel like she could trust herself to make the right decisions now. She'd decided to run for mayor, and look where it had gotten her. Some part of her felt free though. She'd harbored so much guilt and shame about what happened with Felix for so long. Now everything that had happened would be out in the open.

She pulled into her driveway and stepped inside her home, where she planned to stay for the indefinite future. She didn't want to see or talk to anyone. At the exact moment she thought this, her cell phone buzzed inside her purse. She walked over to the counter, pulled out her phone, and read the screen.

> *Gil:*   I'm still here. In case you were wondering.
>   Not going anywhere.

She stared at the screen for a long time. Then she tapped back a reply.

> *Moira:*   Do you want to come over tonight and
>   watch the six o'clock news with me?

So much for being alone. Gil would probably think this was a crazy invitation. She suddenly didn't want to watch the news story by herself tonight.

> *Gil:*   Sure. If it means spending time with you,
>   I'm there. Is there a reason we're watching
>   the news?
> *Moira:*   Yes. I'll be on it.

Chapter Thirty

Gil had spent the day with Doug, touring the Somerset cottage one more time and watching Doug sign his first lease agreement. Doug also met his neighbors-to-be. He knew them already, of course. Doug was one of those people who knew everyone. It was one of his strengths and the reason why he made a great campaign manager for Gil. One of the reasons, at least.

This was going to be a good thing. Gil remembered when he was barely eighteen and wanted to leave his parents' home so badly he could hardly stand it. Not because they were hard to live with but because it was a rite of passage. Doug deserved that as much as anyone.

Doug had smiled from ear to ear when Gil had been with him today. It was a good day—for both of them. Topping it off for Gil was the text Moira had sent, inviting him over to watch the news. This had him curious, of course, but just knowing that he was going to spend a little time with Moira also energized him. There was an extra lift in his step and in his heart, even if he didn't think she was calling him over to recharge their relationship.

He took several steadying breaths as he pulled into Moira's driveway, headed up the porch, and rang the doorbell. He wasn't sure what to expect coming here tonight, so he'd skipped the flowers he'd considered buying at the florist shop, and he'd dressed casually in jeans and a T-shirt. Moira was leading; he was following.

He rang the doorbell and waited anxiously for her to answer. He liked to think he was good at reading people. Her eyes and smile would tell him exactly where they stood, which was something he needed to know. Before word had leaked out about Moira's night in jail, they'd been falling hard and fast for one another. Feelings like those didn't just disappear. At least not for him.

The door opened, and Moira offered a hesitant smile. Her hazel eyes were warm and inviting, which made him breathe a little easier. It was all he could do not to step toward her, wrap his arms around her, and give her a kiss. He didn't though. Warm and inviting could mean they were still friends. Or it could mean Moira's feelings for him went deeper than friendship. He didn't want to misinterpret anything tonight.

He offered her a wide smile in return. "Hey."

"Hi." Her cheeks flushed slightly. She looked like she was doing well. There was a glow to her skin, and a twinkle in her eyes. The weight of the world didn't appear to be pressing down on her shoulders the way Gil thought it had the last time he'd seen her.

"I'm here to watch the news with you," he said, inwardly reprimanding himself for sounding awkward.

"Thanks for coming." She opened the door wider. "I've got news-watching snacks for us."

Gil stepped inside her home. She'd rarely invited him in. He wasn't quite sure what to do with himself, so he stood there shifting back and forth on his feet for a moment.

"Have a seat on the couch. I'll bring the popcorn and sodas to the coffee table."

"Okay." He walked over to her couch and sat in the middle, which would have her either sitting close to him or clinging to the far side. "So, you said you're going to be on the news tonight?" he finally asked.

Moira placed a large bowl of popcorn on the coffee table in front of them and sat beside him with their thighs separated by a few inches of distance. She wasn't clinging to the far side, which was a good sign. "I am."

Gil lifted his brows. "Is this a good thing?"

Moira sucked in a shuddery breath. "Honestly, I'm not sure. I think so. Or maybe it's not good or bad, it just is." She shrugged.

"You are being very mysterious right now. Are you going to make me guess?"

Moira angled her body toward him, pulling one knee up in front of her. "I decided to confront my criminal past head-on instead of hiding from it. I didn't give the reporter all of the details, but I provided enough to explain why I behaved the way I did. Not that violence is ever justified," she said, backtracking.

Gil could see the slightest insecurity in her eyes as she looked at him. He wasn't sure he'd ever admired anyone more than he did Moira right now though. "Wow. That took a lot of courage."

"And you know what?" she asked, weaving her fingers together in front of her. "Once I told the truth and put it out there, it didn't seem so big and ugly anymore." She looked at him for a long moment, her smile deepening. "It also made me realize that I haven't truly thanked you for stepping in that night. You could have ignored your gut and given your friend the benefit of the doubt. Most people would have. He was your roommate. Your friend."

"You were my friend, too, Moira," Gil said quietly. "And even if you weren't, you deserved to have someone step in on your behalf and make sure you were safe."

Moira seemed to swallow thickly. She fidgeted with her hands in front of her as she talked. "What you did took courage, too, and it changed my life, Gil." Tears shimmered in her eyes.

Gil was speechless for a moment. He wanted to pull her toward him, but he still wasn't sure where they stood or what she wanted from him tonight. "So are you back in the mayoral race?"

Moira laughed and shook her head. "No. I'm not ready for that. I think what you told me the other day was pretty wise. I need to start small by joining the town council. I enjoyed attending the last meeting. I have ideas, and I want to help the community. I also think you're the best mayor for Somerset Lake right now. You always put the people of this town first. You choose what's best, even if it's not exactly what you want. Like moving Sweetie's out of its location and building a parking lot." She hesitated. "You have my vote. You always will."

Gil's heart squeezed. "It means a lot to me that you would say that after everything. Thank you." He held her gaze, wishing he could read her mind, but he never could seem to know what the woman in front of him was thinking. Each unveiling of who she really was only made him fall deeper for her.

"You also have my heart," she finally said.

∞

Moira wasn't sure what she was doing right now. She hadn't planned on diving back into a relationship with Gil tonight. She just wanted to see him, and she wanted to share the news story with him because it wasn't just her story. In a way, it was his too.

But being with Gil brought back a flood of emotions. She was in love with him. It was undeniable. It wasn't rash or impulsive. It had built up over time, not just these last few weeks but over the last few years. Maybe that's why Moira had avoided Gil so fervently. She'd instinctively known that letting him in was the same as loving him. For her, at least.

"Your heart?" Gil asked, brows raised just a touch, as if maybe he didn't believe his ears.

"Yeah. Gil, I want to try again."

"Try what?" he asked.

She laughed quietly. "You know, being your girlfriend."

A smile flickered at the corners of his lips. "The thing is, we never broke up. So, the way I see it, you are my girlfriend." He scratched the side of his face thoughtfully. "That still feels a little juvenile somehow. Until you, I haven't called someone my girlfriend since early college. Maybe not even then."

"I like it." Moira leaned in to kiss him, brushing her lips to his. "I like you."

"Well, I love you," he said, looking her in the eyes. "I'm *in* love with you, Moira. Some part of me thinks I fell in love the very first time I laid eyes on you. All I know is that the kind of feelings I have don't ever go away. You have my heart."

She swallowed. Saying those three little words wasn't something to do impulsively. This wasn't impulsive or rash though. She knew how she felt about Gil. "I love you too," she whispered. "I've never said that to a guy before. You're the first."

"I'm honored. And I'm humbled that you would love me back." He kissed her briefly. Then he leaned forward and grabbed the bowl of popcorn off the table. "It's almost six. I'm ready to watch my girlfriend on the news."

Moira scooted in closer to him until her thigh was touching his. "Fair warning, Mr. Mayor. I might just kick you out of your office four years from now."

He glanced over. "Assuming that Denise Berger hasn't already done so."

As he said it, the news started with a breaking story that wasn't Moira's. Jessica Marcus stood on-screen talking into her microphone in front of Denise Berger's large brick home.

"Breaking news tonight, Denise Berger has decided to drop out of the mayoral election for Somerset Lake," Jessica said, speaking into her microphone. "What was going to be a tight race this fall is looking like a shoo-in for the current mayor, Gil Ryan."

Moira's lips parted. "What?" She looked at Gil. "Did you know about this?"

"No, I didn't. But I can't say I'm surprised. She didn't seem too thrilled at all her opposition at the town council meeting the other night. I don't think she realized that she wasn't going to win the popular vote. Denise isn't really one to go into a contest that she isn't likely to win."

"I agree. There was no way she was ever going to beat you."

"Whatever the real reason, I'm a lucky guy. I get to keep my job and the girl." He leaned in and brushed his lips over Moira's again.

When the kiss was over, she reached into the bowl

of popcorn and pulled out a piece, holding it up to his mouth. He took it from her in one quick motion. Then he picked up a piece of popcorn and fed it to her as well.

"A happily ever after for you," she said, snuggling in closer and breathing in the scent of him. Breathing it all in. She loved this moment and the feel of his arms wrapped around her. There was no place she'd rather be in all of Somerset Lake or anywhere else, for that matter. On a wistful sigh, she said, "And a happily ever after for me too."

Epilogue

Happy Fall, Somersetters! Here's your daily dose of Reva!

- The grand opening of the new Hannigan Street parking lot happens tomorrow. There will be no claiming of parking spots. Not officially at least!
- There'll be another animal adoption fair this coming weekend! Beth Chimes is your point of contact if you would like to volunteer.
- Who loves a fudge sale at Choco-Lovers? The pumpkin spice fudge is buy one pound, get one free. Run, don't walk, and give Jana all your money!
- Now that our previous Most Eligible Bachelor is off the market, it's time to vote on someone new. Stay tuned to my blog to see who the upcoming candidates for MEB are!

Love & Bullet Points,
Reva

∞

Maybe Moira was partial because November was her birthday month, but there was no place quite like Somerset Lake in the fall. The foliage was a perfect blend of reds, oranges, and yellows, and the air was too warm for a coat but perfect for a lightweight cardigan.

Pulling her current sweater a little tighter around her as she stepped out of her home, Moira's gaze stuck for just a moment on the dent right in the middle of her front door. A tiny little rock could do a lot of damage. It could do a lot of good too though. Because of that rock and a few bored teenagers, Gil was going to make a very important announcement to the town today, after thanking them for reelecting him as mayor and using a jumbo pair of scissors to cut the ribbon for Hannigan Street's new parking lot.

Moira's phone rang as she dipped into the driver's seat of her car. She checked the ID before answering. "Hey, Mom. Are you still meeting me at the ribbon-cutting ceremony?"

"I wouldn't miss it," Darla said, her voice light and cheerful. "Your father and I are going together."

Moira's parents had been doing a lot of things together since they'd both retired. Darla was semiretired at least. Sometimes she worked at the diner when Angela was on vacation, to help a friend and connect with her former customers. Mostly Darla had moved on to shared hobbies with Moira's father though. Like fishing and hiking. They'd also taken up bird-watching, of all things. Moira's parents had even started a board game night at their home with all their other retired friends. It just so happened to take place on Thursday nights when Moira was at book club with her friends and Gil was having wings and drinks at the tavern with his. Thursday was apparently a social night in Somerset.

After a pause in the conversation, Darla asked, "Are you okay? I know how much you loved Sweetie's."

Moira thought about the question for a moment. It had taken her a little bit to get to this point, but she was okay. "It's a bittersweet day, for sure. I'm not as sad about Sweetie's being gone now that I know how much retired life suits you. Sweetie's was just a building. I still have all the memories."

"Me too," Darla said. "How's Gil?"

"He's good. He's already at the new parking lot." Moira started the engine and reversed out of her driveway.

"Well, tell my future son-in-law that I'm proud of him."

Moira and Gil weren't engaged. Not yet at least. The topic of marriage hadn't even come up, and Darla was well aware of that fact. Instead of correcting her mother, Moira laughed the comment off because both of them knew it was just a matter of time before she and Gil were married. "Proud of him for what?"

"For doing what's right for the town. And for making you happier than I've seen you in quite a while."

It was true. Moira was happy. She'd always been so vocal about not needing a man to be content in life. And that was true. She didn't need a man. She'd proven to herself and everyone who would listen that she was more than capable of taking care of herself. She'd discovered that she liked having someone to take care of her once in a while though. She liked having Gil. And she took care of him just as much as he did of her. They were a good team, the two of them. "See you at the ribbon-cutting ceremony, Mom."

"See you there," Darla said.

Moira disconnected the call and finished driving, pulling up to an available spot halfway down Hannigan

Street. The new parking lot wasn't officially available for parking just yet, so she still had to make the long trek to where Sweetie's Bakeshop used to stand. Moira and her friends were meeting up at the diner now, and while it wasn't the same, sometimes change was good.

One thing that didn't change, that never would, was that they gathered in Lakeside Books every Thursday like clockwork under the guise of discussing books. The true discussion, however, went much deeper than words on a page. The book club was about life and friendship. Now that all of them were in relationships—even Tess's employee Lara—there was also a lot of talk about love, marriage, and babies.

"Moira!"

Moira turned toward Reva Dawson's exuberant cheer. Not even the town's nosiest member could dull Moira's mood today. "Hi, Reva."

"Good to see you. If you're looking for Mayor Gil, he's over there." Reva pointed a manicured finger in the direction of where Sweetie's Bakeshop had sat until a month ago. "Doesn't he look handsome?" Reva asked, leaning in to Moira.

Moira tore her gaze from Gil and eyed Reva. "He's taken."

The blogger chuckled, enjoying Moira's mock jealousy a little too much. "He's much too young for me, dear. Don't worry. I always knew you two would end up together."

"You did?" Moira asked, wondering at the comment.

"Of course. When I dubbed him the Most Eligible Bachelor of Somerset Lake last year, I hoped the attention would encourage you to fight for what was always yours."

"And what is that?" Moira asked, intrigued.

"His heart. It was so obvious, dear. Everyone in town could see it a mile away. Even those who aren't as nosy as I am." She dug her elbow into Moira's side.

For once, Moira didn't want to flee from Reva. "Well, you can play matchmaker for some other unsuspecting singles now," she teased.

"Yes, I can. And you better believe I'm planning to." Reva rubbed her hands together. "Matchmaking keeps one young."

Moira could practically see the wheels turning in Reva's brain. She wondered who the next lucky guy or girl in Somerset would be.

Excusing herself, Moira headed in Gil's direction. When he saw her coming, his face seemed to light up. Had it always done that? Was Reva right? Was it always so obvious how he felt about her? Moira wished she had let him in so much sooner. Then again, things always worked out the way they should. Isn't that what her mom used to tell her? In this case, it seemed to be true for everyone involved.

Gil wrapped his arms around her as soon as she was in front of him. "Hey, you," he said in a low voice, his breath tickling her skin. "I have a proposal for you."

Moira pulled back and searched his face.

Gil cleared his throat. "Um, let me rephrase. I have an *offer* for you. How would you like to do the honors of cutting the ribbon for this ceremony?"

"Me?" Moira pressed a hand into her chest, where her heart was still beating fast from the mention of a proposal. Didn't a man know not to utter the P-word without a ring to back it up? "Really?"

"Yeah. I'll be right beside you, but you should be the one." Gil hugged her closer. "What do you say?"

Moira's eyes stung. She wasn't about to cry, but her

emotions felt raw today. It was a bittersweet occasion, and she was glad to share it with the man she loved. "I'd like that."

"Good. Me too."

Moira cleared her throat, eying Tess, Trisha, Lucy, Della, and Lara huddled toward the front of the crowd. "The cutting isn't for fifteen minutes, right?"

Gil followed Moira's gaze. "Say hello for me. You don't have blood-related sisters, but your friends definitely fill that gap."

Moira grinned. "In that case, they'll be your adoptive sister-in-laws one day."

"I like the sound of that."

Moira did too. "Back in a few minutes." She turned away from Gil and headed in her friends' direction.

"Big day," Tess said, stepping forward and hugging Moira first.

"Yes, it is." Moira hugged the other women one by one. "Where are the guys?" she finally asked.

Lucy tipped her head toward the back of the crowd. "Miles is working."

"Same," Trisha said. "Plus Jake told me he knew I'd rather be with you-all anyway." She reached for Moira's hand and squeezed it. "And he wasn't wrong about that."

Moira glanced back toward Gil. "I'm afraid I can't stay. I'm actually going to be the one cutting the ribbon."

Lucy bounced on her heels for a beat. "Wow. That's so cool." She glanced over at Trisha. "I might not be able to stay either though. My patient here could go into labor at any moment." She was referring to Trisha, whose belly was swollen and carrying low.

"I know a few months ago we had said we'd do any-thing to stop this parking lot from happening, but that plan has changed," Moira teased. "No need to go into labor right here in the crowd to put a stop to things."

Trisha's cheeks appeared to flush. "I think we'll be okay. Although I'm predicting book club might have to take place at my home with the baby next week."

The women squealed in unison.

"I'm so excited!" Tess said. "Our first book club baby. I mean, I know you have an older child, Trisha, and Della has two boys, but those boys are half-grown. This will be a tiny human."

"And the first girl," Moira pointed out.

Trisha's smile dropped and then she groaned, pulling a hand to her belly.

"What's wrong?" Moira asked, suddenly concerned.

Trisha looked up and smiled again. "Just a kick. Let me tell you, this girl is tough."

Tess placed her hand on Trisha's belly. The other women all did the same, stacking their hands to cover the baby bump. "Tough just like her mama," Tess said.

"And all her mama's friends," Trisha shot back.

The ceremony went off without a hitch, and then Gil announced the plans for a skate park. Everyone in the audience seemed to love the idea. There was laughter and cheers and lots of excited chatter once Moira cut the ribbon. Afterward, she stopped to talk to several friends and would-be voters while Gil worked the crowd as well. Then they made their way back to one another.

"We have one more place to go," Gil said as he walked her to her car. "My truck is just up ahead. How about I drive, since the next place is a surprise?"

"A surprise?" Moira asked, holding his hand. "I used to think I hated surprises."

"And now?" Gil asked.

"Now I love a lot of things I never thought I liked before."

"Including me?" he asked, one side of his mouth quirking.

"Especially you," she said, wrapping her arm around his.

When they arrived at his truck, he opened the passenger door for her. Moira climbed in and buckled up while he jogged around and got in on the driver's side.

"It's a good surprise, right?" she asked, suddenly feeling a little anxious.

"Mm-hmm. A life-changing surprise."

Moira felt her eyes round. Her life had already gone through so many changes this year. Sweetie's was gone. She'd dipped her toe in politics and joined the town council. And she was in a serious romantic relationship for the first time in her life. One thing that hadn't changed was her job at the emergency dispatch, which she continued to love. No more following up on her callers' lives though. Even though it was difficult, she trusted the system. Somerset's emergency response team was amazing, and if there was ever anything she needed to know, Reva would be sure to get the word out. No doubt about that.

"Life changing?" Moira repeated. Maybe there was another proposal up Gil's sleeve. Was he considering marriage? She wasn't sure she was ready for that just yet.

"You'll see," Gil said in an upbeat tone. He turned the key and started the engine and then drove toward the outskirts of town while Moira's imagination got the best of her. Finally, he pulled into a driveway that led to a log cabin home that sat on a creek.

"Have you guessed what your surprise is yet?" Gil asked, bringing the truck to a stop and cutting the engine.

"I am absolutely bewildered. Where are we?"

Gil pulled his keys from the ignition and dropped them in the middle console. "Beth Chimes's house. She fosters."

Moira shook her head, still not tracking. She had spent a lot of time volunteering with Beth and the rescue animals. She and Beth had become friends, although Moira had never come to her home. It was a beautiful place. "I'm still not following. Why are we here?"

Gil pushed his truck door open and stepped out. "Come on. Beth is waiting for us."

Moira opened her truck door and stepped out. The ground was soft beneath her flats. She was dressed for a ceremonious occasion, not playing in the dirt or creek. Were they here to look at a dog? Moira stopped in her tracks. "Gil, I'm not ready for this."

He reached for her hand. Before he could respond, Beth walked out of her home and headed in their direction. She was holding a leash with a blur of brown and white fur tugging at the end.

"Hey, you two!" Beth said excitedly. "Molly has been beside herself with anticipation. I think she knows what's going on."

Moira looked down and blinked. "That makes one of us."

Beth looked at Gil, concern knitting the area between her eyes. "You didn't tell her?"

He shook his head. "I wanted this to be a surprise. Hopefully, a happy one."

Moira had to blink again because there were tears blurring her eyes. "Is this... Molly?"

"Surprise," Gil said with a small smile.

Moira looked between him and Beth. "What is she doing here?"

Gil took the leash from Beth. "Thanks, Beth. I'll take it from here."

Beth gestured behind her. "I'll just be out back with my other fosters if you need me. I'm going to give you two some time to discuss…things." She winked at him and turned, leaving Moira and Gil alone.

Gil cleared his throat. "Molly's owner ran into some unforeseen life changes. She needed to move, and she couldn't take a pet with her. Turns out Molly here still needs a good home."

Moira swallowed past a tight throat. "I can offer her a good home," she said without even taking the time to consider the decision. She was leading with her heart, which she'd decided would never steer her wrong. If she'd led with her heart the first time she'd met Molly, she'd have taken this little puppy home months ago.

Gil shrugged. "The problem is, Goldie has already met Molly, and she's grown a bit attached. You and I might have to compete to see which of us gets to take her."

"Compete against each other?" Moira asked, jaw dropping. "Again?"

"Or," Gil said, smile growing as he looked at her for a long moment—she could look at this man for a million years and never grow tired of his smile—"we could just join forces and raise our dogs together."

Moira really liked the sound of that. "Dogs make us better humans, right? Isn't that what you told me?"

"Something like that. All I know for sure is that you make me better."

"Well, I'm not marrying you just for the sake of sharing a dog," Moira said without thinking.

Gil tilted his head. There was a humorous glint in his gaze. "Who said anything about marriage?"

Moira felt her entire face flush. Ever since he'd said the P-word earlier, she'd had marriage on the brain. "Oh, I just..." She shook her head. "I only meant that a dog is no reason to commit to one another."

"You're completely right. The best reasons for committing are because you love someone and you don't want to be without them. Because you want to wake up to that person and go to sleep with them. Because you want to share every single moment that you possibly can together."

Moira searched his gaze. "Mm-hmm. Those are excellent reasons."

"I'm glad you think so, because those are my reasons for wanting to share a dog with you, Moira."

A million happy feelings flooded through her body. "Those are the reasons I want to share a dog with you too," she said quietly. The wind tousled her hair, blowing it around her face as Molly barked and wrapped her leash around their legs.

"Just to clarify, sharing a dog means sharing a life, right?" he asked, his expression serious.

Moira laughed as more tears filled her eyes. She could blink them away as much as she wanted, but they would just keep coming, and she was too happy to care. "That's right," she said. Then she bent and picked up Molly, holding the tiny dog against her chest as it attempted to lick her cheek.

"The paperwork is already done," Gil said. "She's ours."

Moira loved the sound of *ours* on his lips. "Perfect. Then let's take her home, shall we?" She narrowed her eyes at Gil. "For the record, home is anywhere that you are."

Gil leaned in and kissed her temple, dodging a sloppy puppy kiss from Molly. "For the record," he echoed back, "I feel the exact same way. And I always will."

Dear Reader,

The characters I write often introduce themselves on the page as I'm creating the first draft. I might know what they look like and a few things from their backstories, but mostly they're a mystery to me—one that unravels as I work through the story. One thing I knew early on about this book and its hero, Mayor Gil Ryan, was that he had a younger brother who has Down syndrome.

As many of you know, I'm not only an author. I'm also an occupational therapist. In my day job, I've met and worked with many young people living with a variety of health challenges and syndromes including this one. When I create these fictional towns, it is important to me that I represent a world that includes and represents everyone. Gil's brother, Doug Ryan, holds a very special place in my heart for that reason. As is the case when developing my other characters, I didn't fully know Doug's story until it revealed itself to me. While living with Down syndrome is not my experience, Doug's desire to be treated as a responsible adult and to remain independent is one I think we all can relate to, regardless of our life circumstances.

Thank you for allowing me to paint a world that reflects a kinder version of the one I live in every day. And I want to take this opportunity to thank you for reading. I hope you enjoyed discovering Moira and Gil and Doug, as much as I did when writing their stories!

Love and Happily Ever Afters,
Annie

Acknowledgments

It's time to thank the endless list of people in my life who have helped me put another book into the world. I certainly could never do this on my own, and wouldn't want to. Writing is a solo activity, but it takes a village to edit, copyedit, proofread, and critique; to design beautiful covers; and to write interesting back-cover copy. There is so much that goes on behind the scenes and so many people to thank.

First, I would like to thank my family. My husband guards my time for writing, and as my children grow older, they have started to guard it as well. My family also inspires my writing and keeps my proverbial well full of all the love and hope I need to draw from as inspiration for my books.

Thank you to my editor, Alex Logan. It is such a pleasure to work with such a talented and professional editor. You hold nothing back and push me to put out the very best book that I can. The same is true for the entire Grand Central/Forever team. A big thanks to Estelle Hallick for finding creative ways to make sure my books find the readers who will love them. I appreciate your hard work and enthusiasm, and I count myself lucky to be on your author list.

I also owe a huge helping of gratitude to my literary agent, Sarah Younger. We've surpassed twenty books together, and I hope that number continues to grow for many years to come.

Thanks to my critique partner, Rachel Lacey, for always being my first reader. I couldn't do this without you. I also want to acknowledge Tif Marcelo, April Hunt, and Jeanette Escudero. Having author friends to chat with makes the journey less lonely and more joyful.

A huge thanks to my virtual assistant, Kimberly Bradford Scott. You have been a tremendous help to me this year, and I am so glad to be working with you.

I would be remiss not to express my gratitude to my readers, some of whom have read all of my books—some have read them several times! I am honored and humbled that you would spend your time within the pages that I've written. Thank you for reading and sharing my books with fellow readers. It means the world to me!

About the Author

Annie Rains is a *USA Today* bestselling contemporary romance author who writes contemporary love stories set in fictional places in her home state of North Carolina. After years of dreaming about becoming an author, Annie published her first book in 2015 and has been chasing deadlines and creating happily ever afters for her characters ever since. When Annie isn't writing, she's living out her own happily ever after with her husband and three children. Annie also enjoys spending time with her two rescue pets, a mischievous Chihuahua mix and an attention-hungry cat, which inspire the lovable animals in her books.

Learn more at:
  AnnieRains.com
  Twitter @AnnieRainsBooks
  Facebook.com/AnnieRainsBooks
  TikTok: @AnnieRainsBooks
  Instagram: @AnnieRainsBooks

Can't get enough of that small-town charm? Forever has you covered with these heartwarming romances!

SUMMER ON SUNSHINE BAY
by Debbie Mason

Lila Rosetti Sinclair returns to Sunshine Bay to share the news that she's engaged—to a man her mother has never met. Eva Rosetti is so ecstatic to have her daughter home that she wants to hide the fact that her family's restaurant, La Dolce Vita, is in trouble. With a business to save and a wedding to plan, their reunion is more than either bargained for. But with support from friends and family, it may just turn out to be the best summer of their lives.

THE GOOD LUCK CAFÉ
by Annie Rains

Moira Green is happy with her quiet life. Then everything goes topsy-turvy when the town council plans to demolish the site of her mother's beloved café. Moira is determined to save it, so she swallows her pride and asks Gil Ryan for help. But with Gil supporting the council's plans, Moira is forced to find another way to save Sweetie's—and it involves campaigning against Gil. As the election heats up, so does their attraction. But can these two be headed for anything but disaster?

Discover bonus content and more on
read-forever.com

FALLING FOR ALASKA
by Belle Calhoune

True Everett knows better than to let a handsome man distract her, especially when it's the same guy who stands between her and owning the tavern she manages in picturesque Moose Falls, Alaska. She didn't pour her soul into the restaurant just for former pro-football player Xavier Stone to swoop in and snatch away her dreams. But amid all the barbs—and sparks—in the air, True glimpses the man beneath the swagger. That version of Xavier, the real one, might just steal True's heart.

SPRINGTIME IN SUGAR LAKE
by Marina Adair

The last thing Glory Mann wants is to head the committee of the Miss Peach Pageant in Sugar, Georgia. Especially when her co-chairman is rugged, ripped…and barely knows she's alive. Single dad Cal McGraw already has his hands full, but he can't deny the strong chemistry he has with Glory. As squabbles threaten to blow up the contest—and the town of Sugar itself—Cal must risk everything to get a second chance at love.

Meet your next favorite book with @ReadForeverPub on TikTok

Find more great reads on Instagram with
@ReadForeverPub

CHANGE OF PLANS
by Dylan Newton

When chef Bryce Weatherford is given guardianship of her three young nieces, she knows she won't have time for a life outside of managing her family and her new job. It's been years since Ryker Matthews had his below-the-knee amputation, and he's lucky to be alive. But "lucky" feels more like "cursed" to his lonely heart. When Ryker literally sweeps Bryce off her feet in the grocery store, they both feel sparks. But is falling in love one more curveball…or exactly the change of plans they need?

FAKE IT TILL YOU MAKE IT
by Siera London

When Amarie Walker leaves her life behind, she lands in a small town with no plan and no money. An opening at the animal clinic is the only gig for miles around, but the vet is a certified grump. At least his adorable dog appreciates her! When Eli Calvary took over the failing practice, he decided there was no time for social niceties. But when he needs help, it's Amarie's name that comes to his lips. Now Elí and Amarie need to hustle to save the clinic.

A LAKESIDE REUNION
by C. Chilove

Reese spent every summer of her childhood in the lake town of Mount Dora, Florida, never realizing that the haven hid a divide between the haves and have-nots. Not until she fell for Duncan, a have-not. Ten years later, she's back and must come to terms with all she's missed. Mostly that Duncan is now a successful real estate developer—and time hasn't weakened the connection between them.

AS SEEN ON TV
by Meredith Schorr

Emerging journalist Adina Gellar is done dating in New York City. So when a real estate magnate targets tiny Pleasant Hollow for development, Adi knows it's the perfect story—one that will earn her a coveted job…and maybe even deliver her dream man. Finn Adams is not a ruthless businessman. In fact, he genuinely wants to help the small town. Only some busybody reporter is determined to mess up his plans. But he can't deny that her sense of humor and eternal optimism are a balm to his troubled past. Will following their hearts mean destroying their careers?